EX LIBRIS

THE ROMANCE TREASURY
ASSOCIATION

TORONTO · NEW YORK · LONDON
AMSTERDAM · PARIS · SYDNEY · HAMBURG
STOCKHOLM · ATHENS · TOKYO · MILAN

These stories were originally published as follows:

A GARLAND OF MARIGOLDS
Copyright © 1967 by Isobel Chace
First published by Mills & Boon Limited in 1967

RED DIAMOND
Copyright © 1975 by Dorothy Cork
First published by Mills & Boon Limited in 1975

THE KILTED STRANGER
Copyright © 1975 by Margaret Pargeter
First published by Mills & Boon Limited in 1975

ROMANCE TREASURY is published by
The Romance Treasury Association, Stratford, Ontario, Canada.

Editorial Board: A.W. Boon, Judith Burgess, Ruth Palmour,
Alice E. Johnson and Ilene Burgess.

Dust Jacket Art by Emile LaLiberté
Story Illustrations by Emile LaLiberté
Book Design by Charles Kadin
Printed and bound by R.R. Donnelley & Sons Co.

ISBN 0-373-04100-4

Printed in U.S.A.

CONTENTS

A GARLAND OF MARIGOLDS

A Garland of Marigolds

Isobel Chase

Susan applied for the job in India on the spur of the moment. But she was well qualified, and it would take her mind off the end of her romance with Timothy.

It was a new world—adjusting to village life there, working to produce better wheat crops, trying to get the necessary water—and it was fascinating. Only Dr. Gideon Wait gave her cause for concern.

Gideon had long replaced the juvenile Timothy in Susan's mind and heart. Yet how could she get the brilliant but always teasing Gideon to see her as a woman—especially the woman in his life!

CHAPTER ONE

On the day I got my degree Timothy took me out to dinner. Tonight, I thought, as we strolled along the Embankment beside the Thames, he would ask me to marry him, and of course I was going to accept. We had been to a Chinese restaurant and the food had not agreed with Timothy's delicate digestion, but he had plied me with enough wine to sink a ship, which wasn't very fair because while I was now in a happy glow, he was as sober as ever.

"What you ought to do is go abroad," he said suddenly.

I pulled his arm closer around my shoulders, marvelling at the way his bones seemed to stick through his flesh as if he were little fatter than a skeleton.

"Abroad?" I repeated blithely. "Whatever for?"

He looked at me sorrowfully. "I should have thought that you would be longing to share your knowledge with the under-privileged," he explained.

I reached up a hand and pulled at his ear. "How can you be so earnest on a night like this?" I asked placidly.

He winced in pain, more from his indigestion than from any action of mine.

"The world today is a thing to be earnest about!" he retorted.

"Nonsense!" I stopped walking and wandered towards the stone parapet to watch a string of barges going past, behind a squat busy little tug snorting under the effort it was making. "Why should I want to leave all this?" I demanded. And to tell the truth it was all very beautiful. The Thames looked dark and powerful that night, hazing in the distance into evening mist. A few lights had come on and it was already dark enough for them to be repeated in the water. Even the more terrible of the new match-box architecture, international and yet a foreigner in almost every land, was softened in the changing hour to more reasonable proportions.

At the back of my mind I was trying to decide how I was going to make Timothy kiss me before we got home. He was surprisingly shy about showing his affection in public and was constantly worried about what other people might think of his choice in tailoring and ties as his mother had once convinced him that it was on these things that one was judged for the rest of one's life. It was the one drawback I knew of in our relationship.

Timothy stared moodily at the Houses of Parliament, allowing his eyes to travel slowly down the river to where we were standing.

"Suki," he said at last, "I've been trying to tell you all evening. I'm going to the States."

At first I didn't believe him.

"I suppose you're going to be an astronaut!" I teased him. Timothy was a space scientist and was madly interested in blasting useless objects into the sky at vast expense, but then I'm prejudiced because I always have thought that the moon was a dead bore outside of its proper romantic place.

He smiled thinly.

"It's to do with rockets, certainly. Part of the brain drain, I suppose," he added, half laughing.

I regarded him petulantly.

"But I don't want to go to America!" I complained. Timothy looked wretchedly embarrassed and he coughed to clear his throat.

"No, I know. Actually I shall only be gone for two years. It's a great experience for me, but they do stipulate an unmarried man. I thought we might put off any proper engagement until I got back."

It was a very bitter blow. Now that I was qualified, I

felt I was ready to be married. I had even turned down a couple of very nice jobs for that very reason. Timothy and I belonged together and, besides anything else, he needed looking after, with proper meals at proper times and a loving wife to mix his stomach potions for him and to comfort him when his chronic indigestion really got the upper hand.

"I suppose," I said in a voice which trembled despite all my best efforts, "I might be able to get a job near by."

Timothy bit his lip.

"But that's the whole point! I can't afford to have any distractions while I'm over there—and you are rather a distraction to me! We've been seeing too much of each other lately and we both need time to think. That's why I think you ought to go abroad too."

I swallowed dismally.

"But we are going to get married eventually, aren't we?"

He brushed away the question as being of limited importance.

"I suppose so. But we need these two years to *know*. Let's see what happens, shall we?"

I tossed my head, my pride coming to my rescue.

"And no strings attached?" I asked him lightly.

He grinned, patently relieved that I had not burst into tears or done anything else to make him feel uncomfortable.

"No strings attached," he agreed.

And so I did not become Mrs. Timothy Black that summer. I remained plain Miss Susan King. However, I did pack Timothy's clothes and possessions for him and saw him off at the airport, receiving a peck on my cheek for my pains. When it was all over, I went to the nearest self-service café and ate a horrid mixture of sausages and spaghetti, before going home and crying myself to sleep.

The following day I decided to go to India.

The advertisement had not been particularly attractive.
It had read more like a University joke. From it I
gathered that someone wished to employ somebody
with my qualifications in an experimental village at
somewhere quite unpronounceable in India. There
was, the advertisement had gone on to say, an experimental irrigation scheme which watered the main farm.
The newcomer would be trying out various new wheat
and maize hybrids to find out which would do best
locally. He, or she, would be paid a pittance for this
privilege and would also have to prove that their qualifications were better than any Indian national's who
cared to apply. Perhaps it was because it sounded so
hopeless that I applied for a job. It was at least in India,
which was where I had decided to go, and as it didn't
sound in any sense a particularly attractive job, there
was every chance that nobody else would apply for
it.

Nobody else did. I received a reply to my letter asking me to ring up a Mr. Gideon Wait at a Putney number, and a sense of excitement gripped me and, for the
first time, I went to sleep without even thinking about
Timothy and wondering what he was doing.

The telephone was answered by the young fresh
voice of a girl.

"Camilla Wait," she said softly, breathing the name
caressingly into the receiver in a way which must have
taken a lot of practice.

"Is your father there?" I asked her.

There was a moment's complete silence, then her
voice came again, more wary and not a little curious.

"No, he isn't. As a matter of fact he never has lived
here."

A prickle of exasperation travelled through me.

"I was told to telephone this number—" I began
crisply.

"Ah yes!" Camilla agreed. "But it's Gideon you
want to speak to. He's my brother."

I made a quick mental revision of her possible age. I

had decided before that she was about sixteen, now I began to wonder if she were older.

"Is he *there*?" I asked her and explained who I was. She giggled, quite unabashed.

"No, he's not. Look," she went on gaily, "the best thing is for you to come round this evening and have something to eat with us. Gideon is sure to be here part of the time." She gave me the address and a few rather wild directions as to how to get there, then I put down the receiver and dashed across to the wardrobe to see what I could find to wear. Anyone would have thought that Gideon Wait meant something to me personally and, in a way, he did. He was the first man I had eaten with since Timothy had gone to America, and I felt as shy and as involved as if he were my first date. Looking at myself in the looking-glass, I thought I had allowed myself to get into a fine mess. I wasn't particularly tall, but I held myself well, giving an impression of more inches than I actually possessed. I had dark, unruly hair and a nose which couldn't be ignored over a wide, mobile mouth that usually gave expression to my normal cheerfulness. There was no doubt that the new lipstick I had recently brought was a great success, and it exactly matched the wispy scarf I intended to tie round my neck, which would look better still. No, it wasn't my looks I was worried about. It was this new vulnerability that Timothy had left me heir to. I no longer felt on top of the situation.

I felt progressively less confident as the bus lurched over Putney Bridge in the general direction that Camilla had told me to go. Supposing I didn't like India? Supposing I couldn't manage the job? Or, even more important, supposing I didn't like Mr. Wait, the man who seemed to be in charge of the experimental farm? I got off the bus in a dream, telling myself how foolish it was to worry, and only succeeding in worrying all the more, as one always does.

I found the house quite easily. It was one of those comfortable, old-fashioned London houses that are sol-

idly elegant and sometimes still have the bars on the
nursery windows on the top floor. Mostly they have all
been turned into flats in these less spacious days, but
every now and again one sees one full of children and
fun and, more often than not, with peeling painted
façades that are hopefully being left yet another year
before they are fully "done up". The Wait house was
one of these. It was actually Gideon's house, but his
sister and her family lived there as he was abroad so
much. Usually there were half a dozen other people
there as well, but who they all were I was never able to
discover.

I walked up the few steps to the front door and rang
the bell. It was a long time before anyone came, and I
was on the point of ringing again when the door slowly
opened and a small voice said:

"Will you come in and tell me why you've come?"

I stared down at the small child who was firmly shut-
ting the door behind me. It was impossible to tell if it
was a boy or a girl as its hair was cut as short as possible
and it was dressed in a shirt and jeans.

"Hullo," I said.

The child glowered up at me.

"That's no answer. Whom have you come to see?"

"Mr. Wait," I said, feeling rather squashed.

"Oh", the child said wisely. "Uncle Gideon. He's
out, but Camilla wants to see you. She wants to make
sure you're the right person before Uncle Gideon sees
you. He'll take anyone who seems keen, you see."

"And that matters?" I asked faintly.

The child chuckled, and I was almost sure he was a
boy.

"He's had a couple of stumers!" he told me. "Camilla says it's all his own fault because he's no judge of
character."

"And Camilla is?" I asked a shade tartly.

The child nodded solemnly.

"There are no flies on Camilla."

He showed me into the sitting-room, still smiling in

that quiet, superior manner that told me he was quite sure that Camilla was going to take complete control of the interview no matter what I chose to do about it. If he was a typical Wait, I thought darkly, the sooner I left the better. I was too sore from my recent experiences with Timothy to want to indulge in personal relationships with anyone else of any age. I was in a mood to be careful, and if I could avoid doing so, I wasn't going to let even this youngster trespass on my affections.

Camilla took me by surprise. She came hesitantly into the room and paused on the threshold, whispering an apology for her freshly washed hair and the state of her clothes.

"I was bathing the children," she explained. "My younger nephews and nieces. Their mother is out."

I cleared my throat.

"Are there—are there many of them?" I asked.

Camilla grinned. "Four altogether," she said cheerfully. "Two of them are twins." She sat down on the chair opposite mine, her deep blue eyes taking in every detail of my appearance. I returned stare for stare, trying to make up my mind if she were as nice and as young as she looked.

"Will your brother be in soon?" I asked at last.

Camilla had the grace to look guilty.

"Perhaps you would like to stay for supper?" she asked.

"Very much!" I agreed warmly. "Does he know I'm even coming?" I went on in conversational tones.

Camilla shook her head.

"I know it's awful of me, but Gideon is so stupid about getting people to go to India. An ounce of good will and he's convinced they're the answer to his prayers!"

I laughed. "And they are not?"

"They haven't been so far. He hasn't had anyone stay longer than six weeks!".

My heart sank. Was it such a terribly hard job, with so few rewards?

"I'm not sure I shall do any better," I said aloud. "I've never been out of England before."

Camilla looked thoughtful.

"I think you'll do very nicely," she said lightheartedly. "You're not going to rush off and get married or anything awful, are you?"

I winced. "No," I replied sharply. "There's no danger of that!"

Camilla's eyes watched with amusement.

"Congratulations, Miss King," she teased me. "I shall give you a drink to celebrate!" She went over to a cupboard and produced an array of bottles. "What will you have? Gin? Sherry?"

I chose a dry sherry and watched her as she carefully poured it out for me.

"Are you going to have one?" I asked.

She laughed, glancing at me over her shoulder.

"Me? Gideon would be horrified! I'm only here at all because I'm in the middle of changing schools. And after that I still have to be finished!" she added with a horrible grimace.

"I see," I said, not seeing at all. "I thought you were about the age to leave school."

"I am", she retorted, "Only Gideon has this thing about education. I would be far more use to him in India. Who wants to be finished?"

"Wouldn't you like to go to university?" I asked her, remembering my own struggles to get an education, remembering too with gratitude the sacrifices my parents had made to make it possible.

"I haven't the brains," she admitted cheerfully "Gideon says it's marriage or stagnation for me. Apparently gentlemen prefer finished blondes—"

"What nonsense!" I interrupted her brusquely.

She laughed. "Isn't it?" A sudden idea struck her, transforming her face into an expression of angelic consideration. "I suppose you wouldn't like to persuade Gideon that India would be much more broadening to the mind?"

"No, I wouldn't," I answered firmly. "But your parents—?"

"They're dead," she replied simply. "They died when I was quite small. Gideon and Rachel, my sister, have practically brought me up. The last word is always Gideon's, though, because he pays the bills!"

I looked down at my glass of sherry, astonished by the sudden soft warmness inside me. Gideon sounded nice, and so perhaps life was not so bad. Perhaps even two years would not be long to wait for Timothy.

"It's a great pity," said Camilla.

Camilla and I put the children to bed. The twins, the youngest, were warm and sweet-smelling from their bath and were no trouble at all. They were not in the least put out at having a stranger to tuck them in and to tell them a long and involved story that pleased me as much as it did them. Camilla had the more difficult task with her niece and the small boy, Jeffrey, who had let me in to the house. The sun was setting when we had finished and a red glow shone over London in a pink and mysterious twilight. Camilla shut it firmly out by drawing the curtains and lighting the lamps. At night, I thought, the drawing-room took on an added elegance because one could no longer see the worn materials that covered the chairs nor the frayed edges of the glowing curtains.

We had only just sat down when we heard a key scrape in the lock of the front door.

"That will be Gideon," Camilla informed me with satisfaction.

I barely had time to gather myself together before the door opened and a larger, incredibly masculine edition of Camilla came into the room. He was fair as she was, with the same well-shaped bones and the same jutting firmness round the chin. He started when he saw me and looked enquiringly at Camilla.

"This is Susan King," his young sister said briefly. "She's going with you to India."

Gideon's face darkened with annoyance.

"Are the children in bed?" he asked abruptly.

"Of course," Camilla answered coolly.

"Then go and find yourself something else to do!" he snapped at her. She rose in one easy movement and went towards the door, winking at me behind his back.

"Susan is staying for supper," she said from the doorway.

"Susan?" he repeated testily.

"Actually," I said, feeling rather sorry about Camilla's curt dismissal, "most people call me Suki. Susan is only for formal occasions."

"Miss King," he said icily, "I hope Camilla has not given you the wrong impression, but I shall need to know a great deal more about you before I decide whether or not you will be suitable for the job I have to offer.

My feeling of warm sincerity fell away from me. I was as cold as I had been ever since I had said goodbye to Timothy.

"Of course," I said.

Gideon frowned over the list of my qualifications and the two letters of reference I had brought him. It was impossible to tell whether he was satisfied or not.

"What made you think of India?" he asked abruptly.

I tried desperately to think of my reasons.

"I have the knowledge," I stammered. "I thought I could be useful."

He looked up at me and his eyes were a dark, dark blue that was very nearly black.

"You have the knowledge," he agreed. "But there's a great deal more to this job than that. Can you *teach* what you know?"

"I've never tried," I admitted. I was beginning to see why none of his other assistants had lasted for longer than six weeks. He obviously expected them to work miracles on absolutely nothing at all! Even the marked likeness between Gideon and his sister faded into insignificance as I thought about how much I disliked him.

Gideon tossed my papers impatiently back on to my knees.

"And then you're a woman!" he said crossly.

I sat up very straight, sure now that I was going to lose my temper.

"Do I have to apologise for that too?" I asked smoothly.

He swung round and surveyed my angry face, surprised that I should have declared battle. His eyes were suddenly amused.

"No," he said slowly, "I don't think you have to apologise for that!" His appreciation was even more unwelcome than his criticism as he added: "No, no apologies needed, I think!"

I was silent. Somehow he still had me at a disadvantage and I was resentful of the fact.

"You have to admit," he went on more gently, "that your sex makes certain administrative difficulties. The village is very much on the open plan scheme of living!"

I blushed. "I'll try not to be too obtrusive, Mr. Wait," I said primly.

"I shall see that you aren't!" he retorted. He grinned suddenly and I was aware that I had been accepted. "You'd better ask me what you want to know about the place."

I hardly knew where to begin. "I know very little about India," I said.

He smiled and I could see a very clear likeness to Camilla.

"That might be a great deal better than knowing an awful lot," he said dryly. "All you'll have to do is produce a bonanza crop of maize!"

In spite of myself I laughed, remembering what Camilla had thought of his previous assistants.

"Yes, sir," I said.

There was a soft knock at the door, followed almost immediately by Camilla.

"All fixed up? How very satisfactory!"

Her brother grabbed her by the hair. "You were listening at the door!" he accused her.

Camilla managed to look dignified if slightly resentful.

"Of course. Now all we have to decide is when we're leaving—"

Gideon stopped her with a look.

"You, young lady, are going back to school."

Camilla made a face at him. "That's what you think!" she growled. "I'm not a child any longer!"

"Then don't behave like a spoiled brat!"

Outraged, Camilla turned to me for support.

"Suki, isn't he impossible! Tell him I'm going with you to India. Tell him you *need* me! You'll need another woman about the place, won't you?" She ended with a shriek as Gideon took a tighter grip on her hair.

"Let me go, you brute!"

"I think," I remarked loudly to no one in particular, "that Camilla behaves with great dignity and restraint."

Gideon Wait turned on me. "Are you backing her up, by any chance?"

"Well," I temporised. I had only just got the job and I didn't want to lose it before I ever saw India. "She does seem a little old for school."

"She's seventeen! She only just scraped through her O levels. Why, she has hardly any education at all!"

"I don't think she'll need much," I said firmly. "She isn't the academic type. She put the children to bed very nicely and she probably does lots of things very well indeed—"

"And I'm not in the least interested in the period of Queen Anne!" Camilla finished for me. "She's dead!"

Gideon looked from one to the other of us and laughed.

"Very well," he yelled at us. "She can come to India! But she'll be *your* responsibility!" He poked an accusing finger in my direction before hugging his sister to him. Helplessly I watched them, wondering what I had taken on. Camilla was really very young and sweet, and surely she couldn't come to very much harm in an obscure village in India?

Camilla held out her hand to me to include me in the little group.

"How nice that you're staying on for supper," she said.

Packing was a nightmare. The days were full enough. If I had had any gaps, Camilla obligingly filled them with her endless questions and even more endless lists of the things she considered quite essential to take with her. Daily, I drastically pruned the pile of things I had decided to take myself, and daily I tried to persuade her to do the same thing. But Camilla was already one of those women who either travel with nothing more than a pocket handkerchief or else with at least ten bulging trunks. Nothing in between appealed to her, and only Gideon's flat refusal to take her with him at all produced a more reasonable list of her requirements.

But at night I was alone and I would wander through the streets of London, retracing the walks I had taken with Timothy. Down that cul-de-sac, beneath the third street lamp on the right, he had kissed me once, and I would remember and weep. It seemed so strange that he should now be in a different country and I should be going to India. In the daytime two years seemed a very short space of time, but in the evenings it would stretch itself out into eternity and I would even doubt that I should ever see Timothy again.

A tin of his stomach powder stood drunkenly on the top of a row of books beside my bed and I hadn't the heart to throw it away. Every day I would search the table down below, where all the tenants' letters were thrown, looking for a letter from him, but none came. He was settling in, I told myself. He was working hard and his tummy was probably upset by the change of food. I could almost see him before me, wincing in pain because of something he had eaten, and he was very dear to me. Sometimes it occurred to me to wonder why he had not kissed me more often before he had gone, but I wouldn't allow myself to ask the question very often. Timothy Black was an ascetic man who seldom allowed his feelings to get the better of him, and that strong puritanical streak had undoubtedly told him that it was wrong to even casually caress a woman to whom you were not yet married. And I couldn't complain, for it was partly this boyish diffidence and exaggerated respect which I had loved. It was only very occasionally that I could see that it was not so much respect for me, but a fear lest he should become emotionally involved in anything outside himself and his work. But this I would never admit. Why should I? I had enough warmth for the two of us! And barriers in love were only made to be broken down.

I cried a great deal in the nights before we left for India and I thought I grew plainer every day. Gideon thought so too.

"What's the matter with you?" he demanded curtly one day, when he came across me lurking in his hallway.

"I—I'm sorry," I had apologised.

He had put a hand on my shoulder and propelled me towards the light.

"I thought so! Burning the candle at both ends, I suppose? Camilla has more sense. You'd better get some colour in your cheeks before we go or I shall be tempted to leave you behind."

"It's none of your business if I'm a bit pale!" I had retorted sharply.

His fingers had dug into my shoulder.

"Oh, isn't it? Well, I'm making it my business!" he had told me, his voice harsh with exasperation. "Are you ill or are you letting your emotions get the better of you?"

I had swallowed. "Someone I know has gone to America," I had told him woodenly. "It's left a bit of a gap, I suppose."

To my surprise he had been quite kind.

"You'll get over it," he had said roughly. He had smiled down at me and his dark eyes had been warm and friendly. "He probably isn't worth all the misery."

I had smiled myself. "It's temporary misery," I had said quietly. "He'll be back in two years."

"And you're waiting for him?"

Too honest to lie, I had shaken my head.

"There are no strings attached," I had said abruptly.

His sympathy had died and he had looked amused.

"Well, let's thank heavens for small mercies!" he had exclaimed. He had flicked my cheek with his finger. "You're not much older than Camilla, are you?"

Indignantly, I had regarded him with something approaching hatred. I wished passionately that I hadn't told him anything at all.

"Does it matter?" I had asked him languidly. "As long as I can grow maize?"

His laughter had rung through the house.

"Not a rap!" he had agreed.

And Timothy did seem to matter less the nearer we got to the day of our departure. On the last day, when we finally shut the suitcases we were taking with us on the aeroplane and said goodbye to our families and friends, I never thought of him at all. The only emotion I was aware of as we made our way to the airport was a burning sense of anticipation coupled with a juvenile feeling of panic that I was bound to lose either my passport or my ticket. Oh, whoops, I thought, India, here I come!

CHAPTER TWO

MOTHER INDIA! I pressed my nose against the awkward window and tried to see Delhi beyond the enormous grey wheeling wing of the aeroplane. The whole of India had been surprising to me from the air. There was so much empty space and huge outcrops of rocks that I supposed grew gradually higher and higher as they travelled north to the Himalayas. Somehow I had always imagined the subcontinent to be crammed full of people and very little else.

I hardly felt it at all when we actually landed and taxied across the concrete apron. Like all the other passengers, I struggled to my feet, smiling at my stiffness from sitting still and trying frantically to find all my hand luggage. Camilla and Gideon were on the other side of the enormous aircraft. They looked almost comically alike as he leaned towards his sister and cracked a joke in her ear. She glanced across at me and laughed, and I was annoyed to discover that I was hurt. It was one thing to be excluded from their family group, it was quite another to be the butt of their humour. But that was what I had to expect for the next two years, I reminded myself grimly. I would be one alone and that was the way I wanted it. I thought hard about Timothy with an increasing sense of panic as I realised that already his features were a trifle blurred in my mind and the pain of memory could no longer be made to ache on order.

The doors were flung open and the incredible heat from the outside rushed into the body of the plane. The sunlight danced in a haze of heat along the edge of the concrete, striking our feet even through the leather of our shoes. Camilla grimaced at me and made her way round a couple of static passengers to my side.

"Super flight!" she exclaimed ecstatically.

"Yes, I suppose it was," I agreed.

She grinned, not taken in for a minute by my lack of enthusiasm.

"For someone who dragged me round Rome for the greater part of the night, that must be the understatement of all time!" she teased me.

I looked around the airport buildings. "It doesn't seem very—Indian," I objected.

Her eyes danced. "You wait! Gideon has been telling me such stories about the people in the village that I can hardly wait to get there! He says we shall have to sleep on the local string beds and we're lucky to have them! *That* sounds Indian and sort of ascetic, doesn't it?"

I laughed. "Very!" I agreed amiably.

"Ah, here he comes!" she went on happily. "I suppose it's the Customs next." Her eyes fell on a group of Indian women dressed in colourful, flowing saris. "There," she exclaimed, prodding me in the ribs, "there's some local colour for you!"

Gideon's dark eyes met mine.

"Disappointed already?" he asked me smoothly.

I flushed. "It isn't that," I assured him hastily, but he wasn't even listening. He had taken off his coat and he walked off across the apron, swinging it easily between his fingers. The heat which had already reduced my crisp cotton frock to a rag apparently had no effect either on him or his clothes.

Camilla and I followed more slowly, determined not to miss anything. A couple of men, dressed in jodhpur trousers and long coat, stood in sober conversation by the entrance to the Customs. Beyond them was a wild character, his hair uncut and unbrushed, and his clothing no more than a sheet knotted over one shoulder. His staring eyes gave him the appearance of madness, but I thought he might be no more than a holy man and walked the long way round him just in case.

It was only when I had achieved my object that I realised that Gideon was watching me. It was too late then to pretend that I had not noticed the holy man or the indescribable odour that came from his body, but I put a brave face on it, hoping that the disapproval on Gideon's face was my imagination. It was not.

"Perhaps you and Camilla had better go outside while I see to the formalities," he said sharply.

Determined, I shook my head.

"I'd rather make sure of my own luggage," I said coldly.

We stood facing each other like a couple of boxers looking for an opening.

"What's the matter with you two?" Camilla asked us, puzzled.

Feeling rather foolish, I turned away and began to walk with her towards the street entrance. A row of taxis had drawn up outside the entrance. The chauffeurs squatted in a circle, gossiping the time away. They looked up when I showed myself in the doorway, jumping to their feet and running towards me, each one anxious that I should choose his cab. I moved back again out of sight and they gathered round the door, waiting, their eyes impassive.

At that moment another car drew up outside and a fair young man, so obviously American that I couldn't help smiling, came rushing into the reception lounge. He went straight across to Gideon and slapped him across the shoulders.

"So you're back!"

Gideon swung around, a wide smile on his face.

"And not alone!"

The American glanced about him with interest. "Anyone I know?"

Gideon beckoned to his sister and introduced the young man to her.

"Camilla, my love, this is my assistant, Joseph Groton. Joseph, my young sister. I brought her after all!"

The American shook her warmly by the hand and then turned to me. His hair was fair and his eyes were so blue that I could hardly believe they were real. There was a touch of weakness in his face, or it might have been the traces of a childhood illness. It had left his mouth too wide and not quite under control, but it was not obvious and to me it was oddly touching.

"And this?" he asked, a particularly charming smile breaking up his face. By contrast Gideon's quick frown seemed all the sterner.

"Miss Susan King," he introduced us briefly.

"In what capacity?"

I laughed, and the American laughed with me at his own question.

"Cereals—maize mostly, I expect, but I'm hoping for a bit of wheat as well."

"I daresay we can oblige you there. Irrigation and beat-up machinery is my speciality."

I could have hugged him, he was so normal and nice. He bent over and picked up my bags which had now been cleared and started to move off with them to the waiting taxi.

"We must get together," he told me lightly. "Two innocents abroad like us should deal famously together."

"I'm sure we shall!", I agreed, quite as enthusiastic as he.

He grinned. "Sticky journey out?" he enquired.

"Not so much that as a sticky arrival," I replied dryly.

Joseph Groton was immediately sympathetic. He too had obviously suffered from Gideon Wait and he was glad to have a fellow-sufferer, somebody he could grumble with, without it meaning too much, but as a safety valve for good of one's temper.

"It'll be swell having you about!" he said. "What's the kid like?"

I looked back at Camilla with a certain pleasure.

"I like her," I said simply.

"That's good enough for me!" said Joseph. He swung the luggage on to the back of the taxi and went back inside for the next lot. When he came back, he had Camilla eagerly dancing beside him.

"Have you ever been so hot in your life?" she demanded of me. "When is the monsoon expected? Or isn't it? This isn't normal, by any chance, is it?"

"It depends on the time of year," her brother informed her. "It's cooler at the village."

"We're a good bit higher than Delhi," Joseph added by way of explanation.

"And when do we get there?" Camilla demanded. She was tired and like the rest of us, except for her brother, was suffering badly from the unaccustomed and oppressive heat.

"We're stopping the night in Delhi," Gideon announced.

Joseph looked at his superior in surprise.

"Oh, but surely, sir—"

"Delhi!" Gideon snapped.

Camilla and I hurried into the taxi, trying to make ourselves as insignificant as possible.

"Gideon's feeling the heat too," Camilla confided in my ear as we settled down.

"Nonsense!" I retorted with some asperity. "Look at that beautiful creaseless shirt and then look at our dresses!"

Camilla giggled. "He *has* been stroking your fur the wrong way! I'll tell him to tread more carefully!"

"You'll do nothing of the sort!" I told her awfully.

She giggled again. "We'll see!"

"Camilla," I begged desperately, "please don't say one word to him. I'll never forgive you if you so much as remind him that I exist!"

Her dark eyes mocked me, and it was with difficulty that I remembered that she was only seventeen.

"Now I wonder what that means?" she said.

Fortunately I didn't have to make any comment, helpful or otherwise, because at that moment the men squashed themselves in on top of us and the taxi made off, with a curious limping motion, towards the road to Delhi. I had never been so close to Gideon before and the experience was a curiously unnerving one. His flesh was as hard as the unpadded sides of the taxi and there was little to choose as to which was doing the more damage to my own more sensitive frame.

The road from Palam Airport ran through miles of deserted land. I craned my neck to try and see the state of the soil, but all I could see was empty country, lying idle, with the occasional tomb dotted about and here and there an obviously new housing development, with that unsettled look of new housing developments the whole world over.

Then we were in New Delhi itself, a large, sprawling garden city, with lots of trees and large flower gardens and, apparently, not very many people at all.

"Disappointed?" Gideon asked me. His mouth was so close to my ear that I jumped despite myself.

"I can't see very much of it," I answered.

He leaned back obligingly and pointed out the main sights to me.

"That's the Prime Minister's house."

I peered round him in time to see the white stuccoed house with its guards in white and crimson with terrific highly starched turbans.

"Where are all the people?" I asked aloud, and then wished I hadn't, it sounded so silly and naïve.

He smiled and his face lost all trace of its former hostility.

"It surprised me at first too," he admitted. "Actually most of the people are in Old Delhi, but Indian crowds are always so silent as almost not to be there at all. I've seen several millions crowding on to the banks of the river on a holy day and there's hardly been a sound out of them."

I felt a tingling sensation of excitement at the picture his words conjured up, but I had no time to day dream then, for the taxi arrived at the hotel where we were staying the night and we drew up with a flourish, the doors flew open and suddenly we were free of the pressure of each other's body and were standing on the burning pavement outside the imposing Victorian entrance to the hotel. A bearer stepped forward with incomparable dignity and signalled to a lesser being to take in the luggage.

"Sahib Wait, you are expected, sir," he greeted us. "And all your party," he added expansively.

We were led gently towards the reception desk and then were taken up by yet more bearers to our rooms in a very grand procession. It appeared that each of us had been allotted a separate room that looked out on to the same terrace where we could all meet for breakfast. Camilla, highly delighted with her new surroundings, ran out to see how much she could see of the city and was pleased to discover that she could look out into the yard of an older and completely Indian house opposite. There a couple of hens scratched in the dust and the children played complicated games, one of which looked remarkably like hopscotch.

"I can almost believe we're here," Camilla sighed with satisfaction.

Her brother grinned.

"We'll go across into Old Delhi and then you'll completely believe it!" he told her.

"Is it terribly old?" she asked him, her eyes round with excitement.

"Well, no, I suppose not," he admitted. "There have been nine Delhis within historical memory, which is one of the reasons one can spend so much time getting from one place to another. New Delhi was built by the British, Old Delhi by a Moslem overlord, and the rest are mainly of archaeological interest only."

Camilla eyed him uncertainly. "You planned this deliberately, didn't you? So that we should see it?"

Gideon shrugged his shoulders. "There won't be much time once we get down to work," he explained. "I'm afraid it may be dull for you?"

But Camilla shook her head, her eyes glowing.

"Never!" she averred. "I'm completely happy to be here."

He smiled at her with real affection.

"Good," he said.

I moved away from them and went into my own room. It was large and spacious and I was secretly rather impressed that it should have been allotted to me. The bed was enormous, a relic from a previous age, elaborately carved with trumpeting elephants. Over it hung a mosquito net, tied in a neat knot to keep it out of the way. On the floor were flung several Indian rugs and a number of rickety tables with collapsible legs. I fingered them experimentally, admiring the heavy brass tops and especially the one made of copper instead, that glowed almost pink in the dim light. Evening was approaching.

From the window I could see the city spread out before me, with its wide streets and the pleasant flower gardens left behind by the British. Once again I marvelled at how few people there were about and wondered where they were all hiding themselves. A young woman dressed in the Punjabi pyjama trousers, now worn very tight to be in the height of fashion, moved slowly past on a bicycle. I leaned out a little farther to see her go, wondering if she were a common sight or one of the few emancipated women who went about on their own.

As I turned away from the window there was a sharp rap at the door. I went over to it and opened it carefully. Joseph Groton grinned cheerfully at me.

"I thought I'd come along and get to know you," he began. "May I come in?"

I stood back to let him enter, a shade doubtful as to whether it was a very good idea to have him in my room.

"Where are the others?" I asked.

He strode over to the window and peered down into the street.

"I suggested they should go off on their own and see some of the sights. Camilla has never had much time with her brother before." He glanced at me over his shoulder. "Do you mind?"

I shook my head, still a little wary.

"Why should I?" I asked abruptly. "It's none of my business."

He swung round on his heel.

"What a prickly creature you are! You wouldn't be averse to making it your business, would you?"

I frowned at him. "I have always found it best," I said coldly, "to leave members of any family alone together."

To my surprise he laughed.

"My, my, what virtue!" he mocked. "Actually the reason I told you was so that you would understand how it is that your evening entertainment rests in my capable hands—"

"You don't have to put yourself out for me, Mr. Groton," I said.

His eyes narrowed with temper. "What's the matter with you? Are you always like this? Or did someone slap you when you expected a kiss?"

I flushed. His words were nearer the truth than I liked.

"I'm sorry. I suppose I'm tired after all that travelling."

He was easily placated. His features relaxed and his weak mouth wobbled into a smile.

"It doesn't matter," he assured me. "I've been looking forward to showing you around ever since I first saw you. And please, it isn't Mr. Groton, it's just plain Joe as far as you're concerned."

He was very sweet, I thought.

"My name is Susan," I told him. "Most people call me Suki, though."

"Okay, Suki!" He extended his right hand and we solemnly shook hands.

"Hullo, Joe," I replied.

He was very easy to be with. From one of his pockets

he produced one of those neat guides that Americans always seem to have, packed with facts written in an easy-to-read style. He leafed through it with deep concentration until he came to the section he wanted.

"Ah, Delhi," he muttered. "We have quite an evening in front of us. I think we'd better get a taxi and go over to Old Delhi first. Will that suit you?"

I abandoned, quite easily, my previous idea of an early night and time to get used to the idea that it was really I who had flown all this way and had alighted in this mysterious sub-continent. It would be much more fun to go with Joe.

"Do you ever get indigestion?" I asked him conversationally as we waited on the steps of the hotel for the magnificent bearer to get us a taxi.

"Sometimes," he admitted. "Why?"

I grinned at him, for the first time feeling quite at home.

"Because I'm an expert at dealing with it," I told him.

Old Delhi was a match for my dreams. The ancient Mogul mosques bore witness to a foreign creed, but it was by no means the only one. The Jains, who refuse to kill any living creature, had a bird hospital beside their temple and, it seemed to me, there were a hundred more, all equally colourful and quite unlike what I was accustomed to. The people too were truly of the East. The raucous traffic strove with a thousand bicycles, the walking skeletons of the holy cows, and the Indian conviction that he would be better off in the middle of the road no matter what the hazards involved. The rickshaws, pulled along by hungry-looking individuals on bicycles, wove in and out of the high-powered cars with a breathless unconcern for life and limb. Cars there were by the hundred, but the Indian heart and mind was still with the ox cart and a more sober pace of living. Speed and death merely gave a tang to the endless excitement of living.

We stopped and watched a pavement barber shaving his customer from top to toe. His tools seemed primitive in the extreme, but his fingers were deft and his patter a source of high amusement to those around him. Both he and his victim squatted in the gutter, in a position that came as naturally to them as standing does to us. If I had tried it, I should have been crippled in a matter of minutes, and that as much as anything else made me appreciate the agility of all their movements.

A cloud of yellowish smoke clung over the city in drifts. It had an evil smell and at each street corner seemed to accost us anew. It was only when I saw a small child lighting a small brazier on the pavement and feeding it carefully with dried cow-dung that I realised that most of the people who lived in the city had no houses to go to. They lived, all of them, on the pavement itself, eating and sleeping, playing and working on the same small patch of ground. Some of them had found shelter in some of the shacks that filled the few spaces between the houses that belonged to the richer members of the community. There was no privacy for anyone, but the families seemed to survive, the younger looking after the youngest with loving hands while the parents looked on with a justified pride.

The whole of life pulsated on those streets. Vendors sold their goods, money-lenders and barbers carried out their several services, tailors sewed their goods, using their toes like monkeys to turn the handles of the battered Singer sewing machines that must first have been used in another era. Saris, brilliantly coloured, were laid out to dry. And there was the movement and enthusiasm of a people who were really alive everywhere one looked.

I stopped at a small store that was selling helpings of curry to the passers-by.

"It smells pretty good, don't you think?" I said to Joe.

He cast me a horrified look. "Don't ever eat any!"

he warned me. "You'd be in hospital with Delhi belly as quick as knife." I believed him, if a trifle reluctantly, quite sure that my English system would never be able to do efficient battle against that acrid smoke and the dust that was being constantly rearranged by the wind.

"Where can we eat?" I asked him, suddenly extremely hungry. "Do we have to go back to the hotel?"

"I'll take you to my favourite restaurant, if you like," he offered shyly. "It isn't at all grand, but it's the real thing."

I followed him eagerly to his restaurant. Joseph knew Delhi pretty well and he had no hesitation as to which of the narrow streets to take. Most of them I should have been afraid to enter on my own, but his breezy confidence reassured me that we were not trespassing on some illicit underworld and, after a while, I got over my fright and was even able to view some of the desperate beggars with sympathy and interest rather than sheer fright.

The restaurant itself was very small. Somehow between the tables a couple of female dancers gyrated madly to the rhythm of an old man on a flute-like instrument that produced a curious, hypnotic sound. The dancers were fantastic and had muscles in their necks, which they could *move*, that I really don't think even exist in mine. Later on, I tried it out in front of a looking-glass and retired to bed a casualty, convinced that I had broken my neck. Actually I had done nothing of the sort, but it was very sore at the time.

Joseph chose a table in one corner. It was lit by a single candle, that added romance if not enlightenment to what we were eating. A singer took the place of the dancers and a severe-looking waiter with very fine features and a thin narrow mouth came for our order. Joseph ordered for both of us.

"It's nice here," he said with pleasure as the waiter went away. "The food really is Indian, not a conglomerate mess mixed with Western cabbage."

I laughed. "I'm expecting great things!" I said.

His hand met mine and took firm possession of it.

"If you could have seen your predecessor—" he began.

It was funny but I didn't in the least mind flirting with him.

"I can guess!" I retorted.

"I nearly fell over when I saw the boss had brought you back with him!" he added, his eyes twinkling.

"I take my work very seriously too," I said.

"Too? You mean you have time for other things as well?"

I coloured. "Yes, of course," I said. There was a glint in Joseph's eyes that I didn't quite like. I had to make it very clear that I had come to work and to wait the two years for Timothy to get home and I wasn't succeeding very well. "But my work comes first," I added defensively.

He leaned towards me over the table. I had a mad anxiety that he was going to burn his tie in the flame of the single candle.

"You're too good to be true," he said. "Tell me all about yourself!"

I licked my lips nervously. "There isn't much to tell. I'd rather hear about you."

His eyes snapped at me. "I'm an American. Isn't that enough?"

I shook my head. "Tell me about your job here."

He leaned back and relaxed in his chair, a slight smile on his face.

"Certainly not. You'll find out all about that quickly enough. I want you to see me as a man, not as a cog in the great Gideon's machine."

I was startled into looking at him more closely. His chin quivered slightly and I was reminded again of the basic weakness of his face. But I liked him very much indeed, if only because, in some indescribable way, he reminded me of Timothy.

"I don't think you'll ever be a cog to me," I said gently.

His smile grew warmer. "Is that a promise?"

I nodded my head solemnly. "It's a promise."

His eyes fell to the table. "I can hardly ask fairer than that," he said.

I was a little embarrassed by his seriousness, but at that moment the waiter brought our food and that successfully distracted my attention. It was certainly the most delicious curry I had ever tasted, not as hot as I had expected, but with so many side dishes that I soon lost count. I recognised the dessicated coconut and one or two of the chutneys, and of course the sliced bananas, but the rest I had never seen before and I was anxious to taste the lot.

"Shall we have some wine to go with it?" Joe asked.

I hesitated, wondering about the price. I had been told that it was impossible to have anything alcoholic in Delhi without paying a great deal of money and I was really wondering if Joseph could afford to throw his money away so recklessly.

"No, I won't," I said carefully.

"Oh, come on! One bottle won't break the bank!"

He gave the order to the waiter and then sat back looking very pleased with himself. "It will be the first seal on our friendship," he added.

"The first?"

He grinned. "Why, yes, I have plans for the second too!"

I blushed, beginning to think that I was rapidly getting out of my depth. A more normal topic of conversation was more to my taste, and so it was with determination that I brought the subject firmly back to wheat.

"What sort of crops can I expect?" I began cheerfully.

But Joseph refused to be drawn.

"It depends on what crops you are referring to," he answered lightly. "If you're referring to wheat, or sugar, or even rice, you can expect practically no return at all. But if you're referring to *other* crops—"

"What other crops, Joe?" I asked innocently.

"Oh, lies, dirt and disease." He winked at me. "Or friends and neighbours, or even people to love—"

My head lifted sharply.

"I haven't time for things like that!" I said sharply.

"Now, Suki," he reproved me, "you just said you had time for other things besides your work!"

"Not those other things!" I said stiffly.

But he only laughed.

"But you forget," he reminded me, "we've set a seal on our friendship. And if that can be broken, here's another bond more difficult for you to forget." He leaned over the table and caught up both my hands in his, kissing me lightly on the lips.

It was unfortunate that at that moment Gideon and Camilla came into the restaurant. I snatched my hands away from Joseph, but it was too late. A single glance was enough to tell that Gideon had seen the whole incident. I greeted him and his sister with flaming cheeks, doubly annoyed with myself. It was not only that I felt that I had somehow failed Timothy, it was more that I had hoped to give Gideon a quite different impression.

CHAPTER THREE

It was still very early when Camilla crept into my room to see if I was awake. She padded over to the shuttered windows and pushed them open to let in the first grey light of the day.

"Gideon has gone to pick up the new jeep," she told her. "We're all expected to be ready by the time he comes back."

I turned over and squinted at her against the light.

"What time is it?" I asked.

"It's nearly six," she said.

I turned back on to my side and thought about it. It was the middle of the night!

"What time will he be back?"

Camilla shrugged her shoulders. "Goodness knows! He *says* the garage is only just round the corner, but he's been gone a little while now. You'd better get up and pack your things otherwise he'll start making rude remarks about the way you spend your evenings!"

I frowned. "Actually I don't," I said sourly. "Joseph—" I hesitated. "I think he was trying to be kind," I ended with a rush.

Camilla chuckled.

"I can imagine!" she agreed enthusiastically. "Poor Joseph! If this place is anything like he described it to me yesterday, you must have come like a gift from the gods to him. I can't think why you're even hesitating about him. *I* think he's awfully nice!"

"Yes," I said, "I suppose he is. I don't want to be precipitated into anything, though. He's in such a hurry!"

Camilla gazed at me solemnly.

"What are you afraid of?" she asked me. "What Gideon thinks of you?"

I shook my head, hoping that she would not detect the lie that was implicit in my response. I didn't *want* to care what Gideon thought, but that was something a little different, as I knew quite well.

"I must get up," I said instead.

She blinked at me, still serious.

"How old do you think Joe is?" she asked.

I swung my legs on to the floor and stood up, pattering over to the window to have a look at the day for myself. Now that I knew where to look, I could see again the yellow smoke of the cow-dung fires and, thicker still, the fires of the funerals that were taking place along the banks of the river. Life and death intermingled throughout the city and both were casually accepted by the citizens as something unremarkable and every day.

"Does it matter?" I replied to Camilla's question.

"Of course it does! I reckon he's about ten years older than I am, and I think that's about right between a man and a woman, don't you?"

"Possibly," I agreed.

"Humph," said Camilla. "Does that mean you have him all staked out for yourself?"

"Well, he certainly isn't ten years older than I am!" I reminded her.

"No-o," she admitted uncertainly. "But you're not *old*, and he is interested. In fact you might say you had a head start with him!"

I went into the small bathroom which was attached to the room and began to dress, leaving the door open so that I could still hear Camilla.

"One could, if it were a race," I said mildly.

She chuckled, a soft, very feminine noise in her throat.

"Not a race," she contradicted me, "a fight to the finish!"

I hesitated in my dressing, wondering if she meant

what she said. But Camilla was still very young and apt
to wring the last bit of drama out of any remark. I finished dressing as quickly as I could and gathered up my
night clothes to pack them away in my suitcase. Camilla
was sitting on the end of my bed, her hair flowing free
and a young and rather touching expression on her
face. She looked up at me and her face fell into a genuine grin.

"I suppose you're cross with me for challenging your
interest?" she said.

It was my turn to laugh.

"Good heavens, no! Joe Groton is nothing to me!"

Camilla was satisfied.

"No," she said thoughtfully. "I dare say Gideon is
much more your cup of tea. The trouble is he never
sees anyone as a woman. My sister is always complaining about it. You see the truth is that we're all dying to
marry him off!"

"Oh, indeed!" I retorted. "Well, there's not the
slightest chance of your marrying him off to me, young
lady! He's a great deal too confident and full of himself
to appeal to my sort of person."

Camilla turned on me, angry at any breath of criticism of her brother.

"What a *smug* thing to say!" she stormed.

I sighed, acknowledging the truth of that. It was the
way I had been brought up, I thought, sensibly and
without much humour.

"Exactly! And your brother may be many things, but
he certainly isn't smug!"

Camilla giggled. "He says he thinks you're a very
cautious young woman," she told me. It was getting up
so early, I know, but I could have sat down and cried.

It was a peculiar experience, having breakfast in the
ornate and gigantic restaurant of the hotel. Two bearers, in braided scarlet coats and with stiffly starched turbans, served us an incongruously English breakfast of
eggs and bacon followed by toast and marmalade. Both
Joseph and Camilla tucked in with concentrated plea-

sure. I myself thought it was rather hot for such a large
meal and I was beginning to wonder what had happened to Gideon and the jeep.

He arrived, hot and more than a little irritable, just as
we were finishing the last of the coffee.

"Are you all ready?" he asked.

"Of course we are!" his sister answered him. "Where
on earth have you been?"

He sat down at the empty place at the table and nodded to the bearers to bring him his food.

"Getting the jeep," he said with tight displeasure.
"It was promised for over an hour ago, but owing to
some death in the family I had to wait for the funeral
party to come back.

I realised that this was only the beginning of the story.

"And then?" I prompted him.

His face relaxed into a smile.

"And then the plugs needed cleaning and they had
to send for a mechanic."

"Didn't they have one?" Camilla asked, entering in
to the spirit of the story.

"It appears not. I did it myself in the end and it's
going, so as soon as we're all ready, we should be going."

In actual fact it was another hour before we were all
settled in the jeep with our luggage in a pile under our
feet. Joe sat in the front beside Gideon and Camilla and
I huddled in the back, both of us a trifle anxious that
there seemed to be so very little to hold on to. We
crawled out of Delhi, dodging the oxen carts and the
weaving bicycles, going so slowly that we had almost
got used to our exposed position by the time we had
reached the outskirts and the open road.

We had not gone very far, however, before my equa-
nimity was rudely shattered by the sight of several large
animals wallowing in a muddy pond.

"What are those?" I asked Camilla nervously.

Camilla looked behind us at the dusty trail we were
leaving across the countryside.

"Where?" she asked vaguely.

"In that muddy puddle." I pointed beside the road.

"That's a tank," Joseph told me.

"The animal?" I was quite prepared to believe him. They looked very large animals to me.

"No, silly, the muddy pools!"

"The animals are water buffalo," Gideon supplied. "They're quite harmless. Do you want to stop and take a look?" He drew up at the side of the road and helped Camilla and me down into the dust, leading the way towards the nearest tank, and there they were, a whole herd of them, slopping about in the evil-coloured water. They were large animals with black and dark brown hides and they spent hours in the water, standing in as deep water as they were able, their big horns about the only thing to show where they were. And they were not alone in the water. A few naked children played in one corner, chasing each other in and out of the water. Women, too, were taking the opportunity to wash both their clothes and themselves, though how they managed to get anything cleaner in the liquid mud I couldn't imagine.

We climbed back into the jeep and sped on along the endless road, through a dozen small and very poor villages and on to our own. I tried to see as much as I could of the various crops as we went along. Sugar cane grew here and there, looking very tired and undernourished. I longed to stop and take a look at it, but that was to come when we came to our own experimental fields and could see better what would have to be done.

The sun grew hotter, until the sky was like burning pewter and the hot, dry wind blew up the dust into our faces and dried our skins and made us long for some cool shade and the splash of running water. After a while Joseph took over the wheel from Gideon, driving with a hare-brained desperation that ate up the miles but left us more exhausted than ever.

At last the heat of the day departed and it was evening.

"Not much farther now!" Gideon said cheerfully.

I tried to smile at him, but the dust had mixed with my perspiration, leaving a tight mask across my face. I rubbed my cheeks with my fingers and they came away red with the same dust.

"Cheer up," he said. "It'll wash off easily enough. Besides, it's rather fetching!"

"Nonsense!" I said roughly.

He exchanged a humorous glance with Camilla and I wished desperately that I had said nothing at all, though why I should care so much I couldn't imagine. I had come to work and to fill in two years—nothing more than that.

So I was stiff and rather wretched when we came to the village. Camilla waved to the children who came rushing out to greet us, but I was too busy looking at the extraordinary buildings, many of them plastered with the ubiquitous cow-dung, and the small central shrine around which the women were gathered, seeking the favours of the little stone figure in their midst, representing which god of the Hindu pantheon I did not know.

The jeep pulled up outside a fair-sized bungalow which had a large verandah going right around it.

"This is the central house of the Station," Joseph told me. "Gideon and I sleep here and the laboratory and the records are kept at the back. You and Camilla are going to sleep somewhere else eventually, but come in meanwhile and we'll raise the cook to get us something to eat."

We accepted the offer gratefully. Enormous fans in every room moved lazily, keeping the air comparatively cool, and it was bliss just to stand beneath one of them and feel the cold current on my face and hands.

"*Memsahib*," said a small, soft voice at my elbow. I glanced down to see the most beautiful little creature smiling gently up at me. It was impossible to tell her age, but the liquid brown eyes held an age of wisdom that contrasted vividly with the youthful firmness of her flesh. She was dressed in a vivid orange sari that was edged with shocking pink and silver that somehow didn't clash but was merely provocative to the eye. With infinite grace she put her palms together and raised them in front of her face in the time-honoured Indian greeting. Her eyes lit up with laughter as I clumsily returned the greeting.

"You have driven a long way?" she asked. "You will need a bath and many clean clothes. It is so hot at this time of year."

The idea of a bath was sheer bliss.

"Is it really possible to have a bath?" I asked her.

The fragile little woman bowed gracefully.

"It will be my pleasure to serve you while you are here," she said in her soft voice. "My name is Lakshmi."

"Lakshmi? The goddess of happiness?" I was proud to be able to show off my meagre knowledge of her religion.

She laughed and smiled.

"She has a little to do with prosperity also," she added. "If you will follow me I shall prepare your bath."

We went out of the main room with its formal chairs and beautiful rugs on the polished floor to explore the rest of the house. One or two pictures, faded photographs for the most part, hung on the walls of the various rooms, decorated with coloured pieces of paper. Closer examination gave no clue as to whom the photographs were of, but they were obviously highly valued by someone in the house.

The plan of the rooms was simple. Somewhere in the centre was the kitchen, a small hole where the cook managed superbly with a small brazier and a few unlikely pots. He squatted on the floor and ground his spices on a flat stone amidst a clutter of utensils. Out of the chaos somehow emerged several meals a day, all immaculately served. It was a constant source of wonder to all of us.

The bedrooms were spartan, furnished only with a single bed, a small table, a chair and a hanging recess hidden by a much faded curtain. There were three of them, all exactly the same. It was easy to recognise Gideon's. Immaculately tidy, it nevertheless betrayed his presence by the titles of the few books and the single strange sculpture that hung on the wall.

I peaked into the second room and into the third. It was exactly the same in every essential as the other, even to the patterns of the dust on the floor.

"You will be comfortable here?" Lakshmi asked.

I looked at her in surprise.

"I thought—I was told that I was sleeping in another house," I said.

"With the little *memsahib*," she agreed. "This is only for your bath. I will bring it to you now."

With a flash of orange she was gone and I was left alone. Down the corridor I could hear Camilla's cheerful laughter and enough splashing to make me envious. It seemed that she was already in the bath and I should have to wait until she was finished. But two seconds later Lakshmi was back carrying an enormous tin bath of the type I had only ever seen in illustrations of old-fashioned books. She laid it on the floor and filled it from buckets of boiling water.

"Thank you very much," I said, expecting her to go, but she did nothing of the sort. Gently she helped me into the bath and cupping her hands together poured the water over me.

"This is from the Ganges. This is from the Jumna." And so on, naming the Indian rivers one by one, the holy rivers of India. It was an attractive custom, but one which is dying out, she told me, half shamefaced. She had been brought up by her grandmother, she told me, and had learned the custom from her.

It was very pleasant soaking in the hot water. By contrast the air seemed quite cool and by the time I had dried myself and dressed I felt quite fresh and anxious to begin at once by seeing where I was going to work and with whom.

Camilla was still soaking in her bath when I went past Gideon's room and so only the two men were on the verandah as I went out. They both stood up to greet me, their cane chairs creaking comfortably.

"Sit down and I'll get you a drink," Joe said immediately.

I frowned at him. "I—I don't think I will," I said shyly.

"Okay," he agreed easily. "On your head be it."

I sat uneasily on the only vacant chair and watched the two men as they joked with each other, tacitly consenting to let me alone until I should proffer a remark of my own. I hunted through my mind for something interesting to say and came up with precisely nothing.

"The *panchayat* is coming up later to discuss the water supply," Joseph told Gideon over his shoulder, helping himself to another drink.

Gideon grinned. "Sheer curiosity!" he laughed. "They want to see the girls!"

Joseph looked straight at me. "This one will keep them in order," he teased me.

I could feel Gideon's eyes burning into my turned-away face.

"The *panchayat* are the village elders," he drawled.

I turned to look at him. "H-how many of them are there?"

"A round dozen. Someone has to represent each of the many and varied interests in the village."

I began to suspect he was teasing me. "And they are?"

He considered for a moment. "Caste," he began, "and sub-castes, and the landowners and the land-hungry, those who want to build a dam for irrigation purposes and those who don't, and so on."

The very idea of having to deal with such a committee appalled me.

"How—how madly democratic!" I said faintly.

Gideon's eyes twinkled appreciatively.

"There's hope for you yet," he said.

But nothing he had said prepared me for the reality of the meeting. One by one the old men trooped on to the verandah, raised their hands in greeting and sat down with their legs knotted before them on the floor.

"Are we ready?" Gideon asked. He looked very strong and inflexible as he towered above them on his chair. One of the old men smiled at him sheepishly.

"The *Swami* is not yet come," he said smoothly.

Gideon frowned. "He does know we are meeting?"

The same old man answered, "Of course."

Camilla, with her hair done up on top of her head and her neck still wet from her bath, came sailing out of Gideon's room and came to join us on the verandah. Her eyebrows rose spectacularly when she saw the assembled party, but although she was so much younger she was much more self-possessed than I could ever hope to be.

"Good evening," she greeted them with a dazzling smile.

The old men rose in a single wave of movement.

"How pleasurable to make your acquaintance," said their spokesman, and the others nodded emphatically round the circle.

"How lovely to see you all!" Camilla responded cheerfully. She clasped her hands together in inspiration. "Is there any lemonade?" she asked Gideon.

It was Joseph who went to the kitchen and came back with a tray of ice-cold bottles and a bundle of straws. The liquids came in the brightest colours of green and raspberry, orange and the deep brown of Coca-Cola. The old men sucked contentedly at their straws and then, suddenly, a young man with wild matted hair and an orange robe that barely covered his nakedness walked in. Gideon greeted him with evident pleasure, and I offered him a bright green bottle which he gravely rejected.

"Though it is good to see such progress and to have all these good men taking refreshments together," he added with a flash in his eyes. "I shall sit here and study the problems we have before us."

He sat down quickly at my feet and bowed slightly to the other men. With his coming everybody had burst into excited laughter, but at his signal there was complete silence again.

"We have come to talk about the well," the spokesman said in his careful English. "We have paid much for this benefit and, as yet, we can get no water there." It was a bare statement of fact, unadorned and uncomplicated.

The *Swami* sat in silence, apparently not listening at all. The others, more confident now the original point had been made, were positively lyrical about their previous expectations from the new water supply and how badly let down they felt. Finally, when the last man had spoken, the *Swami* turned to Gideon.

"Is this true?" he asked quietly.

Gideon nodded.

"As far as it goes. We are waiting for the electricity to be turned on. As it is it has to be manipulated by hand and the women prefer the old tank down by the sugar cane."

"And the electrician?" the *swami* prodded gently.

"Has not been paid," Gideon supplied wryly.

There was an immediate outburst of indignation as all the old men tried to explain why their particular group in the village was not responsible for this omission. With mounting excitement they told how the electrician had come and had done the work and then had removed the operative fuse until his bill had been paid in full. But how could they pay until they got the water to irrigate their crops?

The *Swami* listened to them all, waiting patiently while the flow of words went over his head and gradually stilled to a whisper.

"Be that as it may," he said calmly, "it is very annoying to be deprived of your water. What remedy do you suggest?"

The silence became uncomfortable.

"I am afraid the research station has already exceeded the amount that was set aside for the project," Gideon said. There was a thread of laughter under his words which surprised me. It was not lost on the old men either.

"It is such a simple dilemma," the *Swami* went on as if no one had spoken. "I shall place my scarf on the floor here in the corner and after everyone has gone doubtless we shall find enough money on it to pay the electrician. Now, let us drink and be merry."

The old men obediently drank up their fizzy drinks and then one by one they departed, gossiping happily among themselves. The *Swami* sat upright, with his back very straight and his neck bent so that he could look at his toes tucked into his groin. To all appearances he was asleep and completely oblivious to his surroundings. I looked at the saintly lines on his face and wondered at his asceticism. He wore the saffron robes of the oriental monk which I knew betokened celibacy and a laying aside of all the pleasures of this world. Later I was to discover that he was the local holy man with a reputation for charity and that he deserved every word of praise that was constantly sung of him. Now, he merely puzzled me.

"It was kind of you, *Swamiji*, to come to our assistance," Gideon said when we were alone.

The young man looked up and smiled.

"I think we have more than enough to pay our way now," he said with satisfaction. "And it was my pleasure to come."

Gideon grinned. "Perhaps I should don an orange robe like yours?"

But the *Swami* shook his head. "You will want to marry, my friend. You are ever a practical man!"

"And you are not?"

The wild unkempt hair waved in the wind. "I like to think," the Indian retorted in an affected Oxford accent, "that I can keep my feet on the ground and my head in the clouds!"

We all laughed, and quite suddenly, without a word of farewell, he too rose to his feet and sauntered down the steps and was gone without a backward glance. Joe and Camilla fell over each other trying to grab the money and they solemnly began to count it up. Gideon watched them with a superior smile.

"I'm glad you managed to restrain your western greed until after the *Swami* had gone!" he chided them. But they ignored him, their attention entirely engaged by a number of small coins that added together could only have represented a very minute sum.

"Mr. Wait," I said with a certain firmness, "would it be possible to see where I am going to work?"

His eyes met mine with evident reluctance.

"If you really want to," he said indifferently. He swallowed the remainder of his drink with a gulp and stood up. "I may as well show you your quarters at the same time."

We went another way from the corridor that led to the bedrooms and through a central courtyard that was full of the servants' children laughing and talking together, the small looking after the smallest and making sure that they came to no harm.

"Do they know who belongs to which family?" I asked.

He smiled slightly. "I imagine so."

He pushed open a door and led me into a laboratory. It was cluttered up with papers and useless apparatus and it was quite obvious that it was being shared by far too many people already. Gideon frowned at some evil-looking growth on a tray and shoved it out of sight. His own area was the only neat part of the room. His trays were labelled and his paperwork looked to be in some sort of order.

"I was afraid they would have shoved my stuff completely out of sight while I was away," he muttered. "We haven't nearly enough room."

"No," I agreed, "I can see that."

"In fact," he added, "you will be the final straw!"

I blushed and bit my lip.

"Perhaps I can work in my bedroom," I suggested stiffly.

He put his two hands on my shoulders and turned me to face him.

"Why are you so touchy?" he asked me.

The strength of his fingers burned into my flesh. "I don't think I am—particularly."

"Oh, come now! Let me disillusion you!" He stared straight into my eyes. "Are you still unhappy?" he demanded.

I shrugged myself free. "Of course not!" I denied in a brittle voice. "I know exactly where I'm going. I'm not in need of anyone's sympathy."

"No?"

"No, certainly not! All I want is to be left alone!"

The warmth and the humour vanished from his eyes.

"In that case you won't take it amiss if I tell you not to tease Joseph, will you? Joseph hasn't got your care-free touch!"

His sarcasm hurt, more than I cared to show.

"Why do you think I'd hurt Joseph?" I asked him unhappily.

"He's susceptible. Don't encourage him."

I stood up very straight and glared at him.

"We're friends!"

"Rubbish!" he dismissed me sharply. "Joseph is incapable of being friends with any woman."

I sucked in my cheeks to stop myself from crying. To give my hands something to do I played with the gas tube that fed one of the burners.

"You're not very loyal to him, are you?" I muttered, hoping to hurt him as he had hurt me.

"More loyal than you think! I wasn't thinking about Joseph's well-being when I hired you."

"Too bad!" I stormed at him. "But it doesn't really matter what you say or think. Joe and I have agreed to be friends and I daresay I shall be very much better for him than you think."

Gideon slammed his hand flat down on to the table.

"If by that you mean a repetition of that pretty little scene I witnessed last night, I hardly think so."

I blushed again. I could feel the colour creeping up my neck and cheeks. And then, quite suddenly, I was so blazing angry that I had to hold on to the table to give myself support.

"What a splendidly *scientific* conclusion!" I stormed at him. "Well, as far as I'm concerned you can think exactly what you please!"

His face tightened with temper in his turn.

"Is that so? Then I'll tell you what I think. I think you're on the rebound, young lady, and that one man's attention will do just as well as the next. *And*, what's more, I'll prove it."

He pulled me towards him and kissed me hard on the lips. The funny thing was that, furious as I was, it wasn't quite so disagreeable as I expected.

CHAPTER FOUR

THUNDER rolled round the skies and was mirrored in my own impotent rage. Gideon let me go and took a step backwards. He looked white and a little less sure of himself.

"Shall we go on with our tour?" I asked him in a funny tight voice I could scarcely recognise as my own.

"I think we'd better join the others," he answered.

Deliberately, I lifted my eyebrows.

"Really? *Afraid*, Mr. Wait?"

His fists clenched as he stared at me.

"Dr. Wait, if you don't mind, when we're working. And no, I am not in the least afraid of you. I have the advantage, you see. I can always sack you!"

The small bit of confidence that temper had given me slowly evaporated before him. I bit my lip, reflecting that he was taking a base and very unfair advantage because his kissing me had had nothing whatever to do with our work. The thunder crashed again overhead and I shivered.

"Is it going to rain?" I asked.

Gideon shook his head. "It's a dry storm. If I turned out the lights you could see the lightning tearing the sky apart. The rain will come later when the monsoons start."

He put his hand up to the switch, but I shook my head in sudden fright.

"I—I think I'd like to go to my room," I said.

He gave me a quick look and I was bitterly self-conscious about my mussed hair and the quivering sensation of tears at the back of my eyes.

"I'll call Lakshmi," he said abruptly and, turning on his heel, he walked out of the laboratory.

Left alone, I could get a much better idea of the work that was being done. A few sickly wheat plants had been picked in jars and I looked at them with interest. They were a far cry from the wheat I was accustomed to in Europe. I reckoned that the yield from these plants could only be about a half and they were all suffering from diseases that were easily curable. Nearly half of the specimens showed signs of "take-all", a disease of the roots that has practically been mastered in England.

A shadow moved across the jars and I looked up and saw that Lakshmi had joined me in the laboratory.

"Hullo," I said.

She gave me a mildly reproving look, apparently not sure that such a greeting was entirely proper.

"Do you want me to take you across to the other house now?" she asked me.

"If you don't mind," I responded.

She swished her sari more securely around her shoulders and stepped out of the room, half waiting for me to follow her. Another flash of lightning blazed across the heavens and was followed by a heavy roll of thunder. Lakshmi winced and then smiled.

"I am afraid of thunder," she admitted softly. "It is better when it rains, but these dry storms only make me think that the gods must be angry."

I thought I could see what she meant. There was something eerie and supernatural about the white light and the noise and no resulting rain.

"I'm a bit afraid too," I said. "We have nothing like this in England."

She gave me a glance of concealed scorn.

"In England life is very much easier," she said calmly, and led the way through the house and out across the back verandah.

The very air was tense and electric with the storm. I could feel it prickling on my skin and I hesitated to walk across the open space, but Lakshmi went daintily before me picking her way over the rough ground, and I thought that I could not be less brave than such a tiny, delicate creature. But I was glad when we reached the safety of the second bungalow, much smaller than the main building and built on a similar, though simplified, pattern of a whole lot of rooms all looking out into the central area where the life of the family was mainly lived.

Lakshmi entered one of the small, practically bare rooms and went over to the window, flinging open the shutters.

"If you need anything, you have only to ask me for it," she said almost apologetically. I looked round the room with a feeling of dismay. It was so foreign to my previous ideas. A single bed, low and threaded with string instead of springs, stood in one corner against the wall. There was no table beside the bed and very little in the way of bedding. Apart from the bed there was only a desk and a home-made wooden chair with one leg at least an inch shorter than the other three. An old frayed rug had been spread across the floor, somehow accentuating the poverty of the rest of the furnishings.

"Where do I keep my clothes?" I asked, trying to keep my outraged shock out of my voice.

Lakshmi smiled. She went over to one of the walls and pressed it with both hands. To my surprise it opened at her touch and revealed a spacious cupboard that was almost a dressing-room.

"Everything is kept here," she said. "It is too hot to have much in the room with you."

I was touched by her unspoken sympathy.

"I'm afraid many things will be strange to me," I murmured.

A fresh outbreak of thunder almost brought the house down about our ears. Lakshmi stood, slight but foursquare, and still smiling.

I think you will very soon grow accustomed to our ways," she said.

A lot of things were strange that evening. The storm rolled away to the distant hills and left the air as hot and as sultry as ever. Occasionally one could see a servant sweeping, but the dust never disappeared. It covered everything, white and sandy, making the same inevitable patterns in the corners of the rooms. And then, later, there were the suicide squads of insects trying to kill themselves in the oil lamps on the verandah. A servant came to let down the netting in an attempt to keep them out, but they came through every crack and cranny, in all shapes and sizes, some of them huge and looking like inhabitants of another planet, some of them small but equally frenzied in their attempts to reach the light.

"Now I know I'm home," Gideon said, surveying a particularly nasty specimen crawling up his trouser leg. How peculiar, I thought, that he should think of this strange and rather frightening place as home. I looked from him to Camilla, who had found a moth and was studying the pleasing sable of the fur on its wings with every sign of delight. It must run in the family, I thought, and crept farther away into the shadows to be by myself. I felt very remote from them all and rather lonely. When I thought of Timothy I wanted to cry, and yet when I tried to make myself remember his face I could only recall the most obvious facets as if he had been no more than a stranger.

Joseph had gone to his room much earlier and later on I had heard the sound of the jeep going out and had presumed that he had gone out. I didn't like to ask where he had gone, but I found that I missed him. Once or twice I surreptitiously looked at my watch and wondered when we were going to eat. A variety of highly spiced smells had been coming from the kitchen for hours, but one glance inside had told me why it took so long for the meal to be forthcoming. The cook had to grind every spice by hand to make his curry, which he did with tremendous care, making a fresh lot every time.

"Hungry?" Camilla asked me.

I flushed, aware that I had been looking at my watch yet again.

"I think I must be," I answered her.

Gideon looked up from his drink and smiled. "We have to wait for Joe to get back," he said calmly.

Camilla was prepared to argue the point.

"Joseph wouldn't mind if we started without him," she said impulsively.

"No, but his companion would!" her brother retorted.

I pricked up my ears, astonished. "Is there anyone else here?" I asked.

Gideon's smile became mysterious and quite aggressively masculine.

"Not here. Joe has gone to fetch her for dinner. She comes round quite a lot when we're here." His eyes sparkled. "She's very pretty and a gentle little thing. You're both to be kind to her!"

Camilla gave him a very sisterly look.

"You've been holding out on us!" she accused him. "Who is this mysterious woman? Are you in love with her?"

Gideon gave her a lazy slap. "That's none of your business!" he reproved her. "Her name is Julie Burnett and she lives here. Her father stayed on after Independence. He has a bungalow in the next village—he retired there. I'm afraid it makes for a rather dull life for Julie."

"How old is she?" Camilla demanded.

He looked at me consideringly. "I suppose she's about the same age as Miss King."

Camilla frowned. "I should think she's older than that! Suki's father hasn't retired!"

It was my turn to frown. I was not enjoying having

the two of them discussing me while I was sitting there, especially not as something told me that in Gideon's eyes at least I was only a pale shadow of this Julie, who was quite obviously the love of his life.

"The Burnetts didn't get married until quite late. Julie is their only child and the apple of their eye."

Camilla made an unpleasing face.

"I can imagine!" she said.

Gideon's face lost its good humour.

"Camilla! Julie is a very attractive person, and if you can't be civil you can go to your room." And then, most unfairly, he turned on me. "And that goes for you too, young woman!"

Just what I should have answered, I hate to think, but at that moment we could hear the jeep approaching and, a second later, Joseph's exuberant laugh as he brought Julie round the house to join us.

It is difficult to describe the impact Julie had on Camilla and me. She was very small and dainty and walked with a bouncy little step that somehow made sure that everyone was looking at her. She was something to look at too! Her hair was rinsed the palest mauve and apparently her clothes and her make-up had been chosen to match. With difficulty, I stopped myself staring at her and went through the movements of greeting her. If *this* was what Gideon wanted, I thought, no wonder he disapproved so heartily of me!

"How do you do, Miss Burnett," I said bravely.

Her grey eyes rested gently on mine. It was impossible to tell what she was thinking. I watched her closely as she turned away to Camilla and managed, just in time, to stop myself disliking the faintly patronising smile she gave the younger girl. I would not allow myself to make any impulsive judgements. Not yet!

We all sat down in a little semi-circle. Miss Burnett pulled her chair as close to Gideon's as she could manage, and I was oddly comforted when Joseph did the same to mine, with a proprietorial air that at another time would have amused me.

"Settled in?" he asked me.

I nodded my head, pleased by the attention he was paying me. I felt at *home* with Joseph.

"More or less." I grinned suddenly. "I haven't tried the bed yet!"

He gave me a sympathetic look, joining in my laughter.

"When I first came I didn't get a night's sleep in a week! But after a while you begin to appreciate the simplicity of the arrangements in this dreadful heat!"

To my surprise Miss Burnett giggled and joined in the conversation.

"I suppose they've given you one of the Indian beds, a *charpoy*! But you don't have to be so uncomfortable. You can get anything you want in Delhi."

Gideon hooted with laughter.

"At a price! And who wants an interior sprung mattress here?"

But Julie Burnett was not so easily put off.

"*My* family all have proper beds. We wouldn't have anything else."

Camilla and I exchanged glances. Nothing could have reconciled us to our string beds more quickly. It was with difficulty I refrained from laughing. Poor Gideon! Whatever he felt about Julie Burnett himself, his family were all going to hate her! She was not at all their style. I thought back to the house in Putney and his sister's family and the children and, frankly, I couldn't see Julie there at all!

But Gideon couldn't leave well alone.

"Why ever not?" he demanded.

Julie looked decidedly sulky. "Someone has to keep up some kind of standards," she muttered. "None of you make any attempt to do so here! Poor Daddy thinks it's dreadful the way you dress and—and everything. He doesn't really approve of my coming here at all, so there!"

Gideon immediately looked contrite.

"I know," he said heavily. "It's difficult for you living here, without many friends of your own kind."

Julie patted her pale mauve hair with a certain sensual pleasure.

"Now, now, Gideon darling, you needn't look so down in the dumps! I shan't stop coming, no matter what anybody says! As I keep telling myself, someone has to keep you up to the mark, and I don't suppose you would eat properly or anything unless I saw that you did!"

I couldn't bring myself to look at either of them in case I should discover that they were both as embarrassed as I was. But Gideon, when he spoke, sounded nonchalant and almost indecently cheerful.

"Good for you! Let's go and eat, shall we?"

We sat at a long table, on hand-made cane seats that were cooler than anything else would have been. Camilla was annoyed because, while her brother sat at the top of the table, Julie had placed herself firmly at the foot with her usual giggle.

"I always act as hostess for Gideon whenever I come," she had explained to us all at large.

It didn't worry me a great deal, because I was sitting next to Joseph and he was a much easier companion than any of the others.

A moth, larger than any I had seen before, swooped over the table towards Julie. She screamed very daintily and Gideon leapt to his feet and flicked his napkin at the winging creature. The attraction of Julie's hair was too much for it though, and it settled on the top of her head, waving its antennae menacingly at the rest of us.

"Keep quite still!" Gideon commanded.

But Julie was quite beyond doing anything of the sort. With frenzied movements she tore at her hair sobbing audibly as she gulped rather than breathed. Camilla watched her with indecent enjoyment.

"I should have thought," she said in clear, young tones, "that someone so accustomed to India would have been able to deal with a *moth*!"

"Shut up!" Gideon said tautly.

"Well, really, it's quite harmless" Camilla argued placidly. "Why don't you scoop it into a glass?"

Gideon looked decidedly put out.

"I don't want to spoil Julie's hair arrangement," he said helplessly.

Camilla looked hard and long at them both. "Could you?" she asked lazily.

It is difficult to say who was the angrier, Gideon or Julie.

"I hate your sister!" the girl sobbed hysterically.

"I'm not surprised!" Gideon agreed grimly. And then, quite suddenly, his lips began to quiver and his laughter rang through the house.

"I'll never forgive you! Never. Never!" Julie stormed at him. "I'll never forgive any of you!"

I felt decidedly sorry for her. Because I was not in the least afraid of flying things myself, I picked the moth up by the tips of its wings and put it firmly outside the shutters.

"You ought to do something to keep them out," I said to Gideon.

He gave me a quick look which I thought held admiration.

"Are you always so calm and collected?" he asked me softly.

I shook my head, suddenly tongue-tied. He was very charming when he wanted to be—too charming for my comfort!

"Well, we can all be grateful to you this evening at least," he went on. Deftly he encouraged Julie back into her seat, smoothing down her hair with gentle but efficient fingers. "Let's get on with dinner, shall we?"

We all sat down again, trying not to notice the red swollen eyes of Julie Burnett, looking reproachfully round the table. Only Gideon paid her much attention, listening to her weak jokes and jollying her along with such blatant flattery that my respect for him zoomed down to zero again.

"Is she here often?" I asked Joseph in an undertone.

For some reason he coloured slightly.

"A fair amount. We provide most of the entertainment hereabouts." He smiled quickly as if he were afraid of what I was thinking. "She won't bother you much," he added. "She only ever has time for Gideon."

Camilla frowned at him across the table and he blushed to the ears, realising that the whole table had probably heard what he had said.

"What I mean is that you'll be pretty busy," he went on desperately.

"And me?" Camilla asked him coolly.

"Ssh!" said Joseph.

Julie Burnett became suddenly aware that something was going on. She stopped fussing at her face and hair and glared at Camilla.

"Gideon always said you were a spoilt brat, but I don't care what you say. A silly little chit of a girl doesn't bother me!"

I glanced sharply at Gideon.

"That's enough," he snapped. "This is meant to be a pleasant occasion. I guess the heat is getting the better of us. Camilla, ring the bell and clear the soup plates. Perhaps the heat of Gobal's curry will cool us all down."

The curry was very hot and the meat was tough. I ate it slowly, washing it down with some of the buttermilk that was on the table. Unexpectedly, I liked it, for I should never have tried it on its own. I tried as much as possible to ignore everybody else at the table, talking only to Joe, and that worked very well because the others fell into an uneasy silence and then began to speak of the local crops and village affairs until even Camilla joined in with a sudden spurt of interest in the condition of the local soil.

But I was glad when the meal was over and Gideon and Julie went back to the verandah to sit by the spirit lights in the black darkness and to gossip about the days they had spent apart. Joseph excused himself by saying he had to work and I dragged Camilla off to our own house while the going was good.

"I suppose they're all right alone," she said wistfully.

"They'll manage," I agreed heartlessly.

"You mean *she* will! Suki, we'll have to do something about that blue-haired doll."

"But what?" I asked.

Camilla put on a scheming expression and I knew she was beginning to enjoy herself.

"We'll think of something," she said sweetly.

Lakshmi had turned down my bed. Apart from the cover there were two natural-coloured cotton sheets stretched over the thin khaki mattress. There was no bedside light, only a single unshaded electric bulb hanging from the ceiling that buzzed at intervals as the voltage changed. I had been accustomed to some kind of discomfort in my digs, all the time I had been studying. But this, coupled with my weariness of mind and body, was enough to reduce me to tears.

I undressed slowly because I was still unaccustomed to the stuffy heat. The storm had started up again and I could feel its electricity against my skin. In a peculiar way it was exciting and I was sure that sleep would be a long time coming even when I had got into that uncomfortable bed. But I had underrated my tiredness. All I could remember was that the bed was not nearly as bad as I had expected, and then I was asleep, heavily and dreamlessly asleep as only the very tired can be.

When I awoke it was pitch black. I lay on my back and listened to the peculiar sounds of the Indian night. The curious scratching noise of some insect on the ceiling, the wild howling of some large cat outside the settlement, and a variety of undertones, all so different from the softer nights I was accustomed to at home. I turned my pillow over, looking for coolness, and was surprised to hear the sound of the jeep going towards the main house. As it passed the yellow headlights came flooding through the windows on to my bed and passed on again. I glanced briefly at my watch. It was a little after three o'clock. I supposed bleakly that it was Gideon returning from seeing his girl-friend home.

And a fine time of night it was too! I thought crossly, and then berated myself for being narrow-minded. But even so I couldn't believe that he would be really fit to do much work in the morning.

I was awake again at half-past six. The grey light of first dawn was already being broken up by the yellow and orange streaks of the rising sun, a perfect background for the lovely old trees that shaded the settlement of bungalows and a few of the village buildings that were caught up in the research station grounds. I hurried into my clothes and wandered outside to take a look round by myself, before anyone else was up.

The village people were already stirring. I was particularly interested in a small one-storied mud house that clung on to the wall of the research station's kitchen garden. The wall which faced its own small yard was covered with hand-made dung cakes drying in the sun. The woman of the house, bejewelled with bits of gold in her nose and round her ankles, was slapping at a few more cakes with her hands and smacking them on to the wall. It gave the house a very peculiar appearance with a series of hand-prints showing where the dung had been slapped on.

I nodded and smiled, muttering good-morning inadequately. The woman came over to where she could see me better and watched me with intense curiosity as I walked round the end of the wall so that I could see her house better. We stood in silence, staring at one another. Slowly, she drew her sari up over her head in a gesture that meant very much the same as an English housewife patting at her hair before she answers the door. She continued to stare at me with the same unblinking curiosity that I frankly shared but hadn't quite got her self-confidence to indulge it in quite the same way.

Eventually she beckoned me over, putting out a wondering finger to touch my dress and the cheap costume beads that I wore round my neck. Then suddenly she smiled and giggled shyly as I smiled back. Grasping my wrist, she led me into her tiny domain, showing me the pots that she scoured with sand and calling to her children, who had been playing naked in the yard, to go into the house and put on the ragged shorts which were all they had in the way of clothes. Somehow the woman made me understand that she was in some way related to Lakshmi and that therefore she had heard all about me. It obviously struck her as very funny that a woman should be involved in Gideon *Sahib's* work. I don't think she realised that her own Prime Minister was a woman.

I was fascinated by the varied signs of the life they led in that courtyard. Two small braziers in one corner were obviously what she cooked on, and a string-bed standing on its side by the gate, made me think that they slept outside if at all possible also. The woman touched my sleeve and pointed to the door, and so, for the first time, I set foot in a completely Indian household.

There were only two small, airless rooms inside, windowless and smelling heavily of dung. Most of the walls were of unpainted mud with garish pictures of the Hindu gods pinned up here and there. A few essential household effects, like a mortar and a couple of shallow pans mostly used for making *chapattis*, the Indian unleavened bread, and some storage jars, completed her few possessions. I congratulated her on them eagerly, all the more so because I was wondering if I could live on such a little.

We came out into the sunlight again and I saw Lakshmi standing in the yard waiting for me. My hostess said something to her and they both smiled at me.

"My sister is honoured by your visit," Lakshmi said softly.

"Your sister? She told me you were related," I replied.

Lakshmi laughed. "She is older than I, and I am not yet married," she told me simply.

I wondered briefly how the younger sister had managed to learn English and to get some kind of an education.

"I have been admiring her home," I said.

Lakshmi nodded. "It is poor, but she is very happy."

We said our goodbyes and strolled slowly back to the main bungalow of the research station.

"Did they send you to find me?" I asked Lakshmi anxiously. I glanced at my watch to see what the time was, but it had stopped. With irritation I shook it and it started to tick again.

"The *Sahib* is already up, but the others are still in their beds," she answered calmly. "It was the *Sahib* who wished you to come to breakfast."

Gideon was sitting on the verandah when I joined him. A pile of letters rested on his knee and he was looking at them with a curious expression of displeasure mixed with a reluctance to do anything about them.

"How did you sleep?" he asked me abruptly.

I stood pointedly ignoring the question until he rose to his feet and offered me a chair at the table.

"Dr. Wait, where do you want me to begin?" I enquired coolly. "Do you want me to go straight out into the fields?"

He glared at the letter he had at last opened. After a few seconds his eyes met mine.

"Miss King, I have put you in charge of the wheat and maize results. What you do with your time is your own affair."

Quite what made me take him to task, I can't imagine. I opened my mouth and to my dismay my question hung on the air.

"Even if I come in at three in the morning?" I taunted him.

"I gather you didn't sleep well, Miss King," he retorted blandly.

"I happened to see the lights from the jeep, that's all," I muttered.

"Just *happened*, Miss King?"

Furious with myself for getting myself into such a position, I bit my lip and tried to look cool, calm and collected.

"I was turning over," I said.

His amusement was very difficult to bear.

"I see."

"I—I'm not used to the heat yet," I added by way of explanation.

"No," he agreed, half laughing. "And it does such terrible things to one's curiosity, doesn't it?"

"I—I suppose it's a long way to Miss Burnett's house. I'm not really interested," I finished loftily.

Gideon grinned at me, thoroughly enjoying my confusion.

"It takes about twenty minutes," he told me confidentially. "But of course it's very romantic driving home in the moonlight."

"It must be!" I said sourly.

He leaned over the table until he was close enough to touch.

"The trouble with you, Suki, is that you're not half as prickly as you pretend to be. You're plain jealous."

"Nonsense!" I said sharply. "It isn't true."

But Gideon only laughed.

"Some other time I may take time out to find out," he teased me. "Right now I must read this mail." He sat back and laughed at me. "It will be a very interesting experiment," he drawled, "don't you think?"

With difficulty I remained seated.

"No, I don't," I said angrily. But Gideon wasn't even listening. He was reading his beastly letters.

CHAPTER FIVE

CAMILLA decided to come with me when I set off to inspect the fields. She couldn't pretend to any interest in either wheat or maize, but she was set on avoiding her brother for the rest of the morning.

"Gideon is different out here," she complained. "He hasn't had time to talk or anything."

"He was on holiday in England," I reminded her.

"And Julie is part of his work, I suppose!" she retorted tartly.

I had no answer to that! My own burning feeling of injustice was too much with me for that.

"Perhaps we won't see very much of her," I said hopefully instead.

Camilla snorted sulkily. "Would you care to bet on that?"

I pretended basely that I hadn't heard her. I pulled my white overall out of my suitcase and put it on, thrusting my hands into the starched pockets and wriggling my shoulders to make it more comfortable.

"Good heavens," said Camilla, "you look more like a doctor than an agriculturist."

"A plant doctor," I suggested with a grin.

She smiled back. "Something *very* impressive! I wish Gideon could see you now!"

I glanced at myself in the looking-glass on the wall. To my eyes I looked young and very vulnerable and not very impressive at all.

"I don't suppose he would be taken in by any exterior," I said wearily. "It's the results he will be looking at."

Camilla gave me a worried look.

"But Gideon is always fair!" she exclaimed. "Unless that mauve witch has put a spell on his judgement as well," she added.

"He's a grown man," I said carelessly. "He wouldn't let anyone interfere with his work."

Camilla looked young and very tragic. "Other men have," she said.

We went out through the laboratory. Gideon was standing by the window studying a stick of sugar-cane. He was plainly surprised to see Camilla, but he said nothing, much to my relief, bcause Camilla was in a mood to argue whatever he said to her.

"I suppose you know where your fields are?" he asked me.

I shook my head. "I'm on the verge of finding out," I replied cheerfully. "I thought I'd have a look round before I did anything else.

He nodded. "I'll point you in the right direction and then let you find your own way. Has Joe laid on any transport for you?"

"Not that I know of."

He made a quick gesture of disapproval and went to the door.

"Joseph! Have you laid on a jeep for Miss King?"

Joseph appeared in the doorway, a piece of half-eaten toast in one hand.

"Look here," he began, "I haven't even finished breakfast yet!"

"The rest of us have," Gideon informed him coldly. "Go and get a jeep ready now. And *shift* yourself!"

I threw Joseph a quick look of sympathy. He might be slow getting up, but at least *he* hadn't been out until three in the morning.

"And come straight back here," Gideon ordered.

"Yes, sir!", said Joseph.

I grabbed my notebook and prepared to follow him. One glance at Camilla's sulky face was enough to know that her sympathies were all with the young American.

"Come on," I said hastily. "We have a lot to do."

Her eyes flashed, but she said nothing. I grabbed a pen and put it in my pocket, pushing her out of the door before me.

"It isn't fair!" she said under her breath as we walked round to the garage. "What has Joseph done?"

One thing Joseph hadn't done was to get our jeep ready. When we caught up with him he was standing helplessly surveying the vehicle that had been officially designated mine for the next two years.

"Gosh, Suki," he exclaimed, "I'm frightfully sorry. I guess I forgot all about it."

I surveyed the four flat tyres and the generally depressed look of the dusty jeep.

"Can we walk it?" I asked hopefully.

Camilla jumped into the jeep and pressed the starter. There was a soggy squeal, telling that the battery was flat too.

"Surely there must be some way of making it go?" she said.

"None at all," said Gideon's voice from the entrance. He walked forward and glanced at the forgotten jeep. "You'd better take Joseph's while he goes to work on yours."

"But—" the American began.

"But nothing!" Gideon said sharply. "It was your job to get the vehicle ready. Okay, so it's you who has to do without transport today."

"You're not using yours," Joe objected.

"That's beside the point." Gideon handed me a roughly drawn map of the village showing the fields in which I had an interest. "Think you can manage?" he asked with a smile.

I hesitated. I was very much aware of the atmosphere between Camilla and Joseph and the man who was giving all the orders, and yet he had reason, especially if Joseph really was in charge of keeping the vehicles on the road.

"Perhaps Joe could show me the way?" I suggested humbly.

To my surprise he laughed.

"If you want him! But that jeep had better be ready for you tomorrow morning. Did you hear that, Joe?"

Joseph grinned sheepishly. "Right," he said. "I heard."

Joseph drove us straight through the village and out the other side. I got tantalising glimpses of the small industries that went on in the dark little shops that lined either side of the road. The oil merchant and his press which was driven by a single bullock that trudged endlessly round and round the home-made mortar. Next door was a bazaar in miniature, a hundred different colours represented by saris, ribbons, shirts, turbans, and a few odd lengths of material spread out across the narrow pavement in the dust. Beyond that was the tailor, working his sewing machine with one foot as he used his hands to guide the material under the needle and, beyond him, the village potter, squatting beside his wheel and making the few simple pots that the local housewives demanded.

Beyond the village the fields began—dry, dusty tracts of ground that grew little and were so badly in need of water that I almost despaired there and then.

"This is your main wheat," Joseph said, nodding with his head towards the driest of all the fields. "Not much hope for that!"

"No," I agreed. "Where's the nearest water?"

Joseph made a face.

"There's a stream over there. In the monsoon it bursts its banks and washes everything away. In the hot weather it just forms tanks for the local buffaloes to wallow in. It's not much help."

I looked at the deep cracks in the dry earth where the wheat was struggling to get a living.

"It might be," I said.

Camilla didn't want to walk across the baked field to have a look at this rather doubtful water supply.

"I'll wait here with Joe," she said prettily. "It's too hot for all of us to drag round."

I expected Joseph to say that he would come with me, but he didn't. He gave Camilla a shy little smile and shrugged his shoulders.

"Whatever the ladies command of me!" he said with mock gallantry.

Somehow I hadn't got the heart to insist that he came with me. I pulled my hat farther over my eyes and went off alone. It was farther than I had thought. The wheat straggled on for several acres, most of it looking little better than the average seeding grass. At intervals I took samples of the earth, sealing them into separate envelopes and marking them so that I should know where they came from. At intervals I pulled up one of the plants and examined the root carefully. Some of them were badly eaten by various pests, a few suffered from root diseases, but the vast majority were dry and brittle from lack of water. I broke a couple of straws and looked at them gloomily. I had a long way to go if I was going to make a go of this thing, and I was beginning to wonder if I had the necessary knowledge and experience even to begin.

The stream when I reached it was so sluggardly that the water hardly moved at all. A few buffalo were immersed in their tanks, sharing the brown waters with one of the women from the village who was busy washing both herself and her family's laundry. I waved to her and she waded to the bank to return my greeting more formally.

"*Namaste,*" she said.

I placed the palms of my hands together. "*Namaste,*" I replied.

I sat on the dusty bank and watched the woman as she went back to her work, banging the clothes against a large flat stone that effectually blocked up most of the trickling stream. The water behind built up slowly, very slowly, into a muddy outsize puddle. It was remarkable to me that the clothes should ever get any cleaner, but after a while she was apparently satisfied and laid the garments out in the sun to bleach and to dry.

I bade her a tentative farewell and made my way back across the baked field. I could see Joseph and Camilla sitting in the jeep, sitting side by side, intent on their own conversation. They were in no hurry for me to get back, I thought dryly, and wondered why I should resent the young man's light interest in Gideon's sister. It struck me forcibly that two years was a very long time and I had no security that Timothy would come home to me at the end of them.

By the time I had come up to them they had got out of the jeep and walked the last few yards to meet me.

"This heat!" Camilla exclaimed. "Aren't you completely exhausted?"

I smiled, a little amused by that. It would be a fine thing if I couldn't complete a single day's work, having come all this way!

"It's certainly hot," I agreed.

Joseph flapped his shirt against his chest and grinned at the two of us. "Where now?" he asked.

"The next field," I retorted.

It was much the same story wherever we went. Neglect and drought vied with each other to be the main cause of the poverty of the crops. On the whole I thought drought won. Even such water as there was was not reaching the plants, and here lay my first and most immediate problem. Gideon hadn't told me, but I thought that our funds were probably pretty tight. It was possible that the government helped a little, but the sort of irrigation scheme I had in mind was expensive even by European standards. It was not the sort of thing that small villages like this one were likely to ever get.

Joseph and I tried to rally the thoroughly bored Camilla on our way home.

"You can come and help me fix up the other jeep after lunch," Joseph offered, very much in the manner of a small boy offering to share one of his best toys.

"I shall be lying flat on my back trying to get cool," Camilla retorted. She saw Joseph's face fall and took pity on him. "Perhaps I'll come along after I've had a long cold shower," she compromised.

Joseph flushed. "You don't have to," he said awkwardly. He glanced at me and then suddenly began to laugh. "Suki, honey, your face hasn't half caught the sun!"

He was right, of course. By the time we got back to the main bungalow it was already burning. One glance in the mirror was enough to tell me that by tomorrow I would be lucky if it wasn't peeling. And at the back of my mind I discovered that it wasn't the thought of the inevitable pain that disturbed me most, it was that Gideon would see me at such a disadvantage, and that was a particularly humiliating thought. I didn't want to give a rap about what *Gideon* thought. What Timothy thought, thousands of miles away in America, would surely always be much more important.

Gideon was out at lunchtime. We all of us wondered where he was, but there was nobody to ask. We sat on the verandah and played with a vegetable curry and the inevitable buttermilk that goes to make up the diet of the Hindu. The food was very good, but it was too hot to eat, and I made my escape as soon as I could and took my samples to the laboratory to test the content of the soils while I had the place to myself. It was work that I enjoyed. I had always enjoyed mixing concoctions and making magic potions that resulted in accurate information. I was at home in the laboratory; I felt confident and sure of myself, and the rest of the world was very far away.

It was almost dark by the time I had finished. I heard the jeep come in and I listened for Gideon's footsteps to come towards the laboratory, but they stopped at his bedroom. I was bitterly disappointed. I sat in the gloom and waited longer, but there were no further sounds, and after a while I began to see how silly I was being. With a sigh I began to put my things away, neatly coding my results in the appropriate files that I had already prepared. When I had finished I walked through the house and paused for a second on the verandah. There were monkeys chattering in the trees, pulling at the leaves and chasing each other up and down the branches, jumping down on to the ground and up again, like so many bad-tempered children.

"Had a busy day?" Gideon asked from behind me.

I turned swiftly. Gideon's hair was wet from the shower. It stood on end, gleaming in the last of the light.

"Yes," I answered. "It is a depressing prospect without more water."

"Oh, I shouldn't say that," he said cheerfully. "There's a long way to go, I know, but the soil is pretty good."

"I've just analysed various samples of it," I said dryly.

"And?"

"And the sooner we get some nitrogen into it the better!" I said grimly.

"Look, I know that soil—" he began.

"Do you?" I asked him tartly.

"Perhaps you'd better let me have your findings," he sighed. He looked rather depressed and I wondered again what he had been doing all day. "Though where I'm going to conjure the stuff up from I don't know!"

"It's the lack of water that I'm really worried about," I insisted.

Gideon grunted. The water from his hair was dripping down the back of his neck and he pulled out a handkerchief to dry himself. Across one corner was a smear of pale mauve lipstick. My sympathy for him died dramatically.

"The new well will help," he said.

I gave him a scornful look. "It might," I agreed, "if anyone was around to work it!"

"Is that intended as a reference to me?" he asked stiffly.

I shrugged my shoulders. "If the cap fits—" I drawled.

To my surprise he looked amused.

"I'll tell you when it does," he said.

Somehow, I thought dismally, he had managed to get the last word again. But it wasn't that which hurt. It was that small smear of pale mauve lipstick that was the unkindest cut of all.

In the morning my jeep was ready for me and so I was independent of what anyone else was doing. I liked it that way. I spent most of my mornings out on the field and my afternoons checking my findings and working in the laboratory. Gideon managed to procure various chemicals, but it continued to be the lack of water that worried me most. When I was not worrying about my work, I worried about myself. I could feel myself growing daily tighter and more intense, but I didn't feel that I could relax with anyone at all any longer. Whenever I did I got hurt too badly, or so it seemed to me.

I was sitting at the bench in the laboratory when the *Swami* came in. He came and went as he pleased, his saffron robes flapping in the dusty breeze. Everybody respected him and was pleased to see him, including myself. I soon got used to his shock of wild hair and his ability to remove himself from any conversation by the simple expedient of staring into space with his soft, enormous eyes completely vacant of any expression. He came and glanced over my shoulder at what I was doing.

"You work very hard, Miss King!"

I struggled with myself not to notice the matted hair so near to mine, or the strong smell of spicy foods that came from his skin.

"What I need most of all is water," I told him bitterly.

The *Swami* nodded gravely.

"We must all concentrate on that," he agreed. It was funny to hear his pure Oxford accent coming out of such a frame.

I looked up at him beseechingly. "I suppose you wouldn't like to work your magic on the *panchayat* to

make them pay for some kind of an irrigation scheme?"
I begged him.

He shook his head with finality.

"A village this size doesn't have that kind of money,
Miss King. You would need a miracle worker for that
sort of thing."

I sighed. "Would it really cost so much?"

"In money? Perhaps not. But so much more than we
could afford."

Reluctantly, I was forced to agree with him. In a land
where a roof over one's head spelt riches and the possession of a bed and a chair something to be talked
about and envied, where could the money come from
for such a project?

"I suppose so. But, *Swamiji* you do see the necessity
for more water, don't you?"

He looked at me, his eyes doleful.

"I am not a fool, Miss King," he said.

"No," I said, a doubtful note creeping in despite my
very best efforts. "But there must be some way of doing something!"

He laughed. "If you can think of it, Miss King, then
I will be happy to follow *your* lead," he said, thus neatly
returning the problem to me.

"Well, I shall have to think of something!" I agreed.
"That is, if we are to grow wheat here at all."

He said nothing more and after a while I returned to
my work, though I wasn't nearly as able as he at withdrawing from my surroundings. After a while he
shoved a bony finger towards my figures and said:

"It wasn't really to discuss your work that I came to
see you."

I threw him an enquiring glance.

"No?"

"I thought you would like to accompany me through
the village to see the new pump."

I was highly gratified. For a moment I tried not to
show it, but the smile of pleasure spread across my face
just the same.

"Is it really working?" I asked.

He nodded. "So they tell me."

I threw down my pen and stood up immediately. I had been astonished and appalled by the delay in getting the well into action. The electrician had had to come from afar and not even the thought of getting his money had been able to tempt him to hurry back to the village.

We walked through the village as if we owned it. The *Swami* strode on ahead, his robes rippling in the wind; I followed a pace behind, anxious as always to see everything that was going on all round me. The *Swami* must have been more observant than he looked because he stopped suddenly in the middle of the street and I practically walked into his back. As always in the presence of a foreigner a knot of begging children had gathered, more curious than determined. The boldest of them touched my skirts, while the others put their hands over their faces and peered through their fingers.

"It will be well when my people learn to be a little less materialistic," the *Swami* said sternly.

I laughed. "You want too much!" I teased him, a little shocked by my own audacity. "They have to eat!"

"But not by begging."

My lips twitched. I could hardly help it.

"No, but by giving me water for my wheat!" I retorted.

He shook his head at me.

"You must ask Mr. Wait for that."

I sighed. "I suppose so," I said.

There were surprisingly few people at the well. I thought I recognised most of the women drawing water. They were very graceful, filling their pots and carrying them off to their various houses on their heads, but it was plain that the vast majority of them were still using the water from the buffalo tanks. We stood and watched for a while, trying to fight down a feeling of disappointment that the whole village was not making use of it as we had hoped.

I went forward to the edge of the well and peered down into its depths. There was very little to see, for the new electrical machinery took up most of the space and one could only glimpse the water below.

"It is working well now," the *Swami* told me, not without pride. "At first it was difficult to get it going because none of us knew how to prime it."

I giggled, remembering similar pumps in the country where we had spent our school holidays when I was a child. I put my two hands on the edge of the well wall and exchanged smiles with one of the youngest house-wives I had ever seen. Aged no more than twelve, she nevertheless had the proud bearing of one who was sure of her own status. For an instant I thought by her looks that she too might have been a relative of Lakshmi's, but as soon as she had filled her earthen-ware pot and raised it to her head, the likeness went and she wandered away down the street and was lost in the crowd.

I had been so busy watching the first girl, I didn't see the second until she was right on top of me. She had none of the confidence of the first, but was quite scared to actually take the water from the well. I stood up straight to help her, but other hands were there before mine. To my surprise, I recognised them to be Gideon's.

"Will you get me water to drink?" he asked her.

She was plainly overcome by such a request, but his smile reassured her and it was obvious that she didn't like to refuse his request.

"The water is tasteless after the other," she told him shyly.

"It is clean," he replied. "The other water holds many illnesses inside it. This will keep your children well and strong."

She licked her lips doubtfully.

"My husband will say my cooking is not as good as his mother's," she went on.

Gideon laughed. "All husbands say that anyway!"

he teased her. "You try it and see if he doesn't compliment you on your new skill."

She was overcome with feminine amusement at the very idea, but she dipped her pot into the water and offered it to Gideon so that he could drink, which he did with such a natural air that the other women gained in confidence and came closer to see the fun. Gideon was completely at home with them. He was never familiar, but within seconds they all felt at ease with him and he had forgotten that he was a stranger bringing strange ideas into their lives.

The *Swami* watched paternally from the edge of the ring of women.

"I shall leave you in his capable hands," he said to me in amused tones. "He is already managing to do what I came for."

"To win their confidence?" I asked him.

The *Swami* nodded solemnly. "Exactly that."

He was gone almost before I was aware. I saw the flash of his saffron robe as he disappeared down the street and I wondered again at the Indian's ability to merge into his surroundings so successfully as to be practically invisible.

Gideon, suddenly bored with his admiring audience, came away from the well and joined me on the edge of the throng.

"Working hard?" he asked me wryly.

I kept my head with determination.

"There's blight on some of your potatoes," I told him, figuring that the best form of defence was to attack.

He smiled quite affably.

"I know. I'm dealing with it tomorrow." His grin grew bigger. "Afraid it will spread on to your fields?" he prodded me.

"Of course!," I retorted. "My wheat is parched, but it is at least *clean*!"

He was still amused, and I wondered what had put him into such a good temper.

"Famous last words!" he said.

But I refused to be drawn.

"I haven't got enough water on those fields to feed a bug!" I turned to face him. "Dr. Wait—"

His smile died.

"Suki, don't dare to mention water to me again!" he reproved me. "I haven't the time or the inclination to go into it now."

But when would he have? I wondered. I allowed my eyes to drop from his face, but not before I had noted the signs of fatigue in the corners of his eyes and the faint shadows that sketched his muscles in more clearly than usual. If he had been home at a reasonable time, I thought, he would be more able to do his work. I suppose my thoughts must have been mirrored on my face, because he grasped me firmly by the hand and pulled me down the street.

"You and I," he said, "are going to the *pan* seller and there we'll sit in the shade and regain a sense of proportion!"

I didn't know what a *pan* seller was, but I followed him willingly enough. I liked being with him, liked it more than was good for me. It was because I liked his society so much that I fought shy of it, sensing its dangers and rather enjoying the sensation.

The *pan* vendor had chosen an ideal spot beside a bank. Gideon and I sat on the red dust and watched him beside us. He squatted by the side of the road, his little cabinet beside him and with a potful of leaves covered with water. When Gideon nodded to him, he carefully prepared a leaf for each of us, covering it with various spices from the little drawers in the cabinet, lime and cutch, cardamon seeds and cloves and the inevitable shred of finely beaten silver which, for some reason, all Indians seem to think essential to their good health.

Gideon received the first leaf and popped it whole into his mouth, chewing it cautiously at first and then with obvious pleasure. I could smell the spices as he ate them, and, when he had finished, his mouth was as red as if he had swallowed a dollop of red ink. I was not at all sure at first that I liked the taste when I got my own leaf, but the taste was so clean and fresh that I was sorry when I had reduced it to pulp and there was nothing left to wonder over.

"Now about this water," Gideon began.

I waited for him to go on, but he was lost in thought. "Well?" I prompted him.

"We'll have to make better use of the monsoons," he said. "The streams fill up then—too much so."

I thought of the muddy trickle that ran beside the wheat field I had looked at first of all.

"I shall build a dam myself," I announced. The spices from the *pan* had practically blown the top of my head off and I felt quite capable of doing anything. "It isn't impossible," I went on, "the water is *there!*"

Gideon gave me a long, hard look.

"All right," he said slowly. "See what you can do, but don't come crying to me if it doesn't work."

My back stiffened with sheer temper.

"I shouldn't dream of it!" I told him coldly.

CHAPTER SIX

JULIE BURNETT invited Gideon and Camilla to spend Sunday with her parents. For some reason Joseph and I were not included in the invitation. I don't think either of us minded much, but Camilla took immediate offence at the whole arrangement. After the incident of the moth, no one had expected her to become exactly friendly with the other girl, but we couldn't help feeling that a certain tolerance was desirable.

"I won't go!" she told her brother.

Gideon barely looked up from the paper he was reading.

"Don't be ridiculous," he said.

Camilla, who was not often or easily put out, completely lost her temper.

"Nothing will induce me to go! Why should I? Besides, why can't she ask all of us? She's a horrible snob and I won't have anything to do with her!"

Things were not made better by Gideon leaving the room as if he had not even heard her.

"Would you go?" Camilla demanded. "Imagine his *liking* such a person!" A terrible thought struck her. "Suki, you don't suppose he would actually *marry* her, do you? Because no one else in the family will survive the shock!"

"Oh, Camilla!" I protested, because I didn't like the idea of Gideon married to Julie myself. "I imagine your brother will make up his own mind when it comes to marriage."

"Possibly," she agreed tearfully. "But I couldn't live in the same household with her."

I sighed. It wasn't my place, I supposed, to break it to

her that she might not be wanted by her brother once he had married. I half-thought that I might try and prepare the ground, but the very idea of Julie living on various research stations round the world was so ridiculous that I hardly knew where to start. It was funny that we should all think of her as such a social creature when really she lived right at the back of beyond and probably had had as few parties and outings in her life as I had.

"I don't suppose Gideon is really serious about her," I said pacifically. "He has to be polite and so do the rest of us."

Camilla stared at me, wide-eyed.

"You mean I shall have to go on Sunday?"

I nodded regretfully, but Camilla became quite cheerful about it.

"Okay, I'll go. It will be quite interesting to see what sort of people managed to produce a freak like Julie anyway."

I frowned at her, but I had to admit that I would have been interested myself. It was terrible to be so curious and I couldn't help being glad that Gideon didn't know of my interest, for I was quite sure that he would have had no sympathy with my own vivid dislike for the other girl.

I thought Gideon looked grim and strange in a jacket and tie when he got the jeep out on the Sunday. Camilla had excelled herself by producing a filmy nylon dress that clung to her youthful figure and a picture hat that gave her a quaint dignity. It was only when she was stepping up into the jeep that I saw she was also wearing elbow-length gloves and a bracelet which was as valuable as it was ornamental. She caught my eye and grinned.

"Somebody has to keep the flag flying," she said tersely.

"Oh *yes*!" I agreed. I was having difficulty to keep from laughing and I was afraid that Gideon would see. As it was, I thought I caught an answering glimpse of laughter in his eyes, but I knew of course that I must have been mistaken. One doesn't stay out until all hours of the night with a girl unless one admires her.

"What are you two going to do with yourselves?" Gideon asked as he started up the engine. For a minute he sounded quite envious of our freedom to do as we wished.

"I'm going to get the dam started," I said.

Joseph stood with his hands on his hips, twisting his belt with his thumbs.

"I guess I'll help," he said indifferently.

Gideon hesitated, looking worried.

"D'you think you can manage on your own?" he asked.

"Why not?" I asked him.

He smiled slightly at my challenging attitude.

"Go carefully," he bade me. "You can't accomplish everything at once."

I hardly listened to him. I certainly didn't think his caution was important. I noticed how easily he slipped the jeep into gear and in a short while they had disappeared in a ball of dust. Poor Camilla, I thought, what a dull day she was going to have. But my own day was full of the most exciting prospects. I turned to Joseph with enthusiasm.

"Will you go and round up the men?" I asked him. "The sooner we begin the better!"

The gentlemen of the *panchayat* stood in a group at the edge of the field looking with distaste at the hardly moving muddy waters of the stream. They did not understand my plans for the dam and they were plainly suspicious that any female should conceive such a plan.

"The water is small and narrow," they argued. "How will you make it more? It will never be enough to water the whole field."

It was difficult to argue in a language with which they were not familiar. I found it easier to show them. Accordingly I built a tiny dam across one of the trickles that went to make up the stream. I tried to explain how I should build a tank on either side to take up the water and how I would slowly build the two walls towards each other, with sluice gates in the centre which could be opened during the monsoons to control the floods. The old men watched with interest. They nodded their heads and discussed the plan between themselves. One of them had a son who had travelled right across India to see a similar experiment in another district. It had brought prosperity to the whole area, he reported eagerly, and the other men believed him. They knew how important water was to the crops. They also knew what it was like to live in times of famine and they knew that the research station made this less likely in their own village.

"It would cost very little," I encouraged them.

Two of the very oldest men hitched up their clothing and came and stood beside me in the stream. With eager hands, I described exactly where the dam would be built, splashing around in the water and getting myself thoroughly muddy and wet.

"It would need much labour," the old men said finally.

"There are young men in the village," I replied eagerly. I knew that there would be the difficulty of caste, but I was hoping for the best. I wasn't at all sure what sort of a working force I would get, but I was reasonably sure that I could manage no matter how few they gave me.

"We would have to pay for the sand and the cement?"

I nodded unhappily.

"But the field would repay the expense in a single season," I countered.

The old men scuffed their toes in the muddy waters and thought some more.

"We shall do it," they said at last. "We shall do it if Mr. Wait agrees to the plans. We shall discuss the whole matter with him."

I agreed to this, shaking hands with each of the old men in turn. When they had gone, I found myself alone, still up to the ankles in muddy water and completely content because I knew that somehow I was going to make the wretched field productive.

I was still standing there, gloating, when Joseph came to find me. He could not have been mistaken for anything but an American. He wore his hat at that particular angle and his trousers skin-tight with his shirt hanging out. He sat down on the bank beside the stream and took out his cigarette case. It flashed gold in the sun as he opened it and offered me a cigarette. I accepted one gratefully. American cigarettes were so much bigger and I like their more mild tang when I smoked them.

"Thank you very much," I said.

"How did it go?" he asked.

I sat down beside him, trying in vain not to grin too triumphantly.

"Well, I think. The actual decision is to be referred to Gideon."

"Oh well, that was only to be expected. You don't mind, do you?"

I felt quite breezy with confidene and didn't mind at all.

"Not a rap!" I assured him.

He grinned. "Good for you! I'll be right in there, cheering for you!"

But I wasn't as sure of him as I wanted to be. For all the length of time I had been on my own, making my own friends and answerable to no one, I was strangely ignorant of the ways of men. When I thought about it, there had been only one man whom I had really studied and that was Timothy. The thought of him made me wince, because I wasn't even very sure of him.

"I can manage very well on my own," I said to Joseph.

He wasn't in the least put out.

"Nonsense. You're going to need all the help you

can get! Friends on these occasions are half the battle. Didn't you know that?''

"I've heard it," I admitted cautiously. "But how can we be sure of our friends?"

He was hurt. I watched helplessly as he struggled with his feelings. First he was angry and then more chagrined.

"What have I done to offend you?" he asked at last.

I shook my head, searching for some way of easing the wound I had inflicted.

"I wasn't thinking of you in particular," I assured him. "It's more that I never realised how personalities come into this kind of work."

Joseph flashed a look of enquiry at me.

"You can't expect to live in your shell for ever," he said quite gently.

"I suppose not," I agreed abruptly. "But it would be a great deal more comfortable!"

Joseph laughed. He had fully recovered his good humour and was determined to jolly me out of my introspective ways.

"Have you forgotten that we set a seal on our friendship?" he reminded me.

I blushed a little, remembering his kiss.

"No," I said uncertainly. "No, I hadn't forgotten."

"Well then," he began reasonably, "how could you even suppose that I would desert you in any hour of need?"

I thought about it seriously, wondering at my own lack of confidence.

"I'll tell you what it is," I confided in him on a note of sudden levity, "I have the feeling you're the friend of every girl!"

His mock indignation amused me.

"I might flirt a little—but I never hurt anyone, do I?"

I wriggled my feet in the sun. The mud had baked hard around my toes and it was a pleasant sensation breaking out of the cocoon of sandy clay.

"There's Camilla."

Joseph started guiltily. "You ask an awful lot of a guy!" he expostulated. "Camilla is a pretty little thing!"

"Very pretty!" I agreed lazily.

"But too young for me, of course!"

"Oh yes?" I prompted him.

He put his hand on his heart. "What do you want, Suki? A full-blown confession about how I cast a glance in her direction?"

I shook my head. "Camilla isn't my business. You're not either, come to that!"

"But supposing she were?" he prompted me. He rolled over on to his side and gazed at me with innocent eyes. "Supposing we both were, what then?"

I smiled lazily at him.

"I'd warn you off, I suppose."

"Because Camilla is only seventeen?"

"I suppose so."

He plucked an ear of corn and tickled my nose with it.

"And would that be your only reason?" he asked me.

I sneezed. I had never played this sort of game before and I was surprised to find that I was enjoying it.

"I don't know. It might be."

He reached over and kissed my cheek. "I consider myself duly warned off." He kissed me again. "Especially when there's such tempting bait so close to hand!"

"Joseph Groton."

He looked very innocent, young and all-American.

"Are you going to warn me off again?" he asked with an injured air.

He was terribly attractive and I didn't think of Timothy at all.

"I'm not warning you at all," I said.

"Lakshmi!"

The Indian girl came running. She had a new sari on of peacock blue edged with white and silver. She looked as bright and as quick as a kingfisher flashing through sunshine and water.

"My, my!" she exclaimed. "Where have you been, Miss Suki? I'll set the fire and draw you a bath straight away!"

I brushed the red dust off my cheeks and laughed.

"I've been talking to the *panchayat* about building a dam—"

Lakshmi gave me a bright-eyed look.

"Did Mr. Joseph help to persuade them?" she asked. "I am sure he would have liked to have done!"

"He came when it was all over," I replied repressively.

"And very welcome, I'm sure," she said in much the same tones that I could remember my mother using.

I met her teasing, feminine eyes as calmly as I could.

"Perhaps," I admitted.

The bath was glorious. I lay in the hot water, sniffing delicately at the tinny smell of the bath. It was surprisingly comfortable and I began to think that before the days of bathrooms and glamorous tiles, people might have had some quite good ideas about comfort after all.

I was just drying myself when the telephone sounded shrilly in the hall. Annoyed, I waited for someone else to answer it. What could it have been but someone from the main house wondering where I was? But Lakshmi was afraid of the telephone and she ignored the sharp ringing of the bell until I could bear it no longer and, pulling my towel around me, I pattered out into the corridor and picked up the receiver.

"Yes, what is it?" I asked testily.

There was a gulping noise at the other end.

"What's the matter?" I demanded.

"There's been an accident!"

I pulled myself together and clasped my towel more tightly around me.

"Where? What happened?"

"This is Julie speaking—"

"Oh, really?" Despite myself my voice was tinged with ice. "Are you hurt?"

"No, no! It isn't me. Though I must say I was very nearly badly hurt as well. It was so careless and unnecessary. Gideon ought to have known better!"

At the mention of his name I felt cold and all the more impatient for her to tell me exactly what had happened.

"Julie, has anything happened to Gideon?"

She gave a quick, breathless laugh, from nerves rather than from amusement.

"That's what I'm trying to tell you. Gideon would insist on playing polo and I told him that the horses were wild—and—and it slipped."

I had a terrible vision of Gideon lying, twisted, on the ground while Julie wrung her mauve-tipped fingers on the side-lines.

"The pony slipped?" I prompted her hollowly.

"Yes," she gulped. "It was awful! I cried and cried."

That I could imagine.

"And Gideon?" I asked dryly.

"He's broken a leg. And, really it's most peculiar, he wants you to come out immediately and drive him home."

"Me or Joseph?" I asked.

"He said you," Julie answered in the same bewildered tones. "It isn't at all necessary. I *told* him I would drive him and Camilla home and stay on and nurse him, but he said I would be more useful calming my parents. They're terribly upset, naturally."

"Naturally," I agreed. "I'll come straight away."

I could imagine the scene as I put down the receiver. Camilla sulky and unresponsive, the parents annoyed that such a thing should have happened in their perfectly run Indian retreat, and Gideon, impatient with pain, shouting orders at everyone. Julie wouldn't like that at all! It was the centre of the stage for her, or nothing at all, and I couldn't help being sneakily pleased that she had been deprived of her star billing for a while. If it hadn't meant Gideon being hurt, I should have cheered!

My mood of elation died speedily when I tried to get the jeep out of the garage. Joseph had put it away for me and apparently he hadn't noticed that one of the rear tyres was completely flat. I looked at it with dismay. The familiar pricking sensation of heat on the back of my neck was already with me after my bath and the accompanying feeling of helplessness made positive action doubly difficult. I tried to find Joe, but he had already gone out again. Thoroughly dispirited, I went back to the garage and started to change the wheel myself.

I had got the jack working and two of the nuts loosened when one of the workers came in for some of the chemical solution Gideon was using on his potato fields. He took the wrench out of my hands and finished the job for me, talking all the while as he did so.

"Going far, *memsahib*? There is no other spare tyre for you to take with you."

He was quite right, but I really couldn't bother about that at that moment. I thanked him warmly for his trouble and jumped up into the driving seat. I had only the vaguest idea of where I was going, but I was reasonably sure that I could find the way if I started off right, and as there were only two roads leading out of the village, I could hardly go wrong.

The road went through trees full of chattering monkeys. It was difficult to get away from animal life in India. People, monkeys, cattle, birds and insects jostled one another for existence. Even in the most unlikely corners a lizard would suddenly come to life to impale a fly on its tongue. Snakes came and went, seeking peace and solitude and sometimes food, and terrifying everyone they met. Normally I rather liked to see this teeming life all round me, but that day the monkeys became almost intolerable, throwing twigs and stones at the jeep and swinging down towards me out of the trees until I really began to believe they were going to leap in with me.

I was not yet frightened, but unconsciously I hurried more and more until I was going so fast that it was scarcely safe on the inadequate double track. I forced myself to slow down, but then the monkeys came again, and by this time I was really rattled and kept telling myself it was only because I was alone.

I took the most used track when I came to the first fork. The jeep crashed over a half-concealed stone and the engine faltered. So concerned was I to keep the thing on the road that I failed to catch the faltering spark and the engine died completely. Swearing under my breath, I pulled in as far as I could and tried to get started again. The monkeys came closer and closer, inquisitively watching my every movement. One of them, braver than the rest, jumped down on the bonnet and pulled a face at me. I was really scared then. They were so incredibly human in their movements, like so many evil old men, jeering at my vain efforts and the squealing self-starter.

I remembered having been told that monkeys were sacred in India because Hanuman, a demi-god and an ape, had formed an alliance with the god Rama and had helped him to find Sita, Rama's wife, after she had been raped by the demon king of Ceylon. Looking at this particularly large specimen on the bonnet, I began to think that their help had been overrated, or certainly man's gratitude had been, for these animals were completely unafraid of me and came closer and closer, teasing me with bony fingers and chattering movements of aggression.

It was a great relief when the engine suddenly sprang into life. I blew the horn and started off down the road again, scattering the monkeys as I went. I was so hot now that the perspiration ran down my face and tasted salt on my lips. It was farther than I had thought and I was beginning to wonder if I had come the right way. I came to a small village and made enquiries from the only inhabitant I could find. The directions he gave me were vague in the extreme, but I gathered that I was on the right road.

When I finally reached the entrance there was no mistaking it. Two enormous lions, made in concrete, marked the gates, towering over the sign that said this was the Burnett residence. Beyond this imposing beginning was an avenue of trees, now badly neglected, but nevertheless still handsome. I set the jeep up the rough drive and rumbled over the pitted surface towards what had once been a quietly tasteful and spacious house. Now it was painted in a violent pink with the windows and doors picked out in a vivid blue. The roof was overgrown with a mossy plant and a general air of neglect brooded over the place. It was not at all the sort of home that I would have thought would have appealed to Gideon, and I wondered what had first drawn him there.

Halfway up the drive a man leaped out from behind a tree and waved me down. I came to a halt beside him and he jumped up beside me with a flurry of words.

"Missee come very quickly. *Sahib* Wait very sick man. Better you take him home. This house not welcome to a sick man. One sick man more than enough, don't you say? Missee Julie wait for you on the verandah. The *memsahib* gone to bed.

"Oh?" I said weakly. "Really?"

"Not a good day for anyone," the Indian went on with complete satisfaction. "Very sad!"

"Do you know where Dr. Wait is?" I asked him.

"But of course. That is why I wait for you to come, to show you the way. I am the most completely reliable servant. You will see."

I began to think that he might be as he directed me to drive round the house and to park the car in the shade of a large tree to keep it cool.

"I take you straight away to *Sahib* Wait," he told me. "We shall not wait for niceties of various greetings as they are taking too much time. Come with me immediately.''

He led the way, his bare feet completely silent on the stone floor of the verandah, and took me through a door that was swathed with mosquito netting to keep out the flies and other lesser animal life. It was dark inside and very cool after the heat outside and I stood still for an instant just enjoying the contrast. The Indian beckoned me onwards and opened a door into a darkened bedroom.

"The *Sahib* is in here," he said.

It was a minute or so before I could see much beyond the general shape of the furniture. I went over towards the bed as quietly as possible in case Gideon was sleeping.

"Hullo, Suki."

I jumped, terribly relieved that he should sound so very much himself.

"Oh, Gideon!" I gulped.

He chuckled and I was very conscious that I had used his Christian name and not his title.

"Why did you come?" he asked. "I thought it would be Joseph."

I hesitated.

"I answered the telephone. Julie said you wanted me to come." I couldn't have sounded very sure of myself because he hastened to reassure me.

"A much prettier chauffeur, anyway."

I could see him more clearly now. He looked as hale and hearty as ever and not in the least in need of my sympathy.

"Julie said you were hurt!" I exclaimed.

He made a face at me. "So I am! I rather think I've broken my leg. Damned pony rolled on it."

I tried to look sympathetic, but my curiosity overcame me.

"What on earth were you doing playing polo?" I asked.

He grinned. "I do play, you know," he said. "And

anyway, the old man likes a game. I'd forgotten all the same," he went on dryly, "that he couldn't bear to lose. I shot the second goal for my side and then bang, wallop, and this!"

"What *do* you mean?"

"I mean that he tripped up my mount!" he said bitterly. "If I could prove it—but I can't, so what the hell?"

"But that's dreadful!" I exclaimed, shocked. "And where's Camilla?"

"In a state," her brother replied. "I told her to go off by herself and calm off until the doctor came."

I gave him a furious look.

"How could you?" I demanded hotly. "You know she didn't want to come in the first place! I'll go and look for her!"

A strong hand shot out from the bedclothes and grabbed me round the wrist.

"Oh no, you won't! I know exactly how she's feeling, but she has to learn to get on with the rough as well as the smooth. Julie spent all day being nice to her, but she couldn't come out of her sulks sufficiently to see it!"

I tried to imagine Julie being nice to anyone and failed miserably.

"I don't think she will ever like her much," I put in.

"That's beside the point!" Gideon snapped back. "She doesn't like Julie's parents either! Nor do I, for that matter, but Julie is the one who has to live with them day in and day out, and I admire the way she does it, without a word of complaint. She has courage, that girl!"

I felt quite as sulky as Camilla must have done.

"And where is she?" I asked.

Gideon leaned back and closed his eyes. Accustomed now to the dim light, I could see the lines of pain etched in around his eyes and the paleness of his cheeks.

"She's getting a doctor."

There seemed to be nothing to do but wait and so I sat down gingerly on the edge of a chair and looked about me. There was no mistaking the fact that the owners of the house had lived in India for a long time. The only table was mounted on an elephant's foot and various trophies hung around the walls, trailing ribbons that were faded and dirty, relics of an era that had completely disappeared. A tiger's skin lay on the floor, the head realistically growling in my direction.

"I suppose someone shot it?" I said with distaste.

Gideon laughed weakly.

"Mr. Burnett, no doubt! What an impossible girl you are!"

We sat in silence after that, waiting for someone to come and restore our spirits. Gideon was more and more obviously in pain and I getting more and more worried about him. But when Julie and the doctor came it was almost an anticlimax. Julie came running into the room, the tears sparkling in the corners of her eyes and her pale mauve hair prettily ruffled by the wind.

"Gideon, he says you'll have to go to the hospital for an X-ray. What shall we do?"

Gideon opened his eyes and looked at her.

"Nonsense! Tell him to come and set it here and then I can go home."

Julie caught his hand in both hers. "You're so terribly brave!" she sobbed.

I looked at the two of them with growing disgust.

"I suppose you want to limp for the rest of your life!" I said with some asperity. "Of course you'll still go to the hospital. Where is the doctor?"

A small Indian doctor, dressed in a Congress cap and very little else, approached bowing from the doorway where he had been standing.

"The gentleman is in much pain," he said softly. "Perhaps it would be better if the ladies left until I have made him more comfortable.

Gideon laughed shortly. "Perhaps you'd better!" he said.

Julie walked tearfully towards the door with me following, a pace or two behind. I felt sorry for her, knowing the ravages tears can make and that she would care, but, oddly, she cried as easily as a child. The tears welled into her eyes and down her cheeks without a single sign of reddened lids and the headache that I am left with. With her it was actually pretty.

"Poor Gideon!" I said with a sympathetic smile.

The tears came harder and she frowned at me.

"Yes," she said. "But do you know that child actually said it was all our fault! As if it wasn't bad enough for poor, darling Papa. I shall never invite *her* here again!"

Which was just as well, I felt, as I very much doubted whether Camilla would have come.

CHAPTER SEVEN

CAMILLA was decidedly sulky, but she cheered up a little when she saw me.

"How's Gideon?" she asked immediately, and I couldn't help feeling that they had been rather cruel to take her away from him.

"He's all right!" I told her. "What did you imagine? He's more impatient than hurt!"

"Really?" She took a deep breath of relief. "It was awful!" she added, and shivered at the memory.

Julie rounded on her savagely, her face pinched with temper.

"You keep quiet, miss!" she spat. "We've had enough trouble from you!"

I was startled out of the composure I had assumed for Camilla's benefit.

"What do you mean?" I asked.

"You weren't there!" Julie said nastily.

Camilla went scarlet with rage and so I cut in quickly before she was really rude to her hostess.

"Of course I wasn't there and I'm very glad I wasn't. It was obviously a great shock to you all. May Camilla and I go out into the garden while we wait to find out what the doctor has to say? And then I'll be taking her home—and Gideon too if he's well enough."

Julie recovered herself with difficulty. Her face was still pinched and white round the mouth and her eyes blazed with temper as she looked at me, but her voice was as soft as honey as she answered.

"Of course you want to have a look round," she agreed. "I'll go back to Gideon and see if he wants anything."

I nodded my head and she went tripping out of the room, her soft hair bouncing with her steps. Camilla contained herself with difficulty until she had gone and then she burst into tears. There was nothing attractive about her crying and she made things worse by rubbing at her eyes with her knuckles like a child.

"It was awful!" she said again. "Suki, they tripped him because he scored a goal. I *saw* them!"

"But it was only a game," I said easily. "Who was playing?"

"That's what was so ridiculous!" she exclaimed tearfully. "There weren't enough people to play a proper game of polo and so they were really just playing about. Mr. Burnett was on one side, with two of the servants to help him, and Gideon and the other two were playing against them. They set up a couple of makeshift goals, and it was terrific fun at first—all the time Mr. Burnett was winning. He shot a goal almost immediately and we all clapped like anything and he was terribly pleased. But then Gideon whacked two into the other goal almost before he could turn round and he *deliberately* pushed his stick between Gideon's pony's legs. Of course the pony tripped!"

"It could have been accidental," I suggested.

"You wouldn't think so if you'd seen his face!"

I found myself believing her, even though I didn't want to because there was something rather nasty about her story, just as I had thought there was something nasty about the whole house.

"All the same, I think you'd better forget all about it," I warned her.

Camilla gave me a curious look.

"Because you believe me?" she asked.

I hesitated, more than a little embarrassed by the question.

"Hush," I said hastily.

It wasn't any too soon to change the subject because at that moment Julie joined us again, all smiles and without a trace of her former rage.

"How nice it is to see you both enjoying your-selves," she purred. "And I have some good news for you too! The doctor says it's a clean break and he's setting it now, so Gideon won't have to go to hospital."

"Good," said Camilla bluntly, "then we can take him home with us!"

Julie frowned quickly through her smiles.

"Now, now, I know how much you want him with you, dear, but we must consider the patient a little too, mustn't we? He'll be much better off here with us."

Camilla opened her mouth and I knew she was getting ready to argue the point, probably at the top of her voice and with more feeling than would have been proper.

"Of course we shall do whatever is best for him," I agreed warmly.

Camilla gave me a stony glare.

"Traitor!" she whispered under her breath.

I smiled on, until I began to think that my face was setting in a mould and that the strain was beginning to show.

"May we go and talk with him?" I asked politely.

It was easy to see that Julie would have liked to have refused, but as there was no good reason why she should, she nodded briskly and walked quickly off, leaving us to follow.

"You're not going to leave him?" Camilla whispered anxiously in my ear.

"Not if I can help it," I replied grimly. "But Gideon won't do anything on my say-so. He'll make his own decision."

Camilla sighed. "I expect you're right, but it would be *fatal*!" And, even allowing for adolescent exaggera-tion, I couldn't help wondering if she wasn't right.

Gideon was sitting up against a pile of cushions with his leg smothered in wet plaster and a rather foolish grin on his face.

"Lovely mud pies!" he greeted us cheerfully.

Camilla went quickly over to the bed and took his hand in hers, squeezing it hard.

"You're sure you're all right?" she asked him in a funny, tight voice.

He laughed up at her.

"You worry too much, young lady! Give this muck time to set and I'll be sitting beside you in the jeep while Suki drives us both home."

Camilla swallowed tearfully.

"*She* said you would rather stay here!" she said rebelliously.

"Did she though?" He laughed in the most light-hearted way. "That's no reason to make such a mouthful of the whole thing." He gave me a quick look and seemed to be reassured by what he saw, because he threw the whole conversation into my court by saying: "Aren't relatives the very devil?"

It was the wrong question to ask of me, who had been bereft of relatives for some years now.

"You ought to be glad to have someone to care about you," I reproved him.

He made a face at me. "Is that what your Timothy would have said?"

My sympathy for him died. I was nonplussed as I always was whenever he referred to Timothy. For long stretches I forgot all about Timothy myself and I was both edgy and wary when anyone reminded me of him. I felt somehow that they were calling in question my devotion to him.

"He really *needs* someone to take care of him," I remembered. "I do hope he's eating the right things in America!"

Gideon and Camilla exchanged impatient glances.

"Well, really!" Camilla fired at me crossly. "As if it matters that your Timothy lives on stomach powders! Gideon is really hurt!"

Gideon's raucous laughter did nothing to smooth my decidedly ruffled feathers.

"Don't worry, chicken," he said to his sister, "I'll be coming home with you!"

We both sighed with relief.

"I hope you're going to tell Julie," I said feelingly.

His eyes shone with amusement. "You're quite as bad as Camilla," he teased me. "Seeing bogys where there are none! And making such a fuss about it!"

I would have made some retort that would have put him firmly in his place, only Julie rejoined us at that moment, as sweet as ever and as full of smiles.

"I'm so sorry to have left you on your own," she began with that "little girl" charm I was beginning to despise. "I just called in to see how Daddy is getting on. It was such a shock to him. He's lying down, poor darling. Mother was too, but now she feels strong enough to see you two girls before you go home. She's in the drawing room. Shall I show you where?"

Camilla looked suddenly defeated.

"It's all right," she muttered, "I can find it." She stood up with a quick coltish movement. "Come on, Suki, we'd better get it over."

Julie gave her a look of vicious hate, quickly concealed by a mask of sugary sweetness.

"I don't know how you manage to be so charming!" she said quite mildly. "If I were you I shouldn't make one of those remarks to Mother. She doesn't understand modern young people like you. She'd think you were being rude."

Camilla went a fiery red and I pulled her after me, out of the room, before she could think of any other reply that would put her badly in the wrong. I had the feeling that that was exactly what Julie would have liked her to have done and that she was doing all in her power to engineer a situation that would make Gideon side with her against his sister.

"She'd *know* if I were being rude!" Camilla muttered crossly.

I could have shaken her. I slammed shut the door into Gideon's room and stalked down the corridor to where I imagined the reception rooms to be.

"For heaven's sake, Camilla!" I scolded her. "Can't

you see how she loves to put you in the wrong? You're not helping Gideon you know."

She gave me a sulky smile.

"I'm sorry," she said. "Come on, it's this way. Let's beard the old dragon in her lair quickly, before Julie persuades Gideon to stay."

"I don't think she'll manage to do that," I replied with quiet confidence. And I really believed it. However fond Gideon was of Julie, he would be worried about his work and he would be back at the station as soon as he possibly could be. It wasn't quite the reason I would have liked, but I believed in facing facts. Gideon would do many things for Camilla, but I was no more than an employee and, as such, I scarcely impinged on his consciousness.

Mrs. Burnett was half sitting, half lying on the sofa, with a hand woven rug cast loosely over her knees. She was very like Julie to look at, with the same soft hair, grey instead of mauve, and the same soft skin and innocent expression. But the years had written in lines of discontent and disappointment beside the eyes and in the wrinkles of the mouth.

"Come over here, my dears. Camilla, you can sit on the stool and Miss King in the chair."

We obediently settled ourselves where she had suggested, while she looked from one to the other of us with bland amusement.

"And what do you think of our remnant of the British Raj?" she asked slyly.

Camilla managed to show her distaste by being far too enthusiastic in a breathless voice.

"It's *lovely*! Were you really here before Independence?"

Mrs. Burnett winced. Independence didn't seem so very long ago to her and she didn't like the fleeting years being pushed on her so ruthlessly. She sighed in a way that was very reminiscent of her daughter.

"Oh yes, indeed. The wasted years, I often call them. I longed to go home to England, if only because of

Julie. It was only right that she should have friends
among her own kind and meet the right young men,
but my husband is in love with India and *nothing* would
make him leave. I think he would have died in England—can you understand that? He had lived for so
long here that he would be quite out of place in an
English provincial town, and London would have completely stifled him. Besides which, living in the sun,
you know, does queer things to a man— But we won't
think about that, will we?" She hesitated, obviously
unsure as to how to continue. "It's so difficult for me
to ask you this," she said at last. "But I should be so
grateful if you would encourage Gideon to stay here for
a few days. It's not for *my* sake, but Julie so seldom
sees anyone of her own age."

Camilla stared at her with unblinking eyes.

"I don't think either of us could persuade Gideon
one way or the other," I said as gently as I could. "Why
don't you talk to him?"

Mrs. Burnett looked more upset than ever.

"I don't want him to think that we are trying to trap
him into anything! Oh dear, how awkward everything
is!"

I smiled sympathetically, trying to ignore the expression of outrage on Camilla's face.

"We're not so very far away and Julie comes over
quite often," I put in comfortingly.

"It's not the same. She has no *opportunities* here, the
poor dear.

Camilla could keep silent no longer.

"And so you deliberately trip up Gideon's horse!"
she exclaimed.

Mrs. Burnett raised her delicately trimmed eyebrows.

"*I*? No, dear. How could I? I wasn't even playing.
And anyway, it's a pony, not a horse."

Camilla cast her outraged glance on me.

"But *he* tripped Gideon up!"

"It doesn't matter, dear," I said hastily. "*Not now*!"

"But—" she began.

"But really there's nothing to say," I said firmly. "No one can make up Gideon's mind for him. Not even you."

Mrs. Burnett looked sad and worried.

"I'm sure my husband meant it for the best," she said humbly. "He gets so worried about Julie too. You do understand, don't you?"

I felt rather sickened by the whole affair.

"It doesn't matter," I assured her in stifled tones. "Perhaps you will excuse us if we go back to Gideon now?"

Her eyes narrowed and she gave me a look of hatred that was so like her daughter that I gasped.

"I suppose you're after him yourself!" she snapped.

I eyed her helplessly, at a complete loss to know as to how to answer. But Camilla had none of my reservations.

"Suki wouldn't be so vulgar," she remarked with touching dignity. "Would you, Suki?"

I muttered something which could have been either yes or no, took one last despairing look round the too upholstered room, and fled down the passage to Gideon's bedroom. I rushed into his room without even bothering to knock. I felt stifled and dirtied by the scented air of the Burnetts and the kind of life they were trying to keep alive.

"Oh, Gideon!" I gulped.

He was very nice about it. He held both my hands reassuringly and the mocking look went out of his eyes, if not the smile.

"Well, well," he said, "How very flattering! I gather your reactions to our hostess are exactly the same as Camilla's!"

I bit my lip. "It isn't that I don't like them," I hedged.

"No?"

"And it isn't Julie's fault, is it?" I went on with determined objectivity.

Gideon lost his smile and became serious for a while.

"That's the way I look at it," he said. "What chance has the girl ever had? Imagine being cooped up in this museum for long."

Considering that I agreed with him, I wondered why I should resent his interest in Julie so much. I pulled my hands free and sighed.

"Does that mean you're going to stay for a while?" I asked casually.

He gave me a lopsided grin.

"Not exactly. I have a job to do and I reckon I shall be able to do most of it on crutches—somehow. No, I thought perhaps we could have Julie over more often. She might like to come and stay for a spell. She could share the same house as you and Camilla."

"I suppose she could," I agreed gloomily.

"It wouldn't be for long, necessarily," he coaxed me.

I smiled deliberately and said with forced cheerfulness: "It won't matter to me anyhow! I shall be far too busy building my dam!"

"Oh?" he asked cautiously.

"It's all settled," I went on, the words tumbling over themselves. "I explained it all to the old men of the village and they were quite pleased!"

"Indeed?"

I remembered belatedly that his permission was still required and that I wasn't going the best way to get it.

"You do approve, don't you?" I asked him anxiously.

"I don't know," he replied dryly. "You have to tell me about it."

"Yes, I will," I assured him. "It won't cost very much at all. I really think you'll like the idea."

"Possibly," he said with complete lack of interest. "But in the meantime I want nothing so much as to go home."

With compassion I noticed the worn look on his face which had not been there earlier. We were all so interested in our own affairs that we had hardly had time to fully realise that he was the one who had been badly hurt.

"I'm sorry, Gideon."

His smile came back.

"I know you are. You're a soft-hearted creature." He began to struggle off the bed while I watched him worriedly.

"I think I'd better get some help," I suggested.

He nodded, concentrating hard on the sheer physical effort of gaining his balance.

"Get Camilla," he bade me. "And if you can, get the jeep round to the nearest door."

Camilla came running when I called her. She helped her brother across the room and towards the door that I had first come in by.

"I thought Julie was with you," she half-accused him. He leaned a little more heavily on her shoulder.

"To tell the truth I was in pain and wanted to be alone for a while," he told her. "She'll be along to say goodbye."

Mrs. Burnett came too, to wave goodbye to her parting guests. She put a possessive arm around her daughter's shoulders and hugged her close.

"It's been such fun having your friends for the day," she said brightly. "I do hope that poor boy is going to be all right, jolted over these rough roads. You must drive extra carefully, Miss King!"

It was quite a business getting Gideon installed in the jeep. Fortunately the front seat gave him plenty of room for his leg to stick out in front of him and there were a number of cushions that could be used as props. I looked at his ashen face with some anxiety, noticing afresh the lines of pain and his shadowed eyes that his determined smile was not really covering up.

"The sooner we go the better," I said to Camilla. She got into the back after shaking hands prettily with Mrs. Burnett. Julie she just ignored, and I was in two minds as to whether I ought to press her to at least say goodbye. But I need not have worried because Julie was not thinking of Camilla at all. Just as I was on the point of letting in the clutch, she made a rush at Gideon flung her arms round his neck and kissed him warmly on the cheek.

"I'll be over first thing in the morning," she whispered to him. "It won't be so very long to wait, will it?"

I couldn't help noticing that he kissed her back.

"I'll be waiting for you, chicken," he said.

Julie flushed with pleasure and triumph and she graciously nodded her head to me.

"Be very careful of him, Susan. He means a great deal to me!" As if we hadn't all been made aware of that! I didn't say a word. I drove straight down the neglected drive and breathed a sigh of relief when we gained the public road.

"Did you hear that?" Camilla demanded in exasperated tones.

Gideon sat well back in his seat and closed his eyes.

"My, my," he said, "how you girls do carry on!" And I wondered if he meant Camilla and me or Julie Burnett. But somehow it seemed too much to hope that he meant the latter.

Gideon remained unbearable for the rest of the day. He lay in his bed and demanded that everybody went and paid him a visit at frequent intervals all through what was left of the evening. My turn came just as I was putting the finishing touches to my latest drawing of the dam I was going to build. I threw down my pencil, feeling thoroughly cross, and went across to the main house and his bedroom.

"I think you're having far too many visitors!" I greeted him.

He scowled at me through the gloom from the inadequate lamp.

"Is that possible? For heaven's sake, woman, stop staring at me and do something to make me a little more comfortable!"

I humped up his pillows and tried to straighten out the worst of the creases in his sheet.

"Why don't you give in and try to get some sleep?"

He snorted impatiently. "Does that mean you're ready for bed?" he demanded.

I smothered a yawn. "Not at all," I said very politely. "If you like, I'm quite prepared to entertain you for the greater part of the night."

He gave me a suspicious look and was only partly mollified by the innocent expression on my face.

"I suppose you'd better tell me about this dam of yours," he bribed me. I fell for the suggestion, hook, line and sinker. He grinned at me amiably. "Supposing you go and get the drawings," he suggested.

I eyed the black smudges under his eyes with some misgiving, but I went and got the drawings all the same. My enthusiasm for the project bubbled up inside me and I was doubly annoyed that I hadn't been able to finish the drawings off properly.

Gideon snatched the sheaf of papers from me and spread them out on his bed. I tried to explain the main points to him, but he brushed away my explanations preferring to see the thing as a whole for himself.

"Are you planning to line the reservoirs?" he asked.

I hesitated. "I'm not sure. Some of the soil around is clay."

"But it will lead to seepage?"

I nodded unhappily. "The trouble is the lining adds to the cost," I explained.

He glanced down at my figures. "I think it would prove less costly in the end than persistent seepage."

I nodded. It sounded as though he was getting keen as well and that was what I wanted at that moment, more than anything in the world.

"What had you thought of using?" he asked me.

I pointed at yet another piece of paper.

"Possibly butyl. It's easy enough to lay. You just drag the sheets out flat and join them together."

"Or?"

"Or P.V.C. The sun might affect it, but if it's buried under about six inches of soil, with the edges covered even more carefully and compacted, I think it should last a goodish while. It has the advantage of being about a third of the cost of the other and the labour costs of laying it here shouldn't be so very great."

"No," he agreed. "We can pick up enough cheap labour to do the whole thing in a few days. The difficulty will be in getting the materials."

"I'll get them," I assured him doggedly. "I'll get them if it's the last thing I do!"

Gideon lay back, suddenly exhausted.

"It may very well be!" he said. "You'd better take a trip to Delhi and see what you can do!"

I sat very still, scarcely daring to breathe.

"Do you mean I can go ahead?"

He grinned. "I don't see why not," he said.

I couldn't sleep at all that night. Every time I turned out the light, I thought of yet another point to do with the dam. By the grey light of dawn I had modified the whole project into a much more sensible unit that had the potential to water most of the research station and not just the two fields on either side of the turgid stream. A wretched bird that I had never heard before came just outside my window and mocked my restlessness. It was not a songbird in the accepted sense, for its repertoire consisted of a series of strange and intermittent shrieks that sounded more like someone being murdered. I buried myself in my pillow and tried to ignore it, and within a few seconds I was fast asleep.

I awoke only because Camilla was pinching the lobe of my ear. Resentfully, I struggled to get free, but she was persistent, and slowly I pulled myself into full consciousness.

"What do you want?" I asked grumpily.

Camilla laughed. "Considering it's nearly lunchtime—"

"*Lunch-time*!" I sat up hastily and stared at her. "It can't be!"

"Oh, but it is! And brother Gideon would like to see you when you can spare him the time."

I gave an abashed glance at the plans of the dam that had fallen on the floor by my bed.

"Did he say that?" I asked, thinking that I recognised Gideon's touch in the words.

Camilla nodded vigorously. Her eyes were lit with laughter, and immediately I was suspicious.

"What's up?" I asked.

"What should be up? Apart from the fact you're so late that it's hardly worth your while beginning a day's work!"

I ignored that, feeling rather ashamed of myself. When I put my feet on the floor and stood up, I felt heavy and immobile as one does when one has slept too deeply after a restless night.

"How is Gideon?" I asked quite grumpily. If it had not been for him I would have got to bed at a more reasonable time and I could have rounded up the *panchayat* by now and told them that I had his approval.

"Like a bear with a sore head, only it's his leg." Camilla lost the happy note in her voice for an instant. "I do hope that doctor set it properly!"

I was hoping so too. I dressed in a hurry, splashing cold water on to my face to make sure I was properly awake. When I had finished, I gathered up my papers and put them into some sort of order.

"Is Gideon waiting for me now?" I asked.

Camilla's expression of delight came back.

"Yes, he is. Now," she said.

I hurried across to the other house with her close behind me. Just outside Gideon's room I took a deep breath and straightened my hair. Then I knocked on the door.

"Who is it?"

"It's me—Suki. May I come in?"

He was in his dressing-gown, sitting on the edge of his bed.

"Good afternoon!" he greeted my wryly.

I said nothing. It seemed very much better not to.

"D-did you want me?" I asked after a while.

He swung round to look at me, noting the sleepy look that still showed in my eyes and the pile of papers I had hastily snatched up. And he smiled at Camilla over my shoulder.

"Shall I tell her?" he asked.

Camilla giggled. "She wouldn't believe it if anyone else did!" she said happily.

Mystified, I tried to read their minds without any success.

"What is it?" I pleaded, half laughing myself.

Gideon balanced himself with some difficulty on his one good leg.

"I've booked your passage to Delhi," he told me. "While you're there you can get all the supplies we need, and, *incidentally*, you can get the things you'll need for your dam."

And I couldn't even thank him. All I could do was sit on the end of his bed and make desperate efforts not to cry.

CHAPTER EIGHT

It was more a halt than a railway station, with the gleaming curves of the rails running through the two plain platforms that stretched out into the hot sunshine from the narrow strips of shade. Children played all along the lengths of slatted wood, apparently oblivious of the searing rays of the sun; their elders vied with one another for standing room in the shade, waving hand-made fans before their faces, completely composed and self-contained even though their neighbour could hardly help treading on their toes.

I found a very small space of shade for myself and took up as impregnable a position as I could manage. The hot smell of humanity overcame my nostrils at intervals, but, in a peculiar way, I was no longer as vividly disturbed by it as I once had been. A couple of children playing hide and seek seized the hem of my skirts and I was distracted from the rest of the crowd for a moment while I tried to restore order. Camilla's only reaction was to laugh at my efforts and in the end it was she who unclasped their long, agile brown fingers and pushed them out into the burning sun again.

"You are lucky!" Camilla said for the umpteenth time. "I wish I were going with you!"

"Why don't you?" I asked gently.

She wiped the sweat off her brow with the back of her hand.

"Gideon said no," she answered bitterly.

I judged it wiser to say nothing in reply to that. Gideon had his reasons for most of the things he did and he probably had a very good one for not allowing Camilla to go with me to Delhi.

"How many days will you be away?" she asked again.

"Oh, hardly any time at all. I want to get started on that dam the first instant that I can." My eyes caught hers and my own disappointment in her not coming was for the moment as vivid as hers. "I wish the train would come!" I said moodily.

Almost as if it were to order, at that moment the train came into sight, puffing and blowing in the distance, with a swarm of adolescent children running along beside it, almost as if they were willing it to slowly come to a stop the moment it reached the long platform. Immediately it did so the scene sprang to life. People hurried backwards and forwards, tripping over each other in their anxiety to get on to the train, to find their arriving friends and relations and to sort out the fantastic mountains of luggage, most of it wrapped in a cotton blanket and tied with a piece of string.

Camilla opened one of the doors and wrinkled up her nose at the stuffy atmosphere within.

"You can't travel in this!" she exclaimed.

I followed her into the train.

"It isn't too bad," I comforted myself more than her. "And I shall get a seat. It looks even more crowded farther up."

I pushed my suitcase up into the rack and went back on to the platform with Camilla.

"Where's Joseph?" she asked, looking about her expectantly. She quite plainly was getting all ready to worry about me travelling on the train all by myself. "You have got that list of addresses that Gideon gave you, haven't you?"

To oblige her I searched for it in my handbag and produced it triumphantly. Camilla glanced at it with warm approval.

"There! You can hardly go far wrong with those directions in your pocket. You've certainly sold Gideon that dam of yours, haven't you?"

"I hope so," I agreed. I looked at the list myself,

written in Gideon's neat, careful hand, and my eyes filled with sudden tears and for the moment I didn't want to go because Gideon wouldn't be in Delhi. I tried to put him out of my mind—to think of anything else, but the picture of him as I had last seen him, trying to hide the fact that he was in pain and concerned because he was sending a woman on her own into a foreign city, persisted despite my best efforts. I turned my face away from Camilla because I could feel myself blushing and I knew it was not beyond her to find the reason why.

"It's terribly hot!" I murmured.

Camilla gave me a sympathetic grin. "Terribly!"

A pedlar, selling copper and brass and a few silver bracelets, came hurrying over to us.

"The *memsahibs* would like to buy?" he whined.

Camilla brushed him away impatiently, but I was curious to see his goods. The silver of the bangles was not very pure, but they were pretty and intricately designed. I asked him how much they were, but I never heard the answer. The engine suddenly whistled with all its might and Joseph came running down the platform and practically threw me into the train.

"It's leaving!" he shouted. "Good luck!"

I waved to them both, the tears stinging my eyes again. A multitude of hangers-on grasped the outside of the train so that I could hardly see the vanishing platforms with their inadequate shelter. In a moment I could see nothing at all and settled a little unhappily into my seat, trying not to think about Gideon at all, or anything to do with him.

"Forgive me for interrupting you," my next-door neighbour said after a while. "There is someone in the corridor who is trying to attract your attention."

I looked first at my neighbour, a gentleman in a dirty dun-coloured turban. His smile was charmingly decorated with a variety of gold-filled teeth and his fingers were bedecked with a number of large-stoned rings. He smiled and nodded out to the corridor. Standing there, looking in at me and grinning all over his face, stood Joseph.

I stood up hastily and struggled with the door into the corridor.

"What are you doing here?" I demanded when it at last gave way to the insistent pressure of my hand. "What have you done with Camilla?"

His grin grew broader.

"She stayed behind to look after Gideon, but we agreed that somebody had to go with you, so I was elected."

"Does Gideon know?" I asked with grim foreboding.

"Good heavens, no! He'll probably sack me when I get back!"

Or me, I reflected bitterly. It would be far more likely to be me. He would never believe that I had never been a party to this mad, stupid idea! Never, never! For I had to admit that I could hardly believe it myself, that they would play such a stupid trick without my consent. And I didn't want Joe with me. There was nothing for him to do in Delhi and I was more than capable of looking after myself.

"I don't know where you're going to sit," I said coldly. "All the seats in my compartment are taken."

He looked at me, astonishment slowly taking the place of his pleasure.

"Aren't you *pleased*?" he demanded.

"No, I am not!" I snapped. "Gideon is going to be furious. What did you think you could gain by such idiotic behaviour?"

He shrugged uncomfortably.

"It didn't seem right to let you go on your own—and besides," he went on dolefully, "I thought you'd want me to be with you."

And in a way I did, I supposed. I mean that I was glad to know that I should have someone to share the responsibility of finding my way about Old Delhi, even if I did feel that I could manage New Delhi quite well on my own. I suppose, too, I was glad to have Joseph's company. He was my friend and we had sealed the fact with a kiss, and in a way he reminded me of Timothy, and anything that could do that was welcome at the moment. No, the only problem was Gideon's fury. That he would be extremely angry, I never had the slightest doubt. Our only hope was that he would have expended most of his fury on Camilla before we ever got back. But that was a forlorn hope, because his very real sense of justice would soon know that it had had very little to do with her—that Joseph and I were old enough to make our own decisions as to how we managed things. And the truth was that this wasn't very well managed at all! There would be gossip and I wouldn't be able to prevent it. And Joseph would be away from his work for no reason at all, and that was unforgivable.

"Oh yes," I said tartly, "I shall *love* having you with me when I think of Gideon struggling to manage on his own with a broken leg! I shall love it still more when he sacks the two of us—and we shall have deserved it!" I went back to my seat and sat down in it, uncomfortably aware that I hadn't been particularly kind when all Joseph had been trying to do was to make things easier for me.

He followed me into the compartment, frowning at my companions as if he were hoping to frighten them out of their seats.

"Surely you aren't afraid of Gideon?" he asked me resentfully when nobody stirred.

I glared at him, trying to remind him with my eyes that we were not the only people who could speak English.

"I respect him," I said tightly. "Joseph, do go and find yourself a seat!"

He went, but I was no happier left alone. My neighbour tried to engage me in conversation, but somehow I didn't have much to say. I was obsessed by my own emotions, by my own misery. Nothing that Gideon could ever say to me was worse than my own imagin-

ings during the first half of that journey. How could
Joseph have been so stupid?

I was still downright sulky when Joseph came to tell
me that we could have lunch on the train.

"I thought there wasn't a restaurant car?" I said,
surprised.

"There isn't exactly," he admitted. "I got off and
bought some things from one of the station vendors at
the last stop."

I must say I was very glad that I hadn't known about
it. To have Joseph on the train was bad enough, but to
lose him somewhere in India would have been too
much altogether.

"There's more room where I am," Joseph persuaded me. "I'll carry your things and then we can be
together."

It seemed churlish to refuse, so I spent the rest of the
journey sitting beside him and chatting of this and that.
On the whole it was very much better than being on my
own, and as his compartment was air-conditioned while
mine had not been, my temper began to improve and I
started to enjoy myself. When we came into Delhi I was
astonished by how quickly the journey had gone and
the feeling of nervous excitement that had been with
me ever since Gideon had said I could go ahead with
the dam came back again with a rush.

"Supposing I've got my figures all wrong!" I wailed
to Joseph.

He grinned. 'Well, supposing you have?"

I grabbed my suitcase and followed him down on to
the platform.

"You'll have to check them for me before we do any
ordering," I said.

His grin became positively triumphant. "Okay, I
will," he said.

He grabbed my suitcase with his free hand and
started off down the platform with his ticket firmly
lodged in his teeth. He had to stand and wait for me on
the other side of the barrier while I searched for mine

in my handbag. When I had finally given it up to the collector, he had already found a taxi and was telling the driver the name of the hotel we wanted to go to.

> *"If there be a paradise on earth,*
> *'Tis here! 'Tis here! 'Tis here!"*

Joseph found the famous Persian quotation on the walls of the Hall of Private Audience in the Red Fort, the room which had once held the famous Peacock Throne, in its more glamorous days, when the ceiling too had been of solid silver. He quoted the words softly, with a touch of magic, as though he had only just discovered their meaning and that it was somehow wrapped up with the fact that I was with him. I gazed up at the flowing script that spelt out the original words and tried to remember that it was only because time was at a standstill that I was so confused about what I felt and thought, that in fact I was waiting for Timothy.

Joseph took me by the hand and led me towards the Florentine panels, the only one of which I can remember depicted Orpheus playing for the birds.

"You are enjoying this, aren't you?" he asked me. "You would never have come here on your own, would you?"

"No," I agreed, "probably not."

"Then you would have missed one of the finest sights in the world!" he concluded enthusiastically. "If we had it back home in the States, so many people would be falling over themselves to see it it would pay off the National Debt all by itself!"

I grinned, amused by the idea. It had obviously not occurred to him that if you took such a gorgeous palace out of its own setting you would reduce its conception to a tourist's nine-day wonder just like any other. It was the history that spoke through the magnificent walls and the miracle of carvings on the walls, a history that had lived and suffered and had formed part of the race memory of the people. You couldn't ship history around the world with the marble and the stone.

We walked past the marble stall of the emperor's Grand Vizier which stood in front of the throne dais and went on into the private apartments and through into the Rang Mahal, or Painted Palace.

Joseph gave me a mocking smile.

"This is a very appropriate setting for you," he said.

I was intrigued by the central marble basin through which runs a water channel passing right through the palace, its bottom carved in the shape of a lotus flower. It was known as the Canal of Paradise.

"Do I look so much in need of a bath?" I retorted lightly.

Joseph stood back to allow me to pass ahead of him into the royal bathrooms, the *hammams*, exquisite Mogul and therefore Moslem baths, similar in function to our Turkish baths, but for them an essential part of the preparation for solemn prayer. It was no surprise therefore that a short way away stood the Pearl Mosque, designed by Aurangzeb, one of the Mogul rulers, for his personal use and for that of the royal ladies at his court. It was too ornate for my taste and I was glad when we escaped its sugary atmosphere into the gardens outside.

"There is something to be said for purdah," Joseph went on. "I should like to keep you away from the anxieties of working and having to provide for yourself and keep you myself alone."

I was shocked by the very idea.

"Oh, would you?" I said haughtily. "Well, let me tell you the price would be very much too high!"

He grinned and put his arm round my waist. It was very uncomfortable walking along like that, but I hadn't got the heart to set myself free from the casual embrace.

"I wonder?" he speculated. "Wouldn't you really rather like to be petted and privileged?"

I gave the question serious thought, but my independence was too valuable to me for me to be able to turn my back on it, even verbally. It seemed I was fully committed to standing on my own feet.

"No, I'd hate it," I replied simply.

The pressure on my wrist became stronger and he turned me in the circle of his arms to face him.

"I think I could change your mind," he said abruptly. He pulled me closer and tried to kiss me on the mouth. At another time I might have suffered the kiss with better fortitude, but at that moment I was only conscious of the fact that I was hot and that I didn't want to be touched.

"Please don't, Joe," I said gently.

"What? Change your mind?"

I shook my head.

"Please don't kiss me. I don't feel like it."

His pride was hurt and I was sorry. To cover the awkward moment I bent over and picked a flower that was struggling for life despite the heat and I put it in his buttonhole with a flourish. We exchanged slightly embarrassed laughs, both aware that we were not the right people in the right moment, despite the beauty all around us. Almost as if he had come to order one of the Sikh guides, in his white jodphurs and tweed jacket, came across to us over the burnt grass.

"Do you wish a guide?" he asked.

Joseph shook his head. "We have already seen all that we want to."

The guide was unconvinced.

"That is impossible, *sahib*. You have not been here at night when the moon hangs over the palace and little lamps are placed in the niches of the two pavilions. The whole romance of India breathes in this garden then!"

Joseph gave me a sardonic look. I wondered if he had it in mind to bring me back that evening, but I need not have concerned myself. Joseph had only one intention and that was to get rid of the guide as quickly as possible. He was always embarrassed by people asking for *baksheesh*, even when it was justified, and this worry was apt to take precedence over all others.

"Let's go," he whispered to me.

It seemed a pity to depart so soon, but I gave way as gracefully as I could. Timothy had long ago taught me not to argue on these occasions—though in those days I have to admit that it would never have even occurred to me to argue with him. I had learned quite a lot since coming to India.

"Perhaps those other people would like a guide," I suggested as another small group of Europeans came out into the gardens. The guide looked over his shoulder to where I was pointing, saluted smartly, and went off to ask them. Joe took a look at them and went quite white in the face.

"What's she doing here?" he demanded between clenched teeth.

I took a closer look at the little group and was surprised to recognize Julie's blue-pink hair.

"Perhaps it's her twin," I whispered.

And at that moment she saw us too.

"Why, look who's here!" she exclaimed in her "little girl" voice. "They're friends of Gideon's! Well, not friends exactly, but they work with him!"

Her companions glanced at us without too much warmth.

"That fellow who runs the research station?" one of them asked.

Julie's lips tightened angrily. "He's very important in our locality!" she said sternly.

They grinned at her, humouring her. It was obvious that they didn't think anything was important but their own interests.

"Of course! Quite agree!" they murmured.

I was the one who wanted to go then. I forced myself to look dispassionately at Julie and I had to admit she was very pretty. She was busy proving how loyal she was to Gideon. So the only reason why I couldn't find it within me to like her was because I was jealous of her, and that I didn't really like to admit.

"What are you doing in Delhi?" I asked her.

She turned to me immediately and smiled quite charmingly.

"I was so worried about Gideon that my parents thought it would be better for me to get away for a while. I'm staying here with friends." She smiled again, quickly and impersonally. "And you?"

I explained about the dam we were building, trying hard not to get carried away by my own enthusiasm. Julie was not very interested. Her eyes kept sliding over to Joseph as if she wanted to know what he was doing with me, but didn't quite like to ask.

"It must be nice to be able to take a look round while you're here," she said instead.

"It is," I agreed. "We didn't have much time to see Delhi when we passed through when we first came."

Julie sniffed.

"I can't imagine enjoying it much here myself if it weren't for the social life," she said. "It used to be much better, of course, when the British were here in force, but it's still very much better than anywhere else."

I laughed.

"We haven't much time for parties," I admitted. "We had a quite exhausting morning trying to arrange for all the stuff we want to be sent to the research station quickly—"

"Gideon should have come," she cut me off. "Gideon knows everyone here, so there wouldn't have been any trouble." She lowered her voice and whispered in my ear, "What on earth induced you to bring that American? *He* wouldn't be much use!"

There was an awkward silence. Joe had not been particularly helpful that morning. He had obligingly checked my figures, but that had led to his having ideas of his own as to how the dam should be built and we had very nearly quarrelled over the arrangements I had already made. He hadn't been much help in finding the various dealers either, but I had been glad of his presence just the same. It had been nice to know he was there in case anything went wrong. And there had been a lot of things to go wrong and most of them had through various misunderstandings and my complete lack of knowledge about the various government controls.

"Don't you like him?" I asked sweetly, taking the war firmly into the enemy's camp. Julie, however, was not to be so easily put out.

"Oh, I'm quite indifferent, my dear. He's not exactly *important* in any way, is he?"

"Perhaps not," I said.

She looked at me even more closely, screwing up her eyes as if she were a trifle short-sighted.

"I don't really understand you at all!" she complained breathlessly. "I suppose it's because all professional women are so terribly efficient and *unfeeling*! I mean we have so much more time to care about people, haven't we? You have your job to consider first all the time, and having to compete with men in their own sphere. I'm so glad that I don't have to bother with all that!"

I found that I resented the idea that I was unfeminine more than I liked.

"Most women have jobs of some sort nowadays," I said pacifically.

Her eyes glinted. "I'm afraid my father would never allow me to *work*," she said with a tinkling laugh. "Don't your people miss you when you are so far away from them?"

I shrugged my shoulders, refusing to answer.

"Dear, dear," she said. "Poor Gideon! When I get back I shall see that he has some *fun*! I can tell that he doesn't get much with you and Joseph around. I don't suppose you ever talk about anything else but your work and plant diseases. How dull he must be!"

I bit my lip, almost sure that she was right. Poor Gideon probably could do with some light relief, but I didn't think the Burnetts were the right ones to achieve this. It had already cost Gideon one broken leg.

One of the men who had come with Julie pulled at her arm to attract her attention.

"Are we going to stand around here all day?" he asked her plaintively. "Surely you see enough of these two when you're at home!"

Julie tossed her head so that her pale mauve hair was lifted in the wind. It was a very pretty and very well-rehearsed gesture.

"Hush, sweet! One has to be polite!" She giggled, maliciously aware that her remark had been hurtful.

The young man pulled her away, kissing her on the cheek as he did so. She bridled and giggled again, pleasantly embarrassed by his attention. I hope I didn't look as disapproving as I felt.

"Goodbye, Miss Burnett," I said formally. "We shall be going home tonight so I don't expect we shall run into each other again in Delhi."

She frowned at me. I think she was wondering if I would carry tales back to Gideon but apparently she came to the conclusion that even if I did he wouldn't believe me.

"I don't suppose we shall see much of each other—ever," she said simply. "But if we do just you remember that my motto is *tit for tat*!"

So that was it! I grinned wryly to myself. There wasn't much I could find to admire in Miss Julie Burnett.

"Ouch!" Joseph broke into my disagreeable thoughts. "That girl gives me the creeps. What does Gideon see in her?"

I pursed my lips together and said nothing at all. I was battling with the knowledge that I could have cheerfully kicked Julie. And I preferred not to even think about what Gideon could see in her. When she tossed her head in that particular way and smiled up at any man as if she regarded him as some Olympic hero, I should have thought it was only too obvious!

"Oh well," said Joseph. "It doesn't matter to us,

thank God! We aren't important enough to be troubled by her."

I wished I could comfort myself so easily.

On the train that night I simply could not get to sleep. The air-conditioned compartment had been speedily and easily converted into a sleeping cabin. It was comfortable and cool. The attendant had wrought this transformation while Joe and I had been dining in the dining-car that was attached to the train and which served both Indian and English dishes. He had been waiting in the corridor when I had come back to check if there was anything else I wanted.

"The *sahib* is in another car as he requested," he told me. "Is there anything further I can get you before I attend to him?"

I shook my head and tipped him as he was obviously hoping that I would.

"Goodnight, *memsahib*," he had bowed and had sketched a vague salute, carrying his hand to his turban as he left and I had been alone.

To entertain myself I had chased a couple of beetles back into the corridor from which they had dared to enter my compartment and I had played with the mosquito netting on the windows that was trying to keep the various insects out, but was actually keeping quite a number firmly in. I gave up after I had swatted a couple of mosquitoes and their dead bodies had fallen on the crisp white bedclothes. It seemed preferable to allow myself to be eaten alive.

There had been nothing to do after that but to get undressed and get into bed. It was a long time since I had slept on a train and I was terribly conscious of the rhythm of the engine and the wheels: I-think-I-can, I-think-I-can, all the way up the hills and the triumphant I-knew-I-could, I-knew-I-could, all the way down again. For a long time I listened in silence, trying to remember the sort of country we had come through. Then I fell to worrying about the dam and whether I had acquitted myself well enough for Gideon to be pleased. That mattered a great deal because somehow I couldn't get away from the idea that he had trusted me to do something for him. Joe had to be explained away, of course. With a sinking feeling that was more a premonition of failure, I couldn't help remembering how Joseph had neglected to get my jeep ready when I had first arrived and how Gideon had frowned on him. I didn't want to incur the same displeasure myself, and yet how was I going to avoid it? I lay and shivered at the thought. Then I realised that my sheet had slipped and that the air-conditioning was coming straight in on me and was making me cold, so I hunched myself up under the sheet and worried some more.

That day was just inexorably changing into the next when I began to worry about Julie. I thought about her parents and the place where she lived, and I thought about the way her friends had treated her at the Red Fort in Delhi. One thing was quite clear and that was that she wasn't nearly good enough for Gideon.

Gideon, Gideon, Gideon, went the wheel of the train and I became sleepy at the repetition of his name. By the time I awoke the rhythm had changed.

"I love Gideon I love Gideon," I muttered to myself, and was promptly wide awake again. I glanced at my watch in the first light of the dawn and was glad to see that it was time to get up. In half an hour we should be just pulling into the station where we had to get out. There was no one to meet us, but my jeep was parked in the station yard where I had left it. Joseph and I climbed into it in silence. I pressed the starting button and in silence we started for home, back to the research station.

CHAPTER NINE

"MISS KING!"

That's torn it, I thought. I stuck my head round the door of Gideon's room.

"Did you want me?" I said.

He was lying on his bed looking both rumpled and out of temper. I would have liked to have offered to tidy the bed up for him and to make it a little less hot and uncomfortable, but I shied away from the angry look in his eyes.

"Yes?" I prompted him.

"I suppose one has to expect disadvantages when one employs females," he began repressively. "But really! Whatever induced you to kidnap Joseph? I'll bet he was a lot of help to you!"

I frowned. I was going to have to pick my way carefully through this conversation if both Joseph and I were not to come to grief.

"I think he felt sorry for me being so nervous," I began hesitantly.

Gideon laughed sourly.

"I'll believe that when I hear his side of it," he retorted grumpily. "Did you get all the things you need?"

I launched into an enthusiastic report of all the things I had arranged to be sent to us. I told him about the bazaar-like shops we had been to and the difficulties we had encountered in finding suppliers for the machinery we hoped to hire and for things like that.

"But you still feel you can manage?" Gideon asked me.

I nodded my head.

"Really, we can," I assured him. "We can get so much cheap labour locally and they can do most of the digging by hand. It seems the long way round, but actually I think we'll get it done quicker that way."

"Very likely," he agreed. He paused. "You realise I won't be much help to you while I'm stuck with this leg, don't you?"

I tried to tell him how sorry I was, but he cut me off short. He had had enough slushy sympathy from all and sundry without my adding to it, he told me harshly.

"I hadn't realised that I was being *sloppy!*" I exclaimed crossly.

His eyes met mine and the expression in his softened a little.

"Oh, damn," he said. "You know quite well what I mean!"

I grinned discreetly, but he knew the way to take the wind completely out of my sails and basely he asked me:

"You look so pleased with yourself this morning that I suppose you've heard from that boy-friend of yours?"

The smile died on my face.

"What do you mean?" I asked hoarsely.

"That fellow in America," he reminded me.

"Timothy?" I cleared my throat, wondering desperately how it was that I could hardly remember the exact contours of Timothy's face, nor the accents with which he had spoken. All I could think of was that he was really rather insipid when I compared him with Gideon.

Gideon's eyes twinkled.

"Do you know so many people in the States?" he asked.

"N-no," I admitted. "But I hadn't been thinking about Timothy, you see. In fact I haven't had a letter from him since I came to India."

Gideon eased himself into a more comfortable position on the bed.

"Didn't he approve of your coming here?"

I shook my head.

"It wasn't that," I explained. "In fact he suggested that I should come. But since I've been here, I've hardly had time to write to *him*, and I suppose that makes a difference."

He gave me a long, hard look.

"I suppose it could," he agreed. I noted the careful change in wording and blushed. I didn't want him to think that I had made all the running as far as Timothy was concerned.

"He—he won't have much to say about his work, you see," I rushed into speech. "He knows that I don't understand much about what he's doing."

Gideon looked thoughful.

"And he doesn't understand anything about you at all?" he suggested mildly.

"Oh, I wouldn't say that! He was always very kind!" I insisted. "I should never have passed my exams if he hadn't coached me and taken an interest."

"Which hardly makes you the love of his life," Gideon went on firmly. "Why don't you write to him and break off that disastrous arrangement you made between you?"

I tried once again to remember exactly what it was I had felt for Timothy, but memory will play the oddest tricks. I could remember exactly the brand of stomach powder that worked most effectively and I could remember his favourite tunes, most of them classical and rather on the serious side. It came as rather a shock to know that it wouldn't hurt at all if I never saw Timothy again. But I couldn't say so. I certainly couldn't admit anything of the sort to Gideon. Why, in a way it was my only defence, my only weapon against the pale blue attraction of Julie Burnett. I had to keep things firmly in proportion, and that meant remembering that she was the one who was attractive to Gideon—not me. And it was important to remember this all the time.

"It was a very vague arrangement," I said with a laugh. "But I guess I must be the faithful type!"

Gideon snorted. "How you love your illusions!"

I was hurt and I showed it.

"Don't you think I can be loyal?" I demanded.

"I wasn't questioning that," he scoffed. "What I wonder is if you really know your own mind. And that I seriously doubt!"

I was furiously angry.

"I am over twenty-one!" I informed him haughtily.

But he only laughed. "Go on, get out and go and make your arrangements. I want to get my bearer to make me a little more comfortable!"

"Couldn't I help you before I go?" I asked, immediately solicitous.

"No, you cannot!" he retorted. "You'd like messing about far too much for my comfort!"

"Oh, indeed?" I said coldly. "Then be uncomfortable. I don't care! I don't have to sleep in that bird's nest!"

His eyes lit with amusement.

"And aren't you glad?" he teased me.

But it wasn't the sort of teasing that I was in the mood for, so I beat a hasty retreat before either of us said something that neither of us would be able to forget.

Later, I happened to be passing Gideon's door when he was seeing Joseph and finding out from him why he had gone to Delhi with me. It was a very different kind of interview and I couldn't help wondering why I had been let off so lightly. But then perhaps he knew that it had been Joseph's idea and that I hadn't known a thing about it until after the train had pulled out of the station.

It was a moment of great pride when I stood on the edge of the wheat field and dug the first spadeful of earth into the wheelbarrow. The dam project had begun. A variety of Indian labour had come from far and wide to dig the reservoirs, some of them, to my great satisfaction, had actually been sent by their own villages to see how it was done. Joseph suggested that I made a speech, but I was too stuffed up with emotion to say anything at all. Instead, I sat on the bank of the sluggish stream and allowed myself to dream of its future glory. The first of the monsoon rains were not very far away and then we should see the waters swell and slowly gather into the two tanks, offering undreamed-of crops in the future. I hugged the knowledge to me with glee. Whatever I was going to suffer personally when the time came for me to leave India, at least I would have left something behind me that was worthwhile and lasting.

The *panchayat* stood in solemn assembly on the opposite bank worrying about the costs and their own disbelief that a slip of a girl could organise anything on the kind of scale they were expecting. From my side of the stream I could afford to smile and wave to them. To my surprise, and with tremendous dignity, they responded with a bow and waved back.

"Look at them! As proud as peacocks!" Joseph scoffed.

"They have something to be proud about!" I retorted crossly. I was getting rather fond of this group of stiff-necked old men despite myself.

"It wasn't their idea!"

"No," I agreed, "but they allowed it to happen. That's quite something in itself!"

Joe shook his head. "They've got you thinking in terms of symbolic action too!"

"Maybe," I laughed. "But this symbol has to be one of better things to be. And it will be too! You just wait and see."

Joseph shrugged, visibly depressed.

"If I'm here for long enough," he grunted. "The great white chief is after my hide after going to Delhi with you."

I was sympathetic, but I couldn't pretend to be exactly surprised.

"Well, you did ask for it rather, didn't you?"

The hint of weakness in his face was exaggerated by the anger that burned up within him.

"He should never have sent you on your own in the first place! It was an iniquitous thing to do!"

I leaped to Gideon's defence, feeling decidedly ruffled.

"How can you say so?" I gave him a rather sharp, remembering glance. "Who did all the arranging, anyway?"

It wasn't particularly kind, I suppose, and he flushed angrily.

"It still wasn't right that you should go on your own," he persisted. "I told him so too!"

"And what did he say?" I asked curiously. I had heard enough of the two men's conversation to know that it was angry, but I hadn't been able to hear what they had actually said.

Joseph shrugged his shoulders.

"I guess I'd better not tell you," he rumbled. "Not that I agree with a word he said, but I don't suppose he meant me to repeat it all to you."

"Perhaps not," I said stiffly, "as it was obviously something unpleasant!"

He flushed. "I didn't say that!" he denied indignantly. "As a matter of fact it wasn't anything against you at all. It was me he was angry with!"

I said no more, but I was now well aware of the danger signals being up between the two men. And I had no doubt as to who had the right of the matter. That was Gideon, for he was a fair man and not given to being carried away by his emotions as Joseph was only too often.

It was something of a relief when one or two of the old men summoned me to join them on their side of the stream. Joseph showed no signs of coming with me, and I was glad, though I was slightly ashamed of being so, because he had had difficulty in getting on with them recently. He considered them reactionary and they considered him brash. There was something to be said for both opinions.

"Are you sure it will be ready before the rains?" the old men asked me anxiously.

I assumed a confidence I was far from feeling.

"Oh yes!" I said. "It will be a terrific amount of work because the ground is so hard, but everybody is very willing. We shall do it all right."

The leader of the *panchayat*, a very old man with flowing white hair, smiled into his beard.

"Who would have believed that a woman could speak with such confidence?" he scoffed gently. Nevertheless, the *Sahib* says you are to be trusted and will make great things come to pass in our village. This evening we shall honour the gods and gain their favour as the women have been doing all day."

I thanked him warmly, secretly thrilled to bits that Gideon should have shown such trust in me. I left him, glowing with pleasure, just in time to see Gideon himself arriving in the passenger seat of his jeep which was driven by the *Swami*."

I ran towards them, waving to them as I went. Their unexpected presence was very reassuring and it was as much as I could do to refrain from throwing my arms round Gideon's neck.

"How lovely!" I exclaimed as I drew up to them. "I didn't think there was any way for you to come."

Gideon smiled at the *Swami*. "He brought me," he said. "He knew I wouldn't want to miss the great event! How's it going?"

"The ground is a bit hard," I said.

Gideon grunted. "We'll soon see about that!" he promised. Somehow he managed to get down to where the men were working and in a few seconds he had them organised into gangs and they were really putting their backs into moving the earth. The *Swami* and I stood and watched him.

"I do hope he doesn't hurt himself," I remarked, unable to keep my anxiety to myself any longer. "He's a grand man, isn't he?"

The *Swami* smiled his consent.

"He is my friend," he said.

Something in his smile made me wonder if I had

been too effusive and had somehow given myself away—though what was there to give away beyond the fact that I liked and admired Gideon and was glad to be working for him? I refused to even think about anything else. Women, if they were wise, did not until they received some encouragement from a man. And I was wise enough to know the ways that led to heartbreak and despair, even if I wasn't wise enough to know that those ways can't always be avoided.

"Where is the other English young lady?" the *Swami* asked me, uncannily mirroring my own thoughts.

"Julie? She's in Delhi," I answered briefly.

The *Swami* swept his orange robe more closely round his shoulders.

"She is not the one for Gideon," he said decisively. "It would be a pity if he fell into the trap of thinking that she were. One needs compassion, but not for one's wife."

Of course, I reminded myself, the *Swami* was a wise man and accustomed to making prophetic utterances and interfering in other people's affairs, but I was still shy of him and not at all inclined to ask his advice.

"Her family sent her to Delhi so that she could get over Gideon's broken leg," I remarked sourly.

"A bribe. I expect she was shocked," he remarked cryptically.

"What do you mean?" I asked him, intrigued.

"It is more what I imagine," he replied. "I think I had better assist Gideon back to the car." He turned to face me and I was terribly conscious of his fine head topped by his shock of wild, unkempt hair. "It is a good task you have set yourself here. India has great need of such ideas and such people." Then he was gone, running down the slope to where the men were working, exchanging a word with this one and patting another one on his shoulder. When he came to Gideon he said nothing at all, but offered him his shoulder as an extra crutch and almost tenderly helped him back into the jeep and drove away, back to the village and his bed.

That evening the whole village was astir. Little lights, kept going with little more than a dab of oil, lit up the hot, dusty streets, transforming them into a fairy paradise. Now and again a firework lit up the sky, whizzing and banging its way to extinction. The noisier, the better they were liked, and the Catherine Wheels that rose and zipped, revolving like a world gone mad, were the confirmed favourites of everybody. The village had decided to hold a feast, to appease the local household gods, and to have a lovely excuse for dousing each other with water and coloured dyes, a ceremony usually reserved for rather later in the year.

I wandered down the main shopping street looking at the sights. By the village well was the local goddess, patronised mostly by expectant mothers, which smelt usually of rancid ghee, a kind of purified butter that the women offered as a libation to ease their labour pains. Now it was covered by coloured streamers and garlands of marigolds lay at her feet while more of them formed an orange carpet before her. It was a very pretty sight.

Seeing me on my own, Lakshmi came across to me and stood by my side.

"Are you enjoying the festival?" she asked me. "Why isn't the *Sahib* with you?"

I laughed.

"The *Sahib* is having trouble carrying his leg around with him!" I told her. "But aren't the lights pretty? And why are the flowers all marigolds?"

She shrugged her shoulders.

"They are always marigolds. When we greet visitors we place garlands of marigolds round their necks; when we visit Ghandiji's memorial place we drop marigolds on the ground. In a way they are the national flower of India."

I accepted her explanation because in a way they suited India. The colour was brash and effective and refused point blank to be ignored, and the marigold was a common flower, easily grown and without the distinction of a sophisticated perfume to please the more jaded palate. A quieter bloom would droop in the hot sun or would be unable to withstand the long days of pelting rain in the monsoon, and it would therefore never summon up the spice and the will for survival that was all I knew of Mother India.

"I see," I said. "No one gave me a garland of marigolds when I arrived!"

Lakshmi giggled.

"When the dam is finished they'll give you hundreds!" she promised rashly. "The crops will grow and we'll be the richest village for miles around. We are all very pleased and proud. I am especially proud, of course!"

"Oh, why?" I asked.

She gave me a sidelong glance that was at once shy and teasing.

"Because it is I who serve you, why else?" she commented. Another rocket streaked through the black sky and fell practically at our feet, causing us both to laugh. "That is nothing yet!" she assured me. "You wait until later when we really get going!"

"Lakshmi—" I began, and then I stopped. After all, the question I wanted to ask her was personal and she might very well resent it.

"You want to ask something?" she prompted me.

"Well, yes," I said. "Why don't you go to one of the cities? You speak English so well. I'm sure you would make more money!"

She laughed softly.

"I have little need of money," she said. "Compared to my friends I am rich, and soon, when I marry, my home will be near here. Why should I go away?"

My interest was immediately caught.

"But who are you going to marry?" I asked, intrigued.

She laughed again, shrugging her shoulders a little.

"I do not know yet. My family are still considering the matter. All I know is that it is time for me to marry and that the money I earn will make me a fine dowry."

I felt sharply that she would never fall in love and never know the agony of indecision that I was going through. It seemed unfair somehow, for the glory of the occasional moment far outweighed the morose sorrow of knowing that Gideon would never fall in love with me.

"But don't you ever want to choose your own husband?" I asked her.

"Sometimes," she agreed lightly, "and sometimes not. The old ways are better when you have a good family and they are kind to you. I will have many years in which to fall in love with my husband."

Another sparkler roared through the sky and fell over Lakshmi's sister's house. It made me think of the poverty of that family and I could hardly bear the thought of Lakshmi being destined for the same sort of existence. As if she had read my thoughts, she smiled at me.

"Don't worry, I am what you would call in your country a 'good catch'. My family have worked very hard so that I shall marry well!"

"Marry well, yes!" I couldn't help arguing. "But what about marrying happily?"

Lakshmi was confused by the very idea and hung her head, only cheering up when I suggested that we should go back to the main bungalow for dinner before the festival really got under way. She walked back along the street with me and accompanied me on to the verandah.

"I shall go and tell the *Sahib* you are here," she said softly, and disappeared inside, leaving me alone with my thoughts. And they were not very comfortable ones, because I had grown fond of Lakshmi and I couldn't see that there was going to be much happiness in the future for either of us.

I chose the most comfortable chair on the verandah and sat down in it, luxuriously stretching my tired body. It had been quite a day and the softness of the night was very conducive to dreaming. In the distance I could smell something cooking, but I was not hungry enough for it to disturb me. Not even the thought of failing to get the dam finished before the rains came could really worry me and I was nearly asleep when Joseph came and joined me.

"Where's Camilla?" he asked.

I shook my head. "I don't know. She's probably with Gideon."

Joseph went and stood on the edge of the verandah, jingling his keys and a coin or two together in his pocket. After a while he began to whistle some endless tune under his breath.

"Do you have to?" I complained.

He ended with a note that even he could hear was off-key.

"Sorry." He scuffed his shoes on the top of the steps and jingled his keys some more. "Suki," he said at last, "I'm not getting anywhere, am I?"

I sat up with a jerk.

"What do you mean?"

He smiled wryly, coming close to the lamp, so that I had a completely new view of his face, lit up from below and giving him new and fascinating shadows. Unfortunately it only served to show that basic weakness about the mouth that I had always been aware of.

"You know quite well. I'm not exactly making a success of my time here, as the *Sahib* Gideon was kind enough to point out to me. You're getting all the kudos for your go-ahead vision with the dam and, damn it all, irrigation is supposed to be my field!"

"Well, so it is," I said in matter-of-fact tones. "What have you been doing about it?"

He was moodily silent for a long moment.

"You know perfectly well that I haven't done a thing about it," he said at last. "I've had my hands full with our wretched machinery."

"That's your job too," I reminded him. "You're also the mechanic."

He laughed harshly. "And I suppose you agree with him that I haven't been doing that very well either?"

"I didn't say that."

"You didn't have to," he said gloomily. "I can feel it in the air about me."

"Aren't you exaggerating just a little?" I teased him.

"You might think so, I don't! The only person who has any time for me at all at the moment is Camilla."

I was determinedly cheerful. "Hence your anxiety to know where she is?"

He nodded. "I thought she might like to watch the fireworks with me. I think she's the only person I could bear to have with me, quite honestly. At least she isn't perpetually nagging me to be something that I'm not!"

I sighed. I was puzzled that he should be even more gloomy now than he had been earlier.

"Have you had another session with Gideon?" I asked.

"Wouldn't you like to know!" he retorted bitterly. "You're not even grateful that I stuck out my neck for you by going to Delhi. Women!" he added almost as if it were a swear-word.

I stood up. He had successfully destroyed my moment of dreamy comfort in the chair. Now I only felt that I was at a disadvantage by being so much lower than he was. When I was standing up at least I could meet him on level terms.

"I was grateful," I said clearly. "But I'm not going to fall over myself to prove it to you."

His eyes sparkled with contempt in the light of the lamp.

"No, no. Never be seen fraternising with those who are out of favour! Funny, I had you figured out quite differently. I had a picture of you as a sweet English girl, loyal and without too much ambition. But you're not like that, are you? You're crowing your head off that Gideon's bought your scheme for the dam. But don't crow too hard. If the monsoon is early, your

cheap little success will come crashing round your ears
and your stature will be no higher in the great man's
eyes than mine is now!"

I bit my lip, feeling slightly sick. I had been quite
unprepared for anything like this from Joseph.

"You're jealous!" I accused him sharply, the tactless
remark rising almost unbidden to my lips.

"Of course I'm jealous!" he agreed. "But I wouldn't
have cared so much if you'd been different about it. I
thought you were my friend!"

"I thought so too," I said coolly. "You're making it
rather impossible, though, aren't you?"

"Am I?" He eyed me sardonically. "I'm not the one
who's been spilling tales to Gideon!"

"Meaning that I have?" I demanded.

"Haven't you?"

"Not that I'm aware of!" I denied sharply. "Look,
Joe, what is all this?"

He hunched up his shoulders and sat heavily in the
nearest chair.

"The jeep wouldn't start again. The *Swami* had to get
it going with his own fair hands. It seems he was a mechanic himself before he took to being a holy man instead. Never cease to surprise one, do they? I mean
who would have thought that he ever earned his living
just like everyone else? Well, anyway, it was just about
the final straw as far as Gideon was concerned. I rather
gathered that not even you could find much use for
me."

I was uneasily aware of a feeling of acute irritation that
he couldn't keep the vehicles properly maintained and I
wondered just what it was that Gideon had said to him.

"I haven't said anything," I said.

"Well, I did," he said moodily. "I even told him
about our running into Julie in Delhi. *That* set him
back a bit, I might tell you."

"The *Swami* doesn't think she's the right person for
Gideon either," I said without thought.

He flung back his head and laughed.

"I suppose you're planning to cut her out!" he exclaimed. "You might just manage it if you play your cards right!"

I gave him a look of extreme distaste.

"Gideon doesn't see me like that!" I passed it off casually. But for some reason my heart was suddenly pounding within me. "It wouldn't be fitting anyway," I said gruffly.

For answer Joseph laughed again.

"Well, well," he said, "whoever would have thought it?"

CHAPTER TEN

IF I was pleased when Camilla came and joined us, Joseph most certainly was not.

"What do you want?" he asked her harshly.

She blushed, but she held her ground.

"Not you," she returned pleasantly.

He gave her a rather haughty look and frowned. "What do you mean?"

Camilla gave him a nice sunny smile and refused to answer him directly. Instead she turned rather pointedly to me.

"Suki darling, Gideon says we're to make the most of the celebrations tonight and that he's coming with us to make sure that we do!" She turned almost reluctantly to Joseph. "I suppose you can come too, if you really want to and if you're not too busy sulking!"

"I? *Sulk*?" he demanded indignantly.

"Of course you're sulking! You've sulked solidly ever since you got back from Delhi!" She sat down beside me, hunching up her shoulders to add point to what she was saying. "You know what", she went on, "I should have thought it was a great deal easier to do your work than to worry about the results of not doing it! It's only an opinion of course," she added hastily.

I had some difficulty in refraining from laughing. Joseph looked like a thundercloud and almost as young as Camilla. It came as a shock to me to realise that I could sit back and watch the two of them and feel the next best thing to old and experienced!

"And what do you know about it?" Joseph mocked her, but he was visibly shaken all the same. "You don't have to do anything at all all day!"

"I find myself enough to keep occupied," she answered smugly. "How about you?"

Joseph flushed angrily.

"I don't know what's the matter with me," he complained. "I don't seem to be able to please anyone today."

Camilla looked fleetingly sympathetic, but it didn't last long.

"Perhaps you don't try hard enough?" she suggested.

But Joseph had had enough. He glared at her and then at me and then silently took himself off, his hands in his pockets and scuffing the toes of his shoes as if he more than half expected us to call him back. Camilla looked sadly after him.

"What's the matter with him," she asked impatiently. "Doesn't he know that it hurts when he goes into a grouch?"

I looked at her closely, noticing the drooping lips and the tears in the corners of her eyes. She looked the picture of heartache bravely borne, and I felt terribly sorry for her.

"I don't suppose he thinks," I answered. "Does it really matter to you?"

She closed her eyes and the tears squeezed out on to her cheeks. Restlessly, she wiped them away with the back of her hand.

"Yes," she admitted. "It matters very much."

I felt a hollow sensation in my middle. I could remember only too clearly Gideon's admonition that Joseph was incapable of being friends with any woman. It was only now that I was beginning to see what he meant.

"The trouble is," I began, "that men don't grow up nearly as quickly as we do. Joe is all right, but he doesn't really know where he's going."

Camilla began to cry in earnest, the tears spilling out of her eyes with increasing ease.

"But I'm young too!" she cried out. "And he isn't even interested!"

I sighed, knowing that I was going to have to talk about Timothy and not really wanting to, because he was still so recent in my own past that the scars could hurt a little, when I thought about it, which hadn't been often these last few days.

"You see," I said, "Joseph is just like Timothy, so I feel I know him rather well."

Camilla stopped crying immediately and gazed at me in astonishment.

"Your *Timothy*?"

I smiled wryly. "Yes, my Timothy. Why not?"

"Well, I don't know," she said uncomfortably. "Gideon said I wasn't to ask you about him, though we were both dying with curiosity," she added naïvely.

For an instant I was shocked that they should have discussed me, not because I was afraid of anything that either of them might have said, but simply because I shouldn't have thought that I was an interesting enough topic for their speculations.

"Both of you?" I asked dryly. "I can't believe that Gideon was much interested?"

"Oh, but you're wrong!" Camilla insisted. "He said Timothy didn't sound your sort at all. Oh, do tell me about him, Suki. Was he madly attractive?"

I blushed a little.

"No, he was quite ordinary. He was very clever and he suffered agonies with his digestion. It was important to see that he ate the right things and things like that!"

A look of distaste crossed Camilla's features.

"And were you really in love with him?" she asked.

"I suppose so," I said softly. I was horribly aware that I had just been discussing him in the past tense as if he were dead and I felt guilty. When we had parted we had parted only for two years—not for life!

"I don't think you were," Camilla said practically. "He was just an interest for you. I expect you needed something while you were studying."

I gazed at her with respect. And to think that I had

started out in this conversation to warn her of the dangers of youthful infatuation!

"Well, yes," I admitted. "Like Joseph."

She smiled a rather superior smile and she didn't look young at all.

"And that's why you think they are alike, Timothy and Joseph?" she asked me.

I nodded. It *was* why they were alike. They were both cast in the same mould, lovable but weak, not the sort of man I really wanted at all.

"It's difficult to admit," I went on with decision, "but I've grown out of Timothy. It happens that way sometimes. No matter how much you think you are in love with a person, you change and so do they, and you find you are no longer in love with them at all."

Camilla smiled more broadly.

"And you think that's what will happen to what I feel for Joseph?"

"Well, yes," I said very gently because I didn't want to hurt her. "You see Joseph isn't very mature, is he?"

Camilla shook her head at me.

"You don't really understand at all," she told me. "Timothy was one thing and of course you feel differently out here about him. Gideon says he doesn't believe you were ever in love with him at all! But what I feel for Joe is quite different! You see I know he's silly and weak and a bit lazy, but it doesn't make any *difference* to me."

I tried hard to think back to what I had thought about Timothy. It was surprisingly difficult. It had been a mixture of hero-worship and a fear that I would displease him, I thought. He had been there always, persuading me that I was cleverer than I really was by making clever remarks that I couldn't really understand but would have died rather than have admitted it. And I had felt maternally concerned about him plying him with stomach powders and overseeing his diet like some fussy mother hen. No, I was quite sure now that I had never been in love with Timothy Black.

"I don't see what it has to do with Gideon," I said with a throat that had suddenly gone dry.

Camilla grinned.

"Poor Suki!" she murmured. "You know, of the two of us, you're the poor mixed-up kid! And don't for heaven's sake start worrying about Joseph and me! We'll look after each other perfectly well. *You'd* do better to worry about Julie!"

"Why?" I asked blankly.

Her face filled with impatience mixed with despair.

"If you don't know, I'm not going to tell you!" she exclaimed, and sauntered off into the house to find out what had happened to dinner. I stood up myself and stared out into the darkness. Here and there a firework burst forth, let loose by someone's impatient fingers. As an older woman and a confidante, I had not been a howling success, I thought, and for some reason I could have cried.

Gideon joined us for dinner. With a great deal of laughter he had fashioned for himself a couple of crutches, tipping them with pieces of an old tyre he had cut up so that they wouldn't slip on the floors. He came across the verandah with a flourish of independence and a broad grin on his face.

"Isn't that something?" he demanded.

I laughed. "That's something!" I agreed.

He sat down heavily and chuckled.

"Know something, you're getting quite cheeky!" he teased me. "How does it feel to have a whole village *en fête* for you?"

"Unbelievable!" I told him. "Not that it is for me exactly. I think they're really beginning to realise what this dam could mean to them."

His eyes twinkled. "Well, the dam is your project!" He laughed at my discomfiture. "And a hell of a lot of work you're going to find it! Have they done their full day's quota?"

I shook my head. "No, but this is the first day. It'll

take a day or so to make it clear exactly what has to be done. I'm hoping then it'll go like a bomb, as Joe would say."

The smile died out of Gideon's eyes.

"What do you think of that young man?" he asked abruptly. "Did I hear you and Camilla talking about him earlier?"

I blushed to the ears, wondering what else he had heard.

"It was just in passing," I said.

He looked straight into my eyes. "Have you heard from that Timothy of yours recently?" he asked.

"No, I haven't, though I can't see what business it is of yours!" I added hotly.

He grinned. "I suppose you can't, you ridiculous blockhead! Don't you think it's about time you wrote to him?"

I wondered how he knew that I had put off writing because I had found that I hadn't anything much to say. To talk of my work would have bored Timothy, and to have talked of anything else would only have shown him pointedly how very well I was managing without him.

"I'll think about it!" I said lightly.

"Yes, do," he said. "The sooner you're free of that entanglement the better!"

But I wasn't sure that I saw it that way. Timothy, after all, was a form of defence. He wasn't a very good one, but he was the only one I had got. And at that moment I needed a defence very badly against the charms of Gideon Wait.

"I'm not sure I want to be free," I said stubbornly.

Gideon looked exasperated. "Muddle-headed and ridiculous!" he commented.

"I'm very fond of Timothy," I insisted.

Gideon blew up like a geyser. It was fascinating to see. Whoever would have thought that he held his temper on so light a rein? But he said nothing. He buried his head in his hands and groaned. Then: "Have it your own way," he said at last. "But don't be surprised if someone takes the trouble to wring your neck for you!"

From somewhere I found the audacity to laugh.

"Oh, really!" I protested weakly.

"Yes, really!" he told me.

Dinner passed in a whirl. I puzzled over what Gideon had said, but I couldn't see any good reason why he should care whether I wrote to Timothy or not. At last, when it was all over, I made my escape to my room and sat on the edge of my bed and tried to pull myself together. Outside the crowd was becoming noisier and noisier and the zip of the fireworks more frequent. The celebrations had officially begun.

The village was indeed *en fête*. I had only the haziest notion of what was going on, because the myths and legends of India must be almost as numerous as her extensive population. So who the two giants, stuffed with fireworks and explosive bangs were remained a mystery, though I cheered as hard as any when they went up in smoke, in one uproarious spectacle of flare and colour, finally bursting into flames.

I recognised the King of the Monkeys, very much the noble ally, with his breast flapping in the breeze to reveal Rama's name written on his heart. But this demi-god, this humanised ape, bore little resemblance to the mischievous monkeys that had frightened me in the forest. I was disappointed when he too didn't burst into flames, but contented himself with throwing coloured water at all the pretty girls instead. Lakshmi was soaked in a glowing scarlet and I, to my intense annoyance, ended up multi-coloured like a patchwork quilt. It was all great fun, though, for the villagers, who knew little about fun and a great deal about grinding poverty. For a night they forgot that the uncertain monsoon was still a month away and they became men of substance with a high purpose in life, and their laughter and shrieks of merriment rang through the dusty street and into the deaf ears of the village goddess, now smelling more rancid than ever.

Some time during the evening Hanuman, the King of the Monkeys, lost the head of his disguise and I saw Lakshmi clinging to his arm as they ran through the crowds. So that was the way the land lay, I thought, and I hoped that her family were thinking along the same lines.

I was standing in the middle of the street, watching her, when Gideon came up behind me.

"All alone?" he asked.

I turned quickly. "Why, yes," I admitted. "But I don't mind. It's so colourful that one would almost spoil it all by talking."

"Is that a hint?"

I was afraid I had hurt his feelings.

"Of course not! Are you all alone too?"

"At the moment, but not for very long!" He could scarcely hide his contented grin.

I waited for him to tell me what was happening and when, but he didn't. He stood there, propped up on his crutches and grinned straight into my face.

"You look very pleased about it anyway," I said crossly.

"I am," he chortled. "Julie is coming to stay at the end of the week!"

I could feel my face tightening into a social smile and my eyes go blank. The last thing I wanted was for him to know what I was really thinking and feeling. *That* would have been disastrous!

"Coming here?" I said hollowly.

He looked quite unbelievably pleased with himself. "At my express invitation!" he announced proudly. "She'll have to shack down with you and Camilla in the small house, but she's very adaptable."

I thought of that cloud of mauve hair having to be dressed and touched up every week, and wondered.

"There isn't any room. There only are two bed-rooms."

His grin appeared again, not one whit put out.

"Yes, I know," he said, "but Camilla says she doesn't mind doubling up with you for a week or so—"

"Or so?" I repeated faintly.

His eyes twinkled mercilessly.

"Oh, come now," he said, "I know you two girls blame the whole Burnett family for my accident, but it really had nothing at all to do with Julie—"

"Even if her father did trip you up?" I put in pugnaciously.

"It still wasn't her fault," he went on reasonably. "She was very upset and wept on my shoulder to show just how sorry she was. It will do her a lot of good to see exactly how and where I work. It isn't the same when she comes over for the day, because nobody does anything very much on those days, we're all so busy entertaining her."

"Exactly!" I said bleakly. "Now nobody will do anything for a week or so!"

He laughed out loud

"Don't be silly!" he said. "With the monsoon only a month away we'll all be working flat out. Julie quite understands that. She won't get in your way at all, so don't look so worried."

I gave him a look that was meant to put him in his place, but it seemed that nothing was going to wipe that smile off his face.

"I'll bet Camilla was pleased!" I said viciously.

"As a matter of fact she was—quite," he retorted.

But I didn't believe him! For who in their senses would want to welcome Julie Burnett into their house? It just didn't seem possible!

The feverish pleasure of the evening was beginning to die down. The old men had gathered beside the well, smoking and yarning to each other. Even the oldest of them was able to squat for hours without the slightest fatigue. In India people queued for buses that way, had their hair cut, mended their fishing nets, and they found it as natural as the European does to sit on a chair. But somehow the presence of the old men put a restraint on the younger villagers and their entertainments that were rapidly turning into mobilised hysteria. The young men dropped the hands of veiled young girls and returned to the pretence that they didn't know them or anything about them. I looked around for Lakshmi, but she was nowhere to be seen. Everyone was tired and happy and they smiled as Gideon and I went slowly up the street, I waiting every few steps for him to manipulate his crutches on the uneven surface of the road.

"Well, your dam has been well and truly sent off," Gideon observed. "I hope we can live up to their expectations."

I could have hugged him for taking some of the responsibility on to his own shoulders. I had worried all I knew in case the rains came before we were ready, and the mere fact that someone else was with me in the venture made it all seem more likely to succeed.

"If they'll dig—" I began.

"They'll dig if you get out among them and keep them going," he said.

I nodded seriously. "That's what I intend to do," I said.

The old men called Gideon over to join them. He hitched himself on to the edge of the well and put his crutches thankfully down on the ground. When he had done, he patted the ledge beside him, inviting me to sit down beside him, but I shook my head. The old men were well launched on their stories and they wouldn't have wanted a woman to sit among them. Instead, I walked back down the street and gathered some of the lost coloured streamers into my hands as a memento of the evening. The whole air smelt of joss-sticks and gunpowder and the flat, spicy smell that permeates all India. If Julie hadn't been coming, it would have been the end of a perfect evening.

Camilla was already undressing when I got back to the small house that we shared between us.

"Have you seen Lakshmi?" she called out to me.

"Not recently," I replied.

Camilla appeared in the doorway of her room, clad in no more than a light chiffon robe.

"That's the trouble with this country," she said. "One can't do anything by oneself. I thought I'd have a bath, but if Lakshmi isn't here who will scrub my back for me?"

I laughed.

"I will if you like," I offered, knowing that it involved a great deal more than that. It was a question of finding the bath and heating the water.

"Have you really got the time?" Camilla asked me. "It's terribly late!"

"Never mind. It will be soothing after all those hectic crowds," I said.

She giggled and padded back into her room, leaving the door open for me to follow her.

"I'll go and raise the bath," she began.

I took one look at her and pushed her farther into the room.

"Not like that! I'll go and get the bath and arrange for some hot water. You can be thinking of a good story to explain away your sudden enthusiasm for Julie!"

She sat on the edge of the bed with her mouth half open and a look of consternation on her face.

"But it wasn't like that—" she started to assure me.

"Oh, wasn't it?" I said grimly, and I set off for the bath, slamming the door behind me.

Lakshmi still hadn't come in when the water was boiling happily and I had dragged the bath down the corridor to Camilla's room. She pulled it inside and set it down on the floor while I went back for the first lot of water.

"Whatever makes you think I want Julie here?" she demanded when I returned.

"Your brother! He told me quite positively that you didn't mind doubling up with me for a week or so!"

"Well, no more I should!" she said, still puzzled.

"So that *Julie* can have your room?"

"Certainly not! What is all this about Julie?"

I swooshed the hot water into the bath with such energy that it very nearly went over the edge on the opposite side.

"Gideon has invited Julie *here*. He thinks it will do her a lot of good to see the sort of conditions that he works under. Besides," I added maliciously, "she's very upset!"

From the look on her face it was easy to see that Camilla shared my revulsion.

"He couldn't *want* her here!" she said faintly.

"He seems to," I said bluntly.

She shook her head. "I just don't believe it! I'm sure he has some ulterior motive and is just not telling us." She giggled suddenly. "I'm not at all sure that I can't guess what it is!" she exclaimed.

I helped her into the bath and poured some water down her back.

"Aren't you going to share the joke?" I asked with some asperity.

She looked round at me, her eyes alight with mischievous laughter.

"No, I'm not," she said. "You wouldn't appreciate it anyway!"

With some difficulty I recovered my good humour and doused her with a spongeful of water.

"Oh, wouldn't I?" I said. "And why not, please?"

But she only shook her head.

"I think I'll ask Joseph what he thinks," she said.

It took time to finish the bath to Camilla's satisfaction. She liked a cloud of bath-salts followed by a cloud of talcum powder and she had no intention of being cheated out of either.

"It takes time to soak the heat out of your skin," she complained when I tried to hurry her out of the water. "Why don't you come in after me?"

I was tempted, but it was already terribly late.

"If you come out right now!"

"Oh, all right!" She stood up and accepted the towel that I offered her, drying herself efficiently and with great speed, hopping into bed and under the single sheet that was all the bed proferred.

I went along to my own room to collect my night things and when I came back Lakshmi was there.

"Will I bring you more water?" she asked. Her eyes never quite reached mine and she looked suddenly shy.

"Why, Lakshmi," I said, "it's happened, hasn't it?"

She nodded. "It is very bad! My family will never agree!"

I sat on the end of Camilla's bed and she squarked as she guarded her feet from me.

"Isn't the King of the Monkeys good enough?" I asked.

Lakshmi giggled. "You saw me!" she accused.

"Uh-huh!" I teased her. "Was it to be a big secret?"

Camilla looked from one to the other of us. "Lakshmi has fallen in love!" she concluded. "Oh, how lovely! Tell us all about it, Lakshmi. Is he tall and brave and handsome?"

Lakshmi giggled again. "That's all you think about, Miss Camilla!" She sighed. "But, yes, he is very beautiful. As Krishna must have been when he walked the earth. He has the softest eyes!"

"Who was Krishna?" Camilla asked.

"One of the gods," I told her. "He was a great one with the women!"

Lakshmi frowned. "Who is human and who is divine?" she asked in a puzzled voice. "All I know is that he is beautiful."

Camilla watched her with eyes gone soft. "I know what you mean," she said. "And I can tell you that I'm strictly human when Joseph is around."

"Camilla!" I exclaimed.

"Oh, nuts! *I* know what I mean!"

"I wish I didn't!" I said, putting on my most disapproving face.

The bath was almost cold by the time I got into it.

Lakshmi fussed around offering to bring more water, but she looked so sad and tired that I felt I would have been imposing on her.

"Don't worry, Lakshmi," I said, when I had finished drying myself and was gathering up my things to go back to my own room. "I'll tell the *Sahib* Wait all about it in the morning. He'll probably be able to sort it all out for you."

Lakshmi's weariness fell away from her with a rush and her dark eyes gleamed with excitement.

"Do you think so? It would be so wonderful! The *Sahib* knows all my family, so perhaps he could persuade them. But I'm not important enough to bother him— Do you think he really would?"

Camilla pulled the sheet more closely around her shoulders.

"Of course he'll help," she said sleepily. "He's my brother, isn't he?"

It was no longer night proper when I went back to my own room, it was already the early hours of the morning. If I were sensible, I thought, I would make the most of the few remaining hours of darkness and get some sleep. It was going to be a long, hard day and I knew it, and yet I couldn't go to sleep yet. When I shut my eyes the fireworks zipped and zooped once more and the smell of gunpowder and the spicy odour of curry assailed my nostrils, mixed with marigolds and rancid butter. It was something to write and tell Timothy about, I thought suddenly. Something to show him that I was making a life for myself without him, that I didn't give a rap.

I got out of bed and found pen and paper and started my letter. It was all so easy once I had begun. It was no trouble at all to tell him that I didn't want two years of waiting, that I wanted to be free. I knew perfectly well that he wouldn't care, on the contrary he would only be mildly relieved to know that at last I had come to my senses and knew finally that we were not made for each other.

I finished the letter, sealed it and affixed the stamp. It was only then that I realised that I had done exactly what Gideon had told me to do. I had written to Timothy.

CHAPTER ELEVEN

THE digging went on at a great rate. I spent most of my time out there with them, trying to ignore the frantic heat, and to do my share of breaking up the concrete-hard surface of the earth. The sun burned my skin a dark brown until I was almost as dark as Lakshmi. Joseph made several teasing references to the dark beauty who had suddenly come among them, but as everybody knew that I was not in the least lovely to look at, they fell rather flat. Camilla, with far more subtlety than I should have expected from her, began a systematic campaign to divert Joseph's attention to herself. Sometimes I wondered if Gideon knew, or had even noticed, but I was far too tired and full of heat and sun to do anything about it. Besides, Camilla often seemed far more capable of looking after herself than I should ever be, so I buried myself in my work and let the world pass by me.

Until Julie came.

It began as a day like any other. I didn't see Gideon at breakfast because I had taken to having my own as early as possible to get as much done before the crushing heat of midday as was possible. In fact I had very nearly forgotten that Julie was coming and what with having so much to do it had become almost unimportant to me. It was probably because of that that it seemed all the more of a shock when I came in to lunch and found her sitting on the verandah, an expanse of neatly stockinged leg stretched out before her and looking unbelievably cool and pretty in her symphony of blues.

Camilla made a face at me behind her back and I gathered that she was not being a very easy guest as far

as she was concerned, but I was too weary to care. I
flung myself into the nearest chair and stared moodily
out at the sun.

"How long before it rains, do you think?"

Joseph laughed.

"You don't have to mind her, Julie! She asks the
same question every day at lunchtime. The trouble is
that she's obsessed by this dam of hers."

"So would you be, if you were breaking your back on
that ground out there!" I grumbled good-naturedly.

"And how you'd hate it if he were!" Camilla put in.
"Perhaps Julie would like to help you while she's
here?" she added with deliberate malice.

Julie shook her head, summoning up a smile.

"I don't think I should be any help at all!" she said
hastily. "Why, dear, I hardly recognised you! You're
burned to a crisp!"

"Yes, I know," I said wearily. "I'm hoping to return
to normal when the rains come."

Julie's eyes widened with memory.

"Oh, but you don't know what it's like *then*," she
said. "Oozing mud and inches of rain every day. Even
my parents long for the green fields of England during
the monsoons!"

Gideon had practically mastered walking with his
home-made crutches, I noticed, as he came down the
verandah towards us. He grinned at Julie and gave her
a downright affectionate look.

"Settled in?" he asked her.

She fussed herself and her chair out of his way and
oversaw his lowering himself down into one of the
chairs with careful solicitude.

"Oh yes, I'm completely comfortable!"she sighed.
"I brought some of my things with me, so that the
room wouldn't be so bare, you know, and they look
just lovely here!"

Camilla giggled and choked. Gideon gave her a severe look, but nothing could muffle her complete glee
over Julie's possessions.

"What sort of things did you bring?" I asked.

She coloured prettily, turning the palest shade of coral.

"Well, you know I'm not *tough* like you," she said, making me feel like the strong woman of some circus. "I couldn't possibly sleep on one of those *charpoys*, so I had to bring a bed with me, didn't I?"

"I suppose so," I agreed, a gurgle beginning at the back of my throat.

Gideon frowned at me. He put out a hand and patted Julie's consolingly.

"Nobody would expect you to sleep on a bed of nails," he teased her gently.

"Certainly not!" I added dryly. I was surprised by the quick flash of amusement in Gideon's eyes, equally quickly suppressed.

I went off hastily to wash my hands before I succumbed to open laughter too and, like Joseph and Camilla, openly derided Gideon's most feminine guest. It was a temptation that had to be overcome because somehow I had to show Gideon that I didn't care who he invited here.

When I saw my room most of my resolution failed me, however. It was piled high with suitcases and household furniture. And, sure enough, a brand new bed had been imported and was taking up most of the space in the centre of the room. An apologetic Lakshmi came running as soon as she heard my footsteps and came to an abrupt halt in the doorway.

"I thought Camilla was moving in with me," I said bitterly.

Lakshmi's wide eyes rested on mine for a second.

"This room is bigger," she explained.

"Ridiculous!" I exploded. "Have you ever seen anything like it?"

She said nothing, and after a while my anger changed to laughter as I thought just how ridiculous the whole situation was.

"You'd better get my bed moved out to give her

some more room!" I said weakly, and was rewarded by a quick giggle.

"I have already taken all your clothes and things," she told me apologetically. "There was no room to leave them here."

"None at all!" I agreed. It came as a wrench to leave that room, though. I had grown fond of its bleak bareness and the way it had refused to respond to the few bits and bobs that I had brought with me. Looking round it now it already looked quite different. A mass of photographs of the Burnett family littered the windowsills, and *her* clothes, quite different from mine with their frills and furbelows, were already draped across every available space.

Camilla's room, on the contrary, was almost as spartan as my own had been and only my own things, hastily moved down the corridor and not yet put away, were out of place. I washed my hands in the bowl on her washstand, flicking the cold water on to my suntanned face to cool myself down. I was just drying myself when Camilla came in and flung herself down on her bed.

"Don't blame me!" she began. "How can Gideon tolerate her?"

"She's very feminine," I said repressively.

Camilla sat up and looked at me. Her eyes were as old as the wisdom of the world. She is growing up too fast, I thought, and wondered what I ought to do about it.

"Julie? Feminine?" she asked scornfully. "She's all promise and very little fulfilment, if you ask me! If Gideon were to kiss her, really kiss her, she'd die of fright!"

I laughed and felt a good deal better.

"You know, Camilla," I said, "there are times when I like you very much!"

She grinned. "I know!" she said. "But then you're in love with Gideon yourself!"

I could feel the blush burning up my cheeks to my hairline.

"Well, what if I am?" I demanded in prickly tones. She got off the bed and hugged me.

"Nothing, I'm really very glad about it. You see, I can't help thinking you'd make a nicer sister-in-law than Julie Burnett!"

"*That* wouldn't be very difficult!" I said sourly.

"No," she agreed. "If only Gideon could see it!"

But Gideon seemed determined to be as blind as a bat as far as I was concerned. At lunch he scarcely said a dozen words to me. But perhaps he didn't have much opportunity, because Julie talked nineteen to the dozen all through the meal, telling us all about her stay in Delhi. There was no doubt but that she had had a very good time there, and I spent most of lunch thinking how nice it would have been if she had stayed there.

The long chain of home-made buckets hesitated and then came to a halt at a signal from the foreman. The men threw down the buckets where they stood and went over to the bank they were creating to lounge in the pitiful bit of shade it provided. One of the older men had brought his *sitar*, a whining and much-loved musical instrument, with him and he started plucking at the strings, catching at a melody here and there to see if anyone would join in one of the ancient and endless songs they all loved so well. There must have been a similar scene at the building of the Taj Mahal or any other monument or mud-hut throughout India. The workers, their clothes the same colour as the dust around them; the richer among them with their midday meal done up in a cloth that had long ago been faded to the same dun colour by the fierce sun; the same separation of the different castes and religions, but the same unity of purpose that had already moved tons and tons of earth to build my dam.

I sat on the bank beside them wondering if the reservoirs were going to be big enough to hold the tremendous volume of water that would be necessary for the needs of the village all through the dry season when the evaporation would be at its height. I wished I were a proper engineer, but it was obvious that any water would be better than none and so I knew that even the small amount that we were doing would transform the local crops.

"We're almost ready for the P.V.C.," Joseph commented from his perch above me. "When's it coming?"

"Any time now," I replied. "Gideon received the dispatching order some days ago."

Joseph grunted.

"It's probably down at the station waiting for someone to go and collect it. I'll take the jeep down and make some enquiries."

"Oh, would you?" I was pleased that he was taking an interest. "Why don't you take Camilla with you?"

"How about my own true love?" he asked.

I frowned repressively. "I have work to do here," I said. "And anyway, why do you have to use such facetious expressions?"

He shrugged. "Ever thought that they might be true?"

"Never!" I said firmly. "Please hurry, Joe. I'll need that stuff this afternoon. The welder too. They promised to send it at the same time, so make sure that it's come, won't you?"

"I can be trusted to do *some* things right!" he grinned at me.

I grinned right back at him. "Yes, I know. Camilla knows it too," I added, and then wished I hadn't. Camilla was so very young still, and what would Gideon say if he knew I was encouraging her friendship with Joseph?

Joseph only looked puzzled, however.

"Does she though?" he said. "May I take your jeep?"

I gave my consent easily enough, though I did wonder what had gone wrong with his own this time. For a mechanic, Joseph was surprisingly haphazard when it came to the combustion engine, but then who was to complain? After the first day he had kept mine going for me and it went well, I had to admit that.

When he had gone, I went down into the bottom of the reservoir to make sure that no stones had been left that would gash the P.V.C. and spoil its waterproofing qualities. Some of the older men were raking the loose earth into patterns that formed symbols of good luck. On some days, they told me, on feast days, their women raked the floors of their houses in the same way, making patterns to please the gods. A youth with the only wheelbarrow—the rest of the men carried everything by hand in their home-made buckets— came trundling by, lethargically picking up the heaviest of the rocks as they were pulled free from the dusty earth. He went off again, jauntily keeping in time with the chanted beat of the rest of the men.

When I came back to the bank Julie had come out in Gideon's jeep to have a look round. I saw her pale mauve fluffy hair and the vivid cerise of her dress from quite a distance, and I am ashamed to say I spent the whole way over to her half looking for an excuse to break away and go off in some other direction.

"Hullo," she said as I plodded up the bank towards her. She looked cool and her face had the well-powdered look that I had long ago despaired of. By way of contrast, I knew quite well that my own face was shiny with sweat and my clothes rumpled and sadly stained by the dusty soil.

"Hullo," I replied a trifle cagily. "What do you think of my pet project?"

"It looks—expensive," she said. "I suppose it has meant delaying quite a lot of other things?"

"I suppose it did," I agreed, surprised by her real interest. "It will be worth it, though. We badly need this water."

She smiled faintly. "Worth it to you, don't you mean?"

"Well, yes," I said, frankly puzzled.

She smiled again. "What I mean is that Gideon doesn't get anything out of it? I imagine all the credit goes down under your name?"

I laughed, relieved that I had caught on to her meaning.

"Oh, we don't work like that!" I told her. "Gideon is running the station, so of course he'll get a lot of the credit—a lot of the blame too if it doesn't work, come to that!"

Julie got out of the jeep, looking really anxious.

"There isn't any chance of that, surely?" she demanded.

I looked round the gigantic earthworks that I had somehow caused to be dug in the dust, away in the middle of nowhere. It seemed a greater gamble at that moment than it had ever seemed. I ran a dusty hand across my hot brow, adding a smear to my already far from clean face.

"It's a distinct possibility," I said. "I'm not an engineer you know."

She lifted her elegant eyebrows and stared at me out of her blue eyes.

"You mean you started all this without knowing anything about it at all!"

"Pretty well," I admitted. "I've seen it done at home in England, but the problems aren't quite the same."

"Look," she said, brushing away my remark. "I want to talk to you. Does anyone around here speak English?"

I shrugged my shoulders. "Some do."

She pouted, patting her skirt into place around her slim hips.

"Never mind, it'll have to do. Gideon doesn't seem to get out much with his leg in plaster, so we never have an opportunity back at the house, do we?"

I sat down on the bank and wished that Joseph would

come back with the P.V.C. The sky looked very odd to
me and I was getting increasingly fearful that the rains
would come before we were ready.

"Do you think it will rain this week?" I asked pessi-
mistically.

Julie made a gesture of impatience.

"Who cares? Susan, I may call you Susan, mayn't
I?"

"Most people call me Suki," I told her carelessly.

"How quaint! Not that it matters. What are you going to do when you've finished this dam?"

My enthusiasm was immediately aroused.

"But don't you see? Once we have water we can
really get to work! I hope to double or even treble most
of the crops in my charge. It will take more than water,
of course. Selective breeding, proper manures and
modern methods will make a tremendous difference
too. It's exciting, don't you think?"

Julie tossed her head and I was pleased to see that
she also was beginning to feel the heat. She was not a
superwoman after all.

"I'm afraid it wouldn't excite me," she said primly.
"I think it's rather a masculine interest for a woman."

So we were back on that again! But this time I felt
more sorry for her than angry.

"Didn't you ever want to do something rather than
stay at home?" I asked impulsively.

She gave me a cynical smile.

"Oh, I think you have to be rather insecure to want
to compete with men in their own fields. My father has
always given me everything I want. Why should I want
to work myself? All I want to do is marry and be a good
wife."

I swallowed down my impatience with the whole
Burnett family.

"Here, in India?" I asked her.

She leaned against the jeep with a secret look in her
eyes.

"It will have to be in India," she said. "I can't imagine England would suit me at all! Servants at a premium and those cold winters! Besides, Gideon has rather turned his back on England, hasn't he?''

I wiped the sweat out of my eyes and looked at her.

"Not necessarily," I told her. "He might go back any time and work there if an interesting opportunity arose."

She bit her lip and trembled, her champagne hair nodding in the wind.

"I'm telling you! He can't go back to England! My parents are here and they would never leave, so you see—" Her voice trailed away and she smiled. "But I forgot," she said. "You don't like my parents, do you?"

"No," I said briefly, "I don't."

"Charming!" she retorted. "Not that it matters. You will be going back to England?"

"Oh? Is that a threat or a promise?"

She tossed her head. She looked very sure of herself, but then perhaps she had reason. Gideon had asked her to stay, after all.

"It was advice really. Camilla will be going back to England soon. If you're wise, you'll go with her. There isn't room for us both, is there?"

"We'll see," I answered. The rains had not yet come and Gideon was still a free man. But I couldn't bear to look at her again in case she knew how she had unsettled me. And I didn't want her to know that I too was in love with Gideon and that unless I was terribly firm with myself I went soft inside at the mere thought of him, and *that* knowledge I didn't want to share with anyone at all!

Julie smiled gently into the distance.

"No, we shan't see at all," she said. "I'm telling you!"

That rather brought the conversation to a close, and I think my relief must have been more than obvious when Joseph came triumphantly back from the railway with the news that the P.V.C. had arrived. He drove the jeep straight up the bank and practically into the reservoir. With a paralysing whoop, Camilla jumped clear and landed in a huddle beside us.

"Are you all right?" I asked her, laughing.

She jumped to her feet, sheer exuberance in living showing in her every movement. Then her eyes fell on Julie and her smile died.

"What are you doing here?" she demanded rudely.

Julie looked at the young girl, noting the dust on her hair and the creases of her face.

"What are you doing, dear?" she returned coldly. "I'm sure Gideon would never approve if he knew you were holding up the great work!"

I interrupted quickly before Camilla could say anything which she might later regret.

"What nonsense! She and Joseph have just been to collect the P.V.C. Where is it, by the way?"

"It's following," Joseph shouted to me triumphantly. He leaned out of the jeep and pulled Camilla back into the seat beside him. "Gideon wants to know when you start welding and he'll be out to help."

A tide of excitement rose within me.

"Tell him I'll be waiting for him," I answered cheerfully.

Joe backed the jeep off down the slope, practically turning it over at the bottom, he was going at such a speed. I grinned and waved at the two of them and then turned my attention back to Julie. To my surprise her face was taut with temper.

"How dare he just ignore me?" she demanded. "How dare he?"

I said nothing. It didn't seem to matter what she said just then. The P.V.C. had arrived at just the right moment and Gideon was coming to help to lay it.

It was a very long job. The sheets of P.V.C. were laid out, edge to edge, until they covered the whole of the dug-out area. Anxiously, I helped to walk out the air pockets underneath before we welded the edges together to form a single bottom to the gigantic tank.

"Right," I said at last. "We can begin welding."

We sat on the bank and waited for Gideon. He came almost immediately. He had come to terms with his leg now and could manage quite well despite the heavy plaster that destroyed his natural balance and made movement so awkward. He came towards us, dragging his leg but otherwise unperturbed by it.

"Is it as hot out here as you look?" he asked me.

I wiped the perspiration away from my brow almost resentfully.

"It's extremely hot!" I retorted. "I daresay one can stay cool with nothing to do but sit on the verandah—" His grin brought me to an abrupt halt.

"I hope you're not referring to me," he said quite gently.

But I refused to answer. He was in love with Julie and I would do well to remember it. Instead I turned away, looking in the jeep for the welder, but Joseph had already taken it out on to the reservoir. Shyly, I glanced up at Gideon to find he was still smiling, so I grasped him by the hand and pulled him down the slope and on to the P.V.C. bottom. It was black and shiny, reflecting the sun into our faces. Gideon stopped and bent down to touch it.

"Hmm," he said thoughtfully. "It should keep the water in. What else are you going to do with it?"

I explained that I had thought to cover it with a few inches of soil so that it would not be perished in the strong rays of the sun.

"Fair enough," he nodded. "I can see that by this time next year we shall be sitting on the banks and fishing in the waters."

"Oh, do you really think so?" I asked enthusiastically. "It would be great fun!"

"I thought you'd think so," he said with satisfaction.

"If I'm still here," I added uncertainly.

He looked at me in surprise. "Of course you'll be here!" he said impatiently.

But I knew that I wouldn't be, not if Julie Burnett was to come instead.

We worked hard until it grew dark and the gangs of men began to think about lighting their fires and eating their scanty meal before bed. The ones who lived locally started back to the village on the collection of rusty bicycles that was their main form of transport anywhere. A few of the more devout began their evening prayers, the Moslems bowing down to Mecca, the Hindus fulfilling their own ritual. The air was filled with the scent of charcoal and burning cow-dung, mixed with the occasional joss-stick and the hot smell of curry. It was time to go home.

Gideon sat beside me in the jeep as I drove home. I was terribly conscious of him as I pressed the starter and navigated the vehicle through the clattering bicycles and the silent shapes that plodded through the gloom.

Gideon stretched his tired limbs and grunted.

"There may be disadvantages to employing females," he said comfortably, "but this is one of the big advantages."

I held on to the wheel with one hand while I swatted at some insect with the other.

"What is?"

His smile was particularly charming in the dusky light.

"Why, travelling through the darkness with you, what else?"

It would have been bliss if I hadn't known that he was teasing me.

"You'd better let me concentrate on my driving, then," I said primly, "or it might not be such fun after all!"

He chuckled. "Are you planning to ditch me, Suki?"

I could feel myself blushing.

"I—I—" I began. "I haven't the foggiest idea what we're talking about!"

"No? You must be feeling very obtuse!"

I made an irate gesture and we very nearly left the dusty strip that passed as a road. With an effort I pulled at the wheel to find that Gideon's hand was already there. As soon as we were straight he placed his hand over mine and it was as much as I could do to steer at all.

"It isn't kind to play with other people's feelings!" I tossed at him.

His eyebrows shot up.

"Is that what I'm doing? How interesting! By the way, I've been meaning to tell you all afternoon that there's a letter waiting for you at the station."

"For me?" I stammered.

"That's right. A pale blue envelope with an American stamp on it!"

My mouth went suddenly dry. I put my foot on the accelerator and we shot forward. I braked very nearly as sharply and almost stalled the engine.

"Timothy," I whispered.

He grinned. "It seems likely, though if I'd known it was going to have this effect on you I would have waited until we got home before telling you about it!"

I apologised and concentrated harder on my driving.

"It isn't really very exciting," I tried to explain. "It's only the answer to my letter to him."

"So you did write?" he prompted me.

I nodded. "I don't suppose you'll ever understand," I said with a sudden burst of confidence. "I can't understand it myself! I was so sure that I was in love with Timothy!"

He turned off the ignition key and the jeep came slowly to a halt. For a second I thought my driving really had fallen to pieces, but I didn't really care. For the first time that day I felt cool and almost happy.

"What did you do that for?" I demanded.

He shrugged his shoulders.

"I just wanted to sit here for ever and watch the clouds blow overhead."

I looked up too at the sky. The clouds were long and

dark, but I was sure that they would go overhead like all the others had done. I wasn't worried.

"Besides," Gideon went on, "I want to hear about your letter to Timothy."

I bit my lips, forgetting all about the clouds.

"There's nothing to tell," I said. "That's the trouble. There never was anything to tell, but I only realised it a week or so ago. I suddenly couldn't even remember his face properly!"

"Had you ever really looked at it?" he asked.

I was indignant, but I shook my head.

"I was far too busy prescribing his stomach powders!"

He laughed, and I found myself laughing too.

"Okay," he said. "Now that you've admitted that, you can drive us both home and read your letter."

I didn't want to move, but the memory of Julie didn't make me want to linger either.

"Do you think it will thunder?" I asked.

He put out his hands just as the first drops of rain began to descend from the sky.

"I think it's going to rain," he said, and we laughed like a couple of children. I only stopped laughing when I thought of all the welding that still had to be done.

CHAPTER TWELVE

I HAD never seen rain like it. By day I worked on the dam, the water dripping down the back of my neck. As soon as the welding of the P.V.C. was done, the men came behind carrying basketsful of mud to cover the shiny black surface. Gideon, his leg so much better that they had pared away at the plaster until his movements were considerably less restricted, used the roller on the edges, weighting it down and rolling it into the soil until there was no chance of any of it breaking free and tearing. He and I both worked in boots, but the Indians didn't seem to care about any part of their body except their head. This was tenderly wrapped against both rain or any hint of a draught, as was only becoming in such an important member.

The narrow stream swelled into a river and the two tanks of the reservoir began to fill. The actual dam was not yet necessary and would have caused flooding, but everything was ready to control the flow of the water. At last, it seemed, the project was complete and there was no reason why the village should ever be short of water again.

And still it rained. Not the mild, caressing rain of the temperate lands, but it came pouring down, bouncing off the earth again and penetrating everywhere until the whole world was a sea of mud and steaming water.

"And to think that I thought the heat was trying!" I remarked one day to Camilla. We were both lying on our beds and despairing of the clamminess that we met with even in our own bodies and clothing.

Camilla sighed.

"It wouldn't be so bad if *she* would only go home!" she said mournfully.

I didn't trust myself to answer. The thought of Julie was a constant burden, weighing down my spirits and making me less and less sure of myself. She was like a cat in the rain, bad-tempered and spiteful, and she never went out if she could help it. It was only at night that she really came alive and she and Gideon would sit for hours on the verandah until the early hours of the morning. It had become impossible for me to sleep until I heard her high heels clattering down the corridor to what was now her room and the creak of the springs, grown rusty in the rain, as she got into the bed she had brought with her.

"Perhaps she will never go," I said thoughtlessly.

Camilla sat up with a bounce. "What do you mean?"

I got off the bed with decision. "Nothing! Gideon likes having her here, though, so why shouldn't she stay?"

"I could give you any number of reasons!" Camilla said flatly.

I ruffled through the papers that I had left on the table so that I would have to deal with them sooner or later, and came across Timothy's letter. How funny, I thought, that I had hardly bothered to read it that evening. I had been so taken up with what Gideon had had to say and so hopeful of so many things. I spread it out now and saw that the corners were covered with fine mould where it must have got wet at some time or another.

"I think she's mad, like her parents!" Camilla announced quite casually.

"Very likely!" I agreed.

Timothy's handwriting was practically incomprehensible, but I could make out sufficient words to get the gist of what he was saying. He was glad that I was happy in India because it was extremely unlikely that he would ever return to England. The work he was doing was interesting and, he thought, valuable to the West-

ern world. The Western world certainly seemed to
think so, judging by the salary they were paying him.
He was eating better too. The doctors had recommended that he live on a diet of milk, steaks and vita-
min pills and he had never felt better. He thought he
would probably marry in America and settle down
there. If ever I wanted to visit he was sure that there
were any number of people who would be willing to put
me up for a few days, only he thought I would really be
better off in India as I seemed to like it so much. He
hadn't time to write any more, but he would send a
card at Christmas with a picture of some rockets on
it.

"Joseph says she simply hates you," Camilla told me
with relish. "Lucky you, that's all I can say. She seems
determined that we shall be bosom friends."

I laughed. "You're Gideon's sister," I said dryly.

She blinked determinedly at me.

"I wonder what she'll think when I marry Joe," she
mused. "He says we have to wait until Gideon accepts
that his work is as good as anyone else's, but that won't
be for ever!"

I turned quickly. "But Camilla, you're so young!"

Camilla hugged her knees happily. "All the better!
I'll have all the more years with Joseph! Is that letter
from your Timothy?"

I nodded sadly, because it was sad, in a way, that
Timothy had never been mine and never would be.

"He says he'll send a card with some of his rockets
on it for Christmas," I said rather bitterly. It wouldn't
have been so bad if his rockets had been of any use,
like—like taking Julie Burnett somewhere far away into
outer space!

"And you *like* him?" Camilla demanded, wrinkling
up her nose in displeasure.

"Not much," I admitted honestly. "But he was
there, and now there's no one."

Camilla looked very wise and nodded her head.

"Never mind," she said. "You have the dam, and

now that it's finished—all but!—and the rains have come, it'll make you famous!"

Which was cold comfort indeed and not at all what I wanted. With my usual neat, precise movements, I tore Timothy's letter up into little pieces and threw them away in the waste-paper basket. One of the best things about a research station is that there is always work to be done and one can't feel sorry for oneself for long with a test-tube in one hand and a spade in the other. If I couldn't be loved at least I could be dedicated.

"Oh, by the way," Camilla added, "you don't really have to worry about Julie, because I have a plan to deal with her. I'm not having her for a sister-in-law, whatever she might think!"

I gazed at her helplessly.

"I don't think you ought to interfere," I said at last.

But Camilla was not so easily dissuaded.

"How many days is it until the last concrete block is placed on the dam? That will be when she decides to go, you'll see!"

I must say I hoped that Camilla was right, but it seemed very unlikely. Julie spread her possessions about the house, like a spider wrapping up its victim in its web. Nothing escaped her soft sweetness or her cloying endearments.

I met her on the way to the village to discuss with the old men our plans for working the dam when the monsoon finally came to an end.

"Are you going out again?" she asked me.

I smiled and nodded. "Have you seen Gideon?" I countered.

Her expression didn't change, but she became very still and watchful.

"He doesn't want to see you just now," she said at last. "He's busy with other things."

"I see," I said. "Perhaps you'd tell him that the rice needs weeding at the top of the valley?"

"I'll try to remember," she smiled. "Have you thought any more about going back to England?"

"Not yet." It was so difficult being pleasant to her when I wanted to throw her out of the house, to destroy the pretty image she lived behind and, absurdly, to find out what colour her hair really was when she didn't bleach it and colour it blue. I turned to look at her, lounging on one of the chairs on the verandah. "Would you like to walk down to the village with me? It isn't raining at the moment, for a change."

She retired into herself, looking small and rather pathetic.

"Oh no, I couldn't! The mud would ruin my shoes!" She smiled her secret smile. "I'm not tough like you," she added, her voice tinged with malice.

"No," I agreed comfortably, "you're not." And without waiting to see if the shot had gone home, I started off to the village.

In the few minutes between downpours of rain everybody had come outside to do their shopping and to gossip to their neighbours. I knew a great many of them by now, with their intricate relationships and strict divisions into caste. Lakshmi's sister came running across the street and touched my arm. We smiled and greeted one another and she went off giggling happily.

The gentlemen of the *panchayat* were waiting for me in the metalsmith's small shop. We went through the shop, with its shavings of copper, tin and other metals and that inimitable smell of hot metal, and into the living space behind where one of the more venerable of the old men lived. They were already seated cross-legged on the floor, while an old woman went from one to the other with a damp flannel so that they could wipe their hands before eating the sweetmeats she set before them. My host greeted me with gentle courtesy and I was surprised to see that Gideon was already seated beside him.

"You're late!" he said to me with a grin.

"I was waiting for it to stop raining," I explained. Try as I would I was quite incapable of sitting comfortably on the floor, but Gideon seemed to manage it, his broken leg sticking out in front of him, the other neatly folded into his groin just like any Indian.

The old men watched me settle myself, their intense excitement coming like waves from their bodies, until I became aware of it and wondered what had caused it.

"We have heard from the government," our host told me in tones pregnant with awed complacency. "They are coming to see our dam. They are coming to see for themselves what can be done to preserve water!"

I looked round their solemn faces and felt rather proud of our achievement myself. Gideon was grinning at me and I smiled back at him.

"When are they coming?" I asked.

The old men stroked their beards in renewed ecstacy.

"They are coming on the day of the new moon."

"Next Saturday," Gideon supplied. They all nodded, their eyes shining with excitement, and I was terribly glad that, for the moment at any rate, I was one of them. This was *my* village and I was extremely proud of it.

We were served with little curry sandwiches and Coca-Cola. The women half knelt, half sat on the floor, with their array of plates before them and served us by hand, carefully picking out a morsel to please everyone there. The henna that showed that their hands were clean and carefully disinfected stained their fingers brown like tobacco juice, but it smelt sweet and spicy.

"Will it rain on Saturday?" I asked the old men.

A very old man, his wrinkled face hidden behind an enormous white beard, cackled with laughter.

"No, it will not rain then," he assured me. "The sun will be out when we go and stand by the dam with the government. Many villages will be there. It will bring much honour to our doors and to the door of the research station. We will all rejoice together and the gods will be pleased."

As soon as I awoke on Saturday I pattered over to the window and raised the blind to see what the weather was like. The red soil was transformed by the sudden green growth of plants that had suddenly sprung forth from the earth. The trees looked clean and shining and the whole world smelt of the brightness of the sun when it makes its first appearance after rain. There was no doubt but that it was going to be a lovely day, and I wondered how the old man had known, but perhaps wishing had made it so, just for once, a tiny miracle for me to remember as one of my last memories of India. For I had to go, I knew that now. I could no longer listen through the nights for Julie to come to bed, nor could I smile any more when she teased and scolded Gideon at meal-times, showing me more clearly every day how confident she was of his approval and—I had to face it some time—his love for her.

I stood at the window and thought back to when I had walked back from the metalsmith with Gideon.

"You look pale," he had said. "Is there something wrong?"

I had swallowed.

"We can't all be beautiful!" I had responded miserably.

He had looked me straight in the eyes and had said: "I have always believed that beauty was largely in the eye of the beholder. Wouldn't you say that, Miss King?"

Miss King again!

"No, I don't!" I had exclaimed bitterly. "I think some people can always attract by their looks no matter what they are, and other—and others can only stand by and watch!"

He had looked rather pleased with himself and had grinned.

"Are you hinting at something, Suki?" he had asked.

I had pursed up my lips and had looked disapproving, knowing that that way I looked my plainest.

"I should have thought it was obvious!" I had said. "But you know your own business best! I should have thought she was most unreliable!"

And he had grinned all the harder.

"Now would you indeed?" was all he had said, and I hadn't seen him alone since then. But he had continued to flirt with Julie, that I knew, because I knew the time that she came to bed, and it wasn't Joseph who kept her company out on the verandah!

I sighed and turned away to wake up Camilla. She gave a grunt of dismay when she saw the time and leaped out of bed.

"I promised Joe I'd help him with the bunting," she explained as she tore into her clothing and fussed over her make-up. "Suki, did you know there's to be a proper ceremony and that you're to be the centre of it?"

"Well, a ceremony," I amended. "But it's only someone from the government who is coming to inspect it."

Camilla applied her lipstick with care.

"Joseph says—" she began, her eyes twinkling. "No, perhaps I'd better not tell you what he said! But look out for Julie's wrath, won't you? Something tells me she's not going to enjoy today very much."

"I don't suppose she will," I said. "Do you think Gideon will want her to be on the platform?"

Camilla flicked her hair into position and made a face at herself in the looking glass.

"I'm beginning to wonder if he cares what happens to her," she said flatly.

"But he must do!" I exclaimed.

Camilla threw me a brief kiss as she departed.

"I don't see why! He's no fool, my brother. Hadn't you better get ready? Don't forget that on this occasion it's you who is to be queen of the ball!"

I watched her disappear out of the door, still sitting on the edge of my bed. Then I shook my head. It was too much to hope for that Gideon should have seen through Julie. Why should he when she was always as sweet as pie as far as he was concerned? But Camilla's warning made me feel uncomfortable all the same. I

could have wished that there was going to be no ceremony if Julie was going to spoil it for me.

I wore my very best dress and managed to make my
unruly hair look respectable and even quite pretty.
There was nothing I could do to make my face look
pretty, but I was not displeased with my efforts. If I
couldn't compete with Julie's fair looks, it was better to
be cast in a different mould rather than an also-ran in
hers. By the time I had jammed a hat on, I thought I
looked quite competitive in any society.

Joseph had already gone to the railway station to get
the government official when I made my appearance
on the verandah. Gideon rose slowly to his feet and
came towards me.

"Very nice!" he said quietly, for my benefit alone.

I blushed and he smiled at me. Julie stood up also
and came languidly across the verandah.

"My dear!" she began in a soft, drawling voice. "Do
you think that hat is quite suitable?"

"I wouldn't have it on if I didn't!" I retorted with a
sudden spurt of temper.

She pouted. "We-ell, if you really think so—" She
paused, slowly pulling on her gloves. "My parents are
coming to see the fun," she told me. "Gideon asked
them!"

I was glad of my hat. I could hide behind the brim
and pretend I didn't care who was going to be there.
But I was worried. I looked down at Gideon's leg and
then out to the waiting jeep.

"Is it time to go?" I asked.

It was natural that Julie should sit in the front with
Gideon. He was driving himself again now, providing
he didn't go too fast so that he had to jam on the brakes
in a hurry, and I was glad to have the opportunity to
hold on to my hat in the wind. I was nervous and I was
hoping that it didn't show, because Julie looked every
inch as if she were accustomed to this sort of thing
every day of her life.

The village band, led by a begging blind man who could play the *sitar* almost to perfection, was already in position, sitting on the bank of the reservoir and playing all the best-known songs in answer to the various requests from the onlookers. And there were so many onlookers! They stretched all the way from the concrete heart of the dam that at last blocked the waters, allowing various channels to gush through man-made gates that would eventually control the waters altogether, right down the banks that we had so laboriously made and across the muddy, newly planted fields from which we were hoping so much.

"They'll trample the crops!" I said in dismay.

Gideon grinned at me.

"They won't do much harm. They're all farming folk." He turned and took me by the hand. "You'd better take your place on the platform. They're waiting for you."

Julie stepped down from the jeep ahead of me. She put her arm possessively round Gideon's, pulling him away. With infinite patience he released himself.

"Sorry, Julie. You'd better find your parents and see that they're comfortable. I'm on duty today and so is Susan. I'll see you later."

Julie gave me a spiteful look.

"She shouldn't be here at all," she protested. "I think it's ridiculous to make all this fuss over her. *You're* the man behind it all!"

But Gideon only ignored her.

"Are you ready?" he asked me grimly. I took his hand and jumped down beside him and, without a further glance in Julie's direction, he led me towards the official space that was reserved for us.

"Do you think we ought to just leave her?" I asked anxiously.

Gideon's hand tightened on my elbow. "Why not?" he replied briefly.

He hurried me up the bank towards the dam with a fierce determination. I could hardly keep up in my high-heeled shoes and I was breathless as well as anxious by the time we had gained the top of the bank. I looked back over my shoulder to where Julie was still standing by the jeep. To my relief she waved to us and I was sure that she had forgotten her spite.

"She'll be all right," Gideon said roughly. "Don't worry about her. I'll see she doesn't bother you."

"But—" I protested.

He stopped and looked down at me and his expression was very gentle.

"I told you not to worry," he said. "I'll see she doesn't bother you."

I have to admit that I forgot all about her as we reached the little clearing on the top of the bank. The old men of the *panchayat* stood in a little semi-circle overlooking the rapidly filling reservoir. We greeted them individually, one by one, putting the palms of our hands together in the traditional Indian greeting and then shaking them warmly by the hand. We were only halfway through this little ceremony when the *Swami* came striding through the crowds towards us. His wild, matted hair stood straight on end and his orange robe seemed to hide less of him even than usual, but his air of authority was as strong as ever. As soon as he had come up with us, he sank on to the ground, apparently oblivious of everyone around us, and contemplated a small patch of ground in front of him. Nobody paid the faintest attention to him. They knew he would join us when he was ready.

I could see the approaching jeep bringing the government official from a long way off. Joseph and Camilla had hung it about with scarlet bunting and the Indian flag flew from the windscreen, proudly declaring that this was an official occasion. The crowd, completely silent as Indian crowds so often are, made room for the vehicle to pass, peering over one another's shoulders to look at the occupant to see what he looked like. I found myself as eager as every one else to see him and I took a quick step forward, almost tripping over the *Swami*.

"I'm so sorry," I apologised, but apparently he hadn't noticed.

"Where's Camilla?" Gideon asked me urgently.

I peered down at the jeep coming towards us.

"Isn't she with Joseph?"

He shook his head.

"Never mind, we haven't time to look for her now. I'll go down and welcome our guest if you and the *Swami* will wait here and keep things moving."

The *Swami* awoke from his dreams and stood up. He came over and stood beside me, smiling gently.

"I think this is as much your great day as it is the village's," he commented gravely. "You have made yourself very much one of us. A lot of people would be sad if you were to leave us now—Lakshmi particularly. She tells me you were instrumental in her becoming engaged to some young man?"

I blushed.

"Hardly," I replied, embarrassed by his approval. "All I did was to mention it to Gideon."

He smiled his acknowledgment.

"And that was enough," he agreed. "Nevertheless she is very happy at the outcome."

He turned away to chat to the old men around him, but at that moment Julie came running up the bank towards us, her face white and looking really frightened.

"It's my father!" she gasped. She flinched away from the *Swami* and turned to me. "He's fallen in the water," she said. "It was all a joke! He only wanted to see that Gideon got his fair share of the credit. He didn't see why you should be standing up here, any more than I could. He was going to make sure that the government man was taken round the other way and didn't see you at all. And then Camilla pushed him in!"

"Camilla did?" My first reaction was to want to burst out laughing, and even the *Swami* looked amused. Julie stamped her foot at the two of us.

"He *can't swim!*"

I caught some of her fright at that. I took off my high-heeled shoes and left them on the top of the bank and ran after her to the other side of the stream and up the other bank to where she thought her father was. A little knot of people had gathered on the edge of the water, giggling and nudging one another. I pushed my way through them and ran straight into Gideon's waiting arms.

"My goodness," he said in an amused voice, "we don't want to have two of you all wet and dripping. Where are you going in such a hurry?"

I tried to release myself from his clasp, but he didn't appear to notice. In fact he held me all the closer as though he didn't want to let me go.

"I thought he might have hurt you," I said at last in shaken tones.

Gideon shook his head. "Not twice," he said grimly.

"But what happened?" I asked.

A tiny, birdlike man, dressed in a *dhoti* and a Congress cap, came forward and shook my hand.

"It was very sudden. This man tried to kidnap me, I am sure of it! He kept saying he wished to introduce me to Mr. Wait's fiancée. Then this girl pushed him into the water!" He waved a hand to where Camilla was standing.

Despite myself, I giggled. Gideon's clasp tightened round my waist.

"Suki, my love, take Mr. Singh and introduce him to the *panchayat*, will you? I'll wrap Mr. Burnett in a blanket and Julie can take him home to his loving wife!"

"I won't!" Julie cried out desperately. "I'm staying here. You *asked* me to stay!"

"And now I'm asking you to go," Gideon replied calmly. "Your father will be better off at home in his own dream world of an existence."

Julie said nothing at all. She tore at his arm and tried to pull him towards her.

"I'm not coming, Julie," he said.

"But why not?" she demanded. She turned on me

bitterly. "It's because of you! Isn't it? I suppose you think you can fascinate him with a few grains of wheat for ever!"

But somehow no one was listening to her. Gideon wrapped Mr. Burnett up in a rug from the jeep, pushed him into the vehicle and lifted Julie in beside him.

"Drive them back to their car," he ordered Joseph briefly.

Camilla jumped up and down impatiently.

"I'll go with him and bring him back safe and sound!" she announced.

Gideon grinned at her. "Okay," he said. "Just so long as Suki stays here with me."

The band was still playing when we arrived back at our reserved positions. I felt a little self-conscious without my shoes and I was horribly aware of Gideon's amusement when the *Swami* silently held them out to me. It was Gideon, though, who put them on for me.

"Well, Mr. Singh," he drawled as he stood up, "what do you think of our dam?"

The government official beamed his approval. From somewhere in his *dhoti* he produced the notes of his speech. The band was silent and he began to speak.

I have no idea what he said. Gideon and I stood a little behind him. He held my hand tightly in his and I stood in a dream, wondering what I had done to deserve such happiness.

It seemed a very long time before Mr. Singh came to an end of his speech, but I didn't care. Even when the clouds came rolling back and more rain threatened to spoil the brightness of the day, it didn't seem to matter. And then, from nowhere, Mr. Singh produced a garland of marigolds and placed it carefully round my neck.

"The marigold means much to us," he said. "It is the colour of the rising sun and the beginning of the dawn of understanding."

There were garlands for everyone. Splashes of orange spread through the crowds. The band began to play again and the crowds broke into song. It was very pretty and it made me want to cry.

"I think we can go," Gideon whispered in my ear. "Will you come home with me?"

I nodded. I couldn't have spoken at that moment. It was as if I had never seen him before, and I knew with a trembling certainty that he knew it too. People stood aside as we slithered down the bank and commandeered the first vehicle we came to. Gideon helped me in, smiling at my uncertainty in my high-heeled shoes.

"Darling, could you take that garland off?" he asked me humorously.

I clutched it to me, admiring the clever way it had been made.

"Why?" I asked. "I'm very proud of it!"

He laughed. "I guess I am too," he admitted.

He sat beside me and drove the jeep off at a great pace until we had left the dam and the crowds far behind us. The first drops of rain were beginning to fall again. Great drops of warm water as big as cherries splattered on to the metal bonnet. When it began to rain in earnest, I thought, we wouldn't be able to hear what we were saying.

"Darling," he said, and he already had to shout, "do you love me?"

But I couldn't say it.

"Was it a mistake to be kind to Julie?" he asked. "She was an awful nuisance to me the whole time she was here!"

"I know," I said. "I saw it in your face when you told her to go."

He pulled me a little closer to him.

"And you love me?" he asked again. But he gave me no time to answer. His mouth came down on mine and I was lost in his arms. The pungent smell of crushed marigolds mixed with the rain.

"Yes," I said when I could. "I love you! I love you! I *love* you!"

And he kissed me again.

RED DIAMOND

Red Diamond
Dorothy Cork

None of the things Red Diamond believed about Martyn Verity, and the kind of girl she was, were true. And try as she might, Martyn didn't seem able to change his opinion.

She was young, it was true, and a bit immature, and indecisive about her future. Trying to decide on a career so soon after her beloved father's death was difficult.

Two things, though, she was sure about. In spite of his beliefs she knew that her initial dislike of Red Diamond on her arrival in the outback had turned into love. And more than anything she wanted to stay at Diamond Springs with him forever....

CHAPTER ONE

MARTYN, lying on her stomach on the beach behind the bungalow, took up a handful of golden sand and let it trickle slowly, slowly, through her fingers. Like an egg-timer or an hourglass or something. "When it's all gone, Bastian and Becky will be here."

She concentrated hard on the sand and as the last glittering grains slid away, a shadow fell and her heart leaped. She was right! Here they were! She had actually started to scramble to her feet when she discovered there was no dog, and that the man walking by her wasn't Bastian at all but a deeply tanned, rugged-looking, broad-shouldered stranger. Curiously analytic grey eyes studied her momentarily from the shadow of black eyebrows, and then, feeling slightly disconcerted, she was on her own again.

She expelled her breath gently, disappointedly, and watched this other man saunter on over the beach to-wards the surf, his thick black hair gleaming, the muscles of his broad brown back rippling above the dark blue swim shorts that were all he wore. Then she stretched out on the sand again to return to her vigil and her reflections. In her pale beige shorts, long white socks, and sleeveless cotton top of a deep-sea green that made her blue eyes bluer and her sun-bleached hair paler, she looked like a girl with nothing on her mind—a girl with nothing to do but lounge about in the sun at nine o'clock in the morning. But inside her head her mind was buzzing and busy.

There wasn't anyone much on the beach at this hour on a weekday, and her eyes strayed to the man who had passed by her. He had dropped his towel carelessly on

the sand and was heading for the water. She was sure
she had never seen him before, unless—unless he had
come wading out of the sea yesterday just as she and
Bastian and Becky had finished their walk along the
beach. Anyhow—so what? She had other things to
think about, and when Bastian came she was going to
ask him to think of something to help her out. Perhaps
some sort of *outdoor* job where she could use her talent
for drawing, she thought, knowing even as she thought
about it that she was asking for the impossible. Still, at
thirty-nine, more than twice her age, Bastian would
surely be able to produce some ideas as to what she
could do, now that Rosalind had said so very definitely
that the swimming lessons were no more than a pretence at seriousness.

Rosalind had given her a week—"One week, Bit—
and I mean it," she had warned this morning—to present her case for a reasonable and practical alternative
to taking a secretarial course. If she failed, then it was
off to Manly in the bus each day to learn shorthand and
typewriting.

"Anything but being stuck in an office all day,"
thought Martyn, laying her face down against the comforting warmth of the sand. And not having the faintest
idea just what alternative Bastian was going to suggest
later that morning.

Rosalind was Martyn's sister-in-law, and she had
issued her edict last night.

Two months had passed since Stan had died, and that
was quite long enough for Martyn to expect to be
treated gently, as a sort of convalescent. Stan was Martyn's father—her brother Richard's father too, but
Dick hadn't lived at home since twelve years ago when
he had won a scholarship to university in Sydney and
left the small coastal town where Stan Verity managed
the local swimming baths. Richard had been called
Dick then, and Martyn had been about seven years old—
in the water more often than out of it, licking ice-cream
cones between swims, running barefoot down the

street to buy fish and chips for tea, her sun-bleached hair streaming, her skin white with salt, the taste of it on her lips. A waterbaby from way back who knew and wanted no other life than the one she led with her father. She didn't remember her mother, who had died when she was four, and life seemed always to have been easygoing and carefree for Bit—Little Bit, as they had called her, because she was so much the baby of the family.

Then her father had died, and the whole of her life's pattern was disrupted.

Because Richard and Rosalind lived on the coast too—but in a Sydney suburb—she had thought she would transplant well enough, but she hadn't. With her deeply tanned face and body, her habit of going barefoot and of wearing the sketchiest of clothes and not caring a fig for fashion, she hadn't exactly made a hit with Rosalind, whom she had met at her wedding five years ago and seen only once since.

"Dear God, Bit, you're positively uncivilized—and not one whit older than you were at thirteen," Ros had commented.

They had treated her like an invalid at first, because she had been so obviously flattened by her father's sudden death. Stan, Martyn had always called him. Everyone did—everyone who lived in the small town, all the kids who came swimming to the baths. He had been so husky and fit, a man who rarely wore more than a pair of shorts, sometimes adding a short-sleeved shirt with an open neck; whose body was brown and tough, whose natural background was the blue-green water of the swimming baths, or the turquoise of the Pacific Ocean. A man who, like some gnarled old tree, one somehow expected to last for ever. Never, never to have died so suddenly of a heart attack before he was sixty.

So Martyn had come south to Sydney and didn't realize till she hit the place just what a misfit she was going to be. The sea was there, of course—the same old ocean almost at the back door, but the life was completely different from the casual one she had shared with Stan way up the coast. Rosalind and Richard, as she had learned to call her brother, lived in an attractive bungalow, furnished with good modern stuff, with airy rooms, an up-to-date kitchen and a bar. At the back, there was a tree-shaded terrace that looked across a lawn of coarse grass to the sea. Somehow Rosalind miraculously kept the floors free of the sand that blew in from the beach in white drifts across the garden. Martyn felt guilty every time she came in from the sea in case she carried sand with her. It hadn't mattered at home, but here everything was so tidy, so immaculate. Except her bedroom, though she did her best with that to the extent that it didn't seem to belong to her. No more sandshoes and swimsuits drying on the windowsill—no more shells on the dressing table.

Last evening she had come in rather late from the beach, tiptoeing, looking back to see if she had left a telltale trail of sand after changing on the verandah and hanging her swimsuit in the yard. Then she had gone dutifully to the kitchen. There was a recipe card on the corner of the dresser, conspicuous under a pretty glass paperweight, and apprehensively she had picked it up. Chicken with Cabbage. She had skimmed through the print anxiously. It looked as if she could have it ready in an hour and three-quarters at any rate. In her mind she could hear Rosalind's voice:

"If you're going to live with us, Bit, then you must make yourself useful—at least until you decide what you're going to do with your life. It might be an idea if you got the meals ready at night for a start, seeing you're idle all day."

"But—" began Martyn hesitantly, worriedly, for she had never done much cooking.

Rosalind interrupted her. "Now don't start telling me you can't cook. I know you've always lived on fish and prawns and pies out of a paper bag, but anyone with a little common sense can cook. You don't need to

be an intellectual giant. I've got a file of foolproof rec-
ipes—you'll learn in no time.''

So last night—chicken and cabbage...

It was simmering gently in the heavy covered pan on
top of the stove when Rosalind and Richard came in.
Martyn earned a modicum of praise and retired with a
sigh of thankfulness to set the table while Richard
poured the sherry.

Everything was as usual—or so it seemed. The meal
was good, the other two discussed their day with each
other—Ros was a radiographer, Dick was a psychology
lecturer. Then they discussed a party they had been invited to, and Martyn, who had a good healthy appetite,
relaxed and enjoyed her meal, and after it was over
went into the kitchen to do the washing up, and protested when Rosalind came in to help.

"For heaven's sake," said her sister-in-law irritably—
she was a slim imperturbable-looking girl of twenty-
seven, with an air of confidence and poise that Martyn
sometimes envied—"don't act as if you're paying
gratefully for your keep with humble services. That's
not how we see it at all. But this is *my* home, and if it
pleases me to wipe the dishes, then it doesn't require
any comment. I want to talk to you, anyhow."

Martyn's heart sank. Another talk! She bit her lip
and almost dropped a plate as she lifted it into the rinsing water. She just didn't seem to fit comfortably into
this household. Two months had proved it. It wasn't
simply that they didn't want her, or that a third person
is an intrusion between husband and wife. The fact was
she didn't belong. To her, they were like people from
another planet, brainy, sophisticated. She didn't understand them and they didn't understand her. Ros was
out all day, but all the same, Martyn was in her hair—
under her feet—far too much of the time. And she was
quite sure that if *she* were Rosalind, she wouldn't want
Martyn Verity around, there every night when she
came home from work, there every week-end—

"How did you put in the day, Bit?" Rosalind asked

after a moment of contemplatively drying the dishes.

"Oh, I gave a swimming lesson this afternoon, and I spent this morning on the beach." She stopped short. It was futile to recite it all. The swimming lessons brought in "pocket money", Ros said scornfully, and other than that there were things that Martyn simply didn't tell them about, because they would be scorned too. About Bastian, and the drawing lessons. She knew that Ros would think of that—"wasted time"—though she loved drawing, and Bastian said she was coming on well. At the back of her mind she had, too, an uncomfortable idea that neither Ros nor Richard would approve of Bastian, because he was older, and divorced, or for some silly illogical reason like that.

She looked through her lashes at Ros, who was frowning.

"That's fine," Ros said vaguely, and then added briskly, "All the same, it's time we started thinking of your future. You must have some sort of life of your own. What do you really want to do?"

Martyn could have said, "I'd like to draw a children's picture-story book." But she didn't, because she just knew that Rosalind would *not* say amen to that. So she said, "There's the swimming. I could find some more pupils, answer some more ads—"

Ros's pretty eyebrows went up a notch. She commented with her usual cool control, "I don't *really* think that's the answer, Bit. I was thinking of something that would eventually make you more or less independent. Until you get married, of course. You don't want to live here with us indefinitely, do you? I mean, it's really a more or less temporary arrangement—till you find your feet."

"Yes, I know," Martyn said.

"Well, then, you've had enough time to pull yourself together, and if you don't have any brilliant ideas yourself, it would seem the most sensible thing to enrol yourself at that secretarial school in Manly. With a little hard work you could be out earning your living in no time—meeting people, doing something useful, instead of frittering away your life in the water. You'd make friends—meet some nice girls of your own age, maybe get a flat together.''

Typing. Secretarial school. To an outdoor girl, what could sound more dismal? Was it any use suggesting a course in art as an alternative? She hadn't been smart enough at school—because she hated being indoors studying had been her excuse—to get an art scholarship. And in her heart she hadn't been sorry about that, because she had loved her life exactly as it was. All she really wanted artwise, after she left school at sixteen, was the bit of tuition she had from a "lady artist"—Mrs. Turner, who had retired up the coast with her husband. The rest of her time Martyn had spent happily in a swimsuit, helping at the baths, in the shop or the locker rooms, on the turnstiles. Smelling the sea, hearing the sound of the waves night and day, tasting salt on her lips, running round with kids her own age; looking after Stan. Of course Stan, who doted on her— Little Bit, the unexpected addition to the family— thought she was just about a genius with her drawings of seagulls and cats and dogs and kids. He was so proud of her drawings it was embarrassing. He'd have had every second one framed and put on exhibition, if wishes came true. And if it was what she had really wanted, he'd have sent her off to Sydney to live with Dick and attend some private art school no matter what it cost. Martyn had never wanted to go. "No, thanks, Stan—life's great just the way it is. Mrs. Turner says I have the talent to do a children's book, and I don't need to go away anywhere to do *that*!"

But time went by so quickly in the sun, she'd never even got around to starting a book.

And now—secretarial school—

Richard had come to stand in the kitchen doorway and she knew they'd been making decisions. It was time for Bit to be given a push in the right direction.

"Give it a go, Bit," her brother said encouragingly.

Martyn looked at him perplexedly. "Not *typing*, Dick. It wouldn't—I couldn't—"

Ros cut in sharply, "What else *can* you do, for Pete's sake? You haven't been brought up to use your brains, and let's face it, you're your father's daughter."

Martyn's face crimsoned with hurt and anger. "I'd have thought secretaries need brains like anyone else," she flared. "So—" She pulled out the plug and the water began to disappear with an enraged gurgle.

Richard said placatingly before Ros could speak, "So they do. And no one's saying you're brainless. But the point is, if you're going to be awkward about typing, then you'd better think hard what you're going to take up instead. You know as well as we do that this just can't go on for ever."

Even he sounded exasperated, and Martyn turned away to dry her hands on the kitchen towel. "I'll think hard," she told Richard. "I promise I shall."

"We'll give you a week," Rosalind said. And she didn't smile...

So now, this morning, Martyn was waiting for Bastian—the only mature and sympathic person she could think of who might come up with some helpful ideas. Because a week wasn't very long to make plans.

Fifteen minutes later she and Bastian and Becky, his Great Dane, were walking along the sand. This was a morning ritual. Bastian brought his dog down from the plateau for exercise, and Martyn, since the day she and Bastian had met some five or six weeks ago, always went along too. They covered almost the full length of the long beach, Bastian throwing sticks for Becky, Martyn sometimes racing along on the hard wet sand, the dog at her heels. The walk over, they would get into the car he parked in a dead end street near the bungalow and go up to his house on the plateau for coffee and for Martyn's drawing lesson. And, for Bastian, the beginning of the day's work.

Today was no different, and somehow or other they

had finished their walk before Martyn said a single word about Rosalind's edict.

"You've been quiet this morning," Bastian remarked when they had returned along the beach. He put his arm lightly around her waist and she looked up at him. He was not very tall, with grey-green eyes and crinkly light brown hair that had a touch of premature silver at the temples. Martyn thought him a rather nice man, and it seemed sad that he was divorced from his wife, Laurie. It had happened not long ago, he had told Martyn, but he had talked little of his personal life, and never about Laurie. There were two children, but they didn't talk about them either, and Martyn didn't pry. After all, her relationship with him was not really a personal one, partly she thought, because he was so much older than she was. But she imagined that behind his silence he was probably still hurt and unhappy about his broken home, and that could be one reason why he liked her company. To fill a big gap...

Now she said, "Oh, I've got things to think about."

"Such as?" He smiled down into her face.

"Such as that my sister-in-law's pushing me to change my ways," she began. She glanced down towards the sea and saw that man with the strangely penetrating grey eyes emerging from the breakers and come striding over the sand. She turned away from him quickly and looked back at Bastian, and discovered he was frowning.

"Meeting me, do you mean? I thought you said you were keeping quiet about us—about the lessons. What does she suspect, for heaven's sake? God, I haven't even so much as laid a finger on you," he finished, his lips twisting wryly.

Martyn coloured. "Oh, it's nothing like *that*—it's not about you, of course. It's just they want me to learn typing or something ghastly like that. And stop—frittering away my life in the sun. I haven't told them about the drawing—they'd think it was silly. But now I'm wondering, you see, what I can do. I don't want to do typing, and they've given me a week to make up my mind." She stopped. He had removed his arm from her waist and stooped to pick up a piece of driftwood and throw it for the dog to fetch, and when he straightened he looked at her quizzically. "I thought *you* might have some ideas," she told him hopefully.

"About you?" he said.

"Yes. Well, about what I could do," she said, a little confused for some reason. "I don't know anyone else to ask. Only you. You—you understand—"

"I'm flattered you feel that way." They walked on a few paces, and arrived at the Veritys' back fence, half submerged in blown sand. "We'll talk about it over coffee, shall we?"

"Later will do if you like," she said quickly, vaguely uneasy. "Tomorrow—I don't want to be a nuisance."

"A nuisance?" he repeated, and she recognized something new in his tone. "*You* a nuisance?" Becky had brought back the driftwood and looked at them inquiringly. She was a young dog—Bastian had acquired her after he and his wife had parted. He continued dryly, "Surely you must be aware that's not how I feel about you, Martyn. You're not altogether a child."

His eyes went briefly over her body in the green top and beige shorts—to her brown thighs that contrasted so stongly with the white socks, and she looked back at him blankly. There were days—many of them—when she felt herself no more than a child. The day she had first met Bastian had been one of those days. She had been sitting on the sand, dumb and dazed and bruised, thinking of Stan, whom she would never see again—never, never, never. And she had been drawing seagulls with a desperate clumsy intensity as if by so doing she could dull her pain. Becky had come racing up and startled her, and Bastian had followed with a quick command to the dog and a reassuring, "She won't hurt you—she's only a playful pup," to Martyn. Then— "What's that you're drawing?" It had been—comforting just then to have this older, mature man take a kindly interest in her drawing, and in herself. It had been almost miraculous to discover that he was an artist—and to have him offer to give her lessons, quite free... Now he was saying, "You're not altogether a child," and she was far from sure that he was right. Besides, what had that got to do with being a nuisance or otherwise?

"I never begrudge a moment spent with you," he said.

"But you've always got a load of fascinating things to do," she protested, disturbed. "I know I must often be just a—just a pest."

"I don't know how you got that idea." He paused for several seconds. "As a matter of fact, you've been absorbing my mind utterly—utterly—for some days now."

"Me?" They had nearly reached the car, and she couldn't quite think how this conversation had begun. "When half the time you're so wrapped up in what you're doing you don't even know I'm there?" she said with an attempt at laughter.

"I'm always well aware of that. How could I not be? It's the law of nature," he added with a slight smile. He opened the car door and she slid in the front while he let Becky in the back, and then he walked around the bonnet to get in the other side. Martyn felt puzzled. Bastian had never talked this way before, and she had an uncomfortable awareness of having disturbed the status quo, quite unintentionally.

Neither of them said anything as he drove away from the beach, down the main road past a few shops, then up along the winding road that led to the plateau. Up here was where she gave some of her swimming lessons, at private pools. This afternoon it would be to Tom and Nanda Fleet, and they passed the Fleets' house before Bastian reached his own garage. He lived alone in a two-storied house with a fair sized garden and a lovely view of the ocean and Martyn preceded him up the steps as she always did, he unlocked the

door and let Becky run through to her bowl of water
and thence, when he had opened the back door, into
the yard. Martyn stopped off in the kitchen to start the
coffee, and forage in the cupboard for biscuits. She had
always enjoyed this little ritual, it was somehow different from doing things in Ros's kitchen, but today—today she was disturbingly conscious that once this had
been—another woman's kitchen. A woman of whom
she knew nothing. Laurie.

Bastian came to the door just as she had everything
ready.

"Upstairs," he directed, smiling at her—just the way
he always smiled, she assured herself. Everything was
perfectly all right. She loaded up the tray and carried it
carefully along the short hallway and up the stairs, and
no matter how much she reassured herself, deep down
she had this feeling that somehow she had started an
avalanche falling.

Upstairs there were three bedrooms, a bathroom and
a shower room, and upstairs again there was a big room
like an attic. Bastian had had this house especially built
for him, and the attic, which had a wide window that
looked from the plateau over houses and gum trees towards the ocean, was his studio. He worked for a correspondence art school, correcting lessons, and in his
free time he did some easel painting. Martyn was always fascinated to see what his correspondence stu-
dents had produced. Some of them were skilled and
some were clumsy, but Bastian gave the same serious
conscientious treatment to them all.

This morning as she poured the coffee and passed
the biscuits, he opened his post as usual. He had put on
his glasses which made him look businesslike and quite
a bit older, and was slitting open packets and glancing
quickly at one or two drawings. Martyn thought with a
feeling that vacillated between relief and puzzlement
that he had forgotten her quandary, and her appeal for
his help. On a small easel at one side of the room was a
portrait he was painting in oils of Martyn, and she

studied it thoughtfully while he was occupied. A girl with rather round blank blue eyes, straw-coloured hair, a brown face and a string of coral around her neck. As a matter of fact, she looked as if she were wearing nothing but that string of coral, and there was something in the expression portrayed by mouth and eyes that made Martyn feel slightly uncomfortable. It just wasn't really her.

She finished her coffee and felt sure now he had forgotten her problem completely, until with a positive action he pushed his papers aside and looked at her over his dark-rimmed glasses.

"Do you want to draw this morning? Or are we going to deal with this problem of yours?"

Martyn looked at him helplessly, no longer sure she should have asked his advice. She said, stammering a little, "It—it doesn't matter. I don't—I don't really expect there's anything much you can suggest. I mean, it's not as if I were good enough at art to do anything— I shouldn't have asked."

He took his glasses off and his grey-green eyes met hers. "Don't panic. Of course there's something I can suggest, and it's perfectly simple. You don't have to run away and learn typing. I'd like you to—belong to me."

He smiled faintly as he said it, and Martyn stared uncomprehendingly. Her mind seemed to have gone quite blank with pure astonishment. Her mouth fell open, but she was incapable of uttering a sound. He was telling her—he was telling her he was in love with her! And she had never even suspected it. Not for a single moment.

He said wryly, "Is it really so surprising? Surely you're aware that you're very very pretty, and very very desirable." He spared a glance for the portrait and then his eyes returned to her.

"But," said Martyn, her head whirling, "you've never—you've never even kissed me."

"I've wanted to," he said. "It's been a—noble deference to your rather tender years. And perversely, I've even enjoyed the exquisite torture. To have you here, to look at you, and not to touch... Well, what do you say? That you'd prefer the typing?''

Martyn shook her head bewilderedly. If this was a proposal, then it was an unconventional one, to say the least. But then Bastian was an artist, and as well, he'd been married before. As for whether or not she was in love with him, it was such a completely new idea that she just didn't know. She said, ''I don't know, I've just— I've just never thought about getting married, not for ages. I'm not—I'm not old enough.''

He raised his eyebrows. ''I wouldn't worry about that,'' he said, not very explicitly, after a moment. ''The point is do you like me enough to consider it? If you want some time to think it over, then of course you may have it, but I'd rather gathered the matter was urgent in your young life. Was I wrong?''

''No,'' she said helplessly. She hadn't even the vaguest idea what she felt about him. Could she be in love with him? Was that why she had enjoyed her mornings with him so much? Was it even, perhaps, why she had kept it all a secret? The fact was, she didn't know even the first thing about love, and so far he hadn't taught it to her. Out of deference for her tender years! She looked at him almost shyly, trying to see him anew. His narrow face, his long grey-green eyes, his light brown kinky hair. Suddenly none of it was familiar any more. It was like looking at a stranger. And odder still, superimposed on his image was that of another man—heavily built, darkly tanned, positive. Where on earth had she seen *him*? Down on the beach this morning, of course. She blinked the image away impatiently.

Bastian reached across the table and took her hand, his thumb stroking her palm. ''You're sitting here looking so stunned. Are you shocked? Aren't you interested? Would you rather forget it?''

Martyn swallowed. It all seemed so unreal. Bastian in

love with her! Girls were always supposed to be flattered when someone wanted to marry them, but she couldn't take it in. It was as if she had given herself an extra problem in turning to him for help. She withdrew her hand from his and from the unnerving tickling of his thumb. "I'll have to think about it," she said huskily.

"Do that," he agreed. "I can see I've turned today really upside down for you. We won't have a lesson. I don't think either of us could concentrate. You run off home and think it over, and tomorrow we'll talk again, and lay a few more of our cards on the table."

He smiled at her and she smiled back, feeling relieved, even reprieved. She gathered up the cups and put them on the tray just as she always did, he put on his glasses, and she went downstairs to the kitchen.

While she was rinsing the cups, she tried to remember exactly what he had said. Had he said he loved her? He had asked, she thought, if she loved him enough to "consider" it—not simply if she loved him. It was—odd. The trouble was, he was so experienced, and she was so horribly *in*experienced.

She tidied the cups away, and looked around the kitchen, clean and shining and neat with its breakfast nook, where once Laurie and the two nameless children had sat with its coffee percolator, and pop-up toaster, its big gleaming two-door fridge and the latest in electric stoves. Everything always looked nice and clean and she knew that a housekeeper came in three times a week to keep it so. Why had his marriage broken up? What had gone wrong between him and Laurie? Marriage, she reflected soberly, was a pretty serious business.

Feeling unaccustomedly nervous, she went to the foot of the stairs to call out, "I'm going, Bastian. I'll see you tomorrow."

She supposed he answered, but she didn't hear him, and of course he was already immersed in his work. Rather meditatively, she wished he had kissed her. It

might have made all the difference. She might have
known then how she felt about him. And he had said
that *not* kissing her had been exquisite torture.

Suddenly, now she was on her own, it all seemed
exciting, thrilling, but she knew she wasn't going to be
able to talk to Ros and Dick about it. She would have to
do all her thinking for herself...

In the afternoon, she went back up to the plateau to
give her swimming lesson at the Fleets'. Tom and
Nanda had been her first pupils and their lessons were
nearly ended now. They had both become quite confident in the water, but all the same Martyn gave them
her full attention that afternoon, and refused to think
about Bastian. It was a bad thing to be preoccupied
when you were dealing with small children and water.

Mrs. Fleet had not put in an appearance at all today,
and it was only when the lesson was over that she became aware of someone watching her from beyond the
shimmering blue water of the small pool. She looked
across the garden as the two children scrambled on to
the black and white tiles that divided the pool from the
lawn, and then she blinked hard. She must be seeing
things! But she wasn't. Most definitely, it was that
powerful-looking deeply tanned man she had seen this
morning on the beach. Standing in the feathery shade
of some wattle trees, smoking, and looking at her in
such a speculatively intent way that suddenly as never
before she was conscious of herself in her simple black
one-piece swimsuit. Conscious of her long brown legs
and tanned face, of the silver-straw hair that, stiff with
salt, fell against her cheek and over her shoulders. And
she remembered, strangely, that Bastian had said she
was pretty—and desirable.

The children were racing for the house, for lemonade and chocolate biscuits and goodness knows what,
and in a moment Martyn would follow them. Not for
lemonade and biscuits, but for the clothes she had left
in the bathroom, and for the money she would be paid
for the lesson. And to report to Mrs. Fleet on Tom's

and Nanda's progress. She had to pass by the man who was watching her on her way to the house, and she felt oddly defensive. Surely he must remember seeing her this morning—and yet there wasn't even the glimmer of a smile on his face. On the contrary, he continued to regard her through half-closed, glittery eyes, in a way that, taken in conjunction with the cynical set of his mouth, suggested there was something decidedly unlikeable, or maybe worse, about her.

"What's biting *you*?" she asked silently, as she came towards him. But all she said was a careless "Hi!" when she was really close.

His heavy eyebrows slanted and he took the cigarette from his lips but didn't return her greeting. Nor did he remark, as she had somehow suspected that he might, that he had seen her at the surf earlier in the day. Instead he told her with a cold indifference, "When you're ready, I'll drive you home."

Mrs. Fleet always insisted on doing that, and she looked at him questioningly, disturbed by something in his attitude. It wasn't just his offhandedness that bothered her. It was something else entirely, something that she couldn't analyse. From this close, she saw he was far from being a conventionally good-looking man. In fact, she didn't think you could call him good-looking at all. She guessed he must be round about Bastian's age, though it was hard to tell with someone as big and muscular and assured as he was. But his eyes—she thought they were the hardest eyes she had ever seen in her life. They were like grey steel, yet they had a curious brilliance. Diamonds, she thought. Smoky diamonds. It was not till later that she knew how apt her thought had been. The thick waving black hair she had noticed earlier in the day was ruffled now, but so shiny she knew he had washed the salt from it, and his tan looked darker still against the bronze and viridian of the classy shirt he wore, open almost to the waist, revealing a dark hairy chest.

She took in everything about him with extraordinary

speed while he spoke to her, and then, as a kind of retaliation to his unfriendliness, she said, cool too, "You don't need to bother driving me. I can walk—or take the bus."

He shrugged his too-broad shoulders carelessly, and told her, "I'll be ready when you are. Don't rush it. There's a glass of lemonade for you on the verandah."

Martyn blinked her blue eyes, hesitated for the fraction of a second, then moved on. Some city people—not Bastian!—could be so distant and unfriendly and patronizing. Though *he* didn't look exactly a typical city-dweller! He didn't accompany her to the verandah, but stayed where he was, and she poured lemonade from the bottle into the single glass that stood on the tray and drank it standing, her mind alert. She could hear the children romping and squealing somewhere inside the house, and a woman's voice speaking to them, but their mother didn't appear. She wondered about the matter of her pay as she set down her empty glass and headed for the bathroom where she had shed her clothes. She needed the money—if only to justify herself to Rosalind, to prove that she was earning something. Or didn't that matter anymore? If she decided to marry Bastian—

In the bathroom she got out of the black cotton swimsuit, put on panties and bra, her beige shorts and the green top—her long socks and canvas shoes. She met her own blue gaze squarely in the mirror and thought with utter amazement, "Someone wants to marry me!" What would Stan have thought? What would he have advised? Quick tears sprang to her eyes and she dashed them away. She could imagine Stan's frown—his surprise—

The dark-haired man was waiting for her on the verandah when she came out, and she found herself going over his points. He would make a good swimmer. He was broad-chested, muscular, a little over Stan's height—maybe an inch under six feet, she judged, not all that tall. But tough-looking. Tougher than anyone she had ever met. She didn't think she liked him much, he was too forbidding. Maybe he found girls as young as she was a bore, or else he had a down on modern youth.

"Ready?" he said, as she appeared, and those adamantine eyes passed over her as impersonally, now, as the beam of a torch. *Didn't* he remember her? Not even now she had on the same gear she had worn on the beach? She was sure he must, but he was too lordly, too high and mighty, to acknowledge it. Well, who cared?

She said firmly, "No, I'm not quite ready. I have some money to collect."

"That's right." One hand, broad, brown, powerful-looking, went to his shirt pocket, and he added mockingly, "I've got your pay packet here."

"Martyn—Martyn Verity," she supplied, thinking he had paused for her name. But she was wrong, because he didn't repeat either part of it, but handed her an envelope which she tucked away quickly in her beach bag. "Thanks."

He followed her down the steps and told her back, "If you're wondering, my sister had to go out. Hence the delegation of duty."

His sister. So Mrs. Fleet was his sister. Well, that was the first bit of information he had offered. She supposed it would be too much to expect him to introduce himself.

"How far do we have to go?" he asked as he opened the car door for her a minute later.

"Only down to the beach," she said, and added pertly, "Near where you saw me on the sand this morning. Remember?"

He waited till he'd got into the car beside her, slammed the door shut and started up the motor before he said, with a swift appraising flick of his eyes that seemed to take her all in anew, "Sure I remember." He added gratuitously and disagreeably, "You know, I wonder about kids like you. You flit around older men

like moths around a flame, playing with something you
don't know a thing about. God knows how many of
you get burned—and burned badly. You now—obviously green, indecently, horribly young—haven't you a
family who cares what you get up to, who you kick
around with?''

Her blood had frozen at his tone, and she felt herself
immediately on the defensive. What sort of a mind did
he have—after merely seeing her walking on the beach
with a perfectly respectable man, and a dog? Possibly
he had seen Bastian put his arm around her waist, but
so what?

She told him icily, and with a feeling of slight triumph, just to take him down a peg or two, "As it happens that—*older* man I'm *experimenting* with wants me
to marry him.''

"Good God!'' The car swerved slightly as he took
the last wide turn from the plateau, and then he braked
before swinging into the main stream of traffic. "You
can't mean it! You're no more than a school kid. Are
you sure it's marriage he wants? And what do your
parents have to say? I wonder they even let you associate with Bastian Sinclair. Or don't they know?''

She was taken aback to discover he knew Bastian's
name, and said with heightened colour, "If you know
Bastian, then I can't think what you're going on
about.''

"Can't you?'' he grated. "Well, I don't know him
personally. I'm sure he's very charming, but I've heard
quite enough about him and his affairs from my sister
to know he's not a man I'd have allowed either of my
younger sisters to run around with.''

"Really?'' Martyn was shaking inwardly. "Well, I *do*
know him personally, and you have no right to talk like
that about anyone you don't know. It's—it's unforgivable, and I'm not in the least interested in your nasty
second-hand opinions. I don't want to hear any more of
them, thank you. This is my street,'' she added haughtily, glancing from the car window.

He swung the wheel and with tyres squealing they were round the corner, and in seconds he had pulled up at the end of the street facing the beach and turned in his seat to face her grimly.

"I've a good mind to go right into that bungalow and have a word with your mother. Someone should give you a down-to-earth talking to."

Martyn's skin prickled with anger. "Go ahead. But there's no one at home. I'm staying with my brother and his wife, anyhow, and they're both at work." She reached for the door-handle and struggled with it for a second till he leaned across, and putting steel-hard fingers round her wrist dragged her hand away.

"Just hang on. So there's no one I can tell tales to. Well, you're not getting out yet. I'm going to do some talking. Come on now, are you actually considering marrying this man? And are you sure it's marriage he's after? Frankly, I hope to God you're shortly going back home to your parents and school and safety, and a decently supervised life."

She jerked her hand away from beneath his. "I'm nineteen. I don't go to school. And my parents—I don't have any. My father died a little while ago—" Her voice broke slightly and she turned away. "Now let me out of here—"

It was a useless plea. "So you're in your brother's care," he pursued remorselessly. "And does *he* know about this idiotic affair?"

"My friendships are my own concern," she said angrily. "I don't have to tell Richard about everything I do and everyone I know."

"At *your* age? And in your obvious—well, one would *presume* obvious—state of unsophistication? And when you're babbling about marriage, or most likely some state far less permanent? What utter drivel!" Those hard eyes bored into her. "You make a full confession to your brother—I don't want to hear it—and listen hard to what he tells you. Bring your boy-friend along to meet the family before you rush into marriage or any other arrangement. My own advice would be to forget all about Sinclair as from right now. Your heart won't break, I'll promise you that. Young hearts are very pliant. You'll do yourself irreparable damage if you're besotted enough to get seriously mixed up with him. You're a good-looking kid—there are plenty more romances ahead of you."

Martyn opened her mouth to utter some sort of protest, but he went on relentlessly, "You tell this man no, you hear me? He has no right to ask *anything* of a girl like you. Get out while you're still in one piece. Don't fool yourself that a kiss is just a kiss, either. After the kiss there's a further step, and then another, and before you know what's happened, you've been eased all the way from the patio or the beach or wherever right through the bedroom door... Does he come to the bungalow when you're here alone?"

Martyn said tightly, her cheeks crimson, and not caring in the least what interpretation he put on what she said, because he was so hateful it was just humiliating—and she was hurt, hurt right through at being treated to this by an absolute stranger— "*No!* I go to *his* house up on the plateau. We're alone *there*."

A nerve twitched on his jawline. "Good God! And it hasn't happened yet?"

"*What* hasn't happened yet?" she asked furiously.

He closed his eyes for a second. "Are you equivocating? Or don't you know anything at all about your—would-be lover?"

She waited for a moment for self-control. "If you mean he's divorced—yes, I know all about that."

"All?" he quizzed.

"What do you mean?"

"If you knew it all, you just mightn't be so damned complacent. Though I don't know—you just could be more depraved than seems possible, from those desperately young heaven—blue eyes."

She reached for the door and again he had her by the wrist.

"Let go," she commanded. "You're hurting me."

She added fiercely, "Bastian is perfectly nice—he's never—"

He had released her instantly but without apology. "Perfectly nice!" he mocked. "Despite a reputation that states the opposite? I know something about that, I assure you, though I only visit the coast once or twice a year."

Martyn looked back at him wide-eyed, scornful, heart thumping. "Reputation? What do you mean?"

"With women, of course. That was what the divorce was all about. Not one woman, but—" He stopped. "Yet he had a decent wife, a couple of nice children."

Her cheeks crimsoned, her head was spinning. She knew nothing about the divorce. She hadn't even, when she came to consider it, the faintest idea whether or not there were other women in Bastian's life—beside herself. She saw him in the morning. What he did with his evenings, his weekends, she wouldn't have a clue. The truth was it had never bothered her. And now she wished she had never mentioned Bastian to this man, whoever he was. Julia Fleet's brother.

She said with an attempt at dignity, "I don't listen to gossip."

"Very virtuous of you," he snapped back. "But you'd have to have the charms of a siren to turn him into a faithful husband—or a faithful lover—overnight. And while I'll allow you're attractive—your eyes are devastating, your figure likewise—in worldly experience I'd say you were at a very heavy disadvantage."

Martyn turned her eyes away from him. "Will you please let me get out of this car?"

"Certainly. But I hope you'll think about what I said. Though I suppose you'll go ahead and do what you damned well please and ruin your life, if that's how you feel. You kids just won't believe you're asking for trouble when you pick up with an older man. Until hard experience brings it home to you—"

"Bastian's no older than you," Martyn retorted determinedly.

"So what's that to do with it? Believe me, I could twist you *right* around my little finger if I had a mind to it. You just wouldn't have a clue what was happening to you. But I don't happen to have a taste for corrupting waterbabies," he concluded disparagingly.

Martyn bit her lip and wished she could think of something utterly killing and obliterating to say. But she couldn't so she opened the door and slithered out.

"Thanks for all the free advice—Methuselah," was the best she could manage. "But I can handle my life without your interference."

"Then you must be a lot sharper than you look—or act," he shot back. He slammed the door shut and drove off without even bothering to say goodbye.

CHAPTER TWO

To her intense annoyance, as she went inside Martyn found she couldn't stop thinking about that man and all the things he had said to her—hurled at her! Everything was confused. *Did* Bastian have a reputation with women? More important still, *had* he asked her to marry him? She had, she supposed, taken it for granted, but now, rack her brains as she might, she couldn't remember that he had put it in plain words. So what had he meant? Did he just want her to go and live with him? Did he think she was that sort of girl? It was unbelievable. They had got on so well together, had such happy mornings on the beach and in his studio. And all the time he had been wanting to kiss her but not doing it. Uneasily she recalled occasions when she had caught him looking at her in a funny sort of way. She had thought it had been an artist's way—that he had been seeing her as subject rather than as a person.

Oh, that man had spoiled everything, she thought frustratedly. Tomorrow she would see Bastian again and she'd discover that everything was as ordinary and straightforward as she had believed before. The only problem was to decide if she was even a little in love with him. She wished and wished that Ros hadn't pushed her into so tight a corner...

She hung her swimsuit in the garden, determinedly discarded her troubled thoughts and went into the kitchen to discover what culinary feat she had to perform tonight. There were still the ordinary tasks of everyday life to be done, thank goodness.

Lamb cutlets with pineapple rings, the recipe was

headed. And presently, in the midst of patting crumbs on to the cutlets with a knife, she stopped to reflect with a faint smile—"Love and lamb cutlets!" Yet she hadn't, when she came to consider it, been thinking of Bastian—she'd been thinking of a few things she'd like to say to that man, for putting horrible thoughts and suspicions into her mind.

She was slicing the rough outside from a big fresh pineapple on a chopping board when another irrelevant thought surfaced. *He* had said he only came here once or twice a year. So where was he from? And would he still be at the Fleets' next time she went to give a lesson? She hoped *not*. Because if he was, she was going to ignore him. Completely. And if he asked any interfering personal questions, she would tell him quite plainly to mind his own business...

The following morning, feeling unaccustomedly nervous she went out to meet Bastian as usual. As she crossed the garden, she noticed she hadn't brought in her swimsuit. Last night Rosalind had said impatiently, "Bit, please don't leave your bathing things draped around the garden. You make the place look like a—like a slum, or a laundry."

"I'm sorry," she had said automatically.

Well, her bathers could stay there till later on, so long as she brought them in before Ros came home... She climbed the low fence and plodded across the dry sand, barefooted, her sandals in her hand. Bastian must be there already, because Becky came bounding up from nowhere, to put her big paws up on Martyn's chest, and nearly knock her over as she tried to lick her face. Then Bastian appeared, and they took their walk as usual. He didn't refer to what had been said yesterday, and they threw sticks for Becky, and Martyn raced along the hard wet sand with the dog just as if nothing had happened.

But later she caught herself looking covertly at the man with whom she walked, trying to find out—

something about him. What Stan would have thought of him, perhaps whether she was in love with him a little—or more than a little—or not at all; and—yes, if he looked like a man with a reputation with women.

It was annoying to be bugged by such thoughts, and that man was to blame. He was to blame too for her nagging suspicion that it had not been marriage Bastian had been proposing to her yesterday.

Her glance had strayed away to the prancing dog, and then to the sea. And to a lone swimmer, away out beyond the breakers. *That man*—she was positive it was he. "Spying on me—on *us*," she thought, as Bastian put his arm casually around her waist so that she was conscious of the touch of his slim artistic fingers through the thin stuff of her shirt. Disconcertingly, she wanted to pull away, but with a deliberate effort of will, she didn't.

A quarter of an hour later they were in his house. He went upstairs while she made the coffee, and the kitchen seemed strange today. She listened in the hallway and when there were no sounds from above, she went into the sitting room. Looking for what, she didn't know. She already knew there were no photographs there, nothing to show what Laurie and the children had been like. This morning, she could smell carnations very faintly, though there were no carnations to be seen. So—another woman? Last night? Suddenly she hated herself. She was developing a suspicious mind rather quickly, wasn't she?

She went quickly and silently back to the kitchen and took the tray upstairs. Bastian was already at work on some of his correspondence lessons—as though he had something to catch up?—and he drank his coffee abstractly. Martyn, when she had finished hers, did some drawings from sketches she had made a couple of days earlier. They were just about the worst drawings she had ever done, and when, a little later, Bastian interrupted his work to take a look at them, he finally removed his glasses and said with a faint smile, "Hopeless! Your mind's not on it. I think I'm going to have to excuse you today. And while mid-morning's not generally considered the best time for talking of love—or making it—we more or less promised each other yesterday, didn't we? Unless you've decided in the meantime to give me a brush-off. And I don't think you have, have you?''

He looked at her steadily and she coloured and swallowed, feeling her mouth go dry.

"No," she said uncertainly, and without really knowing what she was doing she stood up and reached for the tray.

He came round the table swiftly. "Forget the cups, Martyn. Now we've started on this we'd better have it right out. I can't wait a week." His hands moved to her elbows, anchoring her arms against her sides. He was very close to her, his eyes on her lips, and she felt her heart begin to hammer. Then with a deft and unexpected movement he had her locked hard in his arms and she was being kissed—horribly, savagely, as if he were going to devour her.

Perhaps three seconds passed before she summoned the strength to push him away, and she did so violently, her elbows against his chest. She had strong arms—she hadn't done all that swimming for nothing—and it wasn't so hard. But she was shaking, and she felt sick—sick—and outraged. She knew now, without any doubt, that her answer to any proposition Bastian might make would be, just as that unlikeable man had insisted, a very loud No. If being kissed by a man is so distasteful, then how could you possibly put up with any further intimacies?

Her mind went with a kind of compulsion to the couch that stood against one wall of the attic. A narrow couch where she had sat while he did studies of her for the portrait he had since painted. The bedrooms were downstairs—and she couldn't by any stretch of the imagination see herself being eased down there.

Neither of them had spoken since she pushed herself

free of him, and she could see his chest rising and falling. He was breathing hard and his eyes looked dark, the pupils enlarged. He said with a crooked smile, "I do believe you've just had your first lesson in love, Martyn. I'm sorry. It's a surprise to find anyone quite so pure. Don't be shocked—I was just a bit carried away. I'll be gentler next time, I promise."

Next time? There wasn't going to be a next time, and she had to tell him so. She had been kissed before, of course—by boys she had known up the north coast. But they had been *boys*. His way of kissing—it was quite new to her and it was—horrible, horrible.

She said with an effort, knowing her face had whitened under its tan, that perspiration had broken out on her forehead and upper lip, "I'm sorry, I don't think I could—" She stopped and shook her head and turned away from his eyes that were watching her so closely.

"I've frightened you," he said. "I've spoilt it all, have I? I rather wondered about that. But the only way to find out is to try it. So where do we stand now? If I promise, most faithfully, to teach you more gently in future, do you feel you could move in with me? Or does the secretarial course seem preferable now?"

Martyn forced herself to look at him. He didn't want her to marry him—he had never asked her. That hateful man had been hatefully right. She said a little pathetically, "You don't want to marry me, do you?"

He didn't answer for a moment, then he said deliberately, "I was going to talk to you about that. If you remember, I said we'd lay our cards on the table. I see it this way—and I speak from personal experience. Marriage is a business arrangement. Love is—love. Love is an art. Love is something to be enjoyed. Young people these days recognize and admit this. So—no. I'm certainly not ready to talk about marriage yet. Not when I haven't even made love to you. You're young. You don't want to tie yourself up with anyone yet. If you moved in with me, you'd be quite free—that's a promise. I'm honestly trying to help you out, Martyn to help you to independence and the way of life that suits you. You're hamstrung while you're living with people who want to dictate to you. Free yourself—act grown-up—make the break."

Martyn listened, completely unconvinced. *This* was not the way to make the break. And she wasn't one of the young people who saw marriage as a business arrangement. Marriage meant love too, and as well it was an old tradition. If it needed effort to make it work, then the very effort had its own value. She knew this instinctively and very positively, so she told Bastian what that man had told her to say. She said simply and unequivocally, "No."

His look changed to one of frowning impatience. "So the whole thing's to be over, is it? Just because of one kiss. I suppose you won't trust me now—won't want to come here again, or even meet me on the beach."

"I think it would be better," she said stiffly, knowing he would think her prudish.

"So it's off to the typewriter for you, is it?" he said with faint contempt. "I'd have expected more character from you, Martyn. It's a shame about the drawing. You were a good pupil with a lot of talent. I'd have liked to see it develop."

He paused and she stood with eyes downcast. She had never felt so gauche, so much at a loss. It seemed a crazy thing to have happened, and it had happened so suddenly. She had *liked* him—and she had been happy about their relationship. And now it was ending like this—vanishing as completely as a soap bubble.

She heard him sigh, and looked up, and when he spoke again his voice had lost its derision, its contempt.

"You're not feeling at all grateful to me just now, are you? But one day you may look back and decide I wasn't altogether a villain. It's been a very great temptation having a beautiful young girl like you captive in my attic week after week... Well, go in peace." He flung out his long-fingered hands. "Perhaps you're right. It wouldn't work. For me it would be too close to fantasy. For you—to sordid reality. You want to dream a little longer." He looked at her long and levelly. "Good-bye, Martyn."

He turned abruptly and went back to his work, and she bit her lip. When she said, "Good-bye, Bastian," the words were scarcely audible. She had a feeling of anticlimax—and of unreality. The curtain had come down on a play that had been a lamentable failure. Bastian didn't look up, so she took the tray downstairs, and though she had intended to dump it in the kitchen and disappear as fast as she could—to run, because she felt like running—she didn't. She washed up, wiped out the sink, put everything tidily away. And then, just as on any other day, she went to the foot of the stairs and called out, "I'm going, Bastian." But this time, instead of adding, "I'll see you tomorrow," she called a clear and final, "Good-bye."

He didn't answer. And that was that.

She walked slowly back home from the plateau, and thought about love and about being young, and about acting grown-up and freeing herself, as Bastian had said. But this was no way to go about it. Stan would have told her that. Sooner secretarial school than playing such dangerous games with something as important as love. When it came to love, she had always kept right in the shallows. She'd paddled, innocently. She'd never struck out from shore into the deep waters. Oh, she knew plenty about love—theoretically. She'd listened to girls talking, she'd been to films, read books, had schoolgirl crushes and other crushes that were a little more real. She hadn't been wrapped in cotton wool; she hadn't buried her head in the sand. The thing was, she had never wanted to hand over her body to anyone. Stan had told her long ago, "You respect your body, Bit, and other people will respect it too. That way, you need never be afraid of sex or of love." It was a kindly if rough-and-ready way of giving her a little of the instruction that perhaps her mother would have

given her, and it was something she had always believed in and hung on to.

With Bastian, she reflected, as she walked down the
long hill in the hot sunshine, she had honestly thought
she had an uncomplicated and totally platonic friendship. Without actually putting it into words even in her
thoughts, she had seen him as a sort of older cousin, or
a rather young uncle. That kind of thing. Safe, and to
be trusted. Sex had never come into it—yet it had been
there in his mind all the time. And she had made it so
easy for him to bring it out into the open. Now everything was spoilt. But *not* because she had played around
with an older man, and irrationally she hated that man
who had preached to her and whose advice she had so
quickly and unintentionally taken. She wished now she
had never let him in on her private life.

Back at the bungalow she made herself a sandwich,
drank a glass of milk, then got into her bathing gear.
Not the black cotton, but a pert green swimsuit she had
acquired since coming to Sydney—a present from
Dick. She hopped over the back fence and went across
the sand toward the surf. She felt disturbed and shaken
up, and the sound of the sea was soothing. The beach
was almost deserted and she spread out her towel and
lay face down on it, soaking up the hot, hot sun, determined to keep her mind a blank. She was back with her
predicament, and she could see only one end to it—
Martyn Verity, typist. So she wasn't going to think
about it. Not now.

She fell asleep in the sun, and she didn't know how
much later it was when she awoke. *Something* had wakened her, and she sat up and stared around her and
blinked hard.

There, not twenty feet away, was that man. His back
was towards her, but she recognized him instantly as he
stood there, his muscular torso gleaming bronze against
the turquoise sea.

She sat quite still, hugging her knees and watching
him, as if bemused. After a few seconds he tossed

down his towel and ran down to the surf, the muscles of his back rippling. He waded into the water amongst the few other surfers, dived under a towering wave, and surfaced beyond the rush of white surging foam. Then with a powerful stroke he began to swim out. What a swimmer he was! Despite herself, she was impressed, and illogically irritated.

Without really thinking what she was doing, she refastened the clip that held her blonde hair back from her face, got up and kicked some sand over her towel so it wouldn't blow away, and went into the sea. Soon she too was swimming out beyond the waves, her hair, darkened by the water, sleek against her head, her eyelashes glittering points, the sun striking spangles of light from the sea around her.

Waterbaby? She could handle the ocean as well as he could!

Well out beyond the line of breakers, she paused to look around and locate him. He was swimming away from her, parallel with the shore, and Martyn took a breath, put her head down, and began to chase him, swimming as fast as she knew how. He was a powerful swimmer with a good clean style, but she thought she could catch him up. What her purpose was, she didn't stop to think, but there was some vague idea at the back of her mind about "showing him".

She was within fifteen feet of him when he stopped swimming, trod water, and turned in her direction. Martyn kept her head down, put on a spurt, and glided past him. Then she too trod water and swivelled round blinking the sea from her eyes and staring as if it had just struck her who he was.

"Hi!"

He tossed the thick hair back from his forehad, and those strange grey eyes reached for her across the dazzling water, cynically informing her that she couldn't fool him. Her little act was just too amateurish for a man who could, if he wanted, twist her round his little finger.

"Well, it's the waterbaby," he marvelled, making no attempt to remember her name. "Or should I say mermaid, seeing you're well out of a mere waterbaby's depth? Is our meeting just a happy coincidence, or have you possibly been chasing me?"

Martyn drew a hand across her eyes, partly to dash away the salt water, partly to hide her red face. She said shortly, "What do *you* think?" and tried to imply by her expression that he was flattering himself if he thought she was chasing *him*.

He looked back at her mockingly. "I think you've been chasing me. So what do you want?" His eyes were bright and hard in the sunlight. "To tell me I was right the other day? That you've taken my advice and broken it off with your Lothario? Let's have it quickly. I'm not interested in floundering about here. In thirty seconds I'm swimming back to the shore."

"You can go now if you like," Martyn retorted. "I'm not interested in taking your advice, past, present or future. It just would seem a shame the ocean isn't bigger, wouldn't it? Then we wouldn't have bumped into each other." She did a quick turtle dive, and was soon riding a wave in to the shore and pretending to herself that she didn't feel snubbed. She tumbled to her feet in the shallow water and was about to trudge out on to the sand when he arrived on the next wave, almost at her feet. She waited till he too was upright, and when he made to walk past her she asked aggravatingly, "What's biting you? Why are you so scared of me? Are you married or something?"

He faced her, hands on his hips, his dark chest glistening with water. "I'm not scared of you. I'm not married. I'm not divorced either. Any more questions? No? Right, then get this straight—when I suggested you should forget your Don Juan I wasn't suggesting you should attach yourself to me. Understand?"

"Don't worry, I wouldn't think of it." Martyn was no longer smiling and bright. She was seething and more put out than ever. Why on earth hadn't she stayed in the sun on the sand, where she was warm and comfortable and at peace? She couldn't think what incomprehensible impulse had made her go racing off into the sea thinking she could make an impression with her swimming. But she wasn't going to step down, and as he left the water she walked along near him. She said bitingly, "I suppose even if you're not married, an older man like you might be embarrassed to have a kid like me tramping along at your side like a moth flitting around a flame."

"Not at all." His mouth, which was wide with a rather full lower lip, curved slightly. "I've lived too long to be embarrassed by a little thing like that, mermaid—"

"My name's Martyn," she reminded him coldly. "Martyn Verity."

He shrugged as if he couldn't have cared less. "Go find someone else to play with—preferably your own age. I'm not interested." He had reached the place where he'd left his towel, stooped for it, mopped up his face, tossed it down again and took up his shirt instead— a dark navy one. In the pocket he found cigarettes, a lighter, sunglasses. Martyn, lingering for a parting shot, reminded him with slight triumph, "I thought you were a bit *too* interested yesterday."

He sent her a scathing look, put on his sun-glasses, took a cigarette from the packet, and as he lit it said carelessly, "I gave you some avuncular advice, that's all. Now, on your way, mermaid."

Martyn turned her back on him and marched off.

Next day Bastian didn't appear on the beach. She had watched from the window and she was conscious of a certain sadness that their friendship had ended so needlessly and so abruptly. When she was quite sure he wasn't coming, she walked along the beach by herself, and then she sprawled idly in the sun, the legs of her jeans rolled up, her cheek supported by a cushion of soft warm sand, the sun burning down on her with its steady loving heat. She was smarting from several hurts and yet she thought persistently of a man with black hair and grey eyes and a tanned face who had said, "On your way, mermaid". Who had said he had no taste for waterbabies. Who had thought yesterday that she was chasing him into the sea...

When at last she staggered up to go back home—because she was excruciatingly hungry—her legs and arms and one cheek were freckled with the glistening clinging fragments of shell and coral that made up the golden sand. She looked about her as she swung across the beach, but she didn't see that man. She wondered uneasily if he would be there at Julia Fleet's again, and she told herself she didn't care a jot either way. "He's not my type," she thought decidedly.

Back home, she made herself an enormous salad and added some cold meat left over from last night. She drank her usual glass of milk, and went outside to fetch in her black swimsuit. It was too early yet to leave for the Fleets', so she went to her room and brushed and brushed her hair. She had washed it this morning under the shower, so it was free of salt, soft and silky. She studied her reflection for a moment, then went into Rosalind's room to borrow some of her waterproof eye-shadow and mascara. Just for something to do, she told herself, and looked critically in the mirror to see what difference it made to her appearance. It added a touch of sophistication, she decided, and she could do with *that*.

Ready at last, and too impatient to sit around waiting, she decided to forget the bus and walk up to the plateau, despite the heat.

When she reached the Fleets' house, she went straight to the side garden where the pool was, because by now she was five minutes late and they would be ready and waiting for her.

But they weren't, and she stood stock still and stared.

Mrs. Fleet, Tom and Nanda—none of them were there. But *he* was, sitting in a cane chair wearing white shorts, his brown torso bare; smoking, and leafing through a magazine that looked like *The Land*. He looked up when she appeared, his dark eyebrows lifting.

Martyn swung her beach bag and said carelessly, "You again! Where are Tom and Nanda?"

"Their mother's taken them to Manly to the dentist. Why do you ask?" he said maddeningly.

Martyn's heart jumped a little. Something was wrong! Perhaps one of the children had bad toothache. But— both of them? And they hadn't let her know not to come? She raised her darkened eyebrows slightly. "Why do you think? I'm expecting to give them a lesson."

He smiled faintly and folded his magazine firmly open. "Then someone's slipped up. And I'm afraid it's you."

"What?" Martyn stared at him blankly, trying to take it in. And then the truth struck her—she had come on the wrong day! However had she come to make such a silly mistake? And to have this man witness it. She said idiotically, "What day is it?"

"Do you really not know? Or are you fooling? It's Thursday."

"I thought it was Friday," she said lamely, colouring deeply and furious with herself for the mistake. Particularly as it was plain now he didn't believe her. He made no comment but drew on his cigarette, and she noted abstractedly that he was as deeply and darkly suntanned as anyone she had seen up the coast. Legs and arms that were all muscle, a chest so broad and deep she wouldn't mind betting he could just about swim across the Pacific Ocean and back without drawing a new breath. "You'd have got on with Stan," she thought irrelevantly. But with Martyn Verity—nix! Yet if things had been otherwise—

She jumped when he remarked, "You *are* done up today, aren't you! Like a dog's dinner. I hope you're not drooping those lovely painted lids for my benefit."

"Sorry, not a chance of it," she said tartly. She

looked at the lovely beckoning blue of the pool and sighed frustratedly. No children, no lesson. Without bothering about goodbyes, she began to move off when he said unexpectedly, "The water looks good, doesn't it? Go ahead and have a swim before you leave. Don't let me put you off—what's your name again?"

"Martyn Verity," she said warily, and taken by surprise.

"Well, then, Verity"—it was a deliberate mistake, she was sure—"jump in and cool down and I'll see if I can find you a lemonade."

She smouldered inwardly. Cool down! He was the most aggravating person she had ever met. And offering her lemonade! She said, "My first name's Martyn— M-a-r-t-y-n. And you needn't put yourself out fetching lemonade. I can live without it."

"Fine. Well, the pool's ready and waiting," he reminded her mockingly.

She stood irresolute, unsure of what to do. To about-face would maybe seem childish, and the pool did look inviting. She wouldn't mind a swim.

His eyes flicked over her—the clean off-white jeans, the dark violet hand-crocheted top—a cast-off of Rosalind's, as a matter of fact—that showed her smooth brown shoulders. "You're a ball of muscle, aren't you?" he commented, and returned to his reading.

With a shrug, and slightly disconcerted, Martyn moved away. She might as well have a swim. She had walked all this way for nothing otherwise. The back door of the house was open, and in the bathroom she changed into her black cotton swimsuit. She caught a glimpse of her face in the mirror and looked again. Done up like a dog's dinner! It was hardly flattering— and she didn't think she'd made a bad job of it. She hoped that eye make-up really was waterproof. If it wasn't, she was going to look a sight. But she wasn't going to wash it off and have him laugh to himself. He probably wasn't going to bother watching a kid like her swimming about in a pool.

"I should have just gone home," she thought a little dismally, and wondered why she was letting herself in for this. She wondered too how it had happened she'd come here on the wrong day. That was something she'd never done before. She was uncomfortably sure that Dick, being a psychologist, would find some unpalatable and unacceptable answer to that one. Such as that she really wanted to see the nameless man out there. Which she definitely didn't...

He didn't even look up from his reading when she reappeared. "Great," thought Martyn. She dived into the water and swam up and down several times. Then she swam a couple of lengths underwater. She could hold her breath longer than most girls she knew, and she thought she might even have managed another half a length, but she didn't want to come up spluttering. This time when she emerged, he was watching her for the first time. If her make-up had run, then he was going to make some caustic comment. She pulled herself out on to the tiles and sat, her legs in the water, facing him.

"Not a bad swimmer, are you?" he said. He got to his feet and looked across the corner of the pool at her. "What's the latest bulletin on the love affair? You didn't tell me yesterday."

She blinked with shock at the unexpected question. "There's no bulletin," she said unco-operatively.

"None? Or do you just mean, Mind your own business? I've a good mind to read you another lecture. Maybe I would if you were dressed in something other than that cotton racing costume... Well, I'll see about your lolly water."

He disappeared and after a moment she got up, found her towel, and gave her hair a good rubbing. Then she carefully draped the towel around her shoulders and stood in the sunshine.

When he came back he brought a tray which he deposited on a small white garden table on the lawn. Besides lemonade, he brought a bottle of whisky and a small jug of ice. For himself, of course, not for her. So he was going to drink with her. But if he thought she was going to listen to another berating, then he was mistaken.

He looked over at her. He had got into a dark open-necked shirt while he was away though he still wore the white shorts. "Come on," he ordered. "Sit down. I'll pour your drink."

Martyn stayed where she was. "If you plan on giving me a talking to," she said decidedly, "I'll drink my *lolly water* here—standing up. And then I'll go. I don't want to hear."

His lip curled. "Sit down," he repeated. And as he didn't bring her glass across to her she moved the few paces reluctantly and sat. He fixed his drink, and she swallowed down her lemonade and poured herself another glass, and neither of them said anything. Then he remarked reflectively, "Why don't you find some intelligent and profitable way of filling in time while you're learning about love? Believe me, you've got a long time to wait before you find the right man."

"Really?" She fiddled with her glass and felt her cheeks burning. Here came the lecture! "How would *you* know?"

"How do you suppose? You're not unique—and you're certainly not the first besotted young girl I've been acquainted with. Apart from anyone else, I have three younger sisters who've all gone through the vicissitudes of love."

"I suppose you advised them all," said Martyn sceptically. "And they took your advice and are all now as happy as can be."

He smiled slightly. "I advised two of them," he admitted. "Not Julia who's the wildest and was married before the old man died. But the other two—yes, I gave them some advice on various occasions. One of them is now happily married, the other, Jan, is still having problems."

"Surely you can solve them for her," Martyn suggested pertly. "I'd like to know what makes you such an expert, anyhow—seeing you're not even married. Are you a councillor or something?"

"I'm a cattleman," he said, a glint of hard amusement in his grey eyes. "I'm not an expert on love, but some things are pretty basic. I've had my share of love affairs—one at a time, by the way—and maturity is the greatest teacher of all. As for you, my guess is you're still struggling through the very first primer."

As he finished speaking he got leisurely to his feet, and glancing round, Martyn discovered that someone else had come into the garden. Not Julia Fleet, but a small trim middle-aged woman with dark hair, who was coming towards them with a quick and lively step. Martyn was aware of curiously confused feelings—of slight annoyance at the interruption, because despite herself her imagination was piqued by his statement that he was a cattleman; of relief that she wasn't going to have to battle on with this conversation. She would have fallen off her chair if she had known that this same woman was going to start wheels turning that would change the whole of her future life.

CHAPTER THREE

"You're back early, Poppy," observed the dark man. "How's Jan? Thinking over my suggestions?"

The woman called Poppy gave a little rueful smile. She had a lively, very likeable face, her eyes behind prettily framed glasses were dark brown and intelligent, and before she answered she looked with friendly curiosity at Martyn, who had stood up too.

"Jan wants to come to Diamond Springs with me, now. I'll tell you all about it later... Are you going to introduce me to your friend, Tancred?"

Tancred! Martyn had vague schoolgirl memories of a Tancred who had imprisoned Richard the Lionheart during one of the Crusades, and she wondered briefly if it was a suitable name. She felt a spark of malicious amusement at being referred to as Tancred's friend, but she supposed he would soon straighten out *that* little error.

Only of course he was not sufficiently interested.

He merely said offhandedly, rather surprisingly getting her name right, "This is Martyn Verity. She's been teaching Tom and Nanda to swim, but she came on the wrong day... Martyn, my stepmother, Mrs. Diamond."

Diamond Springs, Tancred Diamond—diamond-hard eyes, thought Martyn abstractedly as he and the older woman smiled at each other. There was something alert and thoughtful in Poppy Diamond's glance at Martyn standing there in her black swimsuit, the striped towel draped across her shoulders and covering her breasts. Then she sank down in one of the cane chairs exclaiming, "Lovely cool drinks! Tancred, I'd love a long, long lime and soda with just the slightest, tiniest dash of gin. I'm feeling absolutely whacked after wrestling with poor Jan and her problems all afternoon."

He said nothing, but disappeared, presumably to fetch the drink. Martyn was thinking, "Jan—that's the sister he mentioned before." She stood irresolute, feeling uncomfortably that she was intruding on a family scene, and that this woman must want to talk to her stepson about his sister. She said politely, "I think I'd better be going, Mrs. Diamond."

"Going? When we've just met? Oh, don't do that. Sit down and tell me about yourself. Did you meet Red here at Julia's?"

Red? Tancred—Red Diamond! He was black rather than Red, thought Martyn—She said, "Yes. And then we met down on the beach, but—" She stopped. That was enough to say. She hoped she wasn't going to be asked if she liked him, or even to agree that he was— well, to agree that he was anything that was in his favour. Because personally she found him infuriating and just too superior for words.

"Now sit down, Martyn. That's an unusual name, by the way. It somehow suits you. Pour yourself another drink. Is it really lemonade?" She sounded amused, and Martyn, remembering her eye make-up, wondered if she was taken for being rather more than nineteen years old. Old enough anyhow for this woman to think she was a friend of Tancred's. More than a mere waterbaby. Adult—and past being satisfied with lemonade.

She said, "Yes, it's lemonade. I've been walking and swimming, and I was thirsty." With sudden honesty she added, regardless of sense or sequence, "He— Red—and I only met on the beach by accident."

Poppy raised her eyebrows slightly and looked amused. "I don't believe in accidents—of that kind. There's usually a bit of planning behind them."

Mine, thought Martyn chagrined. She was the one

who had chased him into the water. But his stepmother presumably took it for granted that any planning had been done by *him*.

"Anyhow," said Poppy, further amused by her obvious embarrassment, "here's Tancred with my drink."

The drink delivered, Red Diamond said, "Excuse me, I'm going in to dress. I'll leave you two to talk. You can tell me about Jan later, Poppy." And he disappeared.

Poppy sipped her drink gratefully. "I'm sorry about this—turning up at the wrong time. You'd reached the stage of talking about an eternally fascinating subject—love."

Martyn coloured. "Not really. He was—your stepson was—just advising me—"

Poppy held up one hand and smiled. "Sh! I don't want to pry... Tell me about this swimming business instead. I never did learn to swim. Is your teaching a full-time occupation or is it a sort of holiday job?"

"Neither really," Martyn admitted. "It's just sort of part-time. It doesn't even earn enough to keep me," she added honestly. And then, without quite knowing how it had happened, she was telling Poppy Diamond about Stan and how she had come to live with Ros and Dick and how she had to find a better way of earning a living very soon.

"The only thing anyone can think of is typing," she confessed, leaning back now and sipping lemonade no longer ice-cold, stretching out her bare brown legs and feeling more at ease. "But—"

"But you're an outdoor girl. Not a city girl?"

"I was brought up on the north coast." A little more encouragement and she was talking about Stan again, and how different life with him had been.

"Ros thinks I've been spoiled—and that I'm a barbarian. And I suppose she's right."

"You're in a period of adjustment," said the older woman when she paused. "Never mind. It will all sort itself out."

"Yes—except I can't wait for that," Martyn agreed. "Ros has given me a week—that's just a few days now— to work something out. I suppose it's fair enough. I have to do something—everyone does. And I expect lots of them do things they don't really want to do. It'll be secretarial school for me," she concluded with a grimace.

"That would be a pity, when you're an athletic type." There was a short pause, then Poppy Diamond looked directly at Martyn. "Would you be at all interested in coming to Diamond Springs?"

"What?" Martyn's blue eyes widened in surprise. She felt flabbergasted. "Diamond Springs?" she repeated uncomprehendingly. A cattleman, she thought—

"Red must have told you that the Diamonds are outback people—cattle station owners."

"Sort of," said Martyn faintly. It began to strike her as faintly funny that she was being invited to Diamond Springs, in the circumstances. It was a good thing Red was not present to hear it!

Poppy Diamond had narrowed her brown eyes as if she were thinking, and while those eye were not actually focused on Martyn, it was as if they were intent on her in some peculiar way and the girl moved uncomfortably.

"Yes, I think I have a plan that could possibly suit us both. Admirably. Though of course it's no use if the very thought of the outback horrifies you. Does it?"

"Of course not," said Martyn rashly. She had never been far away from the sea, but outback was a magical work, and no matter what her other thoughts, it was one that sent prickles of excitement running up and down her spine. It was just a pity it had to be associated in any way with Red Diamond. "It doesn't horrify me at all."

"Well then." Poppy paused for thought again. "I'm planning to spend three or four weeks at Diamond Springs. Would that be a breathing space for you—long enough for you to work something out to suit yourself? I'd try to help too," she promised.

Martyn frowned. "It's very kind of you, but—but I don't see why you should bother about me. Besides—" She stopped. Why bring her hostile relationship with Red into it?

"I'm not being entirely altruistic," Poppy assured her. "I'm being logical too. Believe me, I think things out, and I think them quickly. It's one of my few strong points. I'll explain... You heard Red asking about his sister—"

"Jan?"

"Yes. He may have told you she's been in a motor accident, and that she's broken off her engagement. Now she wants to come home to Diamond Springs—to get away from it all, and to recuperate. She's round about your age—twenty-one—and she needs young company. Her leg is not all that bad and the doctor confirms that one of the best ways of rebuilding the muscle is swimming. Well, she can swim at Diamond Springs— there's a good pool there—but how much swimming is she likely to do on her own? Red's busy, and I'm just not a swimmer—I'd drown if I fell into two inches of water. The only time I cross a river is when there's a drought. So do you see? She's set on coming outback, and if you would come too, it might stop us all from going bananas—you with your problem, me with mine, making it all possible for Jan. Isn't that logic?"

It was, of course. But it was still impossible. Martyn said, "But you don't know a thing about me."

"Now come *on*! When you've been telling me all about yourself for the past ten minutes—when Julia trusts you with her children! When you and I are so obviously *simpatico*! No, Martyn, I'm a woman who makes quick decisions about people and I'm seldom wrong."

"But—" began Martyn helplessly.

"No buts. You'll never persuade me you're a doubtful character. Not with those ultra-honest eyes. And I'll tell you something else, Martyn. I married Red's father eleven years ago, and do you know how long I'd known him? I'd met him exactly twice. Once was at a picnic race meeting, the second time was the day after a dinner party. And neither of us had a single regret in the five years of married life we shared. And all I'm trying to point out in telling you that is that I'm quite capable of making a quick and accurate judgment of character... Anyhow, think it all over, will you? When will you be here again?"

"Tomorrow. It's the last lesson."

"Tomorrow, then," said Poppy with finality. "I'm not giving you a week—just a day's long enough. And I hope you'll say yes." When Red came back a minute later she remarked, "You've taken your time, Tancred. Never mind—Martyn and I have really got to know each other, haven't we, Martyn? You'd be surprised."

Martyn felt too stunned to answer. Poppy's invitation had really put her in a spot. Of course she wanted to go to the outback, and yet her conscious mind warned her darkly, "With that man there? Never! It would *never* do." She felt those *diamond*-bright eyes on her, and she wondered if they were hostile or merely sceptical. She raised her eyes to meet his gaze fully and could almost hear his question—"What have you been up to while I've been away?" But all he said was a laconic, "If you run along and make yourself decent, I'll drive you home, Martyn."

It was the first time he had actually called her Martyn, and it gave her a peculiar sensation. Though she couldn't think why it should be so.

She wondered as she changed out of her swimsuit if Poppy—Poppy? Mrs. Diamond!—was at this very minute telling him all about her brilliant idea. Well, he would quash it, for sure. But she would get in first—he wasn't going to dictate to her, to win another victory. She would tell Poppy she had decided she couldn't come, and she would tell her today—before she left. She didn't care a cent if Red Diamond realized her refusal was on account of him. On the contrary, in fact. She thought briefly of Jan—the motor accident, the broken engagement, the swimming that would help her injured leg. But she couldn't possibly do it, worse luck. Because the outback—well, it would have been fascinating to go there.

Dressed, she flicked a comb through her now dry hair and fastened it back. The make-up was as good as new, and she looked easily twenty-one. Poppy had thought that. She liked Poppy, and that was a shame too. It would have been nice to be able to help.

When she went back outside, he was waiting for her, but Poppy had simply disappeared, so Martyn had no chance of voicing the refusal she had planned. In no time at all she was alone in the car with Red, being driven home.

He didn't waste any time at all in letting her know that Poppy had let him in on her bright idea—or in giving her his opinion on the subject.

"You told me an hour ago there's no bulletin on your current amour. Now I don't know what the hell that meant, but this new idea of dropping everything and falling in with my stepmother's impulsive plans— storming the outback—that's utterly out of the question. Just what's in your mind? I assure you there's no amusement in store for you at Diamond Springs. You'd better tell my stepmother tomorrow that you're not coming."

He hadn't looked at her at all, he simply talked fast and drove fast, down towards the sea.

Martyn had already made up her mind that she couldn't go to Diamond Springs—simply because it would mean putting up with *him*. But she certainly wasn't going to let him tell her what to do. She wasn't dense, and she had the distinct impression that he imagined she had ideas of amusing herself with him. He had already accused her of chasing him into the sea and warned her not to attach herself to him. Well, he appeared to have an opinion of his own attractions that was just too conceited for words. He wasn't even what you would call good-looking! He was too dark and tough—certainly not the type of man she would ever dream about. If he didn't like waterbabies, nor did she like big-headed cattlemen. It was a pity, though, that she had ever been silly enough to blurt out so gratuitously that Bastian Sinclair wanted to marry her. That had really got her offsides with him!

She drew a deep breath and told him with all the composure she could muster, "Here's what's in my mind, Mr. Diamond. Or rather, who is. And that's your sister Jan. She's the one and only reason I could just possibly consider coming to Diamond Springs. You see, swimming just happens to be great exercise for people in all sorts of conditions, if properly supervised. It's not too strenuous, because water supports the body. It's the one thing I know backwards, and if swimming's needed to help your sister recover from her accident, then this could be just the—intelligent time-filler you said I needed, couldn't it?" She sent him a triumphant glance and concluded, "I know you think I'm a silly kid with nothing in my head but love affairs, but even a big-time cattleman can't always be right."

There was a second's silence. "So it would seem," he said. "However, you could have spared me the pseudo-scientific speechifying." Then—"You look like emerging as something of an enigma. I find it difficult to make sense of you."

"I'm not asking you to make sense of me," retorted Martyn, feeling she had really scored a point this time. "We just aren't—*simpatico*, are we?" she added bitingly.

"You express my thoughts exactly," he agreed lightly. "Unfortunately, I can't see you keeping altogether out of my way at Diamond Springs—you won't be spending all your time at the billabong. So do me a favour, will you, and tell my stepmother no."

By now they had reached the point where he would let Martyn out of the car, and her hand was ready on the door. As she got out, she said offhandedly, "No is your favourite word for me, isn't it? Sorry—I'm not particularly interested in doing you a favour—you're not the one I'm aiming to please... Thanks for the lift. Good-bye." And without a backward glance, she walked quickly towards the bungalow.

What a positively detestable man, she thought. The calm, arrogant way he had told her to say No—for the second time—made her almost determined to say yes, just to aggravate him. After all, Poppy had asked her along mainly for Jan's sake. The fact that it would also, temporarily at least, be helpful to Martyn was only of secondary importance. Yet to go would, in a way, be cutting off her nose to spite her face. She didn't think she could put up for long with that man even in very small doses.

Well, she would think it through carefully and reasonably, weighing all the pros and cons, after dinner. She would take a calming walk by the sea, and there she would get the whole thing into perspective and decide what it was worth to her. She had always loved walking by the sea at night, hearing the softened roar of the waves as they creaped stealthily in over the sands— gently, peacefully, after their restless flaunting power of the day. She loved to feel the softness of the night air flowing over her limbs and face, and to see the stars hanging in the darkness of the heavens, remote and mysterious and beautiful as they had been before man had learned too much and landed on the moon.

But as it happened, she didn't do any quiet thinking after dinner. Unexpectedly, her mind was made up for her when her brother came into the kitchen to dry the dishes for her.

She had a feeling Rosalind had sent him along—to finalize things. She had been very conscious during dinner that she was an intruder in the house, a positive pain in the neck to Ros, who could probably visualize her staying for ever and ever. She sympathized with Ros quite heartily and wished herself free and independent, and years and years older. Unfortunately, she had never been the sort of girl who is ready at eighteen to kiss her parents goodbye and go out into the world. All in all, she thought it had been pretty noble of Ros to put up with her so long. But the irritations were beginning to surface now, and tonight she had been home too late, and the *pot-au-feu* had not been properly cooked. Now to explain that she had mistaken the day and gone to give a swimming lesson that was scheduled for tomorrow?

"Well, Bit," Richard said with a kind of cheerful determination, "have you made any weighty decisions about this career of yours? It just won't do for you to continue with this aimless, lazy life, you know."

Martyn listened to him a little regretfully. She thought that, if she could get to know him well, she would quite like this brother of hers. But it wasn't going to advance their relationship if she stayed here too long.

She admitted, "I haven't really, Dick. I'm sorry. I know that the swimming's not enough, but apart from that and drawing and helping at the baths, I don't seem to have any particular talents."

He frowned slightly. He had a rather austere and scholarly face—not in the least like Stan's—but there was a little softness, and a lot of concern—for Ros? for her?—in his blue eyes. He said briskly, "Neither swimming nor drawing's going to make a living for you. I think we'll just have to make your mind up for you. And I'm pretty sure you'll find that after all there's nothing so deadly dull about secretarial work. There are lots of jobs to choose from, and I'll possibly be able to wangle something interesting for you one way or another. So what do you say? Shall we arrange for you to start next week, if possible?"

"No." Martyn said it so determinedly that she gave even herself a start. "I don't want to do typing. How would you have liked it if Stan had said you had to be a—a plumber, or a dentist or something, when you wanted to be a psychologist?" He was staring at her as if she had suddenly changed into a hobgoblin or something, and she hurried on, "But don't worry, I won't bug you any longer than I can possibly help. I'll think of something, and in the meantime, I've—I've been invited to stay at a cattle station, anyhow."

"Who on earth by?" he exploded. "What's this all about? Now look here, Bit, what have you been up to all day on your own?"

Martyn bit her lip. "It's too late to go into all that now, isn't it?" she said thinking of Bastian and the bother she *could* have struck there, in her innocence. Then at the alarm in his face, she reassured him, "But it's perfectly all right, Dick. Don't get apoplectic. I've been invited outback by the grandmother of some kids I've been teaching, that's all."

"*Is* it all?" Richard looked quite fierce. "Well, before you start making any arrangements, I'd like to meet this grandmother and find out what it's all about. You're not in search of a holiday, you know, Bit. We're trying to bring you down to earth."

"But too quickly," Martyn protested. Now she had said she was going outback, she knew she wouldn't go back on it. Her mind was made up, and Red Diamond could go jump in the lake or the billabong or the dam, or something, if he didn't like the idea of her "storming" his cattle station. "I know I'm a problem to you, Dickie. I suppose I'm just—slow at growing up, but I can't help it. I can't sort it all out in a few days, and I *do* want to get out of Ros's hair—" Suddenly there were tears in her eyes despite her defiance, and Richard, who naturally had more feeling for her than his wife, softened at once.

He said clumsily, "Don't cry about it, Bit. It's a pity you don't fit in with us, but you just don't and that's all. So as long as I meet this woman and can be sure there's no funny business—"

Martyn dried her eyes and smiled a little. "There's absolutely no funny business, Dick." She didn't really think Red Diamond would qualify as "funny business"!—and anyhow, he simply didn't come into her plans, and when she talked further to Dick about the reason why she had been invited to Diamond Springs, she didn't even give him a mention...

To her relief, he wasn't there the following day when she went to Julia Fleet's. Poppy was delighted she had decided to accept her invitation and agreed to come and meet Rosalind and Richard the next day, and plans were outlined. Tuesday Poppy would pick her up at the bungalow to go to Kingsford Smith airport. Poppy would arrange the flight and the expense would be hers.

"Bring enough clothes for a month, and remember it will be hot and you'll be doing lots of swimming—and some riding too, if you'd care to." Martyn didn't mention Red and his injunctions not to come. He might be the boss of the cattle station, but this was between her and Poppy. Diamond Springs, Poppy told her was way out west. "Too far from the coast, really. After my husband died, I left Red in charge—well, he'd taken over a year previously, really—and came to Sydney with the girls. Julia was married but Belinda was at university and Jan was still at school, and I reckoned they needed me more than he did. You can imagine—Red wouldn't want an organizing stepmother around the place. He's a very competent man," she added, and Martyn forbore to comment.

Ros and Richard were both impressed by Poppy Diamond, though Ros made the point that this was to be a breathing space only for Martyn, who when she came back would have to knuckle down to secretarial school if she hadn't found any suitable alternative. Poppy listened seriously, and said she was sure everything would work out satisfactorily.

"She's a nice woman. Sensible too," Rosalind remarked when Poppy had gone. "You're lucky, Bit—and lucky we're letting you go off on a holiday like this. Because for sure it's going to be more holiday than work. I wonder who runs Diamond Springs?" She paused, and Martyn shrugged as if she hadn't a clue. "I just hope you might meet some nice uncomplicated outdoor type there, and get married. That would solve everyone's worries, wouldn't it?"

Martyn supposed it would, but she couldn't see it happening. Besides, after her brief experience with Bastian, she didn't really think she was ready for love and marriage. Red Diamond was right—she had years to wait for the right man, and she liked it that way. She didn't care how slowly she was developing. Her main problem was going to be how to fill in the years between, and she thought for the first time in days of that children's book she used to talk about. *Not* an acceptable alternative to knuckling down to hard work, of course.

Ros and Richard had rather alarmingly decided Martyn should have some new clothes, as she had nothing sophisticated at all apart from a few of Ros's cast-offs, and though she protested, Rosalind took Monday off from work and accompanied her to town. There, her sister-in-law selected clothes for Martyn that she considered suitable for the country, and Martyn wondered secretly if she would ever feel at home in them. She was quite sure she would never wear either of the two pretty semi-evening dresses. She had the uneasy feeling that Ros had that "uncomplicated outdoor type" very much in mind, particularly when she insisted Martyn should have her hair professionally styled at a hairdressing salon—for the first time in her life.

She hardly recognized herself with her shorter, sleeker, cleverly cut hairstyle. Was this *blonde* the waterbaby from the north coast? It had been no use protesting that it was all costing too much. "Your father left you a little money, Bit—you're not completely penniless," she was reminded.

"Maybe I should have told Poppy no," she thought once or twice. But it was too late now, and besides, it would have been straight off to secretarial school, and as well, she'd have stayed under Ros's feet. Everyone was more pleased with her this way.

Everyone, that is, but Red Diamond. She didn't expect *he* would be exactly delighted when she turned up with Poppy and Jan.

Tuesday morning after Ros and Richard had wished her a happy time and gone to work—and reminded her to lock up carefully—she spotted Bastian and Becky on the beach, and on an impulse went over the fence to say goodbye. Bastian stared when he saw her in the pretty faded-rose knitted cotton dress that Ros had instructed her she was to wear on the flight.

"Martyn! You're bewilderingly beautiful. And your hair—you've had four inches cut off it. But what style! What's happened in your life that you're suddenly so grown up! I'm prepared to believe you've taken up fashion modelling."

Martyn felt embarrassed at what she saw in his eyes. Covetousness. Desire. And she would die of horror if he kissed her good-bye. She said quickly, keeping her distance while even Becky stared in puzzlement instead of jumping up, "I'm going away. I thought I'd say good-bye. I've got a sort of job in the country—a temporary one. Teaching a girl to swim," she added, simplifying it so he would not start asking questions.

He was still looking at her. "I've missed you. When you come back, look me up, won't you? Both of us might be interested in love, marriage, by then. I'm an emotional cripple at the moment, having just finished with one marriage."

And another love affair? she wondered, even while she told him, "I don't want to get married for years and years."

"If you should change your mind, think of me then. Give me first option," he said lightly, and added, "You're lovely! Really lovely. Do I get a good-bye kiss?"

She said awkwardly, "I'd rather not," and wondered

what had made her force this encounter. To try herself
out in her new guise? She didn't like the thought. "I
have to go—I haven't finished my packing and I
mustn't leave my bedroom in a mess."

It was a relief to get away, and yet she thought about
him when she was safely back at the bungalow. He had
looked at her differently—*so* differently. As if she were
a woman with—she sought for words to express. A
woman with a woman's power. Whereas before she had
been completely at his mercy. But she wasn't a woman.
She didn't have a woman's power. It was all on the outside. Clothes, a new hairstyle, make-up. Inside she was
as unsophisticated as ever. She still didn't know the first
thing about love, and she knew *his* kisses couldn't teach
her that...

When the taxi came at last, Poppy Diamond was the
sole passenger. Without being entirely aware of it, she
had been tensed up to face Red and Jan, and it was a
relief as well as an anticlimax when they were not
there. Poppy confessed to hating flying, and was all
nerves, and though in the taxi Martyn babbled with determined cheerfulness about her new clothes and her
excitement and so on, she knew that the other woman
took in scarcely a syllable of it. At Kingsford Smith airport, once they had checked in their luggage—Poppy
had two suitcases, both of them surprisingly large, Martyn one, brand new, very smart, and bought yesterday—
they went for coffee.

Poppy swallowed down a tablet with hers. "It will
make me dopey, but it can't be helped. I can't face the
trip without it. I hope you're a good air traveller, Martyn."

For Martyn Verity, this was the first air trip she had
ever made, but now didn't seem quite the time to admit it, so she merely smiled and said, "You don't have
to worry about me—I'll be perfectly okay."

It was not till some time after they were airborne and
Poppy was dozing—or appeared to be—that Martyn got
round to thinking about Jan and Red again. They must

have left a day or so earlier, but she was determined not to spoil her enjoyment of the flight by thinking about the meeting ahead of her. With Red, of course. She was looking forward to meeting Jan and making friends with her. She couldn't possibly by anything like her brother!

Looking down from the air she marvelled at her first ever sight of anywhere from this high up. It was fantastic. First there had been the sea, sparkling, blue, patterned like fish scales, as the plane flew east; then they wheeled around to fly west over the city, then over a floor of white cloud and across the ranges and the tablelands. Finally the plains, incredible flatness and emptiness, fewer and fewer signs of habitation. Martyn looked down, reading rivers from lines, scrub from dots, homesteads from tiny cubes, towns from glittering iron roofs. The sea was hundreds of miles away, and she wondered if she was going to miss it terribly.

At last they put down at an outback airfield, and from there they had to take a feeder flight. Poppy was groggy and uncommunicative and able only to stagger from one aircraft to the other, and Martyn felt sorry for her. For her part, she was feeling on the tips of her toes—elated, excited, amazed at her own good fortune. The *outback*! And here it was, first of all, around them in the hot dry air that was so different from the moist coastal air; in the small isolated airfield, and then below them again after they had boarded the little feeder plane. It was a fairly smooth ride, but Poppy looked sick and kept her eyes closed, and Martyn wasn't able to ask her any questions about the country they were passing over where away below, on red earth patched with green and grey, she could see the thin silver line of a river, the shimmer of a dam, the red or silver-roofed buildings in their surrounds of toy trees that were homesteads.

Something in her heart began to sing. She had forsaken the sea, her first love, for this adventure, and it was going to be wonderful, in spite of everything. Everything meaning Red Diamond.

They came down in the middle of nowhere—or so one would have thought. Though Martyn had seen a tiny town—a straggle of houses with galvanized iron roofs that glittered in the sun—and the red ribbon of a road.

Poppy opened her eyes as the plane bumped to a standstill. "Thank God that's over!" And then it was no time till they were out in the sizzling heat and a big dark man was striding across to meet them. Red. Martyn's heart beat out a small tattoo of apprehension.

He kissed his stepmother briefly on the cheek and looked at Martyn twice as if checking who she was. The first time with interest, foxed, she thought, by the dress and four inches off her straw-coloured hair; the second time with animosity and cold condemnation. He gave her an unsmiling nod and then proceeded to ignore her.

"Are you all right, Poppy? You don't look *quite* as green as usual... My God, whose is all this luggage?" His raised brows and silver sharp glance told Martyn he thought it was hers, and she said quickly, defensively, "I've just the one case—I'll take it."

"Oh, the brand new one," he said sardonically. "The honeymoon one." His eyes, screwed up in the fiercely bright sunlight, flicked over her as urgently as naked blades, and he remarked so that only she could hear it, for Poppy was moving groggily ahead, "And you're done up to match it, aren't you, Martyn Verity?"

She crimsoned and hated him. He looked broader, bigger, darker than she remembered, and his thick black hair gave him a barbaric air. No, she thought, he certainly didn't have film-star looks. He was horribly tough and hard. Jan, she presumed, had been left behind at the homestead. Ignoring his gibe, she asked, "Do we have far to drive?"

"Forty odd miles." He added, "You certainly made up your mind to get here, didn't you?"

"I certainly did," she agreed, her head up. "Everyone doesn't have to take your advice, you see."

Poppy was waiting and now they had reached his car—a station wagon. Red allocated the seats, Poppy in the front—"I want to talk to you about Jan"—Martyn in the back. Well, that suited Martyn, who was now feeling really jumpy and on edge. It was the unpleasant effect Red Diamond had on her. She hoped he wasn't going to make life miserable for her just because she hadn't been intimidated by him. She was going to listen to what they said in the front seat, anyhow, and she didn't care if he knew it. Anything about Jan must be of interest to her, since the object of her coming here was to be helpful.

They didn't talk at all at first. Poppy was leaning back against the seat and had asked for ten minutes' peace to settle her nerves. Martyn stared out at the scenery. Red earth, gum trees, plains that stretched to infinity. A sun that had a different brilliance from the sun at the coast, because here it was reflected back from a different coloured landscape. The road was rough, and it was a long time before she saw any cattle at all. Once there was a river—wide, with sloping red banks shaded by great gum trees. The road went straight across, and the brown water splashed coolly and noisily up around the station wagon. A few dragonflies darted about, and some white cockatoos flew against the blue of the sky, and finally Poppy sat up straight and ran her fingers through her hair and sighed. The man beside her remarked almost at once, "Feeling better?" Then, "I took it for granted you'd have come unaccompanied."

Martyn didn't hear the first part of the Poppy's reply, only, "I'm always better not travelling alone, Red. You know that."

Martyn saw him shrug his broad shoulders. Her cheeks were burning.

"Well, how about Jan?" he said after a moment.

Martyn moved fractionally forward in her seat. If she was going to be any use to Jan, then the more she knew about her the better, so she was going to listen hard.

She very soon discovered that she wasn't going to be any use at all, and that she didn't need to know even one tiny little thing about Jan Diamond.

Because Jan wasn't at Diamond Springs, and she wasn't coming.

CHAPTER FOUR

MARTYN'S blood ran cold. No Jan, no reason for Martyn Verity to have come to Diamond Springs.

Red had known, Poppy had known, but Martyn had not been told. She simply couldn't understand it. Why hadn't Poppy telephoned, or come to the bungalow and explained that she wasn't needed after all? Instead, she had simply arrived in the taxi, watched her and her luggage being loaded in, talked about the disagreeableness of air travel, and uttered not a single word about altered plans.

And Martyn had made an utter fool of herself with her pert report to Red's unfriendly greeting.

Now here she was, an unwelcome, useless visitor to his domain. And she knew exactly what he must be thinking. She was chasing him—first into the ocean, now to the outback. It would be no use protesting, "I came for Jan's sake".

What had happened, she gathered from her eavesdropping—if it could be called that—was that Jan's engagement was on again. She had seen the doctor—"after that stern lecture you gave her before you left, Tancred"—and this time she hadn't been over-emotional or refused to listen. She was convinced now she was going to be neither deformed nor a cripple, and when Barry turned up she at last agreed to see him. Result—she was wearing her ring again, and had gone off to Terrigal to stay with him and his parents, where she would have plenty of sun and sea and swimming and love, and be whole, body and mind, in no time.

Red listened to Poppy's recital in almost complete

silence. "So—happy ending," Poppy concluded, and he nodded.

"When she rang that it was all on again I was relieved, but I'm glad to have the details. Barry's a good bloke—definitely the man for Jan. I told her that, and confidentially, I told Barry too."

Martyn in the back seat kept perfectly silent. She was glad that everything was ending happily for Jan, even though she didn't know the girl personally. But what she felt most keenly about was her own false position. The thought of that made her grit her teeth.

Poppy turned round and rested one arm along the back of the seat. She looked a better colour now, and she smiled brightly as she said, "Sorry for excluding you, Martyn. I was just bringing Red up to date about Jan. Are you all right there?"

"Yes, thank you," said Martyn stiffly. She thought, "You could have brought *me* up to date too—before it was too late." Why hadn't Poppy done that? And how on earth was she going to put in three or four weeks on Diamond Springs? Her heart sank at the prospect.

Somewhere along the line they went through gates and along a double red track that crossed an enormous paddock. Away off under some trees, Martyn saw cattle, and then there was another gate—horses—and beyond, on a slight rise, the homestead sheltering amongst trees, with a straggle of buildings a little way off where, she presumed, the stockmen and station hands must be quartered.

She didn't know what sort of a homestead she had pictured, but this one was long and low, green-roofed, and surrounded by a very wide, open verandah with insect screens all round.

Someone came down from the verandah as they all moved from the car to the house—a grey-haired woman with a weather-worn face, who embraced Poppy and was introduced to Martyn as Mrs. Hall, the housekeeper. The two women went ahead talking into the house, and Martyn was left to follow with Red, who was carrying one of his stepmother's suitcases, and hers. She walked a little away from him, uneasy and resentful. She felt a fool, but she wasn't going to start protesting innocence. He could think what he liked. He'd soon discover she wanted as little as possible to do with him.

He said coldly, "As Jan wasn't coming, we weren't expecting you, so we don't have a room ready, but Mrs. Hall will soon get one of the girls to make up the bed. Fortunately, we do have several empty bedrooms."

Martyn swallowed, and said equally coldly, "May I please have one a long way from yours?" and was only a little ashamed of her own rudeness.

"Certainly," he said crisply. She followed him round the verandah. "We'll put your things in here. It's the best I can do for distance. Tidy yourself up—hang up your clothes when you get them out of that beautiful honeymoon suitcase. There's a bathroom along the hall if you want to freshen up. We'll expect you on the verandah for a drink when you're ready. Are you sticking to lemonade or have you promoted yourself to stiff drinks?" His grey eyes quizzed her ironically.

She looked back at him for an instant, and she didn't see anything in his face that resembled in the slightest degree Bastian's expression when he had seen her in the faded-rose—and very expensive—outfit she now wore. For Red Diamond she certainly wasn't a woman with a woman's power. She was just an obnoxious—kid—whom he positively disliked.

She said with an attempt at bravado, "To celebrate this particular occasion—yes, I think I'll promote myself to stiff drinks."

He smiled slightly, cynically, and left her alone.

She didn't change. One thing she did, though, and that was take off her sheer tights. It was just too killingly hot in them. Then she went along to the bathroom for a wash. There was a clean face towel there and she removed the make-up she had put on earlier in the day—for what reason she could not now imagine. It was a fresh-looking, modern bathroom, everything was spotless. She thought it must be a second bathroom—a guests' bathroom. Somehow she hadn't thought there would be such things on a cattle station. There certainly hadn't been in the tiny timber residence at the swimming baths, where she had lived with Stan! She felt a little afraid about what she had inadvertently let herself in for, and wondered if she would possibly be able to leave in a few days. If she did, what an ovation she would get from Ros and Richard, she *didn't* think! Especially when they had laid out all that money on her wardrobe—in hopes of the uncomplicated outdoor type she might meet!

Well, it was her money in a way, but seeing she had lived with them for over two months, she didn't really think they owed her anything. Dick had said earlier, "We'll keep your money as a nest egg for you, Bit. Then when you need it, for training, or for anything special or extraordinary that arises, it will be there." She thought her nest egg must have been diminished somewhat by this spending spree Ros had taken her on—for a special occasion!

When she came back from the bathroom it was almost dark and she had to grope for the light switch in the bedroom. She looked around the room for the first time. Muted blue bedspread and curtains, off-white walls, vinyl flooring in a pale pretty floral pattern, two simple string-coloured rugs. Funny after the rough and tumble with Stan up the coast, and the small room it had been a battle to keep tidy in Richard's house.

She went out to the verandah and walked around, and when she found a lighted area she was relieved to find Poppy there alone. That man, who figured in her mind like some dark devil, wasn't in evidence. She said immediately, "Mrs. Diamond, why didn't you tell me Jan wasn't coming? If I'd known, of course I wouldn't have come."

Poppy was leaning back in a long chair of fine cane, looking very civilized and very composed—which she had not looked during the journey. She said wryly, "Yes, that's why I didn't tell you. It *was* a little bit underhand of me, but I know you're going to love the outback, and you struck me at once as being just the girl for—" She paused fractionally and then went on, "For this sort of life. You'll soon discover the spell the country puts on you." She smiled persuasively at Martyn who stood with her back against the verandah rails, feeling on edge because she knew that Red would soon appear.

"Besides," said Poppy, "the idea was to be helpful to you too, wasn't it? You still have your little problem to solve."

"Yes, but it's not *your* problem. You don't really *know* me, Mrs. Diamond, and Red—"

"Please call me Poppy," the other woman interrupted. "And don't worry about Red. We'll all soon get to know each other—though I feel I know you already.... Anyhow, I like to have another woman around the homestead when I'm here. It's good for Red, too. That's one reason I visit every so often, and I generally bring someone along."

Martyn wasn't convinced. Mrs. Hall was here, and Poppy appeared to be on very good terms with her. She couldn't pretend to herself that having *her* here was going to be good for Red, and she wondered fleetingly who else Poppy had brought.

When Red appeared with sherry, she accepted a glass, ignored him, and looked out into the darkness. Dinner was ready so they didn't linger, and the meal was bearable because Poppy talked. About what, Martyn hardly knew. She was worried and she was tired and confused, though the sherry had picked her up a little. Poppy talked about somewhere called Jindi-yindi— "That place has a hex on it," she said. She talked about the extraordinary rains that had fallen in the past few weeks.

"Luckily we didn't get too much," Red said. "parts of Jindi-yindi were just about swamped out."

"I told you there's a hex on it. It's a place I'd leave *strictly* alone if I were you, Red."

To Martyn, it sounded singularly like a challenge, but Red didn't answer it. His eyes sought her out across the table fleetingly, and then he told Poppy, "It's quite like old times, isn't it?"

There was a tiny silence.

"What do you mean?" Poppy said.

He raised his dark eyebrows. "When Jan and Linda came home for holidays, wasn't there always an extra girl or two as well?"

"Well, what's so wrong with that? There's not much company here. It's good for you."

His eyes glittered and Martyn looked away. She thought, chilled and appalled, "Girls invited here for *his* benefit—"

"What became of that last desperately eager girl, by the way?"

He reached across for the coffee jug, very casually, as he spoke. "What was her name? Very pretty—very sexy. Stephanie Gray?"

"That's it," Poppy agreed. "She's married now. But I'm surprised you even ask. I thought you hadn't liked her."

The corners of his mouth lifted slightly in amusement. "Now come on, how could I have helped liking her? Your trouble is, you expect too much—love to order, wedding bells—and after all, she was never *my* guest, was she?"

His stepmother blinked in annoyance. "Oh, guests! Must we always put everyone into compartments?"

He smiled crookedly. "That's something I rather thought *you* liked doing... I hope you've made plans for entertaining Martyn, anyhow. I'll be out tomorrow, by the way. I haven't had an opportunity up till now for going over to Jindi-yindi, and it's something I must do."

"Then that'll do for entertainment for a start," said Poppy promptly. "You can take Martyn and me with you."

"Not me." Martyn almost said it aloud but not quite, it would sound too rude. But how on earth was she going to spend the days now that Jan was not here? And now that she no longer felt she could trust Poppy Diamond who was always inviting girls along for Red's benefit? What on earth had she let herself in for? She squirmed at the thought of how she had arrived complete with new hairdo, pretty clothes, smart travelling case, and she eyed Red covertly through her lashes. He was so sure she was chasing him, but oh no! She would be scared stiff to do *that*. She was willing to bet that anything Bastian had handed out was nothing—but nothing!—compared with what she'd get from this tough man if she ever got tangled up with him.

Meanwhile, he hadn't bothered answering Poppy's suggestion that he should take them with him to Jindi-yindi, wherever that was. He merely said cryptically, "I thought you didn't like *That Lot*, Poppy."

Martyn had pushed back her chair. The meal was over, and she badly wanted to escape. She said awkwardly, "Can I go and help with the washing up?"

Red looked at her quizzically. "The girls will see to that. Forget about making yourself useful. There's nothing for you to do—not a thing." His eyes mocked her and she coloured furiously.

"Martyn has a problem," Poppy interjected quickly. "A *personal* problem to sort out. Haven't you, Martyn?"

Yes, there was that, she remembered almost with a shock. But she didn't want to air that just now, so she nodded and quickly excused herself. "Do you mind if I go to bed early? I'm tired, and—" She stopped. *He* was looking at her so—sceptically, so inimically, it was almost more than she could stand. She heard herself say with a rush, "And I don't particularly want to go to Jindi-yindi tomorrow, thank you very much... Goodnight." She turned away and left the room and found she was on the verge of tears. *Why?* Because she had been made a fool of... *What* a fool! And she had liked

Poppy! But Poppy had been treacherous. It was not really a fair criticism, she knew, but just now it was how she felt—let down. Her pride pricked. Well, she'd get over it.

In her room, the bed had been made up, there were two big fluffy towels, and in a vase on the dressing table some hardy yellow and white and pink wild-flowers with prickly leaves.

One thing she didn't have new was pyjamas. Just the thin old striped cotton ones she had worn up the north coast. They were familiar and comforting, and when she'd got into them she felt more herself and she went to stand on the verandah and look out at the dark. It was her lucky night, because a big cheese-coloured moon was just rising over the plains and flooding the land with soft golden light. It was very silent and lonely and just a little bit like looking at the sea when the moon made a path across the waters. When she was a child, she used to think you could walk across it, using the black flecks as stepping stones. Tonight there was no shining path, but there was all that beautiful awe-some light spreading out and out, and there were sounds that she didn't know. Not the hush-hush-hush of the waves, but a weird owl's cry, the howling of a wild dog far away, the lowing of cattle. And a sound like a drum, isolated, vibrant.

She wasn't even aware of it when someone came walking along the verandah till Red Diamond's voice said dryly, "Romantic, isn't it? I can guess the kind of thoughts that are going through your mind."

"Can you?" she said sarcastically. She had shed a few tears, but they had dried on her cheeks. "I'll give you a check list if you like."

"Spare me that, for God's sake." He was beside her now, but not too close, and he lit a cigarette. In the glow of the lighter she could see his eyes on her, hard unamused, assessing. The last because of her schoolgirl pyjamas, she supposed.

She ran her fingers through her hair and said nervily,

"I'd rather you knew than have you guessing. I was just regretting I ever came here. I hadn't an idea your sister wasn't coming—not until I heard Poppy telling you in the car."

"No? That's a bit hard to believe."

"It's true," she flared. "Ask Poppy. If I *had* known, I assure you wild horses wouldn't have dragged me here."

He leaned nonchalantly against the verandah rail, and quite obviously he didn't believe her. Neither, if the truth were told, did she really believe her own words. Because the thought of seeing the outback had been a very tempting one.

"No?" he said cynically.

"No," she repeated furiously.

"All right, don't push it. I won't pile all the blame on you. I know a fair proportion rests with Poppy who made the whole thing possible, and always likes to work things her way." He paused and drew on his cigarette. "Nevertheless, if it should enter your head to pester me, now that you *are* here, I'll tell you right now you'd be as well off chasing shadows."

"Thanks for the advice," said Martyn angrily. "But I never chased a man in my life."

She heard his low laugh. "You're fooling yourself, aren't you? I've never met a female yet, from six years up, who didn't mark down her quarry and stalk it. Females are natural scalp-hunters, it's instinctive. Just look back at a couple of unexpected encounters we've had, you and I. I'm not flattering myself, but facts are facts, and here you are in the outback, despite everything. Well, it's going to take you rather longer to swim back to the shore this time, but take note, as far as Martyn Verity is concerned, I'm not even as good a bet as Bastian Sinclair—and that's something. I take it he's the focal point of this personal problem you have to sort out, here in the peace and quiet of Diamond Springs, and doubtless with my stepmother fouling up the lines in her own inimitable style."

Martyn had opened her mouth several times to protest, but he had swept on relentlessly, and now he concluded, "To get the record really straight, you might like my exact assessment of you—"

Her cheeks burning, she breathed. "I'd love it—and when I've heard it, maybe you'd like to know what I think of *you*—"

She saw the gleam of his teeth as he smiled grimly. "Fair enough, I'll buy that. Well, here goes. I see you as a woolly-minded kid who's asking for trouble. I'd say you've probably been horribly spoiled all your life—by everyone. You haven't had to earn your own living, hence you haven't yet discovered that life is real, and that people are real too—very real." His eyes flicked over her, she could feel it in the almost-dark. "You're very lovely to look at, and you act sexy in an innocent, pretty little girl way, without knowing just what it is you're inviting. Just don't ever invite me, that's all. You might have a freakish taste for older men, but I don't have one for kids."

He stopped, and Martyn counted slowly up to ten, and then she told him evenly, "You've given me good value for an—assessment, haven't you? But don't worry, I'd rather take poison than offer *you* any invitations." She drew a deep breath and tried to do some quick thinking. "I wish I had your—your oratorical gifts, but I haven't. I just think of all the men I've ever met—of any age—you're the least likeable, and the one with the nastiest mind. *Full stop.*"

"You've done well," he said coldly.

They looked at each other through the darkness. Now there was a faint and slightly crooked smile on his mouth, and his eyes looked dark and hard. Martyn's spirits sank down and down. She thought, "We hate each other."

He said abruptly, "I wish to hell you'd listened to me instead of letting my stepmother persuade you into doing something you're going to regret. You must have known the thing about Jan was nothing but a made-up excuse—a very thin story... Well, sleep tight, and if there's anything you want, just let out a yell. Someone will hear you, but it won't be me. I sleep on the far side of the house. Goodnight."

"Goodnight," she echoed almost inaudibly. She could feel the air vibrating around her, and her whole body felt as if it had been subjected to a very slight but unpleasant electric shock. She thought she would sooner be under Rosalind's feet any day than in the company of that man.

And yet—strangely—she couldn't imagine not having come to Diamond Springs. No matter how thin an excuse helping Jan had been. And that, she was beginning to realize, was possibly only too true. Poppy Diamond had had other things in mind when she had invited her here.

She thought, as she left the verandah rail and went in to bed, that she was glad she hadn't set him right about the nature of her personal problem. He was welcome to think it concerned Bastian Sinclair and to consider her as spoiled and as useless as he liked. She hated him...

In the morning, one of the kitchen girls, a pretty teenager in a pale blue cotton dress, came barefooted to her room with a cup of tea and a slice of home-baked bread at some hour not long after dawn.

"Brekfus be ready on the v'randah in half a nour, Martyn," the girl told her cheerfully. Martyn nodded and thanked her. No matter what had happened, she felt great this morning, she had slept well, and now she was eager to see what she could of the outback. She drank the tea, ate the bread and butter, and went along to the bathroom to the shower. She saw no one and heard nothing other than muffled sounds from the direction of the kitchen, and when she came back to her room she saw through the long window that opened on to the verandah some stockmen in wide-brimmed hats and checked shirts riding out across the paddock. She didn't suppose Red Diamond would be amongst them, because he was going to Jindi-yindi. And so was Poppy. But she, Martyn, was not. She had told him last night, and now in the clear light of morning she wished she had not been so hasty.

She got into the soft new off-white jean-style pants that Ros had bought her and a matching short-sleeved jacket. She didn't need to clip her hair back now it was its new length, but she brushed it well and decided to forget about eye make-up. It would probably only aggravate *his* opinion of her as a sex-crazed dolly girl anyhow—and she had half a mind to change out of this gear into a pair of the comfortable old pants she had managed to slip into her case while Ros wasn't looking. She didn't want to give even the vaguest impression of wanting to make an impact on Red, and if that was what Poppy had had in mind when she invited her, then she was sorry, but she wasn't co-operating. If she'd been in some way just a little bit intrigued by Red Diamond, it hadn't counted. She'd come in all good faith to look after Jan—and to think about her own future too, she remembered. It was funny how she could never get her mind seriously fixed on that, mainly because she just couldn't think of one thing she really wanted to do. And how she would hate Red to know *that*. She would probably finish up getting a living-in job minding children. Even if Ros and Dick disapproved, that way she wouldn't be confined indoors all day and she'd have a chance to work on some kind of a children's book...

At last, somewhat in dread of having to confront her host again, she walked round the verandah to find where breakfast was being celebrated. It wasn't difficult, because of the delicious smell of bacon and toast and coffee—and steak! Her step quickened. She was hungry!

Poppy and Red were at the table already and he stood up and greeted her and pulled out a chair for her as if nothing at all had happened between them the previous night.

"Sleep well?" Poppy asked. "All ready for a day out?"

Yes, Martyn said, she'd slept well. She didn't answer the other question, and she felt vaguely ill at ease, because of—everything. Not merely because of Red, who had given her a cool and mocking smile.

"Changed your mind about coming to Jindi-yindi?" he asked her casually. He didn't even look at her but reached for the home-made marmalade and gave his attention to his toast. Martyn noticed his hands, broad and dark with strong-looking fingers. He had showered, and his black hair was damp. He wore a dark red shirt with a celadon-green silk neckerchief that looked rather striking. Martyn was saved from answering his question when the little aboriginal girl came softly round the verandah and placed the most enormous plate of steak and eggs and bacon in front of her.

Poppy said, "Of course she's going to Jindi." She added, "We don't go visiting every day of the week out here, Martyn, as you might imagine, so when there's an opportunity it's good sense to take it."

Martyn smiled and shrugged a little, letting herself be persuaded as abstractedly as if it didn't matter much to her one way or the other, though she had the disagreeable feeling that she had made herself appear childish by her previous perversity.

"Where *is* Jindi-yindi?" she asked as she attacked her breakfast.

"Next door," Poppy said. "How far to the homestead, Red?"

"Thirty-three miles," he said, ignoring Martyn's change of mind. "Rough miles," he added. "We shan't make the journey in a mere hour."

Martyn made no comment. Inwardly, she felt a little excited at the thought of seeing more of the outback. It wasn't till later—when breakfast was over and she had made final preparations in her room—that she discovered Poppy wasn't coming after all.

Red was waiting in the car and Poppy was standing

nearby and smiled apologetically at Martyn when she
appeared. "I'm suffering a reaction from travel and
tablets—I think I'd be better staying home today after
all Mrs. Hall will bring me up to date on all the local
gossip."

From the car, Red looked at her cryptically. "You're
quite transparent, Poppy, and I assure you the whole
manoeuvre's pointless. However, do as you please. But
don't believe all you hear, will you? Local gossip's not
always very reliable." He leaned across and opened the
door for Martyn, who climbed into the seat beside him
with a feeling of slight frustration. It looked as though
Poppy was manipulating her!

"Give my regards to the Bowers, Red," Poppy said
brightly.

Her stepson sent her a lopsided smile. "That Lot?"
Sure. They'll want to know why you didn't come
along . . . Well, so long, we'll be home to dinner."

Another minute and they were alone. Martyn thought
it was really crazy. Her first day at Diamond Springs and
here she was setting off on a day's outing with the very
man she had sworn she would avoid. A man whom she
disliked intensely. She had actually told him so! Poppy
had worked it this way, and he knew it as well as she did,
but he was not going to be allowed to think she was a
party to the plan. She would make a point of bringing
Bastian's name into the conversation (What conversation? she paused to wonder, because so far there hadn't
been any) just as soon as she could. Fortunately she
hadn't burnt all her bridges behind her. She'd never confessed to having broken with Bastian, and it shouldn't be
all that hard to fabricate a white lie or two—such as that
her brother had wanted her to get away for a while so as
to sort herself out. That was true enough in its own way,
except the sorting out had nothing in the world to do
with Bastian . . .

She moved a little and tried to concentrate on the
outside world—on the red earth covered patchily with
tough-looking, not quite green grass, on the ill defined

and decidedly bumpy track, on the groups of belahs and wilgas beneath which cattle grazed or lay in the shade. Heat shimmered, and birds flew against the cloudless blue of the sky, and the land seemed very vast, and very empty.

"What's keeping you so quiet?" the man beside her asked so suddenly that she was startled.

"Oh, I was thinking about Richard," she said quickly.

"Richard?" She saw his brow crease, and was pleased.

"My brother," she began, then broke off, discovering that after all it was not so easy to lie. But by saying just those two words she had said enough, because he said at once, "Your brother's called a halt to it?—suggested you go away and get over your silly infatuation. Is that what you intend to do? I certainly hope so."

She shrugged, coloured, looking out of the car again at the long lines of fencing. "I don't know." She waited to see if he was going to read her another lecture, but he didn't, and after a moment, because it was on her mind, she told him with faint aggressiveness, "I wouldn't have come today if I'd known Poppy wasn't coming too."

His brows lifted cynically. "More protests? But why not? Are you afraid I'll try to seduce you on the way? I assure you I won't."

Martyn's temper rose. "My mind doesn't work along those lines. I just meant—" She stopped. What *had* she meant? Was there to be more talk of dislike? Fortunately, at that moment she saw something that distracted her completely—an emu, the first she had ever seen outside a zoo, resting on the ground in the hot sunshine on the other side of the fence beside which the track ran. As the car drew nearer it got to its feet and began to run along beside the fence, watching the car curiously, keeping pace, its long buff and brown feathers flopping and bouncing like thick silky hair.

Martyn was fascinated. Her fingers fairly itched to get hold of pencil and record that movement. She exclaimed spontaneously, "Oh, it's beautiful! Those flip-flopping feathers! I've never seen such a sight!" The emu had lost the race now and she twisted round so she could watch it through the back window.

Red said dryly, "Beautiful's not quite the word I'd have chosen. However, I'm afraid we can't pull up just now. I want to get over to Jindi-yindi. But don't worry, you'll have all the time in the world for bird-watching while you're at Diamond Springs. There aren't all that many other distractions. It's not exactly the centre of the metropolis."

"I'm not used to city distractions," she said mildly, though she was seething. "I'm from the north coast, not from Sydney."

He didn't comment. He said merely, "Still, you're going to have lots and lots of time on your hands. If wild life really interests you, you'll be able to watch emus and goannas and cockatoos to your heart's content."

She made a small grimace. Till you're at screaming point, he could have added, by the sound of his voice. Time on her hands because she shouldn't have come—she wasn't wanted.

Ahead, she could see cattle in a mob, the smoke of a fire, a group of men sitting in the shade of gum trees drinking billy tea, eating slabs of bread. "Is this Jindi-yindi?" she asked.

"No. We're still on Diamond Springs. Those are my stockmen. We've a muster on, branding the calves. I'm going to stop for a minute."

He pulled up under a big coolibah and got out. Martyn watched him stride across to the camp and talk for a while to a tall stringy-looking character—his head stockman, she supposed. Then he looked about him and picked out another stockman who got up from where he was squatting on the ground to come forward with a wide smile. This was an aboriginal, a man with a broad, dark, shining face, very white teeth, crinkled-up eyes. She saw Red lay his hand on this other man's shoulder and they talked for a few minutes. Then, with a general gesture of salute, Red had left the stockmen who were now beginning to move towards the horses hobbled beyond the trees.

"Who was that?" she asked impulsively as he got back into the car, and started it up.

He sent her a wordless questioning look.

"The aboriginal," she said a little impatiently.

"Drummer. One of my best stockmen. His wife's gone away to town to have another baby—went yesterday with the mail truck. His sister is looking after the other two children."

Some instinct told Martyn that Red hadn't *needed* to talk to Drummer. He had simply wanted to. She had sensed, as she watched them, an understanding—a sort of comradeship between the two men. She didn't know how or why, and Red had nothing further to say.

Some time later they went through a gate, and he said, "We're on Jindi-yindi now. They've had a bad time here the last little while—almost ever since they took over, in fact. I don't know if you read in the papers about the rain we had here in the north-west. Diamond Springs was lucky. It did us nothing but good. But Jindi-yindi was hard hit—suffered a lot of flood damage on the far side of the run, lost a lot of stock and had miles of fencing washed away. These things can be disastrous for a man on the land—they can ruin him."

Martyn listened. She had already heard Poppy Diamond say there was a "hex" on Jindi-yindi, and she had the feeling that Poppy didn't much like the folk there—That Lot. Martyn was sorry they'd had a bad time. Here, you certainly couldn't notice it. There was plenty of pasture, and there were stands of trees that made pleasant shade or sheltered a dam. The cattle she saw looked sleek and well fed.

Red said presently, "They need capital to buy more stock and to repair their fencing." He said it musingly almost as though he had forgotten she was there, and quite suddenly she wondered about the people on Jindi-yindi. Were they young people? Or were they old folks?

It wasn't long before she found out.

CHAPTER FIVE

THE usual thick grove of trees that shelter a homestead appeared, and in minutes they had pulled up outside the garden.

"We're not expected," Red said, climbing out of the car, while Martyn opened her own door and slid out quickly, smoothing down her new pants. She felt the air hot on her head and arms. At the coast, the air was moist and salty, here it felt very dry, but clean and good. As she moved round the car to join Red he told her, "You should wear sun glasses. Those beautiful blue eyes will be ruined and you'll look old before your time if you don't watch out."

"Who cares? Anyhow, I won't be here all that long. At home I never wore sunglasses, not even on the beach. Stan said healthy eyes could stand strong sunlight—and read small print by candlelight as well. And *his* mother—" She stopped because he was staring at her with a sort of quizzical amusement.

"Stan?"

She flushed. They had begun to walk towards the house. "My father."

"Oh. He died recently, you said."

"Yes." She averted her face. He had spoken gently, and if she wasn't careful, she still cried over Stan.

Ahead of them, the screen door opened and a girl appeared at the top of the steps. She called out delightedly, "*Red*!" and came quickly down towards them—almost into his arms, her hands outstretched. He took them in his.

"Surprised to see me, Fay? I thought it was time to pay my respects. Is David about?"

"He's out on the run somewhere," Fay said. Red released her hands and reached out towards Martyn almost absentmindedly.

"This is Martyn Verity. Martyn—Fay Bower."

Martyn said, "Hello," and was aware at once that the other girl was wondering who on earth she was. Red's introduction had been the briefest possible, but after a bright, "Hello," she put her arm through his and invited, "Come in and have a nice cold beer."

Red released his arm. "Sorry, not now, Fay. Lunch later, if Maude can manage it? Right now, I want to catch up with David."

"Oh. Then I *think* he went over to see how the fencing was going. You'll need to drive. Shall I—"

"You and Martyn stay here—get to know each other," he added, and to Martyn it seemed his eyes glinted. "I know my way about. Besides, you'll have to do some planning with unexpected guests to lunch. Poppy sent her regards, by the way—she came home yesterday, brought Martyn with her." He nodded briskly and moved back to the car leaving the two girls together.

While the conversation in which she had taken no part had been going on, Martyn had taken in a few facts about Fay Bower. She was an attractive-looking girl—young woman, rather—with brown hair that had a smoky sheen on it. Martyn put her age at about twenty-eight. Her eyes were the colour of champagne, and she was tall, slim, straight, and lightly tanned—not nearly so brown as Martyn. Even though she hadn't been expecting visitors, she looked immaculate in pale blue cotton slacks with a sleeveless ribbed matching top. Martyn was glad after all that she hadn't sneaked back and got into her old clothes. She'd have felt at a distinct disadvantage. As it was, she somehow didn't feel very much at her ease.

Both of them watched the car move off, and then Fay looked at Martyn. In fact, she looked her over—

from head to foot, and very rapidly. She said briskly, "Come on in and I'll see about some cold drinks."

Martyn followed her on to the verandah, Fay indicated a chair and disappeared. Not very hospitable, Martyn decided. She could have invited her out to the kitchen. She looked around her. There were half a dozen cane chairs, a small round table, a couple of ceiling lights. Everything was a little dilapidated, and the floor, after the clean shining polished verandah floor at Diamond Springs, needed not only a bit of polish but a sweeping and a good scrubbing as well. The Bowers certainly couldn't have as good house staff as they had at Diamond Springs, Martyn thought, as she sat down and waited for Fay to rejoin her.

She waited a long time with nothing to do but stare out at the garden which, though you couldn't say it was overgrown, was certainly not very well tended. She thought of what Red had said about the flood damage, and how the property needed capital, and she supposed that their finances had been affected badly and that possibly they'd had to cut down on staff. Presently her thoughts wandered to the emu she and Red had seen, and she wished she'd brought even a small sketch pad along with her today. She could have done a sketch from memory. Bastian—and Mrs. Turner too—had always said it was a very valuable exercise. It taught you a lot about observation, and made you take in more next time you had an opportunity. But she didn't even have a scrap of paper with her—she hadn't brought a handbag. So—time on her hands. Sounds, voices, from somewhere inside the house. It looked as if Fay had forgotten her and was doing something about lunch.

Someone else joined her on the verandah before Fay did. A man. She saw him come along the gravel path, climb the steps, push the door open and let it swing shut behind him. Then he stood staring.

"Hello!" He all but whistled as he said it. Martyn had heard Hello said with exactly that intonation many

times before—usually on the beach. She never took
any notice because she'd learned it was a sort of opening gambit, and before you knew where you were, you
had someone on your hands that you didn't want to
know. On the beach, she never even bothered looking
up, but here—well, she was on the verandah of the
Jindi-yindi homestead, and she had to be polite, so she
smiled, and didn't turn away. She saw a very good-
looking man in a long-sleeved dull green shirt, narrow
cord trousers, and tan boots that had only a light film of
dust on them. He had the film star good looks that Red
Diamond lacked. Thick burnished brown hair, even
features, a square forehead; good teeth that showed
because he was smiling at her—good, but not as white
as Red's, she noted automatically. Age? About old
enough to be Fay Bower's husband. Of course! That
was who he was, she thought with an odd sort of relief.
And Red must have missed him.

She stayed where she was and he came towards her.
It was then she noticed his eyes—champagne-coloured,
and they licked her over in one swipe and swallowed
her whole.

No, not Fay's husband. Her brother.

He had come to a dead stop in front of her when Fay
appeared carrying a tray, glasses, a jug of fruit juice in
which ice tinkled.

"Oh, David, I heard the door. You didn't see Red?"

As if it needed an effort, he shifted his eyes from
Martyn. "No. Should I have? Aren't you going to introduce us? We haven't got beyond just—looking—
yet."

Fay deposited the tray on the table. "Sorry. This
is—" She stopped, she'd forgotten of course, and Martyn said obligingly, "Martyn Verity."

"She's a guest at Diamond Springs, came over with
Poppy," Fay said, and added somewhat belatedly, "My
brother, David."

He looked at Martyn and raised one eyebrow. "With
Poppy? Not with Red?"

Martyn felt irritated all of a sudden. She hated that instant, insincere, flattery-by-implication thing, and wondered what he'd think if she said—as she'd heard girls say on the beach, at club dances—"Oh, go and get lost!"

She said politely, "I came with Poppy, Red came earlier. I know him, of course. I met him at his sister's house."

There was a tiny silence, then Fay, who was pouring the drinks, said brightly, "Really? So you got yourself an invitation. Well, I suppose it wasn't hard. Poppy likes to bring—*eligible* girls out to Diamond Springs. She thinks it's good for Red." She handed a glass of fruit drink carelessly to Martyn, who immediately had to wipe a few spilled drops from her white pants with a tissue from her pocket. She said evenly, as Fay passed a glass to David, "And isn't it good for him?"

She looked at the other girl, and sipped her drink. She was wondering why she hadn't dropped dead the way Fay was looking at her. So Red was *her* property. Was that the message? She rather thought it was. Well, she was welcome to him.

Fay said in a clipped voice, "Red can manage his own life. He doesn't need an interfering stepmother around trying to push him some way he doesn't want to go."

"I don't think anyone could do that," said Martyn, a little surprised at her own coolness. "Do you?"

Fay didn't answer. She said, "What's the news of Jan? Or aren't you up to date with that? She'd got herself into a very nasty psychological mess last time I heard."

"You'd better ask Red about it," Martyn said carefully. "But I don't really think Jan is in a mess at all."

"Then you don't know a thing," Fay said. "Well, I'd better get back to the kitchen." She turned to David. "I shall never understand why Lewis had that woman working in the kitchen for him. If I wasn't sure of being out of this place before long, I think I'd strangle Maude

with my bare hands. Two extra people for lunch and
she expects me to work out every minute detail. It's
worse than having nobody working for you!"

"Calm down," said David. "Just remember she
started here as a girl under old Annie Bower's rule, and
you'll forgive her everything."

Fay gave him an angry glare and disappeared inside
the house, and he grinned and sat down on the arm of a
chair he had moved in Martyn's direction.

There was silence for a moment and she moved uneasily, knowing she was being looked at again, and
wishing, rather illogically, that Red would come back.
Wishing too that she *had* put her old jeans on today—
David Bower might not have been so fixated then. She
leaned back in her chair, raised her glass of fruit drink
and looked cautiously over it at the staring and oh, so
handsome David.

"Has your family lived here for a long time, Mr.
Bower?" she asked, like a polite schoolgirl.

"David," he insisted. "I'm not that old... No, the
Bowers haven't lived at Jindi-yindi so long, actually. If
you want the history—Annie Bower's father, Old Man
Richardson, was the first owner, and as Annie was the
only child, she inherited the place when he died, and
ran it like a man. She'd always worked with the old
boy—was out on the run with him every day from the
moment she could sit a horse. She married a Bower—
Charles, who was my great-uncle. He wasn't a countryman, so she kept on running the property—she was
one of those frightfully forceful females, and poor old
Charles opted out at forty—was kicked to death by a
wild horse or something. They had a son Lewis, and
that was the beginning of the Bower rule, except that
Lewis was never allowed to reign, his mother did it all
for him. And that," he finished with a wry grimace, "is
why the old place was a bit of a shambles when it came
to me and Fay. After Annie died, Lewis didn't know if
he was on his head or his feet, he wasn't capable of
organizing a fowlyard, let alone a cattle run, and the

first thing he did was sack anyone who knew more than
he did. Which left him with a few half-trained aboriginal stockmen.''

"And then you had the flood," Martyn prompted.
She liked him a lot better when he was being—even
slightly—informative and amusing, instead of acting
the Romeo.

"Yes. Who told you about that?''

"Red, of course.''

"Of course," he repeated. "So I suppose you know
all about Fay and me as well.''

"No." She looked at him directly. "I didn't even
know either of you existed till I met you.''

"No? Well, maybe I'm not worth a mention, but I'd
have thought Red would have had something to say
about Fay," said David, narrowing his eyes.

"Why?" If you want to know something, the best
way to find out is to be blunt and to ask, Stan had always said. But David wasn't putting it into words.

"I'll give you three guesses," he said, and then he
smiled and reached for her glass. "More?''

So he meant that Fay and Red were interested in
each other. Somehow the information sent a little electric shock up and down Martyn's spine.

"Now tell me about yourself," he insisted when she
had refused another drink. "What lured you away from
the city and brought you to the outback? Holiday and
nowhere to go?''

She widened her eyes. "Something like that. And
the outback is special, isn't it?''

"Is it? What about Red? You wouldn't be the first
girl to come here on a visit on his account, you know.''

"I'm sure I wouldn't," Martyn agreed, a little bored
at having her motives made suspect. "But as a matter
of fact, I agreed to come because Jan was supposed to
be coming, and Poppy wanted me to keep her company
and help her with swimming, as a kind of remedial exercise.''

"I see. The poor girl did some damage to her leg,

didn't she? But you came, and she didn't, so I don't quite get it."

Martyn was exasperated. Was she supposed to have come because she was madly in love with Red Diamond? It was absurd to take it almost for granted that every girl who came here had fallen in love with a tough-looking character who appeared to have no heart. He wasn't at all the sort of man Ros had had in mind, she was sure, when she had hoped that Martyn would meet up with some uncomplicated outdoor type.

Meanwhile, however, for what reason she didn't know, David had evidently decided to believe her guiltless and to tell her, "Well then, there's no reason why you and I shouldn't get together now and again since you're here, is there?"

She flushed, but it was mainly with annoyance. She just didn't like his tactics, she didn't understand them. She hadn't found a suitable answer when Red himself arrived back, and the twosome was split up.

Lunch was a very plain salad with cold beef and glasses of beer—which Martyn didn't take, so was given more fruit drink. They ate on the side verandah, and the table was already laid when Fay came to say it was ready. Martyn didn't catch even a glimpse of the bothersome Maude, but she had a break from David's concentrated attention while the talk was of Jan and her mended engagement, and of the fact that the fencing repairs had been started. She picked up the point that Red had recommended a certain contractor, but that David had been lucky and got on to someone who would do the job thirty per cent cheaper.

The reason David hadn't been where Red had expected was because he had been exercising a new mount he'd bought, a thoroughbred named Regal.

"Cost me a packet," said David, "but a good horse is something I can't live without. That's one thing I've missed since Fay and I moved out here. Nothing on the place but stock horses and most of them are only half broken. I don't think there's a good horse breaker on the property either—I daresay old Annie used to do that part of the work herself, I wouldn't put it past her," he added half jokingly. "By the way, Red, I was going to ask your advice about buying some store cattle that are being brought to the sales from Queensland. Should I take a look at them?"

"I'd say so. In fact, I'd intended to mention it to you. It would be a good move. You've got plenty of feed here."

"Great," nodded David. "Feel like coming along with me?"

Red picked up his half empty beer glass. "Sorry, I shan't be buying, so I can't spare the time," he said a trifle tersely. "But you're quite capable of making your own decisions—your own judgments."

David shrugged. "I'm not as well acquainted with inland cattle as you are. Still, if it's not convenient— And of course you have a guest. Eh, Martyn?"

Martyn, taken by surprise at being brought so suddenly on stage and into the limelight, blushed scarlet. The Bowers, both brother and sister, were concentrating their attention on her, and she waited for Red to correct David to say, "Martyn's Poppy's guest." But he didn't. He said blandly, "That's right... But I'm sure you can manage without me, David. Well, I'll let you get back to work. I know you're busy and I have plenty to do myself. We must be on our way."

Fay said almost sharply, "I'm disappointed. I thought I was going to have some company for a change. What about Sunday, Red?"

"Come over and we'll organize a picnic," he said laconically. He pushed back his chair and got to his feet and the others did likewise. "Bring your bathing gear and we'll go to the swimming hole and maybe have a campfire afterwards. We have a swimmer in our midst, by the way, so you'll have to be on your mettle, Fay."

Fay looked at Martyn and in her champagne-coloured eyes dislike was very thinly veiled. Martyn was aware of it behind the sparkling smile.

"I should have guessed you're a swimmer—that accounts for those lovely strong-looking shoulders."

It was a decidedly backhanded compliment, but David cupped a hand over one of Martyn's shoulders at once, and with difficulty she stopped herself from pulling away. She didn't like being handled so casually, so familiarly, by someone she didn't know. He said, "Martyn's a perfect physical specimen."

She bit her lip. How was she supposed to react to that? It was so—dopey, so obvious. Fay looked at Red and Red looked as if he simply hadn't heard. He said, "Come along, Martyn, fetch your jacket or whatever else you've left lying about—"

"My jacket's in the car," she said quickly. "And I haven't anything else."

"No handbag? No make-up kit?"

"No," she said flatly.

On the way out to the car, while she and David went ahead down the verandah steps, the other two followed slowly behind, and when Martyn paused by the car and looked back, Fay had her hand on Red's chest and was looking up into his face. A brief flash of unexpected emotion burned through Martyn like a flame and left her—aching. Incomprehensibly. So he was human—susceptible—despite the fact he looked so tough. Today even his hair looked wild, and his shoulders—they were just that little bit too broad for true masculine good looks. The man beside her—David Bower—was lighter, lither, more civilized in every way. More easily comprehensible too. And yet—a mark in Red's favour—David was not as straight, as blunt and sincere. He was a flatterer, he had a way with him. And Martyn was very well aware of it. So why—?

Her thoughts became indistinct, blurred. She had no idea what David was saying to her, though she didn't realize it for seconds. She was watching Red intently. He was so physically fit, but not in the least like the swimmers she had known. Nor was he like the fishermen who went out to sea from the small north coast town where she had been born and bred. There was a wild, burning steely sort of toughness about him that could never be broken. There would be no tenderness in him, not like there had been in Stan, who had so often tucked her in at night, been gentle and understanding when she had problems at school, or when she was feeling depressed or out of sorts. And even when Red looked down at Fay as he was doing now, he did it in an intent kind of way, not in a tender way. Unless there was a hidden softness in his eyes that only Fay could see...

He came to join her at last, and at last the good-byes had been said and they were on their way. They didn't speak to each other for minutes, and then he said abruptly and without looking at her, "Don't be flattered too much by David's attentions. I know you go for older men, but I wouldn't recommend you should talk yourself into a love affair with David Bower while you're here."

She felt herself bristle with hostility. "Why not? I imagine at least he's a gentleman. And anyhow, it was he who was doing the chasing, in case you hadn't noticed—not me."

His brows tilted. "Admittedly that's a change," he allowed infuriatingly. "But all the same, I'll guarantee you gave him the green light. The woman always does. Perhaps you're too young to be fully conscious of your own wiles yet, but it's a fact."

"You're—cynical," she said. "Hard."

"As diamonds," he agreed. "I've a reputation in the outback, and that's it." He turned to look at her quickly and she felt the fire of his grey eyes, and she wondered nervily if he thought she had ever given *him* the green light. She had no idea what to expect of him or what he might suspect of her, and it was maddening and disconcerting. Then suddenly he dropped personalities as the car bucked a little.

"This car's running like a pig. I'll have to get Harry to give it an overhaul."

Martyn sank back in the seat, relieved to be forgotten.

She went to bed early after dinner that night, but she lay awake in the darkness for a long time. From towards the end of the verandah she could hear voices, and soon, because she had sharp ears and she was sleepless, she began to pick up what was being said. She listened quite deliberately. In real life, people don't block their ears and hurry away too soon—if they're interested. And Martyn was interested. Besides, she was in bed where she had every right to be, and they must know she was there. Because her light was out, they no doubt thought she was asleep, but if they didn't want her to hear, then they should have talked somewhere else.

Poppy said, "I really don't know why you bother with That Lot, Tancred. They're rubbish—weaklings. Not like the Richardsons. Why Lewis was so ineffective he was the joke of the district."

Silence.

Then Poppy again. "I sometimes wonder if Fay would have been so charming to Lewis if she'd known just how far the place had gone down the drain... Of course they want your help, and it would suit David very well to have you part of the show. In my opinion, he's a fool—even though a persuasive one. He's the type who lets other people do the work while he takes all the credit."

"Do you call that being a fool?" Red asked dryly. "In any case, you've got the bull by the tail. From my angle, Jindi-yindi's not more than a side issue. I'll admit I don't like to see a good property going to seed, and I'm convinced that all that's needed is good management and a bit of capital."

"And if you're going to provide both," she retorted heatedly, "then Diamond Springs will be the loser. You're playing right into their hands."

"Oh, for God's sake, Poppy, try to be a bit realistic. I know exactly what I'm doing. I don't need your personal opinions or your interference, however well-meaning they may be. Anything I do, you can be sure I do it because that's what I want to do. I like Fay—she's intelligent, mature and healthy—and those are three of the attributes an outback man should look for in a wife."

"You talk like a man without a heart," said Poppy. "You always have. But this time you're being reckless as well, trying to mix—love—with business. Bad business at that, in my opinion. There are plenty of girls in the world. Why should you have to choose someone like Fay Bower? Oh, when I think of all the other girls— nice girls—you've loved and dropped—"

"Loved? When you're young, love's nothing but a game. And I'm sorry, but I've never worn rose-coloured glasses in my life."

That was all Martyn heard, lying wide-eyed in the dark. The voices faded and she turned on her side. Love's a game—when you're young. How wrong he was! Martyn was positive she took love twice as seriously as he appeared to. He was thinking of marrying Fay Bower—that was clear. Not because he loved her, but because she had the attributes! And because he was interested in Jindi-yindi? Somehow, the thought made Martyn feel sick. Why on earth was that? She turned on her other side and resolutely refused to think of that moment when she had looked at him and Fay Bower standing together and a flame had burned through her heart...

Martyn's knowledge of the Jindi-yindi set-up was expanded a little next day by Poppy, who chose that day also to reveal the contents of the large suitcases she had brought from Sydney. Curtain material.

"I'm going to make new curtains for all the bedrooms," she said firmly. "I don't live here any more, I only visit—I'd drive Red bananas if I stayed for long— but I love the place, and it does need a woman's interest to keep it the way it is. You know what I mean? Or am I crazy thinking there's something special about this old homestead?"

Martyn shook her head, thinking of the feelings she had had at Jindi-yindi. They were on a side verandah where vines made a cool screen against the heat of the day, for outside the sun was blazingly hot. Martyn had risen fairly early, but Red had already gone out on the run—for which she was thankful—and she had breakfasted alone with Poppy. "Jindi-yindi has a kind of—neglected look," she said tentatively after a moment.

Poppy had taken tape-measure and scissors from the drawer of a big table and was spreading out a length of soft pastel green material, and was looking very business-like and determined. Now she looked up briefly.

"Did Tancred tell you about Jindi-yindi?"

"No. But I gathered from David that it had been left to him and Fay by some sort of a relation."

"That's right—Lewis Bower. He was in love with Fay, and although he was about thirty years her senior, she played him along. It may sound catty to say so, but it's true."

"But she didn't marry him?"

"No. His mother, old Annie Bower, wouldn't hear of second or third cousins marrying, and Lewis always complied with her wishes. But of course he left the property to Fay and her brother—which was exactly what she'd hoped for. They've had to raise a mortgage to pay the death duties and they're in a bit of a financial fix at the moment, but Fay has plans for remedying *that*."

Martyn didn't ask how, she already knew. And after a second she changed the subject and asked if she could help with the curtain-making.

"No, no." Poppy was quite emphatic. "You're here to amuse yourself, not to be my offsider. Tomorrow we must persuade Red to take you out on the run, but today, why don't you take a ride, or go down to the swimming pool? Goodness knows, it's hot enough."

That was true, and finally, feeling completely useless, Martyn took herself off and spent a good part of the day at the river. The swimming pool there was wide and deep, its banks fringed with acacias, and willows and tall red river gums, and she swam and wallowed lazily for a long time, then lay on her towel in the shade. She didn't know why, but she felt vaguely troubled and on edge. She thought about her future, and what would happen when she went back to Sydney. "Three weeks will go in a flash," she told herself. "And I shan't be seeing much of *him*." Red Diamond, who was planning to marry a girl who possessed at least three of the attributes required of an outback wife. Intelligence, maturity, and health. Health was the only point Martyn would score, and she wasn't part owner of a neighbouring cattle station either, however rundown. Appalled at the irrational quality of her unexpected thought, she got up and dived into the water again.

When she walked back to the homestead it was not long before sundown and Red had just come in.

He said without preamble, merely flicking his eyes over her suntanned face, completely devoid of make-up, "Sling your swimming things down somewhere and I'll take you to the far waterhole to see the birds. I suppose you ride?"

Protests rose in her throat—"I don't want you to think you have to entertain me"—but they were never uttered, he simply didn't give her an opportunity. He hadn't, in fact, paused as he spoke to her, but kept on walking towards the house, and he tossed back over his shoulder, "Be down at the horse paddock in five minutes' time."

She was there, and she refused to think why. She hadn't ever done any riding, but he helped her up into the saddle and she took the reins in her hands and felt her heart beating fast. As they started off, he sent her a cynical glance.

"You don't ride, do you, mermaid? Only sea-horses and the surf. Well, you won't come to any harm, I'll look after you."

She didn't need his reassurance, but didn't say so.

She felt safe enough riding slowly along the track, over
the paddock and through a grove of smallish twisted
trees. It was the end of the day and the sun was sliding
fast down to the horizon—a flat, limitless horizon—
through a paling, cloudless sky. The air had assumed a
peculiar clarity and every hanging leaf, every blade of
grass seemed sharply outlined. And he, riding a little
ahead of her just now—hatless, his dark hair burnished—he was sharply etched too. Red Diamond. Inside her was an unanalysable feeling of elation, topped
with a kind of cynical amazement at herself and her
own unpredictableness.

The waterhole, when they reached it, was silver-grey
like his eyes, and then, slowly and quite fascinatingly, it
turned rose and finally brilliant crimson. They left their
horses and she followed him, all eyes, to stand entranced as myriad birds began to fly in—from the trees,
from the skies, from nowhere. Tiny jewel-coloured
budgerigars floated down like a storm of bright coloured leaves; noisy white cockatoos, brilliant parrots
alighted on the water in swarms; there was a cloud of
finches, and in the shallows long-legged birds waded.

Martyn watched till her eyes almost fell out and at
last she turned to the man at her side and said on a long
soft breath—"Oh!" Bastian would have said, "What
about a few quick sketches?" but this man wasn't Bastian, he was Red Diamond. His heavy eyebrows curved
up and then descended and his unnervingly brilliant
eyes glinted at her. He reached in his pocket for cigarettes, and suddenly she somehow knew that while she
had watched the birds, he had been watching her. Gap-
ing, infantile, she supposed.

He said casually, "Now you're acting like the kid you
really are."

"I'm not a kid," she said with dignity. "I'm nineteen. These days, that's quite an age, and I assure you
I'm well clued up. I'm not the—neophyte you like to
picture me."

He bit on his full lower lip for a second. "Well, well,

that's quite a word, isn't it? What are you trying to tell me? That you know it all and can handle it?''

There was carmine light reflected on his face and she saw it burn like fire in his eyes as he suddenly whipped around and took hold of her shoulders. Then with a tricky movement he jerked her so that her head was flung back and she found herself staring up into his face, momentarily paralysed, her blue eyes wide, unblinking. Inside she could feel herself quaking and she was afraid. If he should kiss her now—if that mouth, long, curving, deadly, with its tilted corners, its sensual lower lip, should touch her own—if he should press her to him savagely as Bastian had done, force her lips apart—then she would die.

Her gaze, that had become riveted on his lips, lifted slowly to his eyes and she suffered the full force of their dagger-bright regard.

He said, his voice so low that she could scarcely hear the words, "Are you aware that you're inviting me to kiss you—to make love to you, Martyn Verity?"

She stared dumbly. Her mind seemed incapable of operating, but she moved her head almost imperceptibly in a gesture of denial. She saw the darkness of his jaw—he was a man who needed to shave twice a day—and was very much aware of his sheer physical strength, his broadness, his maleness—and of the fingers that tightened and tightened on her shoulders until she could have screamed with the pain of it. His face moved closer to her own, his features blurred, his eyes dazzled her. She could scarcely breathe. And then—

"Because," he said, his voice now crisp and clipped, "I'm not going to. Do you understand—mermaid?"

Anticlimax! She felt herself relax, collapse, and for a second she wanted to laugh hysterically. Her tongue came out to moisten her lips, and unexpectedly her eyes were swimming with tears.

He moved one hand away from her shoulder. A finger, not long and slim and artistic like Bastian's, but strong and masculine, sketched a brief line beneath each of her lower lids as he flicked her fallen tears away.

"What do these signify? Disappointment?"

"Relief," she said huskily, trying to rally.

"You're frightened of me?"

"I could be," she said, and tried to smile. She pushed back her hair with a hand that trembled, though she hoped he wasn't aware of it. The birds had gone, the water was still, and the sky colourless.

"I wonder why," he said, close to her hair.

She didn't answer.

"Another evening," he pursued, "you'll be able to come on your own."

"It will be preferable," she said, her self-control coming back. She moved away from him abruptly and sought the horses that stood beneath the trees. It was maddening to have to allow him to help her to mount, but nerves had given her *some* courage and she was very quickly off and away, letting her horse have its head and take her back to the homestead.

She didn't shower before dinner that night. Instead she lay flat on her back on her bed for twenty minutes, her mind a determined blank—or as near as she could make it. No matter what she wanted or didn't want, there seemed to be *something* between her and Red Diamond—something struggling underground, trying to get through to the surface. She couldn't think why he had touched her as he had, and she wished desperately that he had not. She hadn't invited anything—she wouldn't dare. She could feel her shoulders still tingling from his grip.

She had all but gone to sleep when the sound of voices, the awareness of light falling slantingly across the verandah outside her room, made her struggle and switch on the bedside light. She was sticky with perspiration and wished she had showered after all, but a glance at her watch showed her it was too late. If she hadn't been hungry, she might have decided to go without dinner. Though what was she afraid of, for heaven's sake?

Like a stone, the thought of Fay Bower dropped into her mind. "I needn't be afraid of him," she told herself firmly but indecipherably.

She opened the wardrobe door and looked at the two pretty special occasion dresses Ros had insisted on providing her with. Her hand already outstretched, she withdrew it. She got into pants and blouse instead. She whisked a brush through her tangled hair and saw her eyes staring back at her, like sapphires, from the mirror. Something had happened in her life, something to do with Red Diamond, who had no intention of either kissing her or making love to her. But who was planning a cold-blooded marriage with that girl at Jindiyindi.

After dinner Poppy excused herself and went to the kitchen, murmuring that there was something she had to see Mrs. Hall about. She didn't come back and presently Red rose and disappeared, presumably to the office, underlining the fact, Martyn reflected, that she wasn't *his* guest. Left alone, she made a rueful face, then went to her room to fetch pen and drawing block. She settled herself at a small table outside her room and began to sketch from memory some of the birds she had seen that evening, and to think of her so far non-existent children's story book. As her absorption grew, she relaxed. The outdoor girl slipped into her role of artist, of dreamer—who saw the world through the glisten of her own lashes, saw rainbow, diamond colours as she recreated that vision of the birds flying down, drinking, rising again, feathery shadows against a brilliant sky.

It was only a dawning consciousness of the utter silence of the bush that eventually aroused her, and she sat listening, intensely aware that the one sound that had been part of her life since its very beginning—the sound of the sea—was absent. She felt a surge of loneliness and home-sickness and longing for Stan swept over her in a wave.

CHAPTER SIX

WITHOUT making a thing of it, Martyn simply didn't take up Poppy's idea that she should go out on the run with Red next day—or that she should ride out to the muster later on. Red hadn't invited her to come, and besides, there was Fay—the Bower Bird, as Poppy called her. She got into shorts and long socks, and since her help wasn't required around the homestead, wandered around past the men's quarters. There she came on some little aboriginal children playing in the dust in the shade of the pepper trees. She stood watching them for a while before she wandered on, and in the afternoon she came back again, this time equipped with small sketch pad and fibre-tipped pen.

The kids were there again, there were some noisy clownish galahs in the trees above and there was a puppy—Noosa, they called her, yellowish, skinny, with a tail that wagged like fury. The pup was chewing on a raw carrot but rushed eagerly to greet Martyn as if she were an old friend. She discovered the children belonged to Drummer, the stockman to whom Red had spoken the day they drove to Jindi-yindi. They were being looked after in their mother's absence by Elsey, a large-eyed, skinny-legged aboriginal girl in a pink cotton dress, who appeared from a small verandahed bungalow to make sure they were not getting up to any mischief.

Martyn soon made friends with the children—two small girls—and did some drawings of them. She had never before in her life had the opportunity to draw little aboriginal children with dark shining eyes and shy smiles, and it was an adventure and a delight, and she did a couple of drawings of the pup as well, to amuse them.

She had stuffed sketch pad and pen into her hip pocket and started back up the dusty track for home when she encountered Red.

"What have you been up to?" he asked, his eyes flicking over her disparagingly in her shorts and socks.

"I've been talking to some children," she said, half defiant and thankful he hadn't caught her out drawing. "Shedding my pseudo-sophistication. Finding my own level with three- and four-year-olds."

His face stayed expressionless. "Drummer's children," he commented. "Their aunt's looking after them. Elsey's never worked at the homestead—she's likely to go walking about on the spur of the moment."

Despite herself, Martyn was intrigued. They were walking back to the homestead together, and she asked, "What if she should go now? What would happen to the children?"

"She'd take them with her. They'd be all right."

Later, in the sitting-room, he complained half seriously to Poppy, "You're not looking after your guest very well. She's been down making friends with Drummer's children."

"What's wrong with that? Martyn's free to come and go as she pleases." They were about to have pre-dinner drinks, but Poppy was still busily hand hemming some of the curtains she had been making, light pretty things.

Red sent Martyn a mocking glance. "She's free within limits," he allowed. He picked up a corner of the fabric and rubbed it between finger and thumb. "If these are for here—we don't need new curtains, you know."

"That's what you think," contradicted Poppy. "I got the girls to wash some of the old ones out today—they've fallen to pieces."

"It's that infernal washing machine," he said with a frown. He had poured the drinks and handed one to

Martyn absentmindedly, and she watched him covertly
as he moved and relaxed in a chair—showered, newly
shaved and very much the master of the house. The
room suited him. It wasn't completely masculine, there
were flowers, copper candlesticks, furniture that was
solid and unpretentious and that Martyn suspected had
been there for ever; for ever, in Australia, not being all
that long by world standards, but still, long in the eyes
of a girl brought up in the residence of a small town
swimming baths. "It's as bad as a mincing machine,"
Red said.

Poppy laughed aloud. "And you're as bad as your
father, Tancred. The fuss he made when we had that
washer installed! The old ways were good enough for
Diamond Springs! Well, it's a good machine—still is—
but as a matter of fact, the girls did those curtains by
hand, they're scared of the machine."

He looked at her and shrugged his broad shoulders.
He wasn't really interested, in fact he was irritated by
these domestic details. Martyn sensed it, yet Poppy
would be quite content to prattle on all evening about
curtains, washing machines, the girls who helped in the
house. Through her eyelashes, Martyn caught Red's regard, and it sent strange impulses vibrating through her
veins.

Poppy said complacently, "Anyhow, if I make curtains now, it might save someone the trouble later on.
Does Fay like sewing—decorating?" she added innocently.

He made an impatient movement. "I haven't the
least idea. It's hardly relevant."

Poppy raised her eyes and her eyebrows as if he were
hopeless. "I'm sure *you* sew, Martyn," she persisted.

Red got to his feet abruptly. "Mermaids don't sew.
And dinner is ready," he said putting an end to the
conversation...

Next day was the day Martyn discovered the emus.
She had decided to take a ride, and Bob, down at the
saddling yards, got a horse ready for her and helped her

to mount. She rode off along a track that followed a fence, on the principle that if she followed that, there should be no difficulty in finding her way home again, though as a matter of fact she was a girl with a very well developed sense of direction. She had gone a good long way, without finding it particularly entertaining as both fence and track seemed to continue on for ever. She was beginning to feel more at ease with the horse and wondered if she might possibly see any of the stockmen, or even a mob of cattle, for after all this was a cattle station, and was looking about her with this hope in mind, when she saw an emu appear from a stand of trees some way ahead. Tall, long-legged, it strode confidently along, its feathers flowing back, its small head, on the end of the extraordinarily long neck turning curiously this way and that.

She had reined in the minute she saw it and it appeared to be quite unaware of her presence as it strode along and finally disappeared into another clump of trees. She was deciding whether or not to pursue it when to her surprise another emu appeared, this one accompanied by five small chicks that immediately put her in mind of aboriginal drawings, with their egg-shaped bodies softly striped in cream and brown, and their little curved necks. They reached scarcely higher than half-way up to the scaly knees of the adult whom Martyn took (quite mistakenly, she discovered later) to be their mother.

The little group followed the route the other bird had taken, but travelled more slowly because of the smallness of the chicks. Reaching the edge of the far group of trees, they loitered to pick around in the dirt and the bark, looking for seeds and insects. Martyn urged her horse quietly forward, but the adult became aware of her. It grunted, emitted a hissing sound and turned to face her aggressively, ready to defend its young. She pulled up at once, and the next minute the chicks had been herded out of sight amongst the trees.

She felt a great deal of pleasure in what she had

seen, and determined to do some drawings. More, as she continued her ride, the idea came into her head that she could do a book about two little children lost in the bush—one white, the other a little aboriginal. They would be found by an emu and taken into its care with its other young. That would be great! She felt full of enthusiasm. They could encounter other birds— comical galahs, chattering parrots, those surprised-looking white cockatoos with the sulphur crests, laughing kookaburras. And maybe a goanna or two and a kangaroo.

She swore to herself that in future she would always carry a sketchbook with her, and when she came out riding she would have a definite purpose. It looked as though she had at last found a rather more rational way of filling in her days.

Then it was Sunday, the day of the picnic with the Bowers. For various reasons, Martyn wasn't particularly looking forward to it. She hadn't come out west to socialize, but to help a sick girl. However, there was no means of escape, for who, on a burningly hot day could refuse to go on a picnic by the river? Who, that is, except Poppy, who seemed quite capable of avoiding all social commitments and appeared to have come to Diamond Springs to make curtains and to gossip with the cook. And, on the side, Martyn more than suspected, to upset her stepson's matrimonial plans, if she possibly could.

The picnic was not, as far as Martyn was concerned, a success. They didn't start off till afternoon, and while Fay monopolized Red—or should it have been the other way about?—David was intent on monopolizing Martyn, and weakly, she agreed to take a walk along the river bank with him when she would far sooner have been in the water with the others.

"What do you do with yourself at Diamond Springs all day, Martyn?" David asked as they strolled slowly along. "Do you go out on the run with Red? Are you a horsewoman as well as a swimmer?"

She shrugged. "I'm not a horsewoman, I can ride a bit—now. But I don't go out on the run."

"I'm surprised at that." He added casually, "You do realize, don't you, that he and my sister are probably going to be married soon? It's something you should know, because I'm willing to bet old Red was at least part of your reason for coming outback."

Martyn felt a strange constriction in her chest. She said briefly in an off-putting way, "I'm years younger than Red. And than you too."

His light amber-coloured eyes laughed at her. "That's not so old—Red and I are about the same age, thirty-three."

Martyn felt a little shock of surprise. Red was only thirty-three! She had thought him five or six years older than that. Perhaps it was his heavy build, his air of authority, of power. Subtly, it seemed to alter her focus on him...

David went on, "You should have come to stay at Jindi-yindi instead of at Diamond Springs. I'd have seen to it you had a good time. The old homestead needs a bit of modernizing, but it's not uncomfortable. What about it? Any chance of making a move?"

"Not the slightest," she said, sure he couldn't possibly be serious. "I'm Poppy's guest."

"Does Poppy drive you around?—entertain you?" he asked sceptically—as if he too knew about the other girls, and of Poppy's probably unsubtle tactics.

"Sometimes," she lied. "But I can entertain myself."

"Doing what?" They had slowed to a stop under a giant gum tree, and he had turned to face her, and she was impressed anew by his good looks.

"Oh, I ride around, I swim. As a matter of fact, I caught up with some emus the other day. I'm going to look for them again soon to see if they usually come that way."

"Where was this?" he asked idly, his eyes roving over her face and down the length of her figure.

Nervous under his rather rude regard, she told him
in detail, and found herself chattering on, ill at ease,
with a rather full description of the chicks. "They're
absolutely fascinating," she finished.

He came a couple of steps closer. "Not half as fascinating as you," he said softly. He put his arms around
her, locking his fingers behind her waist and swaying
her towards him. "Are you going to let me kiss you?"

She hadn't even got around to saying a very decided
No when quite abruptly he let her go, for the simple
reason that Red had come striding towards them, saying imperiously and unsmilingly, "If you two don't
come and take a swim, it will be too late."

Martyn snatched at the excuse to get away, but was
furious that Red should have caught her with David's
arms around her. Red-cheeked, she marched ahead of
the others back towards the picnic. Fay had come out of
the water and stood in her bikini in the sun. Ignoring
her, Martyn went straight to the car and changed
quickly into her green swimsuit. Back at the water, she
dived in quickly and was completely disconcerted on
surfacing, to find herself at very close quarters with
Red, whom she had not even noticed in the water. She
flipped back her wet hair and blinked some of the water
from her lashes, confused at encountering the splintery
sharpness of grey eyes.

"Disappointed it's not David?" he asked mockingly.

"Maybe," she said, and added senselessly, almost as
though to cover up something else, "Why did you have
to come and shove your frame in just now, anyhow?"

"I thought it might be prudent," he said unsmilingly.

She gave him an angry baffled glance, then ducked
her head down and swam underwater as far as she
could until lack of breath forced her to surface. She
looked back and he was threshing towards her—swimming fast but with appalling lack of style. He slowed
when he saw her, and when he was close enough she
saw his eyes were blazing angrily.

"You little idiot! Are you trying to drown yourself—to give everyone a fright?"

She stared at him in amazement. "Neither. There's nothing to make a fuss about. There aren't any snags here and I've been swimming since before I could walk, I'm perfectly safe."

He was white about the nostrils. "I just don't like pranks of that kind. You're never to do that again. Never. Do you understand?" He glared, then turned his back on her and swam back towards the bank. Without a second's thought, she followed him, and by putting on a spurt managed to pass him and scramble on to the bank ahead of him with a sense of angry triumph.

"That's not tactful," David said in her ear after she had picked her way across the spiky grass and reached for her towel. "No man likes a woman to beat him at any sport. You're certainly some swimmer, aren't you? Don't ask me to have a race—I'll be completely demoralized." She looked at him, but she scarcely saw him, though she smiled coolly, and she was hardly aware of it when he put his hand on her bare back. "Why do you wear that cover-up thing? Don't you have a bikini?"

"No. My sister-in-law didn't think it would be the best gear to wear in the bush where I might be swimming with the stockmen or—anybody." As she spoke her eyes looked for Red and found him, further along the bank with Fay, half naked in her tiny two-piece. "Bikinis are all right if you don't take swimming seriously. I find a one-piece the most comfortable." She swung her gaze back to David.

"The most comfortable way to swim," he said deliberately, "is in the nude."

She coloured slightly. "Here? One couldn't."

"Why not? On a lovely warm moonlight night—"

Red had moved a few steps closer. He asked coldly, "What are you two talking about?"

David grinned. "Swimming in the nude. Preferably by moonlight."

Martyn felt she could have died, and Fay looked disgusted.

"For heaven's sake, David, remember Martyn's just a kid."

Just a kid? Who had put that into Fay Bower's mind? Martyn needed just one guess. She said smilingly, "What makes you think so, Fay? I'm sure if you ask Red about the things I got up to in Sydney he'll put you straight about *that*."

She could see fury in Red's eyes, and a very curious expression in Fay's. David said, alert, "Oh, so you two knew each other that well in Sydney, did you?"

"No, we did not." Red spoke almost savagely. "Don't jump to the conclusion either that I was mixed up in any of Martyn's escapades. What's more, I won't have anyone swimming nude on Diamond Springs. And that I mean." He turned away abruptly. "Now I suggest we get a fire going. It's going to turn cool here by the water—hardly the evening for stripping off and jumping in, rather fortunately."

No, it was not a successful picnic. Martyn was thankful when it was all over, the last chop eaten, the last bit of mess cleared away, everyone beginning to yawn, herself most of all.

On the way back to the homestead—thankfully a short drive—Red said into the darkness, "You don't beat about the bush, do you, Martyn? A new romance under way already. Do *all* personable older men draw you like a magnet?"

"You mean David?" she asked resignedly.

"Who else? I don't know that I'd consider it the best way to help you sort out your personal problems. It may possibly wean you off the idea that the big romance of your life is connected with a man easily twice your age, but all the same—"

"All the same, if I want *your* advice, the thing would be to say a great big NO to David," Martyn broke in swiftly. Too swiftly, because she didn't stop to think.

"There's an interesting reaction," he said instantly.

"I can't imagine David's asked you to marry him already, so am I to conclude he's made you a different proposition? If that's the case, certainly my advice would be to say No. Further—it would be not to *invite* such propositions in future."

There was silence for five seconds. Martyn seethed and regretted that her lack of experience made it impossible for her to find a smart and worldly retort. Her own fault of course for opening her mouth too wide too soon. It was something she'd have to watch as far as Red Diamond was concerned. Then he said musingly, "I've seen my sisters through various love affairs, various aberrations, but I'll admit, I've never dealt with anyone quite as tricky and enigmatic as you, Martyn Verity. One of these days I'm going to find out whether or not you're somewhat ahead in emotions and experience of the wholesome schoolgirl type you assuredly typify—at least outwardly."

"Are you really? And just how will you do that?"

"You'd be surprised," he said dryly.

She couldn't see his face—only a dim shape and occasionally the glint in his eyes as he turned to face her. The headlights of the car leaped ahead on the track, made ghosts of the trees, intensified the dark of the outback. It was as if she and the man beside her were alone in the world. And yet, just minutes ahead, was the station homestead. Poppy, Mrs. Hall. The men's quarters, the small cottage where Elsey was minding Drummer's children while his wife was in hospital.

Out of her thoughts she asked, "Has Drummer's wife had her baby?"

"Yes." He sounded surprised.

"Is it a boy or a girl?"

"A boy."

"I suppose he's pleased."

"Why on earth do you suppose that?"

"Because he has two girls already. And *they* want a brother. What are they calling him?"

"Tancred," he said, slight amusement in his voice,

though under the amusement she sensed a sort of pride, a gentleness, that were strange in him. "So you've been making friends. You're an odd girl."

"Am I? I don't know how you work that out. What do you expect me to do all day? I have to entertain myself somehow."

"I suppose you do," he conceded. "However, you *would* come."

"Because I thought I was going to be useful," she said quickly. He was driving so slowly the car seemed scarcely to be moving at all. "It's true, even if some nasty suspicious streak in your nature won't let you believe it."

"Okay, okay, we've been through all that before. But just don't hold me responsible for your predicament. If you stop still and think for just two seconds you might remember I warned you not to come to Diamond Springs."

She gave an exasperated sigh. Because he was an exasperating man, and trying to get through to him was like trying to walk through a stone wall. She suggested, "Mightn't it have been better if you'd told your stepmother not to invite me—or to cancel the invitation out? You're the boss here, aren't you?"

He disregarded that. He said, "You're sorry you came?"

Was she sorry? Ahead, she could see the lights of the homestead. At least, there was just one light shining on the verandah. Around the men's quarters there was complete darkness. She heard a dog's bark and then there was silence till from a long way off there came a drumming sound—the sound she had heard her first night in the outback. She thought briefly of his question and it was an unanswerable one, because for some strange reason she simply could not conceive of not having come to Diamond Springs—of not being here, alone in the car with Red Diamond, on this very night— engaging with him in an irritating, bewildering, unsatisfactory yet somehow—*fascinating*—conversation.

So instead of answering his question, she asked one of her own.

"What's that drumming sound?"

"It's an emu," he said. "Probably the female warning her mate of danger.

It came again, just once, and then the silence of the bush closed in. Martyn said softly, "I love to hear it. It's an exciting sound. I don't miss the sea so much when I hear sounds like that."

"The bush is full of sounds," he said. "Can't you hear them?"

They had reached the precincts of the homestead now, and he switched off the engine and the headlights. The car windows were wide open and they sat and listened. It was so dark now when she turned her head a little she could barely see his profile, against the only slightly lesser dark of the night. They were both silent, listening. Martyn heard a faint night wind in the trees, the soft sighing of the leaves as they moved infinitesimally. She heard a stealthy rustling on the ground nearby amongst the fallen gum leaves and strips of bark. She heard the soft hesitant call of an owl.

Yes, the night had its sounds, and she turned slightly to tell him and observed that his profile was no longer towards her. He had shifted a little, so silently and cautiously that she had not been aware of it. Now his arm was along the back of the seat behind her shoulders, and though it was not touching her, she could feel its warmth. Suddenly she was too aware of him beside her in the darkness of the car. Red Diamond—a man who sometimes infuriated her; a man who—she had to admit it—intruded too often on her thoughts. Ignore him she could not. He had some kind of fascination for her.

He spoke, and his voice was rough, edgy. "*I'm* sorry you came, Martyn Verity. You're going to be a problem to more than one person around here. It's a very great pity my stepmother asked you along."

"I don't know what you're getting at," said Martyn half indignantly. "She asked me because of Jan and so that—" She stopped. She had never confided her problems to Red. And wasn't it best to let him think what he did?

His fingers tugged in a disturbing way at a lock of hair that fell almost to her shoulder. "So that what?" he asked remorselessly. "So that you could get away from Bastian Sinclair for a while? Though I'll guarantee you've never told *her* who your boyfriend is." His fingers had released her hair, and now they touched the side of her neck, so delicately that she wasn't sure if she was imagining it or not. Because Red's fingers were simply not delicate. And besides, why would he touch the side of her neck like that? She felt herself grow tense, and though she held her head quite still, something went wild in her. Right now she couldn't get anything sorted out. She wondered why they were sitting here in the dark together—talking about what, she didn't know. Her mind was a mad, mixed-up kaleidoscope of picture and sensation, and she said incoherently, "I—I don't want to talk about it—my—my problems."

"No?" She felt his eyes reaching for her through the darkness, and then he moved nearer and his fingers caught the lobe of her ear and pulled it gently. Yet it was the most excruciatingly tantalizing sensation she had ever experienced. She caught her breath. She wanted to cry out, and she wanted to lay her face, her cheek, against his hand and capture it against the soft bareness of her neck. And that was what she did.

After that, the inevitable happened. She was in his arms, and oh, they were powerful arms. And his mouth—it didn't seek hers, but it was on her eyelids, her temples—her throat. Gently, gently—hovering only. He needed a shave—not badly, but quite definitely—and while one part of her was quite lost, while her hands had gone of their own accord to lie flat, fingers spread, against his back, warm beneath the soft cotton of his shirt—another part of her was almost shocked, and completely bewildered. It had been strange enough to think she was here alone in the car with him, but for this to happen, out of the blue—to be in his arms—

And then she recollected. He was going to find out how she stood in regard to emotion and experience.

It was like a dash of icy water in her face. He was not going to find out. Not anything. Particularly what she didn't know herself. If his lips found hers, she might hate it. She might. But she was doubtful. She just didn't know how she would react—and she didn't want him to make the experiment, to find out—

She stiffened and withdrew.

"Enough?" he said softly—mockingly. She wished she could see his face and in some strange way she hated him because she couldn't. And she hated him for the way he asked her, so coolly and clinically, "Enough?" She had the feeling she was trapped, that he *had* found out something and that whatever it was, it was not to Martyn Verity's advantage.

She didn't say another word to him before they parted for the night.

CHAPTER SEVEN

AFTER the day of the picnic, Martyn was determined to make a really serious effort to avoid even a moment alone with Red. David had warned her that Fay and Red would probably be married soon, and it was embarrassing to think she had been thrown in his path deliberately by Poppy. The slightly humiliating part of it all was that she couldn't really feel herself to be in any way exclusive. Poppy, nice as she was, was an interfering matchmaker, and Martyn was just one more girl in the line—perhaps a last bid at a time when things, from Poppy's point of view, were getting rather desperate. Red had—what was the phrase Poppy used?—"Loved and dropped" a number of girls but Fay Bower looked like not qualifying for the dropped category. As for the "loved", Martyn knew nothing about that.

"And everyone's in the know," thought Martyn, riding moodily out across the paddock the following day. "I'm a late nomination for the position of Mrs. Tancred Diamond." It was a thought that made her singularly uneasy. Mrs. Tancred Diamond. Imagine belonging here—so far from the sea. Impossible? She might have thought so once, but now she wasn't sure...

Earlier in the day Poppy had shown her a big map of the Diamond Springs run, a map that took in the outskirts of the neighbouring properties, including Jindi-yindi, and while she had talked, her finger pointing out a dam here, holding yards there, a river crossing and so on, Martyn's mind had strayed off on journeys of its own. *That* was where she had seen the emus; and there, on the far side of the trees, was a waterhole. So, thought Martyn, the mother emu could have been taking her chicks there. And *that* was the track she had travelled with Red, and *that* was the camp where they had been branding the calves...

Now, though she rode across a seemingly endless paddock, she knew almost exactly where she was, and her thoughts went compulsively to the man she had determined to avoid. A man who was too tough and hard to be sentimental about love, who had never "worn rose-coloured glasses", and to whom the challenge of Jindi-yindi meant much, she was certain, despite the fact he had told Poppy it was a side issue. It was curious how he had touched her last night in the car, his fingers so gentle, his lips so caressingly soft—but *deliberately* so, she reminded herself quickly.

Do things just happen? Or do they happen because you want them to? she wondered. Or *not* happen because you *don't* want them to. Poppy had said, the first time they met, that she didn't believe in accidents of a particular kind—meaning Red and Martyn meeting accidentally on the beach. Well, that *hadn't* been an accident because Martyn had chased him into the sea. So now—had she in fact chased him to the outback? Had there been something else there all the time, hidden under her outward dislike of Red Diamond?

Her thoughts broke off. Away ahead of her, on the far side of the fence, an emu was racing, and to her amazement she saw that one emu—maybe six feet tall, and with the tiniest head you could imagine, but what muscular legs!—kick the wire fence, break it, and go through. Martyn, who had reined in her horse, stopped and stared. In the next paddock there were sheep. She could see them dotted about amongst the hummocks of grass and under the shade of the belahs. They were sheep kept for killing, as a change from the perpetual beef. It was something she had learned that morning when Poppy showed her the map. The paddock where they were kept was small, and she watched the emu stalking across it in a lordly way, looking this way and that, while a few of the sheep looked up and then began to drift, as if drawn by an invisible current, towards the hole in the fence.

Broken fences, as everyone in the outback knew— even Martyn—meant trouble. She stayed quite still, thinking. Sketched on her retina was that map of Diamond Springs. She knew where the men were working today, and that there was a gate in the fence some distance back. But she didn't need the gate, she could take her horse through the break in the fence and make her way to the paddock that was being mustered just a little bit more quickly.

It didn't take much longer than she had thought, and it wasn't hard to locate the working camp. There wasn't all that much dust, because there was still plenty of feed on the ground after the rains, but where there are a lot of cattle there is always a bit of dust.

She shaded her eyes and looked over at the men as she came nearer to the camp. She couldn't see Red, and that was just as well, seeing she wanted to avoid him. Mostly the men with the cattle appeared to be aboriginal stockmen—she couldn't even see that rangy character who was Red's overseer. But she caught sight of one man she recognized, amongst the bright checked shirts and broad-brimmed hats. The aboriginal Drummer, and she rode over and told him what had happened.

His big white teeth showed in a smile.

"Those emus! That two times they done that. I'll tell the boss, miss. He be here d'rectly."

Martyn didn't move away at once, though the thought of Red being here "d'rectly" made her feel guilty. He'd think she was chasing him up when she had determined to do quite the opposite... She asked Drummer, "How is the new baby? You called him Tancred, didn't you?"

"Too right! He's fine—come home soon to Diamond Springs. Teach him grow up to be a fine stockman, work for Red like me." He paused, then added a

word of warning. "That paddock next the killing sheep—
you watch out for emus in the long grass, miss."

Martyn said she would and out of the tail of her eye
she saw Red come riding up, and she turned in the
saddle ready to hear, "What the hell are you after, mermaid?"

Instead, he merely cocked his eyebrows, and asked
laconically, "How did you find the camp, Martyn?"

She coloured a little and put her head up. Drummer
had moved away a little, very discreetly. "Poppy showed
me on the map."

"And Poppy thought you could make it out here
without mishap?"

Her colour deepened. "I had no intention of coming
here," she said aloofly. She knew *Poppy* had had it in
her mind. "But I happened to see a break in one of
your fences, and the killing sheep are coming through
the gap. I thought I'd better let someone know."

His eyes were watching her intently, and now he
frowned. "Those damned emus again, I suppose.
Right—thanks for the news, you've been helpful.
Can you find your way home again?"

"Yes, thank you. Good-bye," she said abruptly, and
wheeled her horse. She sent Drummer a wave, and was
off, away from Red Diamond, forcing herself to forget
him and to think of those emus that she had meant to
look for and to draw.

She was back again the following day. Not at the
muster camp, but looking for the emus and the chicks.
And by late afternoon, with her wild-life drawings
done, she'd sought out a place where she could stretch
out and take a rest—a place where the ground was comparatively soft and red and sandy, in the shade of some
feathery-leaved acacias. She was wearing a pair of old
jeans she had brought and a pink cotton button-
through blouse. Already the jeans were grubby from
the time she had spent crawling about, hiding behind—
or in!—tall clumps of uncomfortably spiky grass, so she
could get closer to her prey.

She had seen two other adults as well as the one
with the chicks, and at one stage one of them had
actually stalked her while she was stalking its friend!
In fact, it had sneaked up on her to investigate while
she was busily drawing. It had approached her from
the side, and peered down to look at her sketches and
she had nearly jumped out of her skin. She had kept
quite still, those weird eyes had blinked at her, one
pearly plastic button was picked deftly from her blouse—
taking a scrap of cotton material with it—and then, its
curiosity satisfied, the emu had gone on its way unhur-
riedly.

After a moment of complete disbelief, Martyn had
laughed aloud.

Now all the excitement was over, the emus had
vanished into the scrub, Martyn lay on her stomach
watching the shadows moving over the red earth and
thinking out her story and its possibilities. A slight
breeze had come up and the trees, where she had left
her horse, made a hushing sound. It wasn't in the least
like the hushing sound made by the sea, it was plainly
and unmistakably an outback sound. A few birds flew
about—no seagulls wheeling and screaming here!—but
little bluebonnets, black and white magpies, a number
of roguish galahs.

The bush. The outback.

Lying on the red sand—on the very bosom of the
land—that received her warmly, securely, steadily. No
lulling rocking motion, no glitter of sun or white coral
sand. And when her tongue touched her lips and tasted
salt, it was the salt of her own sweat. But oh! it was a
fact that sea and salt and sand weren't everything in
life, even if you had been born to them and had lived
with them for the whole of your nineteen years. The
red heart of this country called to her as strongly as did
its golden shores, and it was all confused with the dark
image of a man with eyes that burned with the fire of
diamonds...

Martyn started out of a kind of dream as a shadow

blotted out the sunlight that touched her through moving leaves. She blinked her blue eyes open, her heart pounding, and jerked herself into a sitting position. Against the dazzling blue of the sky, she saw a man on horseback. Red! Then her heart dived. It was David Bower.

He smiled down at her, then swung from the saddle to the ground.

"Hello beautiful. I was looking for you. I saw your horse back there in the trees, but it took me a few minutes to locate you. You're well camouflaged there in your dusty pink, and as still as a goanna sunning itself. What have you been dreaming about?"

As he spoke, he lowered himself to the ground beside her and putting an arm around her pulled her body lightly against his own. Martyn resisted because it was instinctive. She scrambled to her feet, and he got up too, to stand, hands on hips, looking at her quizzically.

"What's making you so edgy? You're perfectly safe with me."

"I'm cramped," she said. It seemed the easiest thing to say. She stretched her arms above her head and wished vainly that she hadn't stayed so long. She had meant to be back at the homestead by this, in time to shower and clean up for dinner. She glanced at David frustratedly. He looked very handsome, very civilized, in his cream shirt, smart riding breeches and boots. His horse, obviously a thoroughbred, stood quietly under the trees.

He said, "I don't see nearly enough of you. You've been on my mind ever since the picnic—when Red came and broke it up just as I was about to kiss you. You didn't give me a chance after that, did you? Was it deliberate?" He stood close to her, half-smiling down into her face. Looking back, she thought his eyes were cold, devoid of expression as if a screen had been drawn across them.

She said indifferently, fidgeting a little, "It just happened that way."

"So why are you trying to avoid me now? On Sunday you were perfectly happy to have me kiss you—"

"You didn't kiss me," she interrupted.

"But I was about to, and you knew it. Yet just now—the way you scrambled away from me—well, it wasn't flattering."

Martyn sighed. "I don't particularly like kissing people," she said, flushing.

His eyes roved over her. "That's something I've never yet heard a pretty girl say—and mean." He took a step closer and reached for her hands, but she put them quickly behind her back.

"*I* mean it," she said.

"I thought you liked me."

"That doesn't mean I want you to kiss me." She glanced at her watch. "Anyhow, it's time I was going home."

"Home," he repeated, frowning. "To Red Diamond? Are you in love with him? Because if so, it's sheer waste. I've told you he and Fay are serious about each other. You're a rank outsider. It's common knowledge that Poppy brought you along because she doesn't like the Bowers, and that's just one more reason why you're not going to do any good for yourself. Red doesn't like to be pushed—and he doesn't like to be chased, either. Did you know that? He's a man who prefers to make his own decisions."

Martyn's colour was high. It was unpleasant to be told she had designs on Red. She said levelly, "I know that. And I'm perfectly satisfied to let him do so." Her eyes challenged him. "Are you?" Because she was pretty sure David was very interested in seeing Red and his sister team up, and Diamond Springs money flowing across the paddocks into Jindi-yindi.

Above, the sky was paling and the tree shadows were lengthening across the ground. Though she hadn't meant to say it, Martyn remarked, "I just wonder why Fay and Red didn't marry long ago."

"Meaning that my sister's older than you are? Well,

my dear, not every man likes to take on the task of teaching love to an ex-schoolgirl. And I don't think you're much more than that yet, are you?''

"Not much," she agreed levelly, but she felt wounded. It was true, and perhaps that was the whole trouble. She had reached the age of wanting to be more than a raw little ex-schoolgirl, and for the first time she wished Bastian had taught her something about love. Yet she had recoiled from the one lesson he had tried to teach her. She was still—Red had put it in words— reading the first primer. Bastian had started too much in advance for her, but David—Her eyes narrowed and she looked at him speculatively. Here was a man who could teach her something, if not about love, at least about its arts. Kissing—So why refuse the lesson she so badly needed? How much had she to learn before she could even *start* to learn! That was the paradox.

David said lazily, "Fay and Red are mature people— they understand each other. I suppose you know that Lewis Bower was in love with Fay—someone will have told you. As for Red, he hasn't lived the life of a monk. But he's ready to settle down now, and she's the obvious choice."

"You mean they love one another?" It was a ridiculous conversation, and Martyn rather thought that later she was going to wish she could forget it. She was aware that David was underlining very heavily the fact that she didn't have a chance with Red, and though when she first came outback it would all have bounced off her, somewhere along the line everything had changed.

David said, "I would presume so." He smiled down into her eyes, and when he reached for her hands this time, she let him take them and draw her towards him. He said softly, "You're young, but not too young for me. You're adorable." And then his arms were around her and his lips touched hers.

It was a flavourless, meaningless kiss. If Martyn had hoped to learn a lesson in love, then she was badly disappointed. His mouth against hers, his arms embracing her—deliberate, calculated—it was *nothing*.

She didn't know till David released her, and with one arm still lightly around her waist turned slightly, that a station wagon had driven up. Now she both saw it and heard it brake to a stop, the door flew open, and Red Diamond got out and stalked towards them, the red light of sundown on his face.

It was the first time she had seen him as red instead of black, and her eyes widened as he covered the few paces between them. His wild black hair, his strong, dark-browned face, his muscled forearms emerging from the rolled up sleeves of a black shirt—all were burnished by the rich red light lavished on them from a sky that had turned into a blaze of crimson and vermilion fire. She caught the flash of his eyes. Red Diamond. How well the name suited him! Something in Martyn's breast leaped up like a living flame to meet him, to salute him. She was totally unaware of the other man who stood so close to her, one arm possessively around her waist. One image only filled her mind. Hard as diamonds? She supposed so. She had certainly never seen a soft side to his nature. And yet—

His voice broke almost brutally into her dizzying thoughts.

"You'd better come along home with me, Martyn, now I've located you—and put Poppy's mind at rest. In her psychic way, she was quite convinced that something drastic had happened to you when you didn't turn up at your accustomed hour," he added dryly. He gestured back to the car. "I brought Drummer along to track you... I thought you were going to the cattle sales, David."

"I changed my plans," said David shortly. "Fay and I talked it over and decided those stores were not for us—we're more interested in buying good breeding stock."

The diamond eyes didn't flicker and there was no expression on Red's face as he said briefly, "I see."

"I'd meant to come and talk it over with you, but—" David shrugged and stopped, and Martyn could practically hear Red's unspoken question—"But what?"

Instead, he said somewhat curtly, "You must run things your way. Jindi-yindi's your show, not mine, and you're"—his grey eyes looked hard at the other man— "you're an experienced countryman. Come along now, Martyn."

Of course she went, but first she looked up into David's face to say "Good-bye. Be seeing you." And then at the car, from which Drummer had emerged to take over her horse, she looked back at David to remark, "That's a beautiful horse of David's. And doesn't he ride it beautifully?"

Red said nothing for a moment. Then— "That horse cost a packet. The man might do better to breed horses instead of trying to resuscitate a hungry, half dead cattle station."

Somehow Martyn knew he disagreed completely with the course David was following in regard to buying stock. For her part, she didn't know a thing about station affairs, but she agreed wholeheartedly with Red's pronouncement that David must run things his own way. Of course, when Red married Fay, then he'd have a finger in the pie—and wouldn't he give it a stirring up! She thought, "There'll be arguments—and I can guess who'll win." David would be driven away. Was that what Red wanted?

She got into the car beside Red. Her protest that she could ride home was ignored. Drummer was obeying orders.

"I want to talk to you, Martyn," Red said uncompromisingly.

She didn't ask about what. Just because David had kissed her, she supposed she was in for a lecture, though what business it was of Red's she couldn't imagine. And was soon to discover.

He wrenched the car into gear, swung it around, and they charged across the paddock.

"How often does this happen?" he fired at her.

Martyn blinked. "It's hardly your business," she retorted. "I don't have to tell you how often another man kisses me—"

He uttered an impatient exclamation. "Forget the kissing game. That doesn't interest me. All I want to know is how often you spend the afternoon with David Bower."

"That's my business, too."

"Not entirely," he snapped back. He turned his head sharply, his glance going to the open neck of her blouse. She raised her hand defensively, and discovered the missing button—the button the emu had nipped off. "You're a guest at Diamond Springs, and I'm not going to turn an entirely blind eye if you come back to the homestead with half the buttons missing from your clothes. However, at present all I'm interested in is how much time my neighbour has been wasting on you—time that would be better spent in an effort to straighten out a property that's badly in need of intelligent handling. I want to know if the delights of your company are so strong as to make him forget a mere cattle sale. Or if the real reason he forgot was because he'd spent too much cash on thoroughbred horses... Had you made a date with him for today?"

"No," said Martyn, her cheeks pink. She felt taken down a peg or two quite decidedly. Her self-interest must make her look very small in his eyes. "This is the first time David and I have met on your property—except last Sunday—so I hope he may be absolved from that particular parcel of guilt. Your honour," she added ironically.

He gave her a sharp look but no answer at all. When she glanced at him he was frowning, and thinking no doubt of David's sins and omissions rather than hers. But when he spoke again, it was to ask, "What do you do with yourself all day? Poppy says you disappear most afternoons—go out riding. You'll get lost one of these days."

"No, I shan't. I have a good sense of direction. Anyhow, I like coming out this way."

"What's out this way?" he asked suspiciously.

"Emus," said Martyn, and was answered by a short laugh of disbelief that *that* could be her interest.

That night after Poppy had gone to bed, and while Red was still in the office, Martyn worked rather frenziedly on her drawings at the verandah table near her bedroom. The whole events of the afternoon had unsettled her in some way, and she didn't want to think about them. She tried hard to become totally absorbed in her drawings of the emu and its chicks and the two small children who were to become involved with them, but it seemed almost impossible to stop herself from thinking about Red and Fay.

It was late when something made her look up, and there almost beside her was the man who had been in her thoughts. He had actually set a tray of drinks down at the end of the table and she hadn't been aware of it. Now he was watching her intently, and she wondered if, from his look of slight amusement, she had been drawing with the tip of her tongue out, a mannerism that had amused Bastian many times. She looked back at him almost guiltily, and the colour flooded her cheeks as she pushed back the fair hair that had fallen across her cheek.

"You're an unknown quantity, aren't you?" he commented. He reached for her sketch pad and began to turn the pages carefully. "These are natty—and they're clever too. Except," he added with a crooked smile, his grey eyes searching hers, "you've got the wrong idea who brings up the chicks in the emu family. That's father emu's task. And in fact it's the male that incubates the eggs. He then looks after the young for about two years while mother emu, except for playing sentry, generally has a good time." He put down the sketch book. "Are you going to have a gin and lemon with me, or don't you drink with the enemy?"

How seriously did he mean *that*? Not too seriously, she decided, as she gave him a wry smile and said, "I will have a drink, thank you."

"I didn't know you were an artist as well as a swimmer," he said a moment later as they sipped their long cold drinks.

"I'm not really," she said diffidently. "Drawing was about the only thing I was good at at school, but I wasn't clever enough to get a scholarship. Stan would have sent me to private classes, but that would have meant going to Sydney and I was happy living up the coast with him."

He nodded, serious now. "You were very close to your father?"

"Yes. I was the baby of the family, you see—well, there were only two of us, and my brother is twelve years older than I am. My mother died when I was small, then Dick went away to university and there were just Stan and me left. He was manager of the swimming baths." As she spoke, she was remembering what he had said about her a few days ago—that she was spoiled, and so on, and hadn't had to earn her own living. She had an idea he was surprised to hear what her father's job had been, and somehow she was glad she had told him. He didn't speak, and she went on rather hurriedly, "Stan always wanted me to have drawing lessons. He had a—a positively inflated opinion of my gifts. He was very—proud of me."

"It's not surprising. You appear to have a lot of talent." He reached for her glass and filled it up again. "You're not going to tell me you're entirely self-taught, are you? These drawings"—tapping her sketch pad with a firm finger—"appear to be practically professional standard."

She flushed with surprise and pleasure at his praise. "Thank you. I had some lessons from an elderly lady who'd retired up the coast, and then when I came to Sydney to live with Dick and Ros—" She hesitated, but he was waiting, so she went on, "Bastian gave me lessons. Free," she added, despite the hardening of his expression.

"Bastian Sinclair. Free private lessons. At his house." He said it almost explosively, and looked at her accusingly.

"Why not?" she said defiantly. "So you see, he's not just—not just an older man." She raised her glass and drank the contents down quickly, knowing that her cheeks were hectic. The gin had something to do with it, but there were other causes as well.

"I see," Red said, looking at her darkly. He had turned the reading lamp away so that there was only the glow of it reflected back from the off-white wall. "And this—proposal of his—you're deciding whether it's worth taking a calculated risk and teaming up with a man who is an art professor as well as a worshipper at the shrine of Aphrodite. I'd say it would be a highly unsuitable match, but you already know my opinion."

He waited, and she didn't know what to say. Having Bastian there in the background was like having a lifebelt, in some way. If she admitted that she had broken with Bastian, that he had never proposed marriage to her, that her problem was something quite other—then she would be on her own. And floundering in waters too rough even for her to battle it out. She would be—swamped. She said uneasily, "No matter what you think about Bastian, he's been—good to me."

His lip curled cynically. "Good to you? Yet your brother stopped the—drawing lessons, didn't he? And I suppose lecturing you makes you more pigheaded than ever. It's the old thing about forbidden fruit tasting the sweetest. And, as no doubt you're going to point out, *I* have no right to interfere in your diet. I wonder," he concluded speculatively, "how much—forbidden fruit you've already swallowed down? And if you've acquired a certain taste for it? Even what David Bower will hand out while you're in the throes of sorting out your priorities. No doubt Bastian Sinclair taught you a lot more than drawing in his house on the plateau. You wouldn't have been his first pupil, either. But of course that doesn't matter to you, does it?" He got to his feet slowly and deliberately, and reaching out took her empty glass and set it on the table. Then his fingers were clamped around her wrists and he pulled her to her feet. "Here's something else for you to digest."

She felt herself pulled against the hardness of his chest, and fear rose in her—fear that he would kiss her as Bastian had, because she was aware of something frighteningly fierce and primitive in his eyes—something too male and savage for her to contend with. If he only knew how limited was her experience in love— that David's kiss had been negative, that Bastian had kissed her only once and shocked the life out of her— that had been the full extent of *his* extra-curricular instruction—she heard herself gasp and twisted her head to one side to avoid the advance of his face towards hers.

Then she was crushed against the warmth of his body, and held so close she could feel and hear the heavy thumping of his heart. He held her hard so that she was completely helpless, and then one arm moved away while he switched off the reading lamp. Now, until her eyes re-adjusted, they seemed to be standing together in total darkness. His arm came back to enfold her. Petrified, she thought—One kiss and another, and then you're eased all the way from the patio to the bedroom. *Her* bedroom door was just a few feet away, and there in the hot darkness her bed was waiting, the cover removed, the sheet turned down. If he wanted he could carry her there and all she would be able to do would be to yell. "If you want something, let out a yell, and somebody will hear you ..."

He spoke against her hair. "What's the matter? Your heart's beating like you were some trapped creature— as if you were a bird that's been swooped on by a hawk." One hand came to rest against her ribs by her heart, and her heart beat faster than ever as the warmth of his hand came through her thin cotton blouse with the heat of fire. Now her eyes were accustomed to the dark, she could see the shadowy shape of his face with its black brows, the wild black hair, the curve of the long mouth with its full and sensual lower lip. She could see the diamond glint of his eyes.

"Who does your heart beat for?" He dropped his face to hers, speaking once more against the silken fall of her hair. "For the drawing teacher? For the handsome horseman from Jindi-yindi? Or is it expectation because I'm holding you like this—as if I were going to make love to you?"

"Don't dare," she said huskily. "I'll—I'll scream, I'll kick—" She paused to draw a much needed breath. "Let me go! I—hate you, Red Diamond—"

"Hatred's a very convenient cloak to wear," he mocked, his hold on her loosening not one fraction. "Haven't you heard it said also that it's close to love? *Love* meaning whatever you choose it to mean... I'm sure a girl who's already played around with a man of the world won't resist long once her senses have been roused by a few tricks."

Martyn bit hard on her lip. His hand still rested where it could feel her heart and she breathed out, "I just pity the girl you marry—you have no feeling—tricks are all she'll get, and tricks I despise—"

"Oh, come on now—David must have used a few tricks today, and you looked happy enough in his arms. If I hadn't come along, who knows what would have happened next? If you invite something you usually get it. Haven't you learned that by now?"

"I—I didn't invite anything from you," she bit out, though she was quaking. She had been right—he was too tough for her, far too tough. "Do you want me to scream? Do you want—Poppy to come?"

He gave a low laugh, a diabolical sound that matched the darkness of his dimly seen face.

"Poppy? To see us here like this would delight my stepmother." His lips moved to her temple and he added softly, "Doesn't it delight you to be in my arms, Martyn Verity? Doesn't it?"

Martyn felt herself slump against him, as if she were about to faint. He was holding her suffocatingly close, and her arms, even with their strong swimmer's muscles, couldn't withstand him. In despair, she heard herself say on a moan, "Do what you like—" Just what she meant by that she didn't know, whether it was surrender or pure defeat. But she thought wildly that if he took her at her word, there would come a moment when she would have the strength she needed to escape him. Because no one—not even Red Diamond—could do what they liked with Martyn Verity. It had never been that way. It never would...

Quite suddenly she was released.

He reached out and switched on the lamp and swung it round so that it shone full and harsh on the two of them. Her face was bloodless, her eyes enormous, their pupils dilated. And she was shaking. He said harshly, "Go to bed. The tricks *you* know just aren't in the book. I'm not going to carry you off by force. I simply imagined I was going to teach you a lesson."

Martyn said nothing. She knew no tricks. *He* was the one who knew the tricks. He and David and Bastian. All of them older men, the older men who he had accused her of—experimenting with, how long ago? But there was something in the way he played that baffled her. The axiom that Stan had taught her—Respect your body and others will do the same—didn't seem to have the same importance when he was around...

She turned away and moved blindly to her room. It was as he had told her back in Sydney. He could twist her round his little finger if he wanted to, and tonight, in fact, he had done exactly that.

And then, when he had done it, he had let her go. Underlining the fact that he wasn't interested in water-babies.

CHAPTER EIGHT

AFTER that, it was as if there were a glass wall between herself and Red. She saw very little of him in the next few days, and even to encounter him briefly around the homestead, away from the dining-room table, was a kind of excruciating agony, they had so little to say to each other. In the mornings, he was gone long before she arose, and Poppy's frequent suggestions that he should take her out on the run were always pointedly ignored.

She no longer went to look for the emus, preferring not to risk encountering David there again, but she still went riding, or swam in the river, and the days went by quickly enough.

Jan Diamond was in the process of deciding on her wedding date. There had been a telephone call from Terrigal, but Poppy had not yet arranged with Red the exact day on which she and Martyn would leave Diamond Springs. Martyn knew that for her it would be all too soon. Her outback adventure was rushing to its end with a frightening speed, and soon it would seem no more than a fleeting dream. One very real thing had happened, however. For the first time in her life she had fallen in love, and she couldn't see herself getting anything more than a broken heart. "The hearts of the young are very pliant," Red had said. Well, it was easy to talk when you were thirty-three ... There were times when Martyn wished she had never come but had accepted without protesting what fate most certainly had in store for her eventually—a course in typing.

When Poppy asked her that day over lunch on the

verandah if she had "nutted out" what she would do
when she went home, she had to admit she was without inspiration. They had not talked together a great
deal. Poppy was always busy, and now that the curtain-
making was over, she had organized the girls into doing
some very thorough housecleaning, which had begun
the day before and was continuing on today. Red had
said impatiently after dinner last night—before he did
his customary disappearing act into the office—"For
God's sake, can't you leave it all to Mrs. Hall?"

"It's not her work," said Poppy definitely. "She has
enough on her hands feeding the men and seeing the
sweeping and dusting are done. The cupboards here are
full of junk that haven't seen the light of day for ten
years or more. Your wife—when you take one—won't
want to move in with all that." She added almost accusingly, "And by the way, Tancred, I'm putting a few
things aside, some of them family things from way
back—history, you might say. I'd like to take one or
two bits of silver or china for the girls, so long as you
don't think it's anything Fay will fancy particularly."

Red frowned darkly at her. "Take anything you
want," he said irritably. "And just don't jump ahead of
me. I haven't announced that I'm marrying Fay yet,
have I?"

Listening, Martyn had wondered exactly what that
meant. Simply that he hadn't *announced* it? Or did he
mean he hadn't made up his mind? Well, either way, it
could hardly affect Martyn Verity...

Now, as they sat over lunch, Poppy commented unexpectedly, "Red says there's a man in your life, Martyn. Is it really serious?"

Martyn coloured deeply at her unexpected remark.
There *was* a man in her life, and for Martyn it was serious. But it wasn't the man to whom Red had referred.
She wondered if he had given Poppy any details and
rather thought not. It had most likely been a stratagem
to persuade his stepmother that it was no use trying to
match Martyn up with him.

She said, deliberately evasive, "Oh, my art teacher. I don't want to get married for ages yet." She hurried on, "I suppose the best thing after all will be to take that secretarial course when I go back." As she said it, it seemed completely unreal. To go back to Ros and Dick and their bungalow—it was impossible to believe that in a very short time she would be whisked back into the other world and into an activity that had no appeal for her whatsoever. Even the thought of her beloved sea didn't comfort her. As for her picture-story book, it would probably never get off the ground. All she would have would be some drawings that were a souvenir of her short stay on Diamond Strings.

"Well, it's your life," said Poppy on a sigh. "I had a silly idea I could help you some way—but I haven't. Still, we mustn't lose touch with you, Martyn. And you must certainly come to Jan's wedding. Tancred will come down for that. And I suppose Fay," she added with a grimace.

Martyn said, "Thank you," and managed a smile, but she knew she wouldn't go to the wedding. She would disappear completely from Red's life, and he wouldn't even be aware of it.

Meanwhile, he was not going to have another chance to play havoc with her feelings. It wasn't as if she didn't know his opinion of her, and while hers of him had changed and changed drastically, to him she was still doubtless, a woolly-minded kid with a kinky taste for older men. "But I don't have one for kids," he had said, and the words were engraved indelibly on her mind. So too was the memory of those extraordinary moments with him when he had held her in his arms and hadn't kissed her. Once she had dreaded the possibility of his kiss, now she longed for it and knew it would never happen.

That afternoon she went down to the men's quarters to look for Drummer's children, meaning to sketch them—and so provide herself with another souvenir to cry over. It was hot and still, the leaves of the tall gum

trees and the feathery pepper trees hanging straight and
motionless. The little dog Noosa, playing in the dust
with a half-rotten orange, growling at it, chasing it as if
it were a ball, came racing up to greet her with a feverish wagging of its tail. But there were no children to be
seen, and presently a fat old aboriginal woman with a
pipe between her teeth appeared and told her, "That
Elsey go walkabout—takem piccaninnies with um."

Disappointed, Martyn thanked her and wandered
back towards the homestead, but on the way decided
she might as well go for a ride. That would be more
profitable than dawdling around in the heat, and it no
longer seemed important whether she should encounter David or not.

Soon she was riding away from the homestead into
the peculiar silence and emptiness of the outback—
over the unending plain that was patterned here and
there by an island of trees around a waterhole, or the
backwater of a river, its solitude and stillness rippled
now and again by shadows as a flock of corellas flew
across the face of the sun; by parrots that showed brilliant colour against a grey-green background, by the
dark shapes of slowly moving cattle.

Reaching trees that sheltered the greenish water of a
billabong, she dismounted and wandered along the
shore, watching the scarlet and blue dragonflies that
hovered silently over the water's surface. Beyond,
through taller trees, she came to the river that flowed
unaccustomedly deep and slightly muddy between its
banks, and suddenly she stopped and shaded her eyes
and stared. A short way up, on the far side of the river,
were two very small black children, clad in bedraggled
cotton dresses. Staggering, they were dragging a great
sheet of bark across the flat stones that lined the low
bank of the river. This side, where Martyn stood, the
bank was steep and made of red earth, but where the
children were moving it was a kind of pebbly beach.
Suddenly their bark raft was launched and by some
miracle they managed to clamber on to it, the older

child almost going under when she missed her footing as she attempted to haul herself aboard.

Now they were both lying on their stomachs and the raft left the bank and began to move fast. It twirled around a few times and then began to float downstream. It all happened very quickly, and even while she was watching, Martyn was stripping off her jeans and cotton shirt. Then she had kicked off her sandals and, slithering down the steep bank, launched herself into the water that flowed even faster than she had thought. Those were Drummer's children, and heaven knew what they were up to, but they were pretty soon going to be in trouble, that was for sure.

She struck out from the bank and swam towards the bark raft, which was spinning crazily downstream. The children were plainly bewildered and beginning to be frightened. The older one was making vain efforts to paddle with one hand, but this did little more than to upset the equilibrium of the raft. And now the smaller child had stopped lying on her stomach and was trying to stand up. As she swam, Martyn kept her eye on them, well aware that any moment now those children were going to tip themselves right into the river. Even if they could swim—and she was inclined to doubt that they could—they were very small and they would be at the mercy of the current. Martyn could only hope that she would be able to deal with the two of them somehow or other when it all happened.

She swam powerfully, and the whole incident took only seconds. She reached the raft in the nick of time—just as it was about to capsize—and managed to steady it. Two pairs of liquid brown eyes gazed at her helplessly, and she said loudly and firmly, "Lie down flat, both of you—and keep still. I'm going to get you over to the bank."

The low bank—where they had come from—would be her best bet, she realized, as gripping the edge of the raft firmly between her two hands she began to propel herself backwards to the shore, using strong leg move-

ments and pulling the raft and children with her. A
glance behind showed the shore was further away than
she had hoped, and revealed also the fact that the
pebble beach had ended, though the bank was sloping
and much more negotiable than on the other side.

The children were babbling to her now, she caught
the words Noosa and Elsey and walkabout, and she
concluded they had tired of the camp life and hungered
for their puppy and the comforts of life near the homestead. So they had run away. And very likely would
have been drowned if she hadn't happened along—
though she hadn't completed her rescue yet, by any
means. She didn't speak but saved her breath for the
strenuous job of pulling the raft diagonally across the
current, hoping desperately that she wouldn't strike
any snags. The heavy rains that had fallen weeks ago
and caused all the damage to Jindi-yindi had flooded
this river too, for she could see debris stranded high up
on the banks.

Suddenly the children became excited, and Martyn,
who was beginning to feel the strain, yelled at them to
keep still or they would drown themselves. She discovered the cause of their excitement seconds later
when two large brown hands reached for the raft and a
voice said commandingly, "Let go, Martyn, I'll see this
through. Get yourself to safety—downstream at least
twenty feet or you'll be in trouble with that old dead
tree."

It was Red, of course, and with a slight gasp of relief
she turned to face him. Across his broad shoulders that
gleamed naked and brown in the harsh sunlight, she
saw a tangle of grey branches knifing wickedly from the
bank. He had taken over the raft and was swimming
the way she had done now, but instead of obeying him,
she swam round opposite him so that she could help by
pushing or steadying, whatever was necessary. After
all, two very precious little lives were involved! Across
the primitive raft, she could see his dark head, his wet
black hair, and the silvery flash of his grey eyes. It

seemed to Martyn that she stared half hypnotized into those eyes for a long time.

Red knew his river well, for he steered the float to a small inlet in the river bank—clear of snags, away from the current, low enough to negotiate. And it was not until that moment, as they reached safety, that she remembered she was wearing nothing but a minute pair of light beige panties and a tiny matching bra. She waited, treading water, while Red picked up each child and dumped her on the bank, and then his eyes found hers and his dark brows ascended.

"You next? Are you too done in to get out by yourself?"

She shook her head. She had sworn to herself there would be no more private encounters with him, and though now at least the children were with them, her heart was beating hard. His face across the dinner table when he was preoccupied with station affairs—or with his plans for teaming up with the Jindi-yindi people, for all she knew—was quite different from the face she saw now, darkly tanned, the sunlit water reflecting up into eyes so that they were more than ever like diamonds. On the bank the children waited docilely, none the worse for their escapade, but obviously a little in awe of the boss and expecting at least a scolding. They looked pathetic bedraggled little mites, and Martyn hoped he would not be hard on them. But she couldn't wait here to see what happened. Her clothes were on the other side of the river, how far upstream she didn't like to think.

Her teeth chattering a little from nerves, she told Red offhandedly, "I'll swim back to where I got in. My horse is there."

His eyes mocked her. "You might rate yourself high as a swimmer, but you're not going to make it up there against the current, mermaid. In fact, I'm just not going to let you try. There's been more rain up north and there could be a few snags drifting down. It's not as safe as the sea, you know."

"Oh, it's all right, I'll manage," she told him determinedly. She looked up at the children whose wet cotton dresses were rapidly drying in the heat of the sun. "You—you look after the children. Forget about me."

"You'll do as I say," he said sharply, commandingly. His eyes moved from her face to her bare shoulders showing above the surface of the water. He certainly couldn't see through this rather muddy-looking water, but she bit her lip vexedly. It would suit her a lot better to battle across the river somehow, but she had the very distinct feeling she was going to have to do as he said.

He said unexpectedly, "I presume you have *some* clothes on, Martyn," and added half humorously, "I did forbid nude bathing on Diamond Springs, didn't I? Well, it's no time to be prudish, whatever your state of undress. Come along now, or I shall have to take matters into my own hands."

He moved towards her purposefully and she set her teeth. It was all very well not being prudish, but her panties and bra hadn't been designed for the beach and they were infinitely more revealing than a bikini. And besides, when you'd had four inches cut off your hair just recently, you couldn't really look forward to riding a horse like a shorn Lady Godiva for heaven knew how many miles across the paddocks that, even if they should by a lucky chance be empty of stockmen, were still peopled by Red Diamond. Nor, near naked, her thoughts continued fantastically, could you expect to enjoy a walk, shoeless, through the bush.

He moved again, and, crazily, she ducked under the water. When she surfaced, to her relief he had hauled himself out of the water, and her embarrassed eyes discovered that he was wearing a pair of dark blue fitting briefs that could easily have been swimming trunks.

"I'll take pity on you, waterbaby," he said with weary cynicism. "I'll see these kids back to their camp in the mulga, and then I'll be back for you. I'll wear the trousers and you can have the shirt. But you're to get out of the water the minute my back is turned. Understand? You're not to attempt to swim back up the river. Do I have your promise? If not—" His eyes and the grim line of his mouth threatened her.

"I—I promise," she quavered, almost ingratiatingly.

She watched him move off, a tall broad-shouldered man with two tiny aboriginal children trotting at his heels. And then she drew a deep breath and climbed out on to the bank.

She stood in the sun and her sparse clothing dried in a matter of minutes, though her hair was still partly wet, and she felt—and looked, she was certain—as naked as could be. If only her things had been black or red or green—any colour but pale beige! Skin colour, in other words, lighter than the colour of her skin, actually...

It was a ridiculous situation to be in, and there was nothing to do but grin and bear it. Even if she broke her promise, and then somehow got across to the other side of the river—even then she'd have problems, because she'd be a long way from her clothes and her horse. No, she definitely needed help. It was just unfortunate that it should have to be his...

When he came back she had lapsed into a daydream, with the heat of the sun on her body and the glare from the water in her eyes, so that she started guiltily when he spoke, his voice remote and cold.

"Good God! For a moment I thought you were stark naked. Here, put this shirt around you and we'll see what we can do about taking you back to your own garments." He stood five feet off, broad and brown and intimidating-looking with his gleaming torso, his black hair, and the narrow-legged trousers and boots he now wore. He tossed a navy shirt across to her and, colouring furiously, she caught it. She fumbled with the sleeves, managed to get into it and to fasten the buttons quickly, aware that he stood, arms folded, eyes narrowed, watching her. It reminded her of the time she had seen him at the Fleets' swimming pool, and somehow been made conscious for the first time of her nakedness.

Like Eve in the Garden of Eden, she thought irrelevantly, slanting a look across at him, through lashes that were glistening gold in the sun. There was a tilted cynical smile on that sensual mouth of his, and he commented, to her discomfiture, "Now, believe me, you look more seductive than ever... Come along. You'll be relieved to know that I've got a vehicle."

Head bowed a little and too much aware of his physical nearness, she moved towards him, picking her way carefully through coarse grass and fallen strips of bark. Had she ever thought that he was not handsome? she wondered dazedly. He was utterly, devastatingly so. He made every other male in the world look insignificant, pallid...

He waited for her, and she edged past him nervily and jumped when he laid a hand on her shoulder.

"You're a funny little animal," he said conversationally, not removing his hand despite the fact that he must be aware of her reaction. "All self-confidence in the water, but on land as jumpy and nervous as a wildcat... Are you going to make it to the car barefoot? I drove as close as I could. Or shall I give you a lift?"

"I'll—I'll make it," said Martyn. And at that moment, unnerved by his touch and moving too quickly, she stepped on a bindi-eye burr and let out an automatic cry of pain. In a flash he had scooped her up into his arms, and though she wasn't a small girl, he carried her as easily as if she had been a child, one arm beneath her bare thighs, the other around her shoulders. She didn't struggle, it would have been undignified, but she felt her own heart thudding and his too, and she felt distinctly naked, under the ridiculously large shirt.

"You've a fine pair of legs," he said with cool admiration when he finally set her down near the car—an old and dusty-looking utility that was obviously general station property. She stood nervously in the red dust, longing to make some perky retort but quite simply unable to do so. Another few seconds and they were both in the car, but instead of starting up he turned and gave her a long thoughtful glance.

"Do you know you were acting quite in the old tradition, transporting those kids across the river on a bark raft? That's the way the aboriginals have been doing it from time immemorial." His eyes, anthracite grey and keen, held something more in their depths than mere inquiry. They were just not quite impersonal, and they were definitely disconcerting. How can eyes do this to anyone? Martyn wondered, as she looked back into them compulsively, simply unable to look anywhere else—fascinated, swooning a little in the strange and almost fearsome delight of answering eyes like those. Eyes that belonged to a man she had begun by hating and now—and now hungered for.

Dazedly, she said, "I didn't know. *They* found the piece of bark—I saw them launch it and I thought they might drown themselves. So—"

"So you didn't have a moment's hesitation in divesting yourself of your respectable clothing and going to the rescue. It was as well you did. I'd probably have arrived too late. I drove over to the camp to check up on their well-being—Drummer was a bit worried, Elsey's not all that reliable, and he hadn't wanted her to take them away. The blacks are camped in the mulga, the kids had grown homesick for their pup— and the good food."

"I guessed as much." She gave the ghost of a smile.

"You did? You take quite an interest in the domestic side of station affairs, don't you? Well, they're back with Elsey now, but someone will pick them up this evening and bring them back to the homestead. Mrs. Hall can take them in tow. Or Poppy. It might give her something a bit more useful to do than cleaning out cupboards." His eyes raked over her once more, and then he added, "I think you've taken to the outback. You get yourself around a bit, don't you?"

Yes, she got herself around. But she never went out

to the muster where she wouldn't be welcomed. She said, "It's not bad. But I prefer the sea."

"Ah yes—the sea and all its associations. Well, are you ready to go back now?"

The question disconcerted her. Of course she was ready. It wasn't her idea they should sit here all day exchanging glances and chit-chat... Or did he mean— was she ready to go back to the coast? She raised her eyes and felt herself quail. He saw too much—his eyes looked too hard.

He said, "Why are you so scared of me, mermaid?"

"I'm not," she retorted. But she was—for reasons she could never tell him. She added, "I just think you're hard—invulnerable—"

His eyes narrowed. "Invulnerable? Well, it wouldn't be good for a man in my world to be too much the other way, would it? And hard—well, we've agreed before, I'm hard as diamonds. The old cliché. Though lately I've begun to question that."

A long moment passed and she thought he was going to reach for her, she saw the muscles of his hard brown arms move, because he was naked from the waist up. Then instead he turned away from her and started up the motor. And she was—yes, she was disappointed, she Martyn Verity! The shame of it! What had happened to her resolve—to her principles?

He drove rapidly along the river bank and finally they reached a rough-looking bridge and rattled their way across it cautiously. He said, "We don't generally need this, only when the river's up," and she nodded. Now they were heading back in the other direction to where she had left her horse, her clothes, and neither of them spoke again.

Her horse was there, and she located her clothes with only a little difficulty and got back into them, then rejoined him. He had left the car and stood, hands on hips, looking out over the paddocks, and now turned to face her, glancing over her as she stood there, respectable again in her old jeans and the green top. She handed back his shirt and as he got back into it, he drawled out, "What's happened to the honeymoon gear you brought along, I wonder?"

"I keep that for the homestead," she said pertly, though she had coloured. "There's no one to impress, riding around."

"No? Well, you've impressed me today. Still, don't bother too much tonight. Any old thing will do." He sent her an enigmatic smile, and helped her up into the saddle. Then with a brief salute, he got back into the old utility and they had parted company.

On Saturday night the Bowers turned up at Diamond Springs; Martyn had no idea whether it was by invitation or not. Dinner was over and Poppy, Red and Martyn were, for once, all sitting together on the verandah.

Red got lazily to his feet the moment he saw car lights outside, and then Fay, with David behind her, came up the verandah steps and the first thing she did was to reach up and kiss Red. Martyn turned away, a feeling of burning jealousy in her heart.

Once greetings were over, Poppy disappeared into the kitchen for coffee. David gravitated towards Martyn, who had remained in the chair, and Fay flung herself down in a lounger exclaiming, "Do you know we came across some vagrants camped in the mulga, Red? On *our* land—with a fire lit and looking absolutely horrifyingly dirty. It shouldn't be allowed—I'll be simply scared to ride around by myself, they look really wild."

"I don't think you need worry," Red said laconically. "They're a harmless lot—some of them are from round the station here and the rest would be relatives. You've got to remember some of them owned the land before we did, and though they're fast losing their old ways and their old freedom, there are still traditions and laws that hang on."

David, who had dropped down on the floor at Martyn's feet and was leaning back against her legs, said lazily, "This liberal attitude. Always seemed lunatic to me. Personally, I don't favour catering to people who have no interest in contributing. It's just too facile an excuse for not working."

"It's hardly a problem," Red said levelly. "From my angle, I wouldn't interfere. You just learn to work with it... If they scare you, Fay, keep out of the way, that's all."

Poppy had brought the coffee, and Martyn, tiring of David's closeness and irritated as well as embarrassed that he had begun to stroke her bare ankle, got to her feet to hand round the cups.

"I should be able to go where I choose," exclaimed Fay autocratically. "Jindi-yindi belongs to me and David, after all. And the way they call me Fay—people whom I've never set eyes on in my life before, I'll swear. It's unnerving. And they *laugh*—at nothing. I never had this experience when Lewis and Aunt Ann were at Jindi-yindi—never!"

"That's not surprising," Red commented, stirring sugar into his coffee. "You didn't rove around in those days. You were over here in the daytime and safe at home with Lewis at night." Martyn looked at him quickly, but his face was quite expressionless, and suddenly the subject was changed when David suggested a picnic the following day.

"Sorry, not for me," Red said. "You're welcome to stay the night if you wish, but I shan't be free tomorrow."

Fay, her cup half-way to her lips stared at him suspiciously, and then looked at Martyn in a hostile way as if she might well be to blame. "Why? What's on?"

"I'm driving to town to fetch Iris and the baby home."

"Iris?" Fay repeated blankly.

"Drummer's wife," Red said briefly.

Martyn's eyes shone. "And the baby—Tancred?" she exclaimed impulsively.

"Sure," he agreed with a grin. "My namesake."

Fay looked daggers. "My God! What a cheek, to call

that baby after you! But surely they can come out with the mail or something. You don't have to go, Red—not on a Sunday when you work every other day of the week and it's the only time we get a chance really to see you."

"Iris is special," Red said, narrowing his eyes. "Remember her, Fay? She used to work in the house here sometimes—a pretty, graceful girl—"

"None of them are *that*," Fay protested, and though she smiled, it didn't reach her eyes. "Anyhow, I wish you'd change your mind, Red, just for once." She turned to Poppy, whom she had more or less ignored. "Red tells me Jan's getting back on her feet again, Mrs. Diamond."

"That's right. All too soon she'll be married and I'll have the last of the girls off my hands. It makes me feel just a little bit sad. I'm sentimental, I suppose. But we'll make it a lovely wedding."

"I'm sure you will," Fay said politely. "You'll be leaving us soon to make the arrangements. And you'll be going too, Martyn," she added sweetly, turning her champagne-coloured eyes in Martyn's direction. "I guess you've had almost enough of the outback by now. It's a lonely place, isn't it?"

"Lonely—but lovely," said Martyn composedly, to her own surprise.

"Hardly lovely," protested David. "I'd prefer to live closer to the coast any time. Still, when you're left a property you don't turn up your nose at it. And if we hadn't taken it up, I'd never have met Martyn Verity," he concluded, pulling the chair he had taken closer to her.

Martyn ignored the compliment which had sounded so insincere to her ears that it made her writhe, and when Poppy gathered up cups and tray and murmured something about seeing to the extra beds, she went to help her. The house girls were by now off duty, and once the rooms had been prepared for the unexpected guests, Martyn slipped off to her bedroom, and gave herself a too early—and consequently rather restless night.

When she got up in the morning, Red had gone and her heart sank. She had had some totally illogical and unfounded idea that he might ask her to go along with him to collect Iris and the new baby. Her spirits sank lower still when she discovered that *Fay* had gone with him—though David was still around. She suffered all that day from a burning jealousy, at the very thought of Fay alone with Red. Just as though *she* hadn't known from her very first day here practically, that Fay was head of the line for being the future Mrs. Tancred Diamond. Her feelings were so acute that she felt positively ill, so much so that Poppy commented on her pallor. It served at any rate as an excuse for rejecting David's suggestion that they should go down to the swimming hole that morning. And once breakfast was over, she retired to her room, where for some time she looked over her drawings with a feeling of dissatisfaction, and wondered when the ache in her heart would go.

Never, seemed the most likely answer.

After lunch the three of them, David, Poppy and Martyn, went out to the waterhole. It was cooler out there, but for Martyn the two hours they put in were scarcely tolerable. She was so utterly miserable and could think of nothing but Red and Fay Bower. He was spending the day—the *whole* day with her! But wasn't he going to spend the whole of the rest of his life with her, very probably? It hardly looked as if he were having second thoughts now, though last night she hadn't thought Fay had showed up in very glowing colours. Red must be pretty tolerant—or else his affair wasn't as cold-blooded as he had made it appear. This time, Martyn reflected moodily, his glasses were at least slightly rose-tinted. And Fay must be really mad about him to have made the trip today, seeing she'd have to come all the way home in the car in the company of an aboriginal woman with a little baby named Tancred! The thought made Martyn smile to herself—and her smile provoked David's curiosity. She hoped she would be able to see that baby before she left Diamond Springs...

She saw him that evening, after they went back to the homestead. Red and Fay had already returned and were sitting in the garden in the shade of a big gum tree, smoking and drinking iced beer. Once again hot jealousy flared in Martyn so that she could scarcely bear to see them together. It would be a good thing when she and Poppy had left Diamond Springs. Poppy was walking ahead, while she and David brought up the rear, his arm possessively about her waist. Well, who cared? She let it stay there. She had been moody and silent all afternoon, and David had been fed up with her unco-operativeness, she was aware.

She slipped away as soon as she could to change out of her swim suit, and rather defiantly got into beige shorts, her sea-green top, and long socks—the very gear she had been wearing the first time she ever saw Red. Then, instead of going back to join the others, she went round the verandah, made her way through the back garden and down to the small cottage where Drummer and and his family lived.

Iris—and she *was* pretty, as Red had said, with big cheekbones and lovely dark eyes—was sitting on the verandah nursing her baby, the pup Noosa was in the dust—wrestling with a large potato today!—the two little girls were admiring their baby brother, and Drummer sat nearby smoking a cigarette and looking very proud. The children were too shy to speak to Martyn, but Drummer got up to welcome her and invite her to come and see the baby.

"This Martyn Red tell you about," he explained to Iris, and Martyn wondered what on earth Red had been saying about her. She stepped up on the verandah, Iris raised her big darkly lashed eyes and told her, "We call him Tancred after Red. Next baby, mebbe Martyn after you. You fished those kids out of the river."

So that was what Red had told her! Martyn smiled.

"Oh, it was nothing. Red did most of it anyhow." Then she admired the baby, agreed that he was like Drummer, and that he looked "plenty clever", and was about to go when Red arrived.

"It's a fine big healthy baby, isn't it? I thought I might possibly find you here. Are you ready to come and join the company now? No more slipping away being antisocial like you did last night."

She bit her lip and they walked back to the homestead together. Her feelings were mixed, just to be with him was both marvellous and unnerving. She had the feeling that the moment they rejoined the others, he and Fay would announce their engagement. "Maybe they'll make it a double wedding with Jan and Barry," she thought, and she longed to run away—to disappear.

"Did you have an enjoyable day?" he asked after a minute or so during which they had walked in complete silence. In the distance, Martyn could hear Noosa barking, and then the baby let out a lusty bellow. She glanced up at Red with a slight smile, but he had no answering one. "I suppose you amused yourself very well with David."

"That's right," she agreed, wounded by his sharp-edged silver-grey look that was so impersonal.

"Yet I gather from Poppy that you've worked out your destiny and decided Bastian Sinclair is the man for you," he said reprovingly. "You're making a big mistake, you know. And quite frankly I find it hard to believe he actually wants to marry you, beautiful though you are. I'd have been prepared to bet one of my prize beasts that his proposition was a very different one."

The colour surged into her face and she turned her head quickly aside. "You always like to be right, don't you? Well, it's a pity, but you're not."

"I'll make another bet, though. I'll bet you never do marry him."

"You can bet whatever you like," she said. They had come within sight of the others now. The blood had receded from her cheeks and she felt more composed and was able to look at him again. "I don't care terribly much *what* you bet, Red Diamond."

His gaze moved to her mouth and he smiled a little. "No? I could make you care—about a lot of things—if I wanted to Martyn Verity."

"You think," she retorted, and wished she could control her heart. He was so right—all the time—and if he once more got her into his arms she would be absolutely and utterly lost.

His eyes flicked over her. "Why did you get back into the little girl gear today?"

"Perhaps because I am a little girl," she suggested, annoyed. Was there nothing about her he could just leave alone?

"Oh no. I'll admit you can get away with it, but you're way beyond the little girl stage these days. You've grown up quite considerably since you came outback... I'm sure David's senses will be titillated when he sees you in that get-up. I shouldn't like to be in Bastian Sinclair's shoes, quite frankly—with you out here playing havoc with all the available male hearts." The last was said almost under his breath, for now they had reached the others.

Martyn's nerves were screaming. She moved quickly away from him and took a chair near Poppy. It was sheer torture to sit there while the others talked and she expected every moment to hear that Red and Fay were engaged.

Dinner was no better and yet eventually it was all over. Nothing had been said about engagements, and the visitors were actually on their way. At the last moment David, in full view of the others, took her in his arms and kissed her. She felt as little as if she had been a stuffed dummy—quite insensible—but over David's shoulders she saw Red, eyes narrowed, lips curling contemptuously. And then he turned away. To Fay.

CHAPTER NINE

RED hadn't gone when she came out to breakfast next morning, though he was on the point of leaving. She had got into some of her new clothes—her honeymoon clothes—a particularly smart tailored cotton top, dark blue with a silky stripe in emerald green to match the very superior pants that went with it. It was a sort of morale-booster, because her morale had been very low during a restless, almost sleepless night.

Finding Red still about was unnerving, yet at the same time her heart leaped exultantly. He had already breakfasted and Poppy had gone to the kitchen for more coffee for Martyn when he appeared on the verandah where Martyn sat alone at the table. She glanced up and felt her face crimson, and saw his obviously amused reaction to that.

He said coolly, "Waterbaby clothes are out today, I see. Who's the super-sophistication in aid of? You didn't know *I'd* still be around, did you?" She hadn't answered when he went on abruptly, "Why don't you ride over to the muster camp this afternoon and we can come home together."

She stared at him, stupefied. He, Red Diamond, was inviting her to the muster! And to ride home with him! She must be dreaming—she positively must! Or else she'd misunderstood somehow.

She said instinctively, without thinking it through, "No, thanks. You might think I was chasing you."

For an instant he looked quite baffled and then he frowned and said quietly, "I'm inviting you, Martyn." His eyes, diamond-hard, bored into hers.

"And I'm—refusing," said Martyn, quaking inwardly, and hoping he didn't know what an effort it cost her to refuse. An immense effort!

"Time's running out," he warned, eyes glinting.

Her heart leaped like a startled deer. Wasn't *that* something she knew with every fibre of her being? Time was running out. Martyn Verity, who had come here a raw, innocent girl, would soon be leaving with a new maturity—admitted to by Red—that had cost her the price of a broken heart... Quickly she pulled herself together.

"If you mean what I think you mean—that I should see all I can of the outback while I'm here—well, I've already seen a fair bit. All I want to see."

He leaned back casually against the verandah rail, a lock of dark hair falling across his brow, those shoulders that were so powerful and muscular straining against the material of the dark checked shirt he wore.

"Are you trying to tell me you don't like it here? That you've only been pretending—"

"Have I pretended? I thought I told you I preferred the sea." She wished that Poppy would come back and break up this tête-à-tête—and yet too, she wished that she wouldn't. These days, in fact, she didn't know what she wanted at all. To spend twenty-four hours of the day in Red's company or not to see him at all. Each in its own way would be torture... "Anyhow, I *belong* to the coast," she said a little desperately. "It's—it's nice enough out here—it's different—" Her glance went past him to the sunlit plain that stretched out and out beyond the garden. "But the sea—the sea is my first and last love," she concluded, conscious of her own artificiality.

His brows tilted cynically. "That sounds really great. Most impressive. Rather like a line from some corny soap opera." He paused. "In other words, it's completely meaningless—empty words. Because one day when you're past the romantic first-love stage—if we can call it that—you'll forget all about the sea. You won't care, in fact, what landscape lies outside your bedroom window," he concluded deliberately.

Her lashes came down defensively and her cheeks flamed. *That* had happened already, if he only knew it. If the truth were told, all she ever wanted to see through her bedroom window was what she was seeing right now...

To cover up her discomposure she told him, "I'm not in the romantic first-love stage anyhow. The man in my life is—mature—" She faltered, and to her relief Poppy came through the door with the coffee.

Five minutes later Red, with no further mention of his invitation, had gone.

The morning dragged by somehow, and Martyn was torn with a searing indecision. Would she ride out to the muster camp? It was a terrible temptation. He *had* invited her—but why? That was what she couldn't follow. Was it to tempt her—to see how she'd react? Because he refused to believe in her love affair with Bastian?—and how rightly! Because he had bet she would never marry Bastian? Or should she calm down and take it all at its face value? He was just offering to show her a little more of the outback. Quite likely she was making mountains out of molehills, looking for significance in something that was quite without it.

Mid-afternoon saw her down at the saddling yard, with Bob obligingly saddling up a horse for her and telling her casually, "Yeah, the boss said you'd probably be wanting a horse. You're to have New Copper now, he said."

New Copper was a little chestnut, and though she had little knowledge of horses it was apparent even to her that he was a finer horse than the one she usually rode, a bay. Perversely, she wanted to settle for the bay today, but the boss's orders were apparently to be obeyed—there was simply no question of Bob's being interested in her personal desire. So New Copper it was, and soon she was riding down one of the tracks that radiated from the homestead, under a blue and cloudless sky.

She told herself she was just taking a ride, that she wasn't going to take up Red's invitation, but she didn't really trust herself. When she came to a gate and had a choice of two ways to go, she chose the way that would, at least, take the longest time to get to the muster camp— *if* she should finally decide to go there. Almost by instinct, she headed in the direction that led to where she had seen the emus and chicks, and when she reached a certain clump of trees, she dismounted indecisively and walked her horse through bright sunlight and shadow, her hat hanging down her back, her blue and green shirt opened a couple of extra buttons to keep her cooler.

Presently a movement on the bright sunlit plain caught her eye. A horse and its rider were coming briskly in her direction. For just a moment her heart stood still, as she wondered if it were Red. But eventually it turned out to be Fay Bower—the Bower Bird—on a well-bred high-spirited horse—that had no doubt cost a high proportion of the money that should have gone towards the restocking of Jindi-yindi. Fay rode beautifully, like a girl from a high-class riding school. She looked poised, sophisticated, and very sure of herself, and as well groomed as her horse—cream shirt, tobacco-brown riding breeches, shiny dark tan boots, on her head a soft cream felt hat with a plaited snakeskin band and chin strap. Ros had tried to equip Martyn adequately for the outback, but riding breeches and boots had not come into her calculations because Ros just hadn't reckoned on Martyn's taking up riding.

Fay reined in when she reached the trees, dismounted, tossed her reins carelessly and with a practised hand over a branch, and came towards Martyn.

"Hello. Where do you think *you're* going?" was her insolent greeting.

Martyn's chin went up. "Why?" she asked flatly.

Fay coloured brightly with anger. "I suppose you're

planning to run down Red at the muster camp. Why
can't you be satisfied with collecting just one scalp in
the outback?''

"I don't know what you're talking about," said Martyn.

"No? You've got David at your feet—but you want
Red too."

The two girls looked at each other with hostility.
Martyn didn't think she had David at her feet, and she
was sure Fay didn't think so either. As for Red—she
was worried about him quite needlessly.

"So if you're chasing my man," breathed Fay,
"*don't*. Aren't you aware that Red and I are going to be
married? If you aren't, then I'm telling you, and you
might as well accept the fact and save your energy."

Martyn felt herself trembling, partly from shock at
Fay's—announcement, partly from the way in which
the other girl addressed her. As if she hated every
smallest bone in her body, every cell... She said in a
voice that was far from steady, "Don't worry, I'm not
chasing—your man, I'm—I'm looking for emus."

Fay uttered a disbelieving exclamation and Martyn,
who had had enough, turned her back, mounted New
Copper as skilfully as she could manage—which was
certainly not very skilfully—and cantered off. Fay
called after her spitefully, "Red won't be pleased to see
you mishandling one of his best horses, I warn you!"

Martyn didn't bother to answer. It might have given
her pleasure to tell Miss Bower that Red had left instructions that she was to have this particular horse, but
she didn't come back to do so. Because she disliked Fay
too much. And that, she admitted to herself as she
gave New Copper his head and let him carry her out of
the shade and into the heat of the burning sunlight, was
completely and stupidly irrational. Fay was just a normal, likeable young woman. She must be, or Red
wouldn't be marrying her. And *that* of course was the
reason why Martyn hated her so much. Martyn's heart
felt torn to shreds. It hurt her almost physically that

Red was going to give his love—his passion—to Fay Bower. Yet it was going to happen, and even though she had more than half expected it, the fact was unbearable, searing.

She let New Copper go where he would, and then, when they reached more trees, she reined in and tried to think rationally. But she discovered she was beyond rational thought. She was quite simply filled with a burning determination to go to that muster camp—to see Red—no matter who he was going to marry, and no matter what Fay Bower said. She sat quite still in the saddle, breathing evenly and trying to decide which way she had to go. Fay and her horse were not to be seen anywhere. In fact, there was no moving creature in sight, not even an emu, except far off across the plain, so far as to seem unreal, a few cattle moving slowly and feeding in the shade.

At this moment Martyn knew herself filled with the same compulsion that had made her swim out into the Pacific Ocean in pursuit of Red Diamond, weeks ago. *Then* she hadn't known what possessed her, what had driven her. Now she suspected it was the same emotion she was feeling now—that even at that early stage she must have responded to Red's attraction, at some level way below the conscious one. *Now* she admitted to physical attraction and to a whole lot more. She had fallen in love with Red Diamond, so madly, so helplessly that nothing else mattered—nothing. She had thought not so long ago that she would most assiduously avoid him for the rest of the time she was at Diamond Springs, but now she knew that she wouldn't. That she couldn't. Despite Fay, despite everything, she had to see him—to be with him—all she could. Pride was forgotten.

Eyes narrowed against the glare, Martyn chose her way unerringly. She touched New Copper's side gently with her knees, pulled lightly on the reins, and they were away off across the red plain with its covering of spiky grass clumps and near-green, after-flood growth.

Her mind went briefly to Stan. What would he have thought to see his daughter thus possessed by love—riding dementedly after a man who was going to marry another girl? To know that his daughter hungered to have that man's hands on her body, and his mouth against hers? A brief pang of shame struck through her, but she knew she had progressed far beyond the rough moral guidance that Stan had handed out. Love—passion—whatever you liked to call it—such as she harboured for Red Diamond put her way outside the influence of decent homely morals such as Stan had preached. This was—the law of nature, she supposed, and she felt her lips and her cheeks burning as she rode on.

She didn't know what she expected from Red. All she cared was that she should find him. He could lacerate her with his tongue—he could take a stockwhip to her. She would pay any price for a few moments of being real to him. His invitation of the morning now seemed no more than a challenge. He would not really expect her to come—not her, Martyn Verity.

But Martyn Verity never got even as far as the next paddock. Deep in thoughts that were driving her crazy with their insistence, she urged her horse away from the track to cut through long grasses that skirted a group of dark-leafed belahs, and suddenly—suddenly—right under New Copper's feet an emu rose up with a grunt and a hiss. The startled horse bucked and bolted, and Martyn was thrown clean out of the saddle. She hit the ground with a thud and every atom of wind was knocked out of her body.

She lay there unconscious, a crumpled heap in the long grasses. She didn't know that the emu, with a warning grunt to the chicks he had been sheltering in the sun, sauntered over curiously to look down at her; to stoop his long neck and methodically, though not very neatly, pick every button except one from her pretty blue and green shirt. And then, after another long stare from his double-lidded eyes, to return to his small family and bustle them off across the plain in search of another place where they could rest in the heat...

When at last her lids fluttered up, she saw nothing but an intense and unending blueness. Her body felt weightless, curiously numb and non-existent, and for a while she thought she had been killed. She thought she could see waves rolling in to the beach and seagulls flying, and she saw her father, Stan, his leathery skin, his wise and kindly blue eyes. And then she moaned because there was a fire in her breast. With an effort she moved one arm and discovered painfully that she had not been killed after all. The sea, the gulls, and Stan's face disappeared, and a shadow came across the blue of the sky.

A man with dark glinting eyes was stooping over her. "For God's sake, are you all right?" Red Diamond asked.

Martyn struggled to sit up, groaning at the pain she felt. Instantly he had an arm around her to support her, then to lower her to the ground again. "Stay where you are and tell me, if you can, what's happened—what's hurt you." His voice was sharp, his eyes had narrowed to slits that glittered frighteningly. "Has David Bower been here?" His fingers were pulling the edges of her shirt across her breast, and widening her eyes she saw that her blouse was completely unbuttoned. She stared with bewilderment. What *had* happened? For a moment her mind was completely blank and then remembrance came flooding back.

"The horse—New Copper—threw me. I'm—I'm all right."

"Lie still," he commanded when she tried to sit up again, and she obeyed weakly. His fingers were examining her now, gently, competently searching for broken bones. Her ankles, her legs, her ribs, her collarbone— she could feel those brown fingers on her bare skin. Then he was saying, "You appear to be all in one piece. I'm going to get you out of the sun. Now just relax—"

His arms were around her as he lifted her from the

ground, and she winced a little. There were no bones broken, but her body felt shocked right through, sore and bruised, and her ribs hurt when she breathed deeply.

"You were lucky to be cushioned by the grass," he said close to her ear. This time when he held her she couldn't feel his heart beating, but she was aware of the dull shocks that shook her body as with long careful steps he carried her to the utility and settled her gently on the seat. She leaned back, closing her eyes, feeling perspiration break out on her forehead and upper lip. Automatically her hands went to her blouse, but when she tried to fasten it, the buttons weren't there.

Her eyes flew open and she met his hard quizzical gaze. As though it were a curious dream, she remembered his saying to her, "I'm not going to turn a blind eye if you come home with half your buttons missing." Now—it was just a little bit funny, but *all* her buttons were missing—all except one, and she knew exactly what he thought, and she knew— Of course! It was all coming back. The emu—hadn't Drummer warned her long ago of disturbing an emu in the long grass? And she had ridden blindly, carelessly, because she had been thinking so absorbedly of Red. Who now thought the worst of her...

He told her carefully, "I came to look for you when New Copper came trotting up riderless. And I want to know—was David Bower with you before you took that fall? If so, I'll hunt him up and I'll—"

She stared at him wildly. Uncontrollable tears had welled up in her eyes and were spilling over. "No, Red, it wasn't that at all." She stopped, remembering Fay, and a pain struck through her heart. She had forgotten what Fay had told her, and now it was a new torture to look at the dark-faced man who stood by the open door of the utility and was reaching into the glove box. He took out a flask, unstoppered it, and held it to her lips without speaking. Martyn took a swallow and spluttered. She closed her eyes and hoped he wouldn't see her weak tears. She heard the car door shut, and then she sensed him getting into the seat beside her. The motor started up and the utility began to move slowly across the paddock.

"I'll get you home," he said as if from far off. "We'll have this out later."

Martyn hardly remembered getting back to the homestead. Everything had become rather hazy. She knew that Red carried her to her room and that someone got her out of her clothes and into her old striped pyjamas. She remembered drinking some hot milk laced with some sort of spirit, and after that she supposed she slept.

When she woke again, the room was nearly dark and she could hear voices on the verandah. Red was saying something about "shock".

"She'll be about as good as new tomorrow."

"About? What do you mean?" asked Poppy's voice. In her room Martyn struggled to sit up and, wincing, reflected that *she* knew what he meant. She was going to be covered in bruises. But her head, fortunately, felt almost perfectly clear.

"Are you sure there's no concussion?" Poppy asked, the words sharp with anxiety.

"Pretty sure. I'll have a talk with her when she wakes and see if there are any signs. If there are, then of course she must go to hospital."

Martyn discovered she was listening to his voice but hardly taking in what he said. That voice—would she ever be able to forget it? It was like Red himself. You couldn't say it was a beautiful voice any more than you could say he was a good-looking man. It was just—Red. Tough and masculine and uncompromising. And she, Martyn, loved it, and she loved his eyes and his hair, and the way his jaw was dark in the evenings, and she loved his big strong-fingered hands, and his broad shoulders, and his very toughness and maleness.

And all of it—*all of it*—was for Fay Bower.

She leaned across and switched on the bedside light,

and almost instantly he—not Poppy—came through the verandah door into her room. She felt her breath catch in her throat just to see him.

"Well?" He looked at her from six feet away. His jaw was dark, he hadn't shaved this evening, she noted, her eyes taking him in from the cover of her lashes. He still wore the dark checked shirt and narrow trousers he had worn that morning, though that morning now seemed a lifetime away.

"Well what?" she asked, leaning back on the pillows, modest in her neat unfussy pyjamas.

"Have you recovered?" he asked dryly.

"Yes, thank you."

"Any headache?" He came further into the room and sat on the side of the bed, his eyes looking at her searchingly.

"No. I didn't fall on my head."

"You didn't exactly fall on your feet either, did you? Do you remember what it was all about? We hadn't finished talking, and now you're rested. I asked you if David had been around—"

"I told you no."

"So you did. But I doubt whether it was a true answer. It's puzzling me what made you go galloping off at such a mad pace that New Copper threw you. And blouse buttons—let's face it—don't fly off of their own accord. Not in those quantities."

She crimsoned. "I wasn't galloping off anywhere. It was an emu—Drummer told me to watch out, but I forgot. It got up from the grass so suddenly—New Copper took fright—"

"I see." He said it half abstractedly, his eyes watchful. Not—trustful, she thought wretchedly. "And now, to return to the matter of your shirt," he continued conversationally. "How do you explain that away?"

She looked back at him unblinkingly. "I suppose the emu could have picked off the buttons."

He looked at her incredulously, his lips twisting cynically. "You think I might believe that?"

She felt despair. She saw quite plainly that he had convinced himself she and David had been—wrestling, or making love or something. Well, she couldn't force his belief, but it was infuriating. She flared, "Yes, I thought you might. Anyhow, does it matter all that much?"

"Yes, it does," he grated. "You're my stepmother's guest and more or less under my protection while you're here, and I don't hold with rough love games being played on my cattle station. No matter what goes, down at the coast," he finished brutally.

"You have a nasty mind." Her voice shook a little. "I'm not like that. And I'm not a liar either."

It was a relief when Poppy appeared in the doorway bringing a tray loaded up with supper for Martyn—tea, creamy scrambled eggs, bread and butter. She deposited it carefully on the bedside table, and Martyn dashed away the angry tears that had come to her eyes, and wondered how much her hostess had heard of their rather heated discourse.

"Are you all right, Martyn?" Poppy asked. "I should hate to send you home not completely whole."

Martyn caught Red's eye and his caustic expression made her fume inwardly.

"I'm perfectly whole." She added deliberately, "It was just a fall. I'm a bit bruised, but otherwise fine." To prove her point, she reached for the plate of scrambled eggs and began to eat.

"Should we let anyone know?" Poppy was still anxious. "Your brother? Your boy-friend?"

"Just what were you planning to let her boy-friend know?" Red wanted to know, his eyes glittering unpleasantly. "Don't meddle, Poppy. The girl's told you— she was tossed by a horse, she's bruised but healthy, and she was lucky enough to fall in the nice soft grass."

Martyn couldn't look at him. She felt her heart beating fast with anger, and for a second she had an impulse to bring the argument into the open. The thought struck her that Poppy must have noticed the mishap to her blouse when she was getting her to bed. *Poppy* would believe her story. She had parted her lips to speak when Red said dryly, as if aware of the direction her thoughts had taken, "Poppy was down admiring Iris's baby when I brought you in. Otherwise she'd have tried to whisk you straight off to hospital. I think you'd sooner be here, wouldn't you?"

She couldn't answer. She lowered her head and continued eating her supper, though now it seemed tasteless. So Red had undressed her! It was the final indignity.

With a lazy movement, he rose from the bed.

"I'll leave you to enjoy your supper in Poppy's tender care," he drawled out, and then he was gone.

She spent a couple of very quiet days after that. She didn't admit it to anyone, but the bruises on her shoulder and arm, the muscles of her back—all were painful. She wasn't up to riding or swimming, all she could manage was a bit of unenergetic walking. Down to see Iris and the children, out to the waterhole to see the birds. She had to have some exercise even if her shaken body would have preferred to remain supine. From the way Red avoided her, she was wretchedly convinced he didn't believe in her innocence.

Well, she supposed none of it mattered in the long run. He had never had what you would call a high opinion of her anyhow...

A couple of afternoons later he came home unexpectedly early. Martyn was sitting in the garden working on some sketches she had done of the children—largely in an attempt to give her mind something else to deal with besides the obsessive and unrewarding subject of Red Diamond. He crossed the lawn and looked over her shoulder, then took a nearby chair. He said, without even greeting her, "I hope Bastian Sinclair will duly admire all the work you bring back—and be convinced that his innocent little paramour has spent her entire absence from him doing pretty drawings."

Martyn flushed but said nothing. If he had come here simply to be unpleasant, then what was there she could do about it?—apart from packing up her things and going inside, and she simply wasn't Spartan enough to do that. She had seen too little of him lately not to be grateful for his company in any circumstances.

She gave herself the pleasure of looking at him openly as he sprawled in his chair, his legs stretched out in front of him, his glittering eyes narrowed as they looked back at her. He hadn't showered, he hadn't shaved, he hadn't changed. He looked rough and tough and overpoweringly masculine with his heavy, broad-shouldered build, and she wondered how she had ever come to fall in love with him. How could any girl be in love with a man who treated her the way Red did Martyn Verity? He even thought she was a liar—he had absolutely no faith in her—

Neither of them said another word. They simply stared at each other for what seemed an eternity. She was on the point of breaking, of demanding what he wanted of her, when David Bower walked into the garden.

"Well, Red. Hello, Martyn, my cherry." He stopped to drop a kiss on her forehead before she knew what he was about. Red's eyebrows descended, his mouth set in a hard line and he got up from his chair.

"Let's get into the office and discuss this business," he said shortly. And in two seconds flat, Martyn was alone again.

Her peace of mind had completely disintegrated. She couldn't have cared less about her drawings. Her arms hung limply down, and she stared ahead of her, thinking, her heart leaden, "Business, Jindi-yindi. And Fay."

At last she stirred, dropped her sketchbook into her room, and walked through the garden and down towards the horse paddock. She had become fond of riding, but right now she couldn't have sat on a horse as

far as a hundred yards, her body had taken too much of
a thrashing the other day. She simply walked—slowly,
and she had no idea where. Anywhere to get away from
her thoughts.

On the way back—it was just before sundown—she
saw David's car rattling along the track towards her. As
this was not the way to Jindi-yindi she had the feeling
that he was looking for her, and she was right. He
pulled up when he saw her, got out of the car and came
towards her where she had paused under some trees.
He had lost some of his civilized suavity, she thought,
watching him come towards her. The thought somehow sprang into her mind that he'd been in a fight, and
her heart quickened. Had he and Red been brawling?
And if so, what about? Red had said they were going to
talk business... Now she could see that one of his eyes
was distinctly swollen, and she felt alarm. She had an
impulse to turn about and run—an impulse, but not the
strength. She wouldn't get far with her muscles in their
present condition, and so she stayed where she was.

He stopped a few feet away from her. His amber
eyes, one of them looking smaller than the other and
marring his very good looks, were fixed on her almost
menacingly.

"I was looking for you, little miss snake-in-the-grass
Verity—just so I can tell you what I think of you."

Martyn was taken entirely by surprise. Her head
went up.

"Yes?" She hadn't the least idea what it was all
about, knowing only that his attitude to her had
changed drastically in the last little while—since he had
called her "my cherry".

"You're a scheming little bitch, aren't you?—with
your tinsel virtue, your spurious chastity. You've thrown
a spanner bang into the dead centre of the works out
here—and all with that innocent little-girl look on your
face!"

Martyn's face whitened. "I haven't the least idea
what you're talking about—not the least."

"No? What about the tales you've been telling Red about me behind my back? That I've been doing my best to rape you!"

"That's not true," she breathed, frightened at what she saw in his face. "I said—I said I hadn't seen you—"

"Then you didn't say it very convincingly. Besides which, I can't see there was any need for discussing me at all. Well, if you will tell lies, I can pretty soon make them into truths." He took a couple of steps towards her and she drew back. "Right now, Red Diamond hates my guts, thanks to you. He's withdrawn his promise of the financial help we need on Jindi-yindi."

Martyn heard him with a feeling of bewilderment. "It has nothing to do with me. Didn't you—didn't you tell him there was nothing between us?"

He laughed briefly. "When you got in first with your story, what would my word be? The damage was already done . . . No, Miss Verity, your spit's blown back in your face this time—you'll find your lies have boomeranged on you." His eyes ripped over her from head to foot as if they would tear her to pieces. "God, what a little hypocrite! I bet you've been setting your cap at Red ever since you dropped down on Diamond Springs— I'll bet you came here with the express purpose of snaring him, even though that slippery stepmother of his must have told you he intended to marry my sister. You've certainly gone out of your way to make sure the Bowers are out of favour, haven't you?"

Martyn was shaking. No one had ever looked at her with such venom in his eyes before. Her heart quailed at what he must have told Red. Yet it was all so crazy! If he had denied it, everything would have been all right. Surely. It was absurd to think that Red would turn against the Bowers simply on her account. She said shakily, "I've never set my cap at anyone. Not at Red— or you—or anyone. If you've told lies to Red about me—" She stopped because he had moved again and the expression in his eyes had intensified.

"Don't bother speculating," he said between his

teeth. "I did. They were lies then, but they needn't stay that way. I'm going to dish out to you just what you deserve—"

Another quick step and he had seized hold of her and twisted her arms violently behind her back. She cried out in pain, and the tears rushed to her eyes. She was completely helpless as he kissed her in a way that made Bastian's kiss seem positively innocent. He had wrenched her arm, done violence to her stiff back, and the tears were running down her face. The next minute she was on the ground and he was crouching over her when a car screeched to a stop, and everything happened fast.

Red—it had to be Red!—hurtled out of the car, dragged David to his feet and dealt him a cracking blow on the jaw. Then with a strength and swiftness that seemed practically superhuman, he had swung David's unresisting body across the track and hurled it into the front seat of the car.

"Get going," Martyn heard him rasp, as he slammed the door shut. He stood dark and threatening while the other man got the car going, and moved off erratically.

Only then did Red give his attention to Martyn. She had struggled to her feet and straightened her clothing, and she knew her face was ashen. Her whole body was trembling and though she had wiped the tears from her cheeks, her lashes were stuck together in points and her heart was thumping as though it would burst. Red's intervention seemed like a miracle, but now, as his diamond-bright eyes raked her over, she knew what he must be thinking and she was ready to crumple up and die.

He jerked his head. She had never seen his mouth set in such a hard and cynical line.

"Move. Into the car. I'll take you back to the homestead. It will be a good thing when you're back at the coast and someone else's responsibility. I see now why your brother was all too ready to hustle you off to the outback. Personally, I'm not going to concern myself over you any more—Bastian Sinclair may be just what you deserve.''

The sun had almost gone down, and the sky was flushed red. Reflected on Red Diamond's face it gave him the air of a terrible and powerful god—an avenging god. Martyn forced herself to move, though to walk, to keep herself upright, seemed to require an immense effort. She had almost made it to the car when she tripped over a tuft of grass and all but fell. Red's arms caught her, his hand was against her fast-beating heart, and then he had whipped her around and she was in his arms and he was kissing her.

Violently at first—and then in a different way. So that from stunned unbelieving shock, she found herself carried into a different mood. She relaxed, melted, felt herself slowly absorbed into his being. The blood came back to her face, his arms supported her, and for a crazy moment she had a feeling of the utmost safety. Of more—of heavenly, peaceful bliss.

Then his mouth left hers and he released her slowly, and his eyes burned down into her face as she leaned back against the support of his iron-muscled arms.

''You melt against my body,'' he said indistinctly. ''Your lips are honey—you could persuade me that to love you would be heaven . . . But love's not a word you understand, is it?'' His voice grew harsh, he chose his words with cold deliberation. ''As David Bower told me, you're a very willing little girl. I think I've been wasting my time getting angry over insults to your— virtue.''

To Martyn, the world seemed a crazy place. Red still held her firmly and though her bruises hurt, she was thankful, for otherwise she thought she would have slipped to the ground. Her eyes held by his, that flashed pinpoints of fire reflected from the flaming sky, she breathed out, ''I didn't want anything to happen with David. Can't you believe me? There's never been anything between us—and the other day, the day New Copper threw me—''

"David threw you first," he said brutally, crudely, and she closed her eyes in shame. "Oh yes, I checked with him on your story, and he wasn't in the mood for being gentlemanly and protecting your name. And to think that once I found you so modest—prudish, even!"

"He lied to you," Martyn said huskily, a spot of bright colour in each of her cheeks. She thought that to die now would be good.

"*You* lied to me," he said, unmoved. "What sort of a girl are you? You responded even to me, just now. I wonder if you'd fall into the arms of any man who wanted you. My God, were you already like this when you came to Diamond Springs, or has it all happened since you've been in my care?"

"Your care!" she accused. "You never cared what I did."

"And did that matter to you?" he flung back. "When you considered me the least likeable man you'd ever met?" He felt for cigarettes, and she took the last few remaining steps to the car and clambered in, mind and body agonized.

He didn't join her for several minutes, and when he came, it was almost dark. She was shivering with exhaustion and misery, but she made one more effort to clear herself.

"What happened just now—I couldn't stop David—he was angry because—"

"Don't protest, don't explain," he said with a savage weariness. "You're a strong girl. You could have evaded David Bower if you'd wanted to. You told me once—or have you forgotten?—that you'd fight for your virtue."

"You forget I was hurt when New Copper tossed me the other day," she flung back, angry now.

"I haven't heard you complaining," he said with deadly coldness.

Martyn gave in. If he wanted to believe the worst of her, there was nothing she could do. Just now the fact that he was unjustly withdrawing his promise of financial help to the Bowers didn't seem to— concern her. David had lied, but she didn't know why. The whole thing was an incomprehensible muddle. "When I've left," she thought wearily—and she hoped it would be soon—"they can fight it all out amongst themselves." Her body flagged.

CHAPTER TEN

DINNER that night was an ordeal. Martyn had showered
and changed when she came in. Her jeans and shirt
looked disreputable and she thought, staring at her
blanched face in the bedroom mirror, that Red had decided she was disreputable too, and it shook her to the
core.

She wanted to weep, but that would have to wait till
later on, when she was in bed with the long night
ahead of her. Her morale had never been so low, and
going back to Ros and Richard seemed like the promise of heaven. She looked at the two pretty dresses
hanging in the wardrobe. Ros had imagined she might
fascinate *someone* if she got herself dressed up. Well,
she certainly hadn't fascinated anyone—on the contrary. In fact, she hadn't even put either of the dresses
on, and she decided she would wear one of them tonight. To nail her colours to the mast, to prove to Red
that she was not crushed, no matter what he thought
of her.

She chose the one with the long sleeves, it was filmy,
semi-transparent with a matching slip, and it would
hide her shoulders and arms—she hadn't worn a
sleeveless shirt since her fall. It was deep green in colour, with a low neck and a beautifully cut skirt that had
a delicate floating quality about it. She slipped into it
and knew that it became her very well, though the colour accentuated her unaccustomed pallor.

Certainly Red looked at her hard when she came into
the dining-room—she had done a cowardly thing in
missing out on the pre-dinner drinks—but Poppy looked
at her too and remarked, "You look lovely tonight,

Martyn. Makes me feel guilty. We've never given you even the semblance of a party. I'm ashamed."

Red added his comment. "Quite the little mermaid, aren't you, in your pretty green seaweed. Like someone out of a fairytale." His eyes were cold and even Poppy looked puzzled.

Martyn smiled brightly as though everything was just marvellous, and took the chair that Red had pulled out for her when he rose. In her heart she wished she had stayed in her room on some excuse, but it was too late now. Besides, there would be tomorrow night, and the night after that—dinner every night with Red, until at last Poppy decreed it was time to go. And oh, God, Martyn prayed that that would be soon!

Red scarcely spoke to her during the meal. She had no appetite for once, and could only play with her food, good though it was. Poppy accused, "You're not hungry, Martyn! Homesick for your boy-friend? Or aren't you feeling too peppy?"

She smiled palely. "I do feel—just a little bit off colour. I'll go to bed early."

"You must be leading a strenuous life lately," Red said caustically. "What have you been up to, I wonder?"

"Now, Red, Martyn had that nasty little accident the other day. She's probably still suffering from reaction. Isn't that it, Martyn?"

Martyn agreed that it was, and then Poppy went to get the coffee, leaving her alone with Red. She could feel his hard grey eyes examining her, and the colour came into her cheeks, but she didn't look up.

He said very softly, "You are an extraordinarily beautiful young woman, Martyn Verity. More so than ever in that gown. You've blossomed from water-baby to siren almost overnight. I guarantee a score of men will lose their heads over you in the years to come. Bastian Sinclair may have met his match in you after all—*he'll* be the one with the problems this time."

Her blue eyes flashed up. "And you don't mean that as a compliment, do you?"

"I think perhaps I do," he said. And then Poppy was back. Martyn drank her coffee and excused herself.

She slept on and off in short snatches all through the night, waking again and again to lie and listen. Tonight she missed the sea—the friendly, ever-present sound of the sea. The silence of the outback had become strangely hostile. She listened tensely, her body rigid. There was no sound of emus drumming, no cry of owl or dingo, no rustling of leaves—no sound at all. She felt alone in the world, and the silence seemed a terrible kind of condemnation—a reality indissolubly mixed with nightmare.

Round about dawn, she left her bed and went on to the verandah in her pyjamas to look out across the garden and the plain beyond with weary, shadow-darkened eyes. The sky was paling, but the ghost of a moon still hung there, a mere silver wraith. The deathly silence had gone. Subdued sounds came from somewhere in the homestead, she could smell frying steak and toast, and she felt very hungry. Mrs. Hall was cooking breakfast for the men—and for the boss—before they rode out on the run for the day's work. Martyn stayed where she was for a long time, leaning against the verandah rail. She saw the long blue-grey leaves of the gum trees stir in the breeze that rose as the sun lifted itself out of the night, and she knew that despite everything there was a great deal of beauty—beauty that she hadn't even begun to discover—in the outback. She knew that she could become as enamoured of the plains, and this lonely, half harsh, half languorous country as she was of the sea, if she were ever given the chance. She had told Red once that the sea was her first and last love, but it had not been true then, and it was even less true now.

As she stood there, a line of horsemen began to move into her vision—the stockmen of Diamond Springs, wearing broad-brimmed hats, checked shirts, coloured neckerchiefs, all of them riding graceful and erect, most of them aboriginals or half-castes. One of them was different, and that one was Red Diamond. He rode erect too, he was dressed as the others were, but to Martyn's eyes there was something about his carriage that was unmistakable, quite apart from the fact that he was a man of heavier build than any of the others.

Gazing at him then, her heart in her eyes, she had no idea that she was possibly seeing him for the last time. The knowledge was only imparted to her later.

Breakfast with Poppy, the usual inquiry—"Did you sleep well? And then, "You look a bit washed out. I always forget that our outback heat can be devastating. You'll be glad to get back to the coast and your family and your boy-friend. Well, cheer up, Martyn, I have good news for you."

Martyn felt a tiny warning shock in her heart, but Poppy didn't yet drop her bombshell.

"Eat up your breakfast and I'll tell you what went on while you were so peacefully asleep in your room last night... First of all, Jan rang up. Her wedding date's fixed and she wants me to come down as soon as possible and see to everything—the invitations, the dresses, the reception. Well, that suits me, I'm an organizing kind of woman, and I'll be in my element. We'll leave tomorrow," she continued, and looked smilingly at Martyn as if she expected this would be the best possible news that she could give her. "Are you pleased? I think you *do* want to get back, don't you?"

Martyn thought she would choke. Her appetite had vanished. Tomorrow! It was one thing to tell yourself you couldn't get away fast enough, it was quite another thing to know it was going to happen.

But Poppy hadn't finished yet.

"In the morning," she said, "Tancred's going to deputize one of the men to drive us in to pick up the feeder plane. He can't come himself—don't ask me why, but he's decided he has to camp out with the men tonight. I'm afraid it's not the best of good manners not to say good-bye to you, but he asked me to say it for him, and to wish you happiness."

Martyn swallowed, and looked down at the table, sure that the death of her heart must be there in her eyes.

"I hope the arrangements are okay with you?" Poppy asked brightly.

Martyn nodded. "Of course. Whatever you plan," she said huskily.

"Good... I haven't any need to hang on here any longer, either. What I wanted to happen has happened."

Martyn raised her blue eyes, puzzled. What had happened? Her expression asked the question for her.

"The Jindi-yindi Fay-Bower business has worked out satisfactorily—and I might as well have saved myself the bother of worrying about it."

"What—do you mean?" Martyn managed to ask, jerkingly.

Poppy buttered toast and bit into it with enjoyment.

"Red's dropped the idea of dedicating half his energies—and half his finances—to Jindi-yindi. And better still, he's dropped the idea of asking Fay to marry him." Her dark eyes were narrowed and she didn't see Martyn's startled reaction. She had thought he *had* asked Fay to marry him! Poppy was smiling ironically. "He's decided he's not interested in marriage after all. That having lived this long without a wife he can continue on indefinitely... Ah well, he's discovered the truth of what I've been preaching for a long while—the weakness of the Bowers. Personally, I'm glad he's decided not to help David."

"He—he told you why?"

"In detail. And he was ropeable! He had it all out with David yesterday. He says David just doesn't belong out here—he should go back east and buy himself a small going concern. I don't think it will hurt if I tell you about it—it's not as if you lived here." Poppy reached for more coffee. "Things have been going from bad to worse. David's said Yes to all Red's advice and never taken it—got his own fencing contractor and now he's been ditched with the work half finished; wouldn't buy store cattle when he could have got them dirt cheap—spent a fortune on horses, all for show. But what really brought things to a head was the fact he used the Diamond name—unauthorized—for credit at some cattle sales the other day—the day you had your accident, to be exact. And Red found out and called him to account. Yesterday."

So, thought Martyn, a little dazedly, none of the fracas had had anything to do with her, no matter what David had said. And most likely, Red had never made David any promises at all.

"But—Fay?" she asked. "Just because of David, he—"

Poppy shrugged. "He didn't go into that. But isn't it proof that his heart wasn't involved? Well, she's probably feeling sorry for herself and badly done by, but it would never have worked. She's just not the type for Red. For instance, I've heard her say things about Drummer that would upset anyone. And Drummer has always had a special place in Red's affections. Those two have known each other practically all their lives and they've been through a lot together. Once, when they were teenagers, and Red's horse got into trouble in a flood river, Drummer saved his life."

Breakfast was finished, but Poppy stayed on, reflective, content, and quite unaware of the turmoil in Martyn's mind. For Martyn, one fact stood out starkly amongst the others. She was never to see Red again. She was to leave in the morning without another glimpse of him. It was sheer agony—and far more real than the fact that he was not going to marry Fay.

Poppy said presently, "This sleeping out at the camp—I don't like it. I've seen too many men break away from the little civilized decencies of life, gradually become misanthropes. It mustn't happen to Red, simply because he's been disillusioned by the Bowers. He should marry, and have the good life he's earned.'' She was silent for a moment, staring out into the red-gold heat of the morning. ''Shall I tell you something, Martyn? It's a bit in the nature of a confession—''

Martyn supposed she must have made some answer, for Poppy went on, ''When I invited you here, it was because I wanted you and Red to marry.''

Martyn had known that, of course. She had also known there had been other girls, and no doubt Poppy had had high hopes of each of them. This time she had certainly made a mistake!

''When I saw you and Red together that first day at Julia's,'' Poppy confessed, ''you just looked so absolutely right together. I don't know—so utterly beautiful. You so young and blonde and suntanned, Red so dark and masculine and powerful. I just had this utter conviction that you were the girl for him. I'm afraid the excuse I made about Jan was only an afterthought— and the fact you had a problem of your own. Oh, didn't I think I was clever! You hadn't told me about this boyfriend of yours then. I should have guessed there'd be someone else.'' She smiled ruefully across at Martyn. ''It was an idea that went completely haywire, wasn't it? You two aren't attracted to each other even in the slightest degree.''

Martyn smiled back, but her heart was aching. Poppy was only half right. Red was not attracted to her—but she would die for him!

That morning she tidied out her room and did some washing, ready for her departure. It was while she was hanging her clothes on the line—and looking unhappily at the blouse with the buttons ripped off it—that a sudden thought struck her. She stood perfectly still. Poppy had said that David had gone to some cattle sales ''the day you had your accident''. Wouldn't *that* prove to Red that she hadn't lied to him? That she had not been with David before New Copper tossed her? She would put it to him anyhow, and at least try to clear her name.

And then she realized that she wouldn't have the opportunity. Red wasn't coming home tonight—most likely because he never wanted to see Martyn Verity again. She stood in the hot sunlight, her arms hanging limply by her sides, feeling futility, despair.

Then her head went up. She would ride out and find Red, force him to believe her... In her heart she knew it was merely an excuse to see him again, because there were other things he believed of her that were to her disadvantage—and basically, she wasn't going to change anything. All the same, she was going.

Over lunch, she told Poppy a half-lie.

"I'd like to have one last ride around. I may never visit the outback again. And if you would, could you show me the map of Diamond Springs again so I can be sure I've got my bearings?"

That was how she found out exactly where Red would be.

She took New Copper again, and mounted stiffly, newly aware of the bruises and stiffness in her body. She certainly wasn't going to get much physical enjoyment out of her ride, but if she was making a martyr of herself, it was because she wanted it that way.

The sun was hot on her back as she rode off, and though she glanced about her, determined to enjoy her last sight of this part of the country, she was too abstracted to delight in the sight of the shimmering plains, the sculptured shapes of the galahs, the flights of the birds. The only thing that roused her was the sight of two emus stepping it out together by a distant fence, their strange, hairlike feathers ruffled by the wind.

She thought she would find the camp quite easily. It wasn't very far—and that was why it was so meaningless for Red to be camping out for the night. There were two ways to choose from. The shorter way would mean a final ride across an open paddock in full view of the camp, and so she turned off at the appropriate place in favour of the second way. It took in a river crossing, but she would have the shelter of trees along the river bank while her eyes sought out Red and she waited for an appropriate moment to approach him. She knew the river had been rising in the last few days, but she hoped the crossing, that had been clearly marked on the map, would be negotiable.

At last she was riding through the trees by the river bank, following a narrow red track obviously used by horses rather than vehicles, and then there was a sharp little descent to the river. There she reined in her horse to make sure she wasn't asking for trouble. The river was the colour of milk coffee, and flowing fast. There were small eddying patches of foam here and there, and small bits of half-submerged debris spun by, further downstream there were rocks and the banks grew steep and the water looked deeper, and more treacherous.

New Copper appeared undeterred by the sight of the water, and Martyn urged him gently in. There were fresh hoofmarks on the track, and that was a good indication. She aimed for a little further upstream, to allow for the current, and that way felt certain of reaching the track where it emerged across the stream.

It was a piece of cake. The horse was confident and made the crossing without even having to swim, and without stumbling once, and in a few minutes was scrambling up the further bank.

Reaching the shelter of the trees, Martyn dismounted, tossed the horse's reins over a branch and walked forward to get the lie of the land. Some distance away she sighted a mob of cattle, some encircling stockmen and—Red. Her blue eyes, screwed up against the glare, found him almost instantly, and her heart leaped in recognition and joy. And then she recognized the rider of the horse reined in alongside him, to whom he was talking. A girl in a cream hat with a snakeskin band, immaculate in pale lemon shirt and dark riding breeches.

Fay Bower.

No longer riding that thoroughbred horse her brother had bought for her, but an ordinary stockhorse.

Martyn stopped dead in her tracks, pain in her heart where before there had been exhilaration and—she admitted it now—a mad hope. Those two sat their horses in the hot sun, utterly intent on each other. Red's wide-brimmed hat cast a deep shadow over his face, and of course from this far she hadn't a hope of reading his expression. She only knew those two were together again and that Poppy must have been wrong—or Red had been fooling her, for some reason of his own. He couldn't finish with Fay—the affair hadn't been heartless. At any rate, it must be on again or she wouldn't be there at his side, her back so erect, looking, even from this distance, so confident. And he, head inclined, was listening to her.

Martyn knew suddenly she had been an idiot to come racing out here. She might salvage a little of her pride in pointing out that she hadn't lied about David the day of her accident, but it would get her nowhere. Tomorrow she would still be on the plane heading for Sydney, while here in the outback—if Red Diamond wanted to, he could go ahead and marry Fay Bower. Hadn't Martyn heard him tell Poppy, "Anything I do, you can be sure I do it because it's what I want to do?"

She turned away. And now it was not the sunlight that blinded her, but her own tears.

She walked under the trees. In a minute she would go back to New Copper. In a minute. Just now her body ached worse than ever, as if in sympathy with her heart. Though it was riding that had made her muscles ache in reality. And riding back, away from love and hope—foolish groundless hope—was going to be a very different matter from riding towards Red. Suddenly the homestead seemed too many miles away, the thought of sitting a horse all those miles quite intolerable.

She looked back through the trees. The girl from Jindi-yindi was no longer talking to Red. As Martyn

watched, she touched her horse's flanks with her spurs
and was suddenly flying across the paddock straight towards the trees where Martyn waited. Exhilarated, her
hat flying off to hang down her back. Now Martyn envied her.

"She's won him back," she thought. If she had ever
lost him.

The other girl didn't see her. Her horse charged
madly through the trees a little way off and Martyn
heard the clatter of stones as she took him at what was
surely an insane pace down the bank. But surely she
had made a mistake. She was too far downstream for
the crossing. Martyn began to run through the trees in
pursuit. Horse and rider had slithered right down the
steep bank and now the horse seemed to be balanced
precariously over the water and was whinnying in fear
while Fay clung to its back.

Martyn called out, "Fay, don't go in there—it's too
deep! Come back!"

It was useless. The horse, that had been tottering on
the brink, had suddenly plunged into the river. The
water was deep and its nostrils flared with fright as it
floundered, tossing its head up. Fay, even more frightened than the horse, pulled her feet free of the stirrups,
and keeping hold of the horse's mane, slipped out of
the saddle, no doubt with the idea of getting back to the
bank. But by now they were well out into the stream
and the horse lashed out in panic. Fay's hands lost their
hold and the river swept her away. She went under,
then surfaced, spluttering and coughing, while further
upstream her horse, its eyes rolling, struggled on.

Even as it all happened, Martyn had slithered down
the bank, pulled off her shoes and was in the water and
swimming towards Fay. She saw the other girl being
whirled on helplessly, and then she was flung towards
the far bank where the rotten branches of an old tree
showed menacingly above the water. She disappeared
momentarily, then emerged choking, her arms flung
out as she tried to grasp at something to hang on to.

Martyn called out, "Hang on, Fay—I'm coming!" But she didn't know if Fay heard her or not.

Her jeans were heavy with water and her shoulders ached with every stroke she made. It seemed an interminable time till she reached the other girl, whose hands clawed at her desperately.

"My foot," Fay croaked. "It's caught—I can't get it free—help me—help me—!"

"Then let go of me," gasped Martyn, all but winded with the effort she had made and in danger now of being dragged under by those clinging hands. She took hold of them and wrenched them away, then duck-dived down into the muddy water.

Down there, she was in a world of almost total darkness. Fay's foot, in its riding boot, was tightly wedged between two branches. Using both her hands. Martyn pulled and twisted, cutting her fingers on the splintery wood. Then, just when she thought her lungs were about to burst and it was becoming absolutely imperative for her to surface again, she got Fay's leg free. Instantly the other girl kicked out and Martyn received a shove in the chest that made her gasp and take in a lungful of water.

It was a second before her reeling senses told her that something else was wrong. She should have been bobbing up to the surface now, but horror of horrors, something was holding her down, and with her last conscious thoughts she realized that the leg of her jeans was caught on a snag.

Then the blackness became total, everything was blotted out and all feeling left her.

She opened her eyes, and it was dark—pitch dark. She wasn't conscious of having a body. The water—her lips parted and she gave a little choked cry. There was no water. She stared into the darkness, and now it was darkness no longer. A small red glow moved and then stayed still. She heard a gentle click and a light came on—a soft light, though it still hurt her eyes so that she flinched and closed them momentarily, then opened them again.

Where was she? Her eyes wouldn't focus properly. She had been dreaming—having a nightmare. She had thought that Fay—that she—

She struggled to sit up and discovered that a blanket was wrapped closely round her from her neck to her feet.

"Martyn," a voice said, and a hand reached out—brown, very solid and strong—to cover her shoulder again.

Her vision cleared. It was Red's voice, it was his hand, and now she was looking into his face. Impossibly, she was in her room at Diamond Springs. Tears came into her eyes and she sank back on the pillow again.

"What—happened?" she asked weakly.

His hand touched her hair. "It's all over now. You're safe, quite safe."

Her blue eyes stared at him. It was beginning to come back. She had been in the river—Fay had been trapped—she had tried to free her. Her eyes widened in an unspoken question.

"Everybody's safe," Red said. "Even the horse. Fay—you—"

"I thought I was going to drown. Fay must have saved me—"

He shook his head, his expression intensely grave. "No, I saved you, Martyn. You're mine now." He stood up. "We'll talk about it later. I'm going to ask Poppy to see to your needs."

She didn't want him to go. She wanted to ask him to repeat what he had said—something quite incredible. Or else her mind was wandering and he hadn't said it at all ... To detain him, she asked, "What time is it?"

"A little after eight, that's all. You'll have a little supper if you feel up to it, and then you must sleep."

"Because in the morning, I'm leaving," she thought, as other memories flooded back. There was something she had wanted to tell him—about David. She said painfully, "Red—that day New Copper threw me—"

He held up his hand. "I know. David was at the cattle sales. I realized it this morning. I was coming back this evening to ask you to forgive me." Suddenly he was kneeling by the bed and there was an expression in his eyes she had never seen there before. He said, huskily, "Oh God, Martyn, do you know that I love you—that I love you more than life? If I'd lost you today the river could have had me too."

Martyn closed her eyes. She felt hot tears on her cheeks and she knew that she must be dreaming.

Everything was vague after that. She didn't know if she slept again, but Poppy was there looking after her, feeding her chicken soup, bread and butter. She wasn't hungry, but she felt very tired.

"What happened?" she heard herself ask querulously.

"Red says you're not to talk any more tonight."

There must have been something in the tea Poppy made her sip, because she was falling asleep again—deep into sleep, a sleep without dreams.

It was late when she woke in the morning, and what wakened her was the sound of someone in the room. It was Poppy, all dressed up as if she were going somewhere. Martyn suddenly sat up in bed with a feeling of guilt.

"Oh, it's time to go and I'm not dressed or packed up—"

"Re-lax," drawled Poppy. "I'm leaving you behind. You don't have a wedding to arrange—well, not someone else's," she amended oddly. "I just sneaked in to say goodbye. I promise I'll look up your brother and his wife and tell them that you're safe and well and—happy?"

Happy? Martyn frowned a little. And—well? Because hadn't she nearly drowned? But Red had saved her... She said uncertainly, "Couldn't you wait? I can be ready in a few minutes—"

"No way," said Poppy. "Red would never forgive

me. You can't just run away like that. And remember, Mrs. Hall is here." She smiled, and stooping, kissed Martyn on both cheeks. "I have to go. But I'm leaving you in good hands. Be seeing you!"

She was gone, and Martyn leaned back on the pillow thoughtfully. Her mind felt alert, and she thought it was time to sort out what was true from what she had dreamed last night. Red had certainly saved her from the river, and she knew that Fay was safe. But otherwise—she must have dreamed the things he had said.

Yet something insisted that she had not. That Red— loved her. It was nothing short of a miracle.

Suddenly she was terribly hungry.

She showered quickly and washed the river water from her hair. Then she put on the clothes she had been wearing when first she met Red—shorts, socks, a top that was deep-sea green, and that showed the fading bruises on her shoulder. It was a strange, back-to-the-beginning thing to get into that particular outfit. It seemed to wipe out all the in-between things, so that she could start again. With truths. About Bastian, for instance.

Mrs. Hall provided her with breakfast when she put her head around the kitchen door and said in a meek voice, "Please—I'm so *hungry*!"

She ate on the wide back verandah where the men had their meals. She ate steak and eggs and toast, and drank gallons of tea. In the back yard she watched a cat stalking a magpie—a cat with a red bow on its tail and another round its neck.

"Who did that?" she asked Mrs. Hall, laughing.

"Oh, those kids of Drummer's. They're little mis-chiefs."

The sun was shining—and no doubt it was broiling hot outside, and by rights she should have been on her way to the coast where there was always a cool breeze. But there was no doubt in her mind where she would sooner be. In the kitchen, Mrs. Hall was making bread and the dough was rising and Martyn was fascinated.

She had the strangest feeling of freedom in the big kitchen that had, till now, seemed to belong to Poppy. Mrs. Hall was a friendly woman, and—at last she had to ask it or go mad.

"Where's Red?"

"Oh, he'll be in this evening. He left instructions that you were to have a lazy day. My, you were lucky he saw you in the river when he rode over to see if Fay had got safely across, weren't you?"

Martyn nodded. So that was how it had happened! She felt all on edge—a lazy day meant no riding, she would have to wait till evening before she could ask him why she was still here when Poppy had gone. Yet she knew why—though she couldn't believe it.

The day seemed endless.

When he came home, it was nearly sundown and she was on the verandah. She greeted him with a careful and deliberately schooled casualness—as though she remembered nothing of what he had said last night. Because—just possibly—she had dreamed it.

"Well, are you in your right mind again, Martyn Verity?"

"Yes." She kept her face turned to his and tried to persuade herself that she wasn't flushing. "I could have gone with Poppy this morning—I don't need to be kept—under observation—"

"No?" His brows rose quizzically. "I contest that. What sort of a man would I be to let you go back to Bastian Sinclair when you made me a declaration of love yesterday?"

She stared at him blankly. She thought she had been blushing before, but now her cheeks were scarlet.

"I—I didn't," she stammered.

"You did," he said. "In very plain words. Though I admit you were barely conscious. Is it true?"

She looked back at him, straight into those diamond-bright eyes, and there was something there that made it impossible to tell anything but the truth.

"Yes," she said with the utmost simplicity.

"And I love you," he said. "Madly."

He drew her into his arms and kissed her, and it was a kiss that was neither gentle nor fiercely passionate, but very, very possessive.

Of one accord they moved down from the verandah then, and into the garden, away from the homestead and the yellow lights that Mrs. Hall had switched on. His arm about her, he asked quietly, "Can you forgive the unforgivable, Martyn? The things I've thought about you, and none of which, I would swear now, are true. Can you believe that, as far as David was concerned, it was sheer blind jealousy that made me go berserk and suspect what I did?"

They had paused under some loquat trees and she looked up into his face. "I believe you. And of course I forgive you. But why did David lie?"

He shrugged. "I guess he thought if I wasn't going to link up with Jindi-yindi and Fay, then he was going to make sure I didn't marry you, either. I'll admit I'd been thinking seriously of Fay—but I revised my ideas completely very shortly after you turned up at Diamond Springs."

"Yesterday," said Martyn hesitantly. "Why was she there with you?"

"Oh, she'd come to tell me David had a buyer for his bloodstock horses and that he'd used my name as a temporary security only. It's something that needn't concern you—a sort of final effort to—bring me back into the fold."

Poor Fay, Martyn thought briefly, and then dismissed her from her thoughts, because Red was kissing her again.

He said quizzically, "I was right when I said you'd never marry Bastian Sinclair, wasn't I, mermaid?"

"I was never going to," she admitted. One day she would tell him the whole of that story, but not just now.

"No? Wasn't that what you had in mind when you came outback? Wasn't that your personal problem?"

She shook her head. "It was a career problem," she

said meekly. "Ros and Dick want me to do a secretarial course and I don't—"

"Well, that's easily settled, isn't it?" he said, laughing.

Martyn smiled a little. She could just imagine Dick's and Ros's alarm when she told them she was engaged—despite Ros's wishful thinking when she had fitted her out with a honeymoon wardrobe and suitcase! "Getting engaged? After you've been away less than a month? Who on earth is he? Now look here, Bit"—this would be Richard—"you're positively not getting engaged or anything at all until we've met this man."

And what would they think of him when they met him? Martyn couldn't see how they could possibly be anything but delighted. Stan would have been pleased. Because Red was everything a man should be—Red was just out of this world—

He asked her teasingly, "Well, how do you think they'll react to our engagement, waterbaby?"

"They'll be mad about it," she said, idiotically, sliding into his arms.

THE KILTED STRANGER

The Kilted Stranger

Margaret Pargeter

It was just an old gray house among the Scottish mountains, but to Sue Granger it already felt like home. She had come to Glenroden fulfilling her mother's dying wish that she deliver a letter to John Fraser, only to find the father she had always believed dead.

John Fraser had welcomed her even though she was just as much of a shock to him as he was to her. Not so, Meric Findlay.

For someone who was supposed to be the manager of her father's estate, Meric seemed to have a lot of authority. Besides he was rude and overbearing and was highly suspicious of her. Sue disliked him intensely. . . .

CHAPTER ONE

IT was August and the midday sun was hot. Susan Granger's smoky grey eyes followed the dancing rays of it across the white-tabled restaurant. When another diner complained she noticed that the young proprietor walked over to the window and drew the thin cotton curtains, effectively cutting out the glare. The curtains were made of a brown cotton material with a white geometric pattern on it. They were attractive. Sue hadn't noticed them before. They looked new. Carefully, her attention caught, she forgot the man she was having lunch with and stared.

"Susan!" Tim Mason's impatient exclamation made no impact even when it sharpened on the last syllables of her name. It wasn't until he spoke again that her wandering gaze returned to fix itself unhappily on his face.

"I'm sorry," she murmured, shrivelling a little beneath his withering regard, grateful when the waitress arrived with their coffee, creating a diversion. It had been a mistake to come here with Tim today, but he had been so insistent. He couldn't be expected to understand that she still found it difficult to concentrate. Along with other things the shock of her mother's accident had done this to her. That man with the curtains... Was it strange that such a simple everyday performance should bring such a comforting sense of normality? A reassurance which all Tim's effusive sympathy and stringent advice had failed to give.

"I'm sorry," she repeated, as he stirred his coffee angrily, lapsing into a rather sullen silence as the waitress went.

His sandy brows raised and he shot her a quick look, not bothering to hide a faint hint of reproach. "I wouldn't mind, darling, but my lunch hour doesn't go on indefinitely, and old Wilcox will have a fit if I'm so much as five minutes late. You might at least listen to what I'm saying. I was asking you about that letter. Now that you've had time to think things over, you aren't still considering it seriously, are you?"

Looking away from him quickly, Sue gazed uncertainly down at her hands. "And what if I am?" she asked defiantly.

"Oh, Sue!" His eyes probed her pale face despairingly. "To begin with—well, that wasn't hard to understand, but surely it's time you began to think rationally?"

Resentment flared, bringing a surge of colour to her pale cheeks, a healthier sparkle to her sombre eyes. "I did promise." She swallowed painfully. "The last promise that I'll ever make."

Tim's good-looking face darkened and he gave a small grunt. "I think you're being far too dramatic, Sue," he said. He leant nearer, across the table, suddenly intent. "You can tell me to mind my own business if you like, but you've devoted all your life to your mother—she saw to it that you never had much real freedom." As Sue started to protest he threw up a restraining hand. "She asked you to deliver this letter when she was really too ill to have known what she was asking. Don't you see, Sue, it could mean more strings, and I think you've had quite enough of those. You've never even heard of the person to whom this letter is addressed. It could be some old relative—almost sure to be if she wrote it some time ago. Whoever it is they'll probably be in need of care and attention, and knowing you, you'll be unable to refuse!"

Sue's hands clenched nervously beneath the table. Tim had no right to speak to her like this. She didn't belong to him in any way, nor did she want to. Yet probably he only spoke as he did because he was anxious? "Tim," she faltered, "you could be wrong. And

I've told you before, Mother only wrote the letter a few weeks ago. She wasn't a very sensitive person, but she did get these sudden premonitions." She didn't allude to his other remarks, unable to deny the truth of them.

He wasn't impressed. She hadn't really expected he would be. He retorted dryly, his brown eyes sceptical, "We can all imagine that we're going to have an accident, Sue. It's a sort of psychological impact. They happen every day. It must be my turn next—that sort of thing. Your mother was too highly strung to apply a little common sense."

"It's not that exactly, Tim." His voice cut cruelly across her ragged nerves. His air of disparagement set her teeth on edge. She wanted to get up and walk out, only some stubborn streak in her make-up kept her sitting where she was. "You must see," she went on, "that this is something I feel I have to do whether I really want to or not. I don't particularly wish to go chasing off into the wilds of Scotland at the moment, but I did promise!"

"When you were naturally upset! If you'd just consider carefully, darling. Promises..." For the first time he hesitated, uncertain, not really intending to wound.

"Deathbed promises, you mean," she prompted expressionlessly as he paused.

He muttered angrily, sensing her contempt, his eyes suddenly as hostile as hers. "I suppose I do, but I wasn't going to put it so bluntly. Not many people are able to refuse requests at a time like that..." Carefully he spooned more sugar into his coffee, giving himself time to think.

"Look, Sue," decisively he replaced his spoon in his saucer, "can I be frank?"

Numbly, although slightly warily, she nodded, and he continued, his eyes gentler now on her smooth, beautifully boned face. "I know you feel that this letter is very important, but so far as you're concerned I didn't trust your mother when she was alive, and I'm afraid I still don't now."

"Please..."

But he didn't allow her small, protesting gasp to deter him. "Just hear me out, Sue. It's only for your sake I'm saying this. Sometimes I didn't think your mother liked you very much, which seemed strange, considering you were all she had. I've seen her gazing at you with the most peculiar expression in her eyes, almost as if she didn't care for what she saw. As if you reminded her of someone she didn't like, and no one could say you looked a bit like her. But—well, most of the time she was possessive, sometimes scarcely willing to let you out of her sight. Look at how she insisted you found a job in the immediate vicinity after you left college! She always wanted you near, but that doesn't prove how much she loved you. Of course it might just have been that she wasn't very maternal, but can you wonder if I'm suspicious about all this other business now?"

Sue flinched, her lips suddenly dry, her face paler as the logic of his words hurt, the pain spreading insidiously. She hadn't realized he'd been aware of so much. That his interest had been self-motivated she had little doubt. He wouldn't know how much it hurt to have one's private doubts and fears exposed to such cruel analysis. The relationship she had shared with her mother was something she never wanted to talk about, certainly not with Tim, with his methodical, detached way of looking at everything. "I'd rather not discuss it," she answered at last—very coolly.

Impatience flared again as he watched her dark-lashed eyes widen defensively. "Sometimes I think I don't understand you at all, Sue," he muttered, eyebrows and temper shooting up simultaneously.

Most of the time I don't understand you either, Sue felt like retorting. But she didn't; not aloud. After all, he had been kind and helped her a lot during these last few days, and appeared to be the only close friend she had. He had also been the only man in their small circle of acquaintances whom her mother had tolerated reasonably well. She looked at him, her grey eyes solemn. "It hasn't been long, Tim, you could try to be tolerant."

"I'm trying, Sue." Across the table his deep sigh was quite audible. Then suddenly he was softly pleading, changing his tactics, bewildering her as he often did by his complete volte-face. "Darling," his hand crept across the table to cover her clenched one, "why don't we get married? Then I could take care of everything. Your mother would have approved, I'm sure of that. Then I could be responsible for all your affairs, and if you insist we could deliver that mysterious letter— maybe during my next holiday or long weekend."

"Oh, Tim!" Tears came, and she wished she wasn't quite so jumpy. A hint of kindness still did this to her. Tears! Staring at him aghast, she blinked them back before he could notice. She hadn't reached the age of twenty without having gone through a handful of boy-friends. She was young and healthy and enjoyed her fun. Only most of them hadn't been a lot of fun really, not with her mother doing her best to antagonize them, and it had never seemed possible to keep them completely out of her way. Always there had been some fault, subtly yet sharply pointed out, effectively spoiling a gay but easily destructible relationship.

Looking back, Sue wondered why she had often given in so quickly. She sometimes fretted that she had reached the age she had without ever being in love. Was she too much like her mother, without any real capacity for deeper feelings? Or perhaps the emotions she dreamt about were totally unrealistic, the warm, bubbling feelings a myth. She was extremely fond of Tim most of the time. Perhaps this was sufficient? But even as the thought entered her head she dismissed it. She knew that she couldn't agree to marry him, not yet. Not until she was completely sure.

"I'm sorry, Tim," her voice trembled slightly as she attempted to hide her uncertainty, "I just couldn't think of marrying anyone at the moment."

Tim, looking into her pale, faintly flushed face, thought he understood. It was too soon after her bereavement. He had been too hasty. His hand tightened reassuringly over hers. "Don't worry, darling, I'll ask you again. Just keep it in mind. But," he frowned, glancing anxiously at his watch, "you must promise me that you'll do nothing about this other matter without letting me know."

Irrelevantly Sue wished he wouldn't keep calling her darling. It might give people the wrong impression. She felt something like a surge of relief when he didn't pursue the subject of marriage any further, but she didn't particularly want to promise him anything, not even brief details of her movements. It might be good to get away for a little while, but she wouldn't say so. There seemed little sense in hurting him deliberately and he might not understand.

Uncertainly she shrugged, glancing at him swiftly, curiously evasive. "I'm not sure what I'll be doing, Tim," she replied, gathering up her bag as he drained his coffee cup and signalled to the waitress, his lunch hour nearly over. "Not until I've seen Mother's solicitor. I have an appointment with him this afternoon."

A dry, late summer wind blew skittishly along the street as she parted from Tim outside the café and made her way towards the bus stop. It was too fine a day to take the tube, but the wind was disagreeable, whirling untidy bits of litter, stirring fine dust about her feet. Sue, taking a grip of herself, resisted a half-formed impulse to scruff her toes in it as the bored-looking schoolboy in front of her was doing. Instead she straightened her shoulders and told herself resolutely that London, even in August, could be nice. And if she didn't care for life in a huge city, there were thousands who did. Her mother had loved it, finding in the busy streets the anonymity she had always appeared to crave.

Sue sighed uneasily, hopping on to the bus when it came, seating herself precariously on the top deck, staring out through the window at the rows of houses and shops which obtruded on to her vision, then dissolved into a meaningless blur. Mingling with this came an almost tangible sense of freedom, an awareness that for the first time in her life she could please herself entirely as to where she lived and worked. Of course there was the flat, but it was only rented and could easily be disposed of, and her present job was only temporary, in a local bookshop, taken until she could find a more permanent teaching post. Now that her mother had gone, there was nothing and no one to keep her here. Tim would eventually accept that she couldn't marry him. If he still wished to keep in touch—well, that would be up to him.

The solicitor didn't keep her waiting. He was a youngish man with a computer-like brain and a conveyor-like system of dealing with his clients. "Sit down, Miss Granger." He was quick to wave her to a seat and even quicker to offer his condolences, the thin formality of his voice grating. Yet, she found his unemotional courtesy oddly bracing, and a welcome change from Tim's well-intentioned but often suffocating sympathy. She sat down where the solicitor indicated, facing him gravely.

"I would have sent for you sooner," he went on, his pale grey eyes sliding impersonally over her, "but I've been out of town. Actually your mother's estate constitutes no problem, but there's something which I'm not quite clear about."

Sue waited patiently as he paused, appearing to search for a paper on his desk. She hadn't met this man before, although she had known that her mother had consulted him once or twice, mostly about trivial matters concerning rent and such-like. She had never heard of any estate. Of course he was probably referring to the few pounds which her mother might have left in the bank. She had always used a bank account, although usually there had been very little in it. It was then that Sue remembered the insurance.

Startled, she glanced up into the solicitor's sharp-eyed face. "There is an insurance, I believe. My father apparently had a good one and, since he died, my mother received a regular monthly sum. She never said how much. I don't suppose it would be all that much after inflation. My father died, you see, before I was born, but it was a great help—the money, I mean. I expect, now that she's gone too, that the company ought to know about it. It was silly of me not to think of it before." Unhappy with her rather muddled presentation of the facts, and the pain it induced, Sue gripped her hands tightly together on her lap.

Frowning slightly, the man found the notes which he looked for and glanced at her keenly, his eyes resting for a moment on her pale silky head, noting the distress in her wide, clouded eyes. "I shouldn't worry about that, Miss Granger," he said quietly. "A week or two is neither here nor there. Actually, though, this was one of the things I wanted to speak to you about. Your mother did mention an insurance some time ago, but when I consulted her bank I was surprised to find that, stricly speaking, there isn't any. There certainly is money paid into her account every month, but more than that I cannot find out. I wondered if you could throw any light on the matter?"

Sue started, feeling her cheeks grow cold as she stared apprehensively at the solicitor's smooth face. There was a hollow feeling at the pit of her stomach. If there was no insurance, and she saw no reason to doubt this man's word, wherever was the money coming from? "Are you sure there's been no mistake?" she floundered nervously.

"Not possibly." Emphatically he shook his head, waiting patiently.

Defeated she accepted this while her mind searched frantically for a suitable explanation. Her face registered dismay, followed quickly by an unexplainable fear as she found none. Intuitively she knew there was something very much wrong, but she had simply no idea what it could be. "I only have the letter," she whispered uneasily, speaking her thoughts aloud. Guilt surged as she mentioned it, but what else could she do?

"A letter?" A shrewd gleam lit the man's grey eyes. "Perhaps I might see it." He held out his hand expectantly.

"I'm sorry." Sue flinched inwardly as she drew the letter from her handbag. "I promised my mother I would deliver it in person and that I wouldn't open it. But if the address on the envelope is of any help, then you're welcome to look at it." She didn't tell him that she carried it about with her all the time, almost afraid to let it out of her sight.

Gravely he took it from her cold fingers, making no comment on her odd little statement as he studied it closely. "I see that it's addressed to a Mr. John Frazer of Glenroden, Perthshire. In your mother's handwriting, if I'm not mistaken." Swiftly he reached for a sheet of paper, compared the two, then nodded his head, satisfied. "Exactly the same," he murmured, glancing briefly at Sue. "I have here your mother's signature. This letter," he lifted it thoughtfully, "you have no idea what it's about?"

"No, I'm afraid not," Sue's eyes were tensely anxious, fixed on the letter as if afraid he wouldn't give it back to her. "I do intend going to Scotland as soon as possible, though, so perhaps I'll find out. Do you think," she asked slowly, "that it might have some bearing on this other matter, this insurance?"

"It might." Another frown creased his high forehead. "You don't happen to have heard anything about this Mr. Frazer, by any chance?"

As puzzled as he was, Sue shook her head. "So far as I know Mother had never been to Scotland. We always lived in London. She used to say that Scotland was a cold, barren sort of place."

"And you believed her?" His voice was faintly, uncharacteristically incredulous.

"Well—" Sue's pale cheeks flushed, "not entirely. I

think she might have changed her mind if she could have been persuaded to go there. I have seen films and heard other opinions. I'm only trying to explain why I find this letter so surprising. I can't think who this man can be."

"To you he's a complete stranger?"

"I've never even heard him mentioned before."

"And you wouldn't consider opening this letter? You don't think it might save a lot of—er—trouble in the long run?"

"Oh, no, I couldn't!" Why had he hesitated before he said trouble? He must know that he was asking the impossible. Perhaps, like Tim, he thought her too dramatic? Bewildered, she turned her head away from the solicitor's probing eyes. She had promised her mother, and a promise was a promise, no matter what the circumstances.

"I see." He made no other comment, but she was aware that he continued to gaze at her speculatively. "I rather think," he said at last, "that we will wait to see what you make out in Perthshire before we go any further. In many ways this trip of yours could be enlightening. If not—well," he shrugged, "another week or two can't make any difference."

Sue still thought his remarks ambiguous as, a week later, she approached Edinburgh in the late afternoon.

"Keep in touch," he had said, when she had rung to say she was leaving. "Whatever you do, let me know how you get on."

Like Tim, he had seemed quite alarmed when she insisted on going on her own, but she hadn't told either of them that her mother had begged her to do just this. Tim especially had tried to persuade her that such a course was clearly illogical, and had been quite offended when she had refused to listen to him. But this way, Sue decided as she drove along, was much better. If the mysterious letter which she had tucked away in her suitcase contained bad news, then there would be no one around to witness her humiliation. Tim never believed in restraining his remarks when time or circumstances proved him right.

In spite of the controversy about her mission, and her own inner apprehension, Sue glanced around her eagerly as her small Mini ate up the miles. The car was going splendidly, something for which she was grateful. The man at her local garage had serviced it well before she left. It had belonged to her mother, who had actually bought it very cheaply with some money she had won in a competition. She had insisted that Sue learn to drive so that they could go out together at weekends. It was taxed to the end of the year, but after she returned to London Sue knew that she would have to part with it. A car was much too expensive to run on her own, and in any case she probably wouldn't need it.

She sighed, then trying to channel her thoughts more cheerfully, thought about her journey. It had been good so far. Admittedly she would have liked more time in York. The Minister had held her enthralled, but the weather was fine and it had been no great punishment to push on. Northwards, after the industrial murk of Tyne and Tees, the hills and mountains had beckoned. There had been a short stop in the historical border town of Alnwick for lunch, then, since rejoining the A1 after her meal, she hadn't stopped at all.

Now she felt tired and as she drove along Dalkeith Road a small yawn escaped her and quickly she put her fingers to her mouth. Perhaps she had been silly to have come so far in so short a time, but there was something inside her which seemed to be driving her on, a curiosity, deeper than she cared to admit, about this man Frazer, as to who he was, and what he would look like. A curiosity curiously mixed with feelings of anger against her mother because she had never mentioned this man until it had been too late for any explanations. And obviously he must have been someone important to her at some stage of her life. Probably Tim

had been right. Somewhere there might possibly be an
uncle, or a grandfather maybe, whom her mother had
deserted. Certainly there must be someone to have
aroused such a guilty conscience. The thought that
somewhere she might have grandparents living produced more mixed feelings, but resolutely Sue thrust
them away, resolving once again to wait and see.

Edinburgh, grey metropolis of the North, a pictur-
esque and beautiful city. As she arrived Sue received
fleeting impressions of splendid buildings, spacious
streets bordered by high tenements and narrow closes.
The old and the new side by side. She progressed
slowly through a heavy build-up of evening traffic, but
didn't mind. Tingling interest was removing some of
her recent lethargy, and anticipation grew as she gazed
around, her eyes wide, each time the flow of traffic
halted. Over the Waverly Bridge into Princes Street she
felt a positive glow returning.

The glow faded a little, however, as she searched for
somewhere to sleep. She tried several hotels suggested
in her guide book without success. In the end it was
only after consulting the information centre that she
was able to find a room. Gratefully she took it, although it was in a more expensive bracket than what
she had had in mind. She would have to economize
later.

The receptionist remarked that even this one room
wouldn't have been available if someone hadn't can-
celled, so Sue was fortunate. "It's because of the Festival," she explained. "Usually we can manage to fit
people in, but at this time of the year it's almost impossible."

Sue thanked her, making a mental note to book in
advance if she should come back again. In her room
she wondered uncertainly what she should wear for
dinner. She hadn't brought anything very formal with
her; just one long black skirt which she hadn't really
expected to wear. In the end, after considering her
luxurious surroundings, she put it on. With a white,

long-sleeved top it didn't look exactly original, but at least she blended into the general scene. She was hungry and in a hurry and it didn't seem so very important.

Bathed and dressed, she went downstairs, for the first time since she had left home feeling a twinge of loneliness, a feeling brought on by the laughing couples and family parties around her. As the receptionist said, it was festival time and everyone appeared to be in a holiday mood. Oh, well, Sue shrugged, she wasn't here, she reminded herself, for pleasure. She asked for a quiet table and was given one by an attentive head waiter who glanced at her appreciatively. She followed him, quite unaware that in her rather severe dress, with her pale smooth hair drawn back into a velvet bow, she looked like some Victorian Miss escaped from the past.

She was half-way through her Sole Mornay when the man with the kilt came in. In Scotland now, she had been told, she wouldn't see men wearing the kilt. Tourists who expected such a sight were disappointed. Well, "He" was wearing one! A wonderful garment in a dark, striking tartan, the name of which she couldn't begin to guess. It caught the eye, holding it, or rather the wearer did. A high, wide and handsome Highlander! Sue's breath caught tautly, irrationally in her throat. He was a complete stranger, but she had never seen anyone like him. He was tall and dark and there was assurance in every line of his well-made body, in the way he held his head. Before he sat down Sue noticed how his kilt swung gracefully from his hips.

With an effort she dragged her eyes away before he could realize she was staring. He had a companion, a girl much older than herself, but younger than the man, probably in her late twenties. One would have to reach that age, Sue thought wistfully, before acquiring such elegance. The girl wore tartan too, with a dark sash over her shoulder. They might almost have been brother and sister, as the same hard arrogance seemed to mould both their features.

Studiously Sue concentrated on her meal, refusing to

take her emotional impressions seriously, relating her
easily distracted mind to her recent unhappy bereavement, which must be responsible for her acting like an
impressionable schoolgirl.

Then suddenly she became conscious of a pair of
eyes upon her, of a gaze so direct it could be felt, so
that it drew her own magnetically. Unable to stop herself, she glanced up to find the man with kilt staring at
her, almost as she had been staring at him. He looked
directly at her across the space of several feet, his eyes
dwelling on her face with not a flicker of dark lashes,
with a narrowed concentration, as if he were seeing a
ghost.

Quickly but with a great effort, she looked away from
him, a strange shudder sweeping through her, annoyed
that a stranger could bewilder her with his eyes alone.
An embarrassing suspicion that her own former scrutiny had sub-consciously attracted his attention brought
hot colour surging beneath her skin. Hating herself for
being a coward but unable to trust her traitorous reactions further, Sue gathered up her belongings and
scrambled to her feet. Then swiftly, without another
glance towards the other table, she left the room.

In one of the large lounges she sank gratefully down
into a comfortable chair, forcing herself to relax. The
man had barely noticed her. She was making mountains out of mole-hills. Why should he notice a complete stranger when the girl by his side was perfectly
charming? In any case, Sue assured herself, she would
never see him again. Here, among numerous other
guests and a medley of small tables and deep chairs,
she would be lost and able to unwind for a short while
before returning to her room. It was getting late and
she would need to be away in good time in the morning.

With lessening tension she drank her coffee, then let
her head fall back against the soft cushion of her chair.
The lounge was quieter now, and tired from her long
drive, she closed her eyes, almost falling asleep.

His voice when it came startled beyond belief, jerking her upright in sudden alarm, her face flushed with confusion.

"Good evening. I owe you an apology, I believe." His tone was deep, totally masculine, as was everything about him. Tall and erect, resplendent in tartan, now that she was so near him the impact was even more devastating than before. It was as if he had reached out and touched her physically, and fright took hold of her once again as his darkly speculative gaze met her.

"I beg your pardon?" Gripping the arms of her chair, Sue forced the rather inane words through her lips. She could think of nothing more to say. Why should he imagine he owed her an apology? Unless...?

"I thought perhaps I alarmed you in the diningroom." He continued as if she hadn't spoken, moving around in front of her, moving her coffee-cup slightly when he caught it with a flick of his kilt. Mesmerised, Sue noticed how a diamond ring flashed on one wellshaped finger. Yet all the while his eyes never left her, his stare encircled her completely, stripping her of all her assurance. Closely he regarded her smooth oval face, her fair hair, the feathery tendrils curling free at the temples, her smoky, dark-lashed eyes. "I had a feeling that I'd seen you somewhere before. I was trying to place you, but when you left so suddenly without, I think, quite finishing your meal, I immediately felt guilty."

"Guilty...?" Bewildered, Sue blinked, glancing at him uncertainly and not a little suspiciously. The man had the audacity to smile, but surely this was one of the oldest tricks in the world? He had noticed her and wanted to know her, otherwise why should a man like this stoop to such devious behaviour? It was the sort of thing one read about in fiction, not the sort of thing ever to happen to Sue Granger. For one brief, improbable moment, excitement flared, only to be as quickly squelched by common sense. Men of his calibre just didn't pick up girls like this. Nor should girls like her-

self entertain such wild ideas. Why he should approach
her in this manner she couldn't think. Unless—her
face went hot—it was as she'd thought before? He had
known instinctively that she had been attracted?

Her eyes, their colour intensified by dismay, looked
away from him, her clear-cut features remote. Desperately she tried to control a nervous tremor. Perhaps her
best defence was to treat the matter lightly? "I'm afraid
you made a mistake," she said coolly, after a slight
pause. "I'm quite certain we've never met before. It
seems probable that you've seen someone like me.
And now, if you'll excuse me..." She turned her head,
an obvious gesture of dismissal.

Not attempting to deny her assertion, or move on,
he towered above her, watching her closely, his eyes
fixed curiously on her face. Neither of them heard the
girl until she spoke.

Her tones laced with a faint surprise, she demanded
sulkily, "Whatever are you doing here, darling? You
distinctly said you'd wait in the bar." Her gaze dwelt
coldly on Sue's taut face as she added sharply, "I
wasn't aware you knew anyone here?"

Sue, about to retrieve her bag from the far side of
her chair, stopped and her head spun. The girl had approached from behind, she hadn't seen her coming.
Close at hand Sue saw that her first impressions hadn't
been far out. She was no teenager, but she was beautiful. Yet her face had a hardness about it which contrasted oddly with the melting softness of her eyes
when she looked at the man. But Sue was certain now
that she wasn't his sister. No girl would look at her
brother in exactly that way.

Before she could speak the man said shortly, almost
as if he didn't welcome his companion's timely interruption, "You usually take some time to powder your
nose, Carlotte. I've just been having a word with this
young lady. I imagined I'd seen her somewhere before,
but it seems I've been mistaken. However, as she

seems to be all alone, perhaps she would care to join us for a drink?''

His suggestion did something momentarily to Sue's breath. Helplessly she glanced at the other girl, noting the frowning disbelief on her face as she stared at the man disapprovingly. In her eyes there was a clear indication that his action in approaching Sue was entirely out of character. Sue heard her protest icily, "But she doesn't even know us!''

"Which is easily remedied." The man's face hardened with determination as his dark brows drew together. Politely he held out his hand, his glance returning to Sue's face. "I'm Meric Findlay. And this lady," his head tilted fractionally and not very kindly, "is Miss Carlotte Craig."

Sue wasn't greatly surprised that Carlotte didn't even bother to acknowledge the introduction. She ignored it completely, staring at Meric Findlay as if he had taken leave of his senses, her voice rising on an almost hysterical note. "You must have forgotten, Meric, that Mother is expecting us? We're late already!''

"Then a few more minutes won't hurt her." Dismissing Carlotte's plea, he looked back at Sue's embarrassed face. His eyes, threatening pools of cool darkness, held hers against her will.

Sue felt like a fly caught in a web, surveyed by the spider, a relentless pursuer. His dark face loomed above her, his expression enigmatic and irrationally, her heart missed a beat. Quite without volition she felt a peculiar weakness in her limbs. The sensation was alarming, and again a small smile flickered across his lips, almost as if he sensed she was unable to move.

Then suddenly to her numbed brain and body there came a saving flash of temper. For some reason or another she had imagined that this man's curiosity might be genuine, but in an instant it occurred to her that he might possibly be using her for another purpose—perhaps to make the girl by his side jealous, or even to annoy her in some way, improbable though it might seem? Devious methods came easily to some men. Her mother had often remarked on it.

Hastily, her pale cheeks flushed, Sue rose, ignoring his hand along with his invitation as she turned to Carlotte, smiling sweetly. "I'm sorry if I've inadvertently kept you from your appointment," she apologized. "But don't let me detain you any longer. I'm sure Mr. Findlay was only trying to be polite."

Biting her lip resentfully, but the incident so far as she was concerned closed, Sue stooped to gather up her wrap, only to find that the hand which she had studiously ignored had reached down and picked it up for her. Then, with what she considered cool audacity, he draped it about her shoulders before she could protest, his fingers inflicting a tingling thrill through the thin material of her blouse. For a space of several quick heartbeats Sue paused, nervelessly, her eyes wide again as they met his. Through the ensuing silence she said, "Good night..." And then, before he could reply, she fled.

Only one spark of triumph illuminated her mind as she almost ran back to her room. She had had the good sense not to tell this Meric Findlay her name.

CHAPTER TWO

THE next morning was grey and misty with a fine rain falling, drenching the spirits and clothes alike. Yet Sue felt oddly grateful for it, welcoming any concealment that a heavily overcast sky might give.

"Typical August weather!" the friendly receptionist smiled wryly, but Sue paid little attention as she quickly paid her bill before going to collect her car.

There was little to be seen of Edinburgh as she left, even the Castle was barely visible, shrouded as it was beneath a canopy of cloud. Scott's Monument stood out, registering briefly as she went past along Princes Street again, but that was all. As in York, she promised herself more time to explore on her return journey. She sighed as her foot regretfully pressed the accelerator. She supposed she was doing things the wrong way around.

Painfully aware of an urge to be gone, she drove swiftly from the city, across the Forth Road Bridge into the hills of Fife. She concentrated wholly on the wet slippery road and the water that streamed against her windscreen. Anything to keep her mind off the previous evening—the disturbing incident in the hotel. She still shuddered to think of it. Not that she could imagine ever seeing Meric Findlay again. Nor, she assured herself, did she wish to. And yet, by some strange coincidence, her heart still missed a beat whenever she thought of him, and an equally strange flicker of regret warred with her desire to forget.

Obviously Meric Findlay had been beset by regrets of another kind as there had been no sign of him at breakfast. Sue had hurried with hers, apprehensive in case he should turn up, but she need not have worried. The table he had occupied the night before was empty and there had been no sign of Carlotte either. Sue could only decide that her conclusions had been correct. He had been using her like a small spanner to wrest a little jealousy from his beautiful girlfriend. People were capable of surprising things when their affections were involved. In Meric Findlay's case the improbability of such behaviour continued to tantalise, and it took an almost physical effort to turn her thoughts in other directions, to thrust his dangerously attractive face from her mind. She mustn't allow anyone or anything to distract her from finding Glenroden and the mysterious Mr. Frazer.

Because of the rain and fog visibility was limited, and Sue was thankful when at last it cleared and the sun came out. Here, she was surprised to see that the countryside was not particularly rugged. It was rolling country, with enormous fields and good sized farmhouses. After Perth, however, the landscape changed, becoming mountainous and wilder, and after Dunkeld, where she left the main road, she felt the loneliness of moor and forest land pressing in on her. By consulting her map she avoided taking many wrong turnings, but when she came to a village several miles along the road she decided to stop and ask the way. She must be getting somewhere near, she assured herself as she parked her car outside the village shop, but she might save herself many miles by inquiring exactly how to get there.

"Glenroden?" the middle-aged woman behind the counter exclaimed, in answer to Sue's rather anxious query. The shop was full, surprisingly full, Sue thought, considering the loneliness of the surrounding country, and she felt her cheeks go slightly pink as a dozen pair of eyes turned towards her curiously.

"You'll be wanting John Frazer," the woman went on as Sue nodded awkwardly. "Or maybe..."

Another woman nearby interrupted eagerly, "I believe Mr. Frazer has hurt his ankle. My neighbor next door was telling me only this morning. He's turned it on the heather, so you should be finding him at home.''

Sue didn't answer but stood there silently as the two women, between them, supplied the information she needed.

"Straight on for two miles, then twice right and twice left. You couldn't miss it.''

"There are two houses, a big one and the other smaller. John Frazer lives in the small one.'' The woman behind the counter glanced at Sue with a frown as she went on serving her customers. "I seem to think I've seen you somewhere before,'' she added, as she finished speaking.

"I hardly think so,'' Sue replied, trying to smile as she thanked each woman for her help. Nervously she retreated to the tinkling door. "I haven't been here before, so it doesn't seem likely.''

With a final nod she let herself out, almost running to her car, shock stinging sharply through her. She had come here looking for this man called Frazer, but to find him had crushed a slender, scarcely formulated hope that he wouldn't exist. Desperately she resisted an impulse to go back home, knowing that she must refuse to pander to her somewhat cowardly inclinations. She started like a sleep-walker rudely awakened, knowing that there was one thing she must do. Any other course would allow her no future peace of mind.

Automatically her hand went out to the ignition, the sudden noise and thrust of the engine as she turned the switch jerking her back to reality. How foolish she was to sit here shaking like a leaf. All she had to do was to drive up to Glenroden, deliver the letter, then leave. Probably it could all be achieved in less than an hour, a case of simple mathematics, nothing to get in such a dither about, not anything to justify such a predominating sense of disaster. Determinedly she straightened, brushing her fair hair back from her forehead with still shaking fingers, and drove on.

Contrary to what she had expected Sue found Glenroden quite easily. If anything her only difficulty lay in the road which was twisted and turned crazily until she almost felt ill. At one spot she had to cross a ford, where a river ran over the road, and as the water surged strongly against her wheels she knew a moment of apprehension. In full flood she imagined this particular stretch of road could be dangerous to the uninitiated, and she couldn't deny a flicker of relief when she arrived safely on the other side. It would have seemed rather incongruous to have come all this way to get stuck in the middle of a stream—or should she call it a burn? It probably wouldn't matter what she called it, she thought wryly. She wouldn't be here long enough.

The river, she saw, ran into a loch which lay heavy and grey in the distance beneath the gathering clouds. Then a stretch of young conifers cut it from her view and she didn't see it again. She took the last left-hand turn, followed the river back up the glen, and found the houses she looked for half an hour later almost hidden in a circling forest of old pines.

Sue's foot jerked swiftly to the brake as she nearly missed the road end. Caught unawares, she changed gear noisily, without her usual skill, as she concentrated keenly on the glimpse of buildings through the trees. The Mini stopped dead, half tilted on the heathery verge as she turned the steering wheel too quickly.

"Damn!" She spoke aloud, but with resignation as she rested her arms momentarily in front of her. It was several seconds before she became aware of the man who stood on a rocky crag some distance away from her. It must have been a high outcrop as he stood out against the forest trees. With a sharply indrawn breath she took in the picture—a modern Turner, creating a complex scene of high drama! A vivid impression, as the great artist often gave, of energy and violence contained in controlled action, as primitive as the mountains themselves.

Although she couldn't make out the man's features,

she seemed to feel his gaze upon her from his lofty vantage point. No doubt he had heard her bad change and, from his pinnacle, was pronouncing judgement. Oh, well... Quickly Sue looked away. What could it matter? Strangers were probably few and far between in these parts, but if he had nothing else to do then she had. Reversing off the grass, she corrected her steering and drove on. She didn't look again up to the crag.

From the moment when she drew up in front of the smaller house Sue knew that everything was going to be different. She couldn't have explained why, but she had the strangest feeling that she was coming home. The feeling persisted as she walked nervously across the wide stretch of rather unkempt grass which lay between the cottage and the long tarred drive. One wouldn't really call it more than a cottage, she decided, regarding it speculatively as she drew nearer. Maybe this Mr. Frazer was a ghillie or something like that. Certainly the house about a hundred yards further on amongst the trees seemed quite imposing. She wasn't able to see it clearly, but it did appear to be a dwelling of some size.

The door of the cottage stood ajar, something for which Sue felt immediately grateful if only because it confirmed her hopes that Mr. Frazer was at home. Tentatively, not allowing herself time to procrastinate, she knocked, but was unable to restrain a quiver of uncertainty when there was no reply. She tried again, with the same result. Then carefully, not knowing quite what to do, she gently pushed open the door and went inside.

The door opened on to a square hall, not large but beautifully panelled in a warm, dark oak. Apart from a length of Persian carpet there was no furniture, only a narrow oak stair going up from the far corner. The door on her right was closed, but the one on her left was half open, and even as she stared, still hesitant, she saw it open wide, and a man stood there.

It must be John Frazer. Sue's eyes went down curiously to his foot. He hobbled, leaning on a stick. Then suddenly, with a small gasp, her eyes went back to his face, drawn there by something beyond her control, some inner conviction that she should know this man, but did not. She couldn't remember ever seeing him before.

His grey eyes were no less riveted than her own, and before she could speak he asked harshly, "Who are you?"

His sharp direct question jerked Sue back to reality, but she was still bewildered by her own reactions. In front of her she saw a tall man whose hair was liberally streaked with grey. Fair hair, and grey eyes very like her own. Very like her own! Tenaciously the thought seemed to churn through Sue's brain as she stared, startled.

"Who are you?" the man repeated, seemingly as startled as herself, but determined also to discover her name.

For no reason that she could think of her voice faltered as she told him, unable to avoid the issue any longer, "I'm sorry . . . I should have told you. My name is Granger, Susan Granger. Mostly my friends call me Sue." She was not prepared for the obviously traumatic effect of her disclosure. His face went pale and his military bearing suddenly slumped, although his eyes never left her face. For a moment Sue thought he was going to fall, but as she stepped hastily to his side he waved her away. "I'm all right," he muttered gruffly. "I damaged my ankle—nothing to make a fuss about. You must come in."

Jerking out a few more stilted sentences, he turned, and she followed him across the soft blue carpet into a lounge. Unlike the hall, it was an extremely cluttered room with books and newspapers scattered everywhere, but the fact scarcely registered as she paused with him beside the open window where he continued to scrutinize her closely.

Sue stirred uneasily beneath his keen regard. "I'm

looking for a Mr. Frazer. A Mr. John Frazer," she added nervously as the silence stretched. "I have a letter for him...from my mother. Do you happen to be this man?"

He nodded, shock spreading with disbelief across his face, filling Sue with a confused alarm. "Does your mother happen to be Helen Granger?" he asked, his voice odd.

Sue nodded uncertainly. "She was."

"Was?" John Frazer reiterated tensely. "Do you mean what I think you mean?"

Again Sue nodded, not wishing to put it into words. She was not really surprised when he said, tonelessly, "She was also my wife."

But it wasn't until he actually said so that total comprehension struck. Shock flooded through her. She stood gazing at him, anguish darkening her eyes to smoky grey, her cheeks white. Was this man her father? Their likeness might be quite incidental. How could she possibly ask?

Seemingly as shocked as she was, he seemed about to say something, then changed his mind. His hand moved to her arm gently and he drew her over to the fire. "You'd better sit down, my dear," he said quietly, obviously taking a grip of himself. "Before we go any further you'd better give me that letter, but I know now before I read it that you're my daughter. With your looks you couldn't possibly be anyone else."

Numbly Sue sat in the chair opposite him in a cloud of bewilderment. Scarcely daring to look at him, she did as she was told. Finding the letter, she handed it over, some part of her mind resolving never to have it back. In retrospect Tim's warning came loud and clear. But how could she have known what she was letting herself in for? That John Frazer could possibly be her father! Just as he did, she knew beyond doubt, before the additional proof of written evidence, that he was. Rather furtively she glanced at him as he sat reading. He was tall and thin, rather frail, but over-all he looked nice, just the sort of man she had often imagined her father would be. Why, oh, why, she wondered desperately, had her mother never told her? It seemed incredible that anyone could have practised such a cruel deception or even succeeded in keeping such a thing to herself!

As for her father's part in the drama, she couldn't begin to guess. There were so many things she didn't understand. Perhaps it would be better not to try. Maybe he would try to explain after he had finished reading.

Almost as if he anticipated her thoughts John Frazer raised his head and, after another cursory glance at the letter in his hand, folded it and handed it to her carefully. "I don't know that I should let you read it, Susan, but it might tell you a few of the things you'll have to know. Between us, your mother and I, we don't seem to have succeeded very well as parents."

His tone was stilted as if the contents of the letter had jolted him considerably, and his face appeared drained of all colour. Momentarily Sue averted her eyes, unable to suppress the feeling that she was viewing some private bitterness, a grief which she couldn't share. Attempting to suppress her own considerable apprehension, she stared at the pages she was clutching, her eyes clinging reluctantly to the closely written sheets.

She read: For a long time, John, I've had a feeling that something is about to happen. If my intuition is correct, and it has never let me down in the past, then Susan will be left on her own. So I am sending you your daughter. If you have any doubts you have only to look at your ridiculous collection of family paintings to see who she is. I left you, John, because I never loved you, although I did try occasionally, you must admit. Glenroden was not for me, you must also admit this. And when I realized that Susan was on the way I knew I must escape. If I hadn't gone then you would never have let me go, not with a daughter or possibly a son in the offing. It was a big decision to make, but I have never regretted it.

I won't need my allowance any more, John, because if you ever read this I shall be dead. But perhaps you will keep an eye on Susan for me, and, if necessary, give her a home. I'm afraid I've never been able to give her the affection she should have had. Perhaps you can supply that too...

There was more, none of which made much sense. Sue felt too disorganized to try and sort it out. The pages dropped from her nerveless fingers as emotion curled and unfurled inside her. The last thing she had expected to learn when she came here was that she had a father, a man who was still very much alive, contrary to what her mother had led her to believe. The news seemed more than she could assimilate immediately on top of all she had been through. She couldn't even begin to gauge the depth of her father's distress. This would probably turn his world upside down. After all, he had apparently been no more aware of her existence than she had of his. In a way—Sue put a shaking hand over her mouth, quelling slightly hysterical laughter— it all seemed too melodramatic to be true!

As if sensing her need for reassurance John Frazer said tautly, "It might be easier, Susan, if we started at the beginning. You must understand that my surprise is as great as yours. Only I'm older, I don't shock so easily, but I must admit this seems to have rather knocked me sideways."

Sue glanced at him a little desperately. "If you like I'll go. You can't surely want me after all this time. I'm not quite sure myself," she added with a sudden flicker of indignation, "that I want to stay."

"We can talk about that later," he suggested with a faint smile. But his voice was firmer, and held just a thin thread of parental authority, even while his eyes stayed anxiously on her distraught face. "I think it might be a good idea if we went through this quickly.

Just the relevant facts. We can always come back to it another day.''

Recognizing the overruling feasibility of what he said, Sue shrank back into her chair, waiting submissively. His struggle to find the right words was clearly indicated by the way a frown deepened on his already lined forehead. For the first time since she had arrived she forgot her own problems to dwell for a moment on the magnitude of his, finding her heart soften suddenly at the look of extreme weariness on his face.

He rose, with some difficulty because of his ankle, and as if seeking inspiration stood with his back to the fire, thrusting the hand which was not holding his stick deep into the pocket of his tweed trousers. ''Your mother and I married, Susan, while I was in the Army. I was a second son and the Army was my career. Your mother loved the life, moving from place to place. My leaves were mostly spent in London, or abroad if we happened to be there. In those days she only came to Glenroden once, when your grandmother was alive. She didn't take to Glenroden or my mother. But I don't suppose she told you anything of this?''

Silently Sue shook her head, wholly absorbed, waiting for him to continue.

''I suppose I should have been warned, but I couldn't foresee that my brother would go before me. There was nothing I could do but come home. It seemed inevitable. Someone had to look after the estate.''

''Didn't Mother come with you?'' Sue dared to ask as he paused.

He nodded his greying head. ''Yes, but she left after a short time, went to live with her mother. After her mother died she came back—I don't know why, as I hadn't been able to persuade her to before this. Anyway we decided to try again, but again it didn't seem to work out. That last time I followed her we had one almighty row. After that I gave up. I did arrange to pay her a monthly allowance, but the last time I tried to contact her at her old home I found that she'd sold up and moved away. She never let me know where she had gone."

"Didn't you ever want a divorce?"

"No, I did suggest it that last time, but she didn't appear to have that in mind. Or maybe," his glance narrowed reflectively, "it could have been because of you. As she said in that letter, if I'd known about you, things would have been entirely different. As it was," his voice sharpened with bitterness, "it should have occurred to me. Now it must be over twenty years too late!"

"About that," she whispered, as he studied her soft young features darkly. "Perhaps, I shouldn't say this, but I don't think that my mother really loved me all that much. This makes what you've told me all the more confusing."

"Your mother was inclined to be self-centered, Susan, and possessive. I suppose we all are to some extent—I don't want to start a slanging match, particularly now that she's gone. If it helps at all your fault probably lay in your looking too much like my side of the family. You are in fact, almost an exact replica of my own mother, and every time she looked at you she must have seen it. I don't think we must blame her too much if she resented what she saw."

Inadvertently Sue's thoughts flew to Tim, remembering his cynical observations. Quickly, to blot out the image, she asked nervously, "Didn't you ever consider selling the estate?"

Visibly he started and she was curious to see a faint flush of colour mount his pale cheeks, a sudden wariness in the grey depth of his eyes. "Estates aren't sold just like that, Susan. This estate wasn't entailed, but it was some years before even my brother's affairs were settled up. And then death duties took a fair proportion of it."

His voice was steady, and the tenseness in his face had gone. She might even have imagined it. She hadn't meant to seem curious about his property, but it might prove difficult to tell him that she didn't want to talk about her mother any more. Later, perhaps, when she and her father knew each other better. Privately she acknowledged that there was still a lot to explain. He would want more details about her mother's accident, about the letter. He himself would have to confirm that the mysterious insurance had really been her mother's allowance. Relevant details would have to be sent to London, but not now. It seemed enough that he was here, and that this man was willing to accept her beyond any doubt as his daughter. A new emotion, bewildering in its intensity, flooded into Sue's heart. She didn't pause to consider that to many it might seem strange that subconsciously she was already thinking of Glenroden as home.

As if he followed and agreed with her train of thought a warm smile curved John Frazer's rather set mouth for the first time as his eyes rested, with a dawning credulity, on Sue's tense face. Before she could try to explain her feelings, he said softly, "Why try to do it all at once, Susan? Willy-nilly we seem to have an unusual situation, and it might be better to get to know each other gradually, although fundamentally I think we both know that the ingredients for a good relationship are there. Certainly it's a rather wonderful feeling to know that I've a daughter. One can forgive much for such a privilege. I only hope, my dear, that you won't share your mother's dislike for the wilds of Scotland, as I shall certainly expect you to make your home here."

Not wishing to lose her somewhat precarious self-control, Sue nodded speechlessly. His words affected her strangely as she became aware of the perceptiveness behind them, a thread of sensitivity which she had found inexplicably lacking in her mother's make-up. Taking a deep breath, she glanced away from his gently tired face. "I might even be able to help you run the estate," she said.

"The estate..." His voice went tight, the tenseness

returned. His weariness was suddenly, curiously cynical. "I have a partner, my dear, a very able man. I don't somehow think he would appreciate your help. He takes care of everything nowadays—saves me a lot of time and bother, leaves me time for my own pursuits."

"But surely," Sue stared at him, her smooth brow creased, "you must still have a lot to do. I mean..." confused, she groped for the right words, "you must have to supervise everything?"

Evasivly her father replied, "Actually, Susan, I'm writing a thesis of Army manoeuvre from 1745, a bit before your time. There's a deal of research involved and it keeps me busy. Of course I do get around the estate from time to time."

Sue's smoky-grey eyes were puzzled and, though common sense warned it was irrational to pursue the subject, something tenacious inside her wouldn't allow her to leave it alone. "This house," she gazed around her, impressions, ideas piling and merging in her overtaxed mind. "I suppose you once lived in the other one which I saw through the trees, and it got too big for you?"

"Why don't you tell her to mind her own business, John, instead of standing there looking helpless!"

Sue jumped, literally, in her seat, a wildness invading her eyes as she heard that voice. It thundered with open menace, telling her quite clearly that he was her enemy! How long had he been standing there? Her pulses stopped, then shuddered. She didn't need to turn around to see that he was the man in the hotel— and the man on the crag. He was Meric Findlay!

"It's all right, Meric."

As she swung around John spoke, confirming her suspicions, although she seemed unable to hear anything clearly above the hammering of her heart. His forcefulness hit her like a blow as his eyes leapt over her full of inexplicable derision. Stunned, she could only stare. Evidently he regarded her as an enemy. It was much worse than his bewildering behaviour the evening before. Then his antagonism hadn't been quite so obvious.

John Frazer glanced swiftly from one to the other, vaguely puzzled. She could see it in his face as he turned and sat down again in his chair. Pulling herself together with an almost visible effort, she said coldly, "I think Mr. Findlay must be jumping to the wrong conclusions. I would even go so far as to say that he could owe me an apology. Unless, of course," her chin tilted contemptuously as her smoky eyes met his dark ones, "he can produce a logical explanation!"

"Sue! Just a minute!" her father interrupted with frank astonishment. "I think I'm the one who needs an explanation. You two apparently know each other, although I'm sorry you don't appear to be on the best of terms."

Meric Findlay cut in ruthlessly, "I met this girl only last night, John, but I knew at once who she was."

"She happens to be my daughter. You couldn't possibly know that." John's eyes flickered with growing perplexity.

With dark eyes narrowed Meric Findlay ignored Sue's wrathful face. "She didn't say who she was, John. I still don't know her name, but I could see by her looks that there was some family connection. I was convinced that she would arrive here today, and I haven't been proved wrong. In fact I saw her coming. If I hadn't been up on the Crag I might have been here in time to stop her."

"You did hear me say she's my daughter, Meric?" John broke in with quiet insistence, oddly defensive.

"I don't care who she pretends to be," Meric Findlay said dryly. "Just so long as you don't believe her without proof. You're too vulnerable, John, always have been. I don't care how many odd relations you collect, but don't ever say that I didn't warn you!"

Sue's blood boiled as her eyes came alive with a helpless kind of anger. No one had ever spoken to her like this before and she found it totally unacceptable. This man considered her an impostor, but, even if he had been right in his assumptions, it certainly didn't give him any right to be so rude. She winced almost aloud as she deliberated on his attitude. He had been more than ill-mannered. He had been devastating, clearly bent on destroying a relationship which might as yet be too fragile to withstand the onslaught of his calculated attack. And, if the glint in his eyes was anything to go by, he was obviously enjoying his campaign of destruction! There was a slight tremor in Sue's voice, but she managed to look straight at him as she retorted hotly, "I can assure you, Mr. Findlay, that my visit here was, to begin with, a mere formality. That John Frazer happens to be my father was as great a surprise to me as it obviously is to you. And as to whether I stay or not, that can't possibly be any of your business!"

There was complete silence as she finished speaking. His eyes still holding hers, he crossed the room to rest his weight on the edge of the cluttered table. The glint in his eye had developed into a positive glitter, and she could almost physically feel the impact of his unyielding personality. She might have been a fly which he was preparing to swat at his leisure, as his eyes travelled over her from head to foot full of cool derision.

"But you have decided to stay, have you not, Miss— er—is it to be Frazer?"

"Of course she's going to stay, Meric," John Frazer injected stoutly. "If you'd just hang on a minute until I explain..."

"Of course she's going to stay," Meric Findlay repeated sarcastically, his eyes turning to John Frazer as if Sue didn't exist. "She'll stay until she decides whether she likes it here. And if not, she'll be trotting straight back to London."

"I would not!" Stung beyond control, Sue jumped furiously to her feet, ignoring her father's plea for rationality as indignation bubbled over inside her. She could at least cope with her own enemies, and if she was to stay here, it might be better to start as she meant to go on. Certainly she didn't intend to be dominated by Meric Findlay. As she stood near to him it didn't help to see herself reflected in his sardonic dark eyes, or to feel so ridiculously small beside his large bulk. But what she lacked in stature he would find she made up in temper! John Frazer was obviously overruled by this man. Turning to glance at him as he sat anxiously back in his chair, Sue knew a faint prickle of irritation that this should be so. "Do you always let your manager dictate to you like this?" she accused, sparks flying from eyes curiously now more blue than grey.

"Susan!" There was a moment's electrified silence. Sue flushed, her temper suddenly fading. It seemed that she had committed the unforgivable, and must apologize. But before she could do so, her father added, his face paling strangely, "I told you before, Susan, that Meric is my partner."

"Oh, well," Sue's long lashes blinked uncertainly, "it's all much the same thing, isn't it? And," she added bleakly, still looking at her father, "I'm sorry if I've seemed rude, especially as I've just arrived, but Mr. Findlay hasn't been exactly pleasant himself."

The observation did not go unheeded. Mr. Findlay replied coolly, with a wry twist of his firm lips, "She could be right, John. Instead of indulging in a slanging match it might be better if Susan and I agree to a truce, juvenile though it seems. No doubt there'll be plenty of time for explanations later. I do know that you've been married, John, so it seems quite feasible that you should have a daughter. We'll leave it at that for the time being and concern ourselves with arrangements for tonight."

Slightly dazed by his change of tone, Sue stared at him wordlessly for an instant. Why should he worry where she spent the night?

"I'm afraid I haven't made any arrangements," she admitted tonelessly. "But I'm sure it must be possible to find accommodation in the village. I didn't realize it was so late."

John Frazer interrupted abruptly. "Of course you can't go to the village, Susan. From now on your home is here, with me. I don't want to lose you just when I've found you."

Sue's heart was suddenly heavy with remorse. He looked tired and frail. The news which she had brought here today must have been disturbing, even though he hadn't seen her mother for many years. She knew a sudden urge to stay to look after him. And surely he must need someone, living here, as he did, all on his own? If only Meric Findlay would disappear instead of towering over them with that superior expression on his face, then perhaps they might get something sorted out.

But it was not to be, although for a moment, as he stalked to the window and stood there framed against the sunset sky, she thought he was about to depart and leave them in peace. Instead, after a brief contemplation of the weather, he turned back, his eyes narrowed over them.

"There's no room here, John, for Susan to stay, and you well know it, but there is plenty of space up at the house. Your own room will still be aired from last week, and if we go now we might catch Mrs. Lennox. She'll soon fix something up for Susan."

"Please." She looked at him uneasily with troubled grey eyes, but his hard, handsome face didn't soften. Instinctively she was aware that he was used to getting his own way and, when he dictated, usually ran to do his bidding. Well, here was one person who would not! She glanced away a little wildly from his dark, taunting eyes, but not because she was frightened of him. If he wanted a fight then she was more than prepared to give him one. He certainly wouldn't find her as docile as her father.

She drew a long quivering breath. "If this cottage has to be good enough for my father, then it's good enough for me. I'm sure I'll be able to find somewhere to sleep without troubling your Mrs. Lennox."

"John!" Impatience tightening his voice, Meric Findlay swung grimly to his partner. "Won't you please tell this girl that I have enough to do without wasting further time! The rooms upstairs are used as attics, junk rooms, stuffed full of your things, and your one bedroom across the hall isn't much better. It would take a month to clear them out, and I haven't time to stand here arguing!"

It annoyed Susan that her father did exactly as he was told. "It would be better, I think, my dear. To stay here wouldn't be very feasible. You see, I use this house more as a retreat, while I'm busy writing. Since my last housekeeper went I haven't bothered very much. I'm afraid I rely too much on Meric."

Which was very obvious! Sue fumed inwardly. He was clearly under this man's thumb, but was it necessary to be so humble? Surely as owner of the estate it was he who ought to be giving the orders? Maybe it was her duty, if only for a short while, to stay, to help him reassert himself against this self-proclaimed dictator. And maybe in the big house she might be in a better position to put Mr. Findlay properly in his place before she left!

She looked at him quickly, her voice silky soft, her cheeks defensively pink. "If it pleases my father, then I'll do as you suggest. But just so long as we can come back here eventually. I shouldn't like to be beholden to you for too long, Mr. Findlay!"

CHAPTER THREE

AWAKENING in her huge canopied bed next morning, Sue allowed herself the luxury of an extra ten minutes to lie and think. The weariness of the previous evening had disappeared, and her eyes were wide as she gazed around the large, well furnished room, feeling that she might almost have to pinch herself to believe that she was here at all.

Her bedroom was truly mediaeval, or so it seemed to Sue, used as she was to modern apartments with their slick, built-in cupboards. The furniture around her couldn't have been changed in a hundred years! Huge dark wardrobes, a wide, brass-handled dressing table; even a washhand-stand complete with china basin and jug, all edging the faded square of unwear-outable carpet, all made to last another hundred years at least! Sue had never seen such furniture outside the country houses which she had occasionally visited—after paying the requisite fee. She had certainly never envisaged staying in one, if only for a few nights.

Curiously she wondered if the rest of the house would be like this. She had only seen the kitchen the night before. Before leaving the cottage, while John Frazer collected a few things together, Meric Findlay had rung the big house, and when they arrived Mrs. Lennox had supper already waiting. Then she had gone to get Sue's room ready. Sue had actually eaten by herself on a corner of the kitchen table. Her father, complaining that his ankle was extremely painful, had decided he would go straight to bed, if Sue would excuse him. Meric Findlay had disappeared with him, not returning until Sue, having finished her meal, had left

the kitchen in search of Mrs. Lennox. Half dazed with
tiredness, she had stood uncertainly outside the door,
not knowing which way to go. She had scarcely been
aware of someone striding into the hall until he stood
beside her.

He had given her a steady look, his dark eyes watchful.

"John's room is along the hall," he had told her
smoothly. "Third door on the right. Do you want to see
him before you go upstairs?"

"Yes, of course," she had stammered, unnerved by
his steely glance, and quite unable to meet it fully. In
spite of all that had been said she had known that she
was still a stranger. She might have found a father, but
as yet knew no great affection for him in her heart, and
the thought of going with Meric Findlay to say good
night filled her with an incomprehensible dismay.

"It's not so easy, is it, Miss Susan?" His stare had
been as disconcerting as his words. Words which he
had used bluntly, with little sympathy for her newly
discovered uncertainty.

"How could it be easy?" she had flung at him with
tired indignation. "If you were aware of the facts, then
perhaps you might understand."

"Oh, John did explain quite a lot as I helped him
settle in," he assured her mockingly. "It's not beyond
comprehenseion. But you're beginning to find, are you
not, that facts and emotions are two different things?"

"You could be right." Reluctant as she was to concede him even this one point, Sue's voice had been
little above a whisper.

His eyes had narrowed sharply on her tense face. "If
I were you," he'd suggested, "I'd look at the situation
through the eyes of a child viewing a foster-parent for
the first time. Then you might not feel so distracted."

"But with foster-parents there are usually no—well,
blood ties."

"Which doesn't always count half as much as we like
to think. It's often the associating ties which are more

important. You and your father haven't any of these as yet. Maybe you never will.''

She had stumbled away from him then without replying, hating him a little for his cruel remarks while unable to deny the veracity of them. He might have succeeded in clearing a degree of confusion from her mind, but she didn't like him any the better for it. "Say goodnight to him for me, please," she had whispered, half over her shoulder as she had run clumsily upstairs. This morning she couldn't somehow remember whether he had answered her or not.

She could scarcely remember getting into bed. Dimly she did recall how Mrs. Lennox had whipped off her clothes with seemingly practised hands, having her between the sheets in minutes. "You'll feel better tomorrow, dear," she had smiled, glancing intently at Sue's tired face. "I've been a nurse and I should know. Mr. Frazer has been telling me the news and I'm delighted. Delighted, too, that you're so pretty. I've often wondered what you would be like.''

Strange words, now that she came to consider them, totally inexplicable. Sue frowned, then shrugged her bare shoulders impatiently. Mrs. Lennox must have a lot to do, and had probably just phrased her thoughts wrongly. Anyway, she could ask her later, after she had had a cup of tea. An unfamiliar longing for one made Sue wonder about the time, and as she groped around for her watch, she remembered also that Mrs. Lennox had added before she went that she wouldn't be here today. Whatever else that might mean it certainly seemed clear that she wouldn't be around with any early morning tea. In any case it was after seven and she must get up and see how John Frazer was feeling.

But before she could move there came a knock on the door, and before she had time to even acknowledge it the door opened and Meric Findlay strode into the room. Utterly surprised, Sue had barely time to pull a sheet up to her chin before he seemed to be towering over her, thrusting a cup of tea on to her bedside table.

Vaguely, in the midst of turmoil, Sue heard herself thanking him as his eyes raked over her stunned face. His glance was compelling, impaling her against her pillows as unmercifully as a butterfly on a pin.

Hardily he disregarded her tentative thanks, not beating about the bush as his eyes met her dilating ones. "You'd better drink that quickly. Mrs. Lennox isn't here, and your father isn't well. And, as you're partly responsible, I'm afraid you'll have to help look after him."

Unnoticed, the edge of the sheet escaped Sue's nerveless fingers as his words jerked her upright, exposing the taut lines of her slim young figure beneath the thin silk of her nightdress. "How do you mean, not well?" Her voice managed to be almost as sharp as his as she stared back at him in consternation. She ignored her tea.

He picked it up again, forcing her to take it. "Get it down," he said curtly. "You still look washed out. I don't want two invalids on my hands. I do lead a fairly busy life, and all this feminine dithering is time-consuming."

Almost choking, yet disconcertingly aware of his dominating authority, Sue did as she was told. She had been about to refuse, then changed her mind. Perhaps if she obeyed he would explain and go. The exploratory inventory of his eyes affected her strangely. Panic was hidden beneath her cool reply. "I'm sorry if I'm wasting your time, but why should you hold me responsible for my father? His ankle, I believe, was hurt before I arrived."

"It's not his ankle. It's his heart." He spoke abruptly, without expression, but leaving her in no doubt as to the authenticity of what he said. "The doctor came last night, after you'd gone to bed."

"You should have told me!"

"Why?" Scornfully he dismissed her exclamation. "What good would it have done? I'm used to John's attacks, and you'd had about all you could take!"

So he had noticed? Somehow his noticing removed a little of the chill from around her heart. Not that he was sparing her now! Half desperately Sue's hands tightened around her cup as she gazed at him, mute inquiry in her eyes. "He might have died!"

"One of these days he might." He refused to give her the reassurance she unconsciously sought. "Some things are occasionally beyond the power of human administration, as Doctor McRoberts will no doubt explain. And if it's explanations you're after you might be interested to hear that apparently the good doctor has known all about you from the beginning."

"From the beginning?"

His eyes narrowed with bewildering inconsistency on her breathlessly parted lips. "If you're always going to repeat what I say it might go to my head. Especially if you continue to look at me as you're doing now."

"Oh, please..." Colour splashed her pale cheeks as she became aware of the subtle punishment which her constant interruptions inflicted. The sudden glint in his eye reminded her that he was very much a man who, if tried too far, would not allow their short acquaintance to deter him from seeking greater penalties.

But then he shrugged, and she went cold again as he said, "It appears that your mother consulted McRoberts years ago, before she left Glenroden for good. John, I'm afraid, doesn't seem to appreciate that, bound by medical ethics, McRoberts was unable to tell him about his own child, but maybe you can make him see reason."

"Mrs. Lennox said..." Totally disorganized, Sue stopped half-way, completely incapable of digesting what he told her, her mind swinging inexplicably back to the evening before.

"Well, what did Mrs. Lennox say?" he prompted smoothly, as she made no attempt to finish, but sat staring at him like a bewildered child.

Uncertainly Sue blinked, her eyes unseeing on his hard, handsome face. "Something about having wondered how I would turn out. How could it have been possible for her to have known? I though I must have heard her incorrectly."

"Not necessarily. Mrs. Lennox used to be the doctor's receptionist and nurse, before she married and moved away, I believe. The information would be down in the surgery files."

"Now she's back?"

"Yes, but not with McRoberts. He's had someone else for a long time. Besides, she's a widow now, and not so young as she used to be. She has a cottage and helps here. Her nursing experience is useful when John isn't well."

There was a short, tense silence as Sue's mind sifted and tangled with the information. Nothing seemed crystal-clear, but one fact seemed to stand out as her clouded vision sought for clarity. "It seems beyond doubt that I am Susan Granger-Frazer?"

He smiled thinly. "Quite conclusively. I'd drop the Granger bit, if I were you. It's not relevant any more."

She said unevenly, "I'm not quite sure yet what I'll do. You knew who I was at the hotel?"

His eyes were suddenly guarded. "Let's just say that I knew you were a Frazer, and knowing about John's heart I was alarmed. And I think for the time being we'll leave it at that, Miss Susan. Right now I'm going to suggest you get out of that bed."

The hardness was back, arousing her resentment, making her aware that Meric Findlay could be more of an enemy than a friend. The brief and obviously senseless but dangerous attraction she had felt for him in the hotel was gone, and she knew a flash of relief. He might have relieved her mind about certain things, but she refused to let even a flicker of gratitude show through. Rebelliously, her chin lifted slightly. "As soon as you're out of the room," she said softly, "I shall do as you suggest with pleasure."

It seemed to Sue to be hours later before she had time to draw another breath. As she washed and dressed quickly her thoughts veered inconsistently from her father to Meric Findlay. Meric Findlay, she decided, was someone whom it would be wiser not to trust, and whom, in her father's interests, it might be better to investigate. It might seem impertinent as well as mercenary to seem too curious about her father's affairs straight away, but it was something to bear in mind. A little bit of private sleuthing as she went along couldn't do any harm. Since her father's health had broken down he had probably left everything in this man's hands, which wasn't a good thing. Well, now he would have someone of his own to help. Mr. Findlay might be a sort of partner, but woe betide him if he took so much as one step out of place! If she hadn't found it possible to love her father yet, then there were other ways of proving herself a dutiful daughter.

Bolstered a little by her brave if highly impractical thoughts, Sue scrambled into a cotton dress, brushed her hair haphazardly with one or two sweeping strokes, then ran downstairs.

There was no one about and she was glad that she knew where to find the kitchen. But with one hand on the door she hesitated, her eyes going to the huge grandfather clock in the hall. It was after eight. Perhaps she should go and see how her father was—if he needed anything? Undoubtedly Meric Findlay with his sweeping efficiency would have taken him a cup of tea, but that might have been some time ago.

Still nervous, she almost tiptoed back along the hall, counted two doors and knocked gently on the third, remembering what Meric Findlay had told her. When there was no reply she carefully turned the knob and looked in, almost ashamed of her relief at finding John Frazer fast asleep. The room had obviously been turned into a bedroom. It was comfortable, and warm from the small fire which burnt in the hearth. Her eyes returned to the man in the bed. He looked exhausted, and had probably had a bad night. She felt an unusual stir of pity in her heart as she studied his worn face, and vowed again to help him all she could.

A tray with the remains of a light breakfast was on
the table by his bed. Maybe Mrs. Lennox had popped
in for an hour or two after all? Swiftly Sue picked up
the tray, closing the door softly behind her as she went
back to the kitchen.

As soon as she opened the kitchen door Sue knew
there was someone inside, but her eyes widened to see
Carlotte Craig sitting by the window, very much at
home, drinking coffee! Since she had never expected
to see Carlotte again or quite so soon, surprise held her
silent while the girl looked her coolly up and down.

"I shouldn't just stand there if I were you," Carlotte
drawled above the rim of her cup. "Come in and close
the door. You seem capable of worming your way into
most places."

Her voice was insolent, her eyes as unfriendly as
they had been in Edinburgh, and her choice of words
clearly reflected her frame of mind. Sue was hungry
amd didn't feel particularly friendly herself, but a
flicker of curiosity controlled an equally sharp reply.
How had Carlotte known she was here? And why was
she here herself? She must surely live somewhere in
the neighborhood to be here so early. Obviously, as on
their previous meeting, Carlotte resented her. But
why? Was she already engaged to Meric Findlay, and
considered Sue an interloper?

Slowly Sue placed the tray she was carrying on the
wide scrubbed table, wishing fervently that she was
more familiar with the general layout of the kitchen.
She couldn't very well start searching for things while
Carlotte sat surveying her with such a cool, calculating
stare.

"Were you seeking Mr. Findlay, or did you come to
see my father?" she asked, a hostile urge to make Carlotte aware of her own position warring with her usual
leaning towards politeness, so that she tempered the
impact of her words with a slight smile.

But if she had hoped to startle Carlotte then she was

to be disappointed. As if she had seen quite clearly through Sue's subterfuge, her thin lips curled contemptuously. "I met Meric on the glen road, and he was telling me you're claiming to be John's daughter. I simply couldn't resist the temptation to come and see for myself. I am, by the way, John's cousin."

"John's cousin?"

"Yes. People do have cousins, you know. And my claim might be much more authentic than yours."

"What do you mean?" As she met the animosity in Carlotte's eyes, Sue's voice was little above a whisper.

"I mean..." There was a furious clatter as Carlotte jumped to her feet, leaving her cup on the window-sill, "that in spite of what John or McRoberts say—or what ever Meric chooses to think—I intend to expose you, even if it takes months!"

Sue sat down abruptly, feeling the strength drain from her legs as Carlotte slammed out without a backward glance. She knew a growing desire to follow Carlotte, to pack her case and never come back. If this house had been so full of intrigues when her mother lived here, then no wonder she had run away. With unseeing eyes Sue stumbled to the window, resting her hot forehead against the cool pane, immediately regretting her hasty thoughts but unable to control them.

Then, lifting her head a little, she looked down the glen. Before her it spread into the blue distance, barely touched yet by the first warm tints of autumn, but full of promise of the vivid colouring which would surely come. Already the heather was purple where it covered the rough, undulating ground against the bare mountains. Last night in the dusk there had been mist on the hills, but this morning the contours stood out, clearly defined against the skyline. Water glinted, catching the sunlight where it ran through rock, and over the lower slopes came the dark green frosting of forest.

A land enticingly beautiful. Sue's breath caught in her throat and, for a minute, she forgot Carlotte's threatening words. The willow trees against the low stone wall outside bent gently to the warm west wind, beckoning her to come and explore. Suddenly she longed to be out, flying through the heather, up into the woodlands, into the world she could glimpse at through the trees.

But of course she could not, though how her mother could have left such a place she could not think. With a sigh she turned from the window and, as she did so, her eyes fell upon a note propped between a teapot and a jug of milk. Slowly she walked across to the cabinet where the teapot stood. The note was addressed simply—Susan, and nervously she picked it up. The handwriting was masculine and before she opened it she guessed it was from Meric Findlay. It was, and he wrote,

"I wouldn't advise you to disturb John. He'll probably sleep until lunch time when Mrs. Lennox could be back. Just look in now and then to see if he's O.K. I won't be in for lunch, so don't start preparing anything for me."

The note terminated abruptly and, equally, abruptly was signed Findlay.

Thankfully Sue put it down, unable to suppress a flicker of relief that she wouldn't see him again for at least a few hours. It would give her time to rally her defences, and, she thought wryly, to try to find some food for herself. He talked of lunch while she hadn't even had breakfast yet! With an indignant hand she swept the remains of his from the kitchen table, carrying the empty dishes to the sink.

When at last she did find something to eat Carlotte's strange behaviour kept spinning through her head, and suddenly she wasn't hungry any more. With a frown she pushed aside her last piece of toast. If Carlotte was really John's cousin and expected to marry Meric Findlay, then she might also expect to inherit the whole of Glenroden, and if the size of the house was anything to go by then the estate itself must be quite large. By coming here Carlotte probably saw her as a threat to all her plans, and, if she was entirely mercenary, no wonder she was bitter.

Sue sighed worriedly, losing interest in her breakfast as she jumped to her feet and started to tidy the kitchen. Anything was better than sitting bothering herself with things which must have happened before she came here. There must be plenty to do. The intrigues of Meric Findlay and his girl-friend would have to wait until she had more time to consider them. But, unaccountably, as she worked her heart ached with a peculiar pain as she pictured Meric on the glen road that morning telling Carlotte all about her.

To her relief Mrs. Lennox arrived back before twelve, earlier than Sue had expected. "I managed to postpone my second appointment, dear," she smiled. "I thought it best, as everything here will be strange to you, and Mr. Findlay would be too busy to show you around."

Gratefully Sue returned her smile. John hadn't woken up, but he had been restless, and Sue had felt a guilty apprehension each time she had peeped into his room.

"Sometimes he sleeps for hours," Mrs. Lennox assured her, "when he's like this. I'll look after him now that I'm back. I know exactly how to go on. But that isn't to say, dear," she added, "that he won't want to see you when he does wake up. In fact it might be better to stay near at hand, as I'm sure you'll be the first person he asks for."

Sue nodded, and helped Mrs. Lennox to prepare a light lunch before accompanying her on a tour of the house.

"I don't rightly know if it's my business to do this," she confessed, as they progressed from room to room. "The trouble is I'm never quite sure where the Major really lives. Whether it's here or down at the cottage."

"The Major?" Puzzled, Sue looked away from the wide precincts of the drawing-room to gaze inquiringly on the nurse's bright face.

"Your father, of course. Didn't you know he was in the Army? The regulars, that is."

"Oh, yes." Understanding dawned as Sue turned her head. "I didn't know his rank."

"Never mind." Quietly Mrs. Lennox closed another door and beckoned Sue back to the kitchen. "It doesn't really matter. You can't find everything out at once. How do you like the house?" She changed the subject abruptly.

"It's nice..." Then, because that sounded insipid, Sue smiled warmly, her small even teeth gleaming white. "I didn't want to say, but it's just the sort of house I've always dreamt of. Big, but not too big. Comfortable without being dreary. Full of antiques which manage to look beautiful as well as old. The whole atmosphere is somehow nice."

Mrs. Lennox nodded approvingly as she stoked up the boiler. "I've felt it myself. It's a pleasant house. Mr. Findlay thinks so, too. He's bought some of the nicest antiques himself, over the years. Perhaps he'll show you some time when he's not too busy."

"Mr. Findlay would appear to be a very busy man." Unaware of the hardness of her tone, Sue avoided Mrs. Lennox's inquiring gaze, her mouth set mutinously. "I suppose," she conceded, when Mrs. Lennox didn't reply, "that when my father is ill he has everything to do himself."

Which wasn't exactly what she'd meant in the first place, and she knew that Mrs. Lennox knew it!

To Sue's dismay John Frazer's attack turned out to be a bad one, and it was several days before they were able to have much of a conversation. During this time she hadn't ventured far from the house, but could find nothing to verify her own suspicions. Although Carlotte was around quite a bit, fussing over-loudly about her cousin, Sue didn't notice that Meric was over-attentive, but then he wasn't the type to wear his heart on his sleeve. He could be spending quite a lot of time with Carlotte for all she knew. Somehow she had a feeling that Mr. Findlay, in spite of his enigmatic exterior, was no hermit. There was something about his mouth which made her suspect that he enjoyed a little dalliance with the opposite sex, even though she herself did not arouse his interest. Nor, she assured herself emphatically, did she want to.

She couldn't deny, however, that even if he seemed generally unaware of her existence she was very much aware of him as a man. She saw little of him. During the day he was seldom in for meals, and in the evening he often went out for dinner, apparently not eager to share a simple repast at the kitchen table. But something about him, each time she saw him, drew the same response which she had been vividly conscious of in Edinburgh. It was probably just those ridiculous kilts which he wore, she decided wryly. In them he looked like some wild Highlander from one of her father's books. Reason enough for any girl's heart to miss a beat, but no grounds whatsoever for imagining that she was irrevocably attracted.

But her heart continued to annoy her by behaving unpredictably one evening when he did come home early. Mrs. Lennox usually went back to the village for an hour or two each night before returning to sleep in case she should be needed. It was quiet, and after dinner Sue sat for an hour with her father, then left him happily studying a huge military tome which Carlotte had brought. She always seemed to be bringing him something, and not always, Sue thought privately, were her gifts very suitable. Not that she ever openly objected as John seemed to welcome the girl, and her gifts gave him much pleasure. Indeed, Sue sometimes thought herself that she might have misjudged Carlotte if it hadn't been for the occasional glances she intercepted. Secretly Sue suspected that her frequent calls had as much to do with Meric Findlay as her father, but it would have been unkind to say so.

On this particular evening a peculiar restlessness made it impossible for Sue to sit still any longer, and after assuring herself that John's bell was within reach, she gently closed the door and wandered into the drawing room. She was standing gazing at a painting of her grandmother when Meric Findlay walked in.

He didn't surprise her as she had heard him moving in the hall, but her eyes swung, startled, as she saw who it was, silently berating her sixth sense for not warning her. At this point she had known there could be no escape. Not that this mattered, she told herself stoutly, yet somehow wishing that he hadn't caught her staring at a family portrait.

"You're home early?" She uttered the first thought to come into her head, a sudden confusion drying her lips. Cautiously she wetted them with the tip of her tongue, embarrassingly aware of his dark eyes on her mouth as she did so. Hastily, when he didn't speak, she tacked on, "Have you had dinner?"

"I've had dinner, thank you." His hard face closed up, inscrutable. Yet something about her naive little speech appeared to amuse him—or was it her appearance? His eyes roved slowly over her, taking their time, indifferent that they subjected her to a disconcerting scrutiny.

The silence didn't seem to bother him, if indeed he noticed it. His eyes probed, exploring each detail of her figure, the fine, clear outline of her face, her hair babyfine, yet heavy, curving on to her shoulders, returning to her eyes, the beautiful clouded grey which contrasted so softly with a gardenia-pale, rose-flushed skin. He seemed bent on a minute examination, and Sue's body tensed as a flickering flame shot through it.

Then suddenly, as his eyes left her, swinging to the painting on the wall, she understood, and his next words confirmed her conclusions, subduing the turmoil in her heart.

"No one could ever deny you are a Frazer," he said slowly. "But how much of your mother is hidden beneath the outer shell, I wonder?"

His eyes were hard again, and his voice, following

the theme, had a deeply cutting edge. A disparaging inflection.

Why should he disapprove so of her mother? He hadn't known her. Why then should he sit in judgment in this lordly fashion? Loyalty dies hard, even harder than affection, if Sue had stopped to consider. Instead she tumbled headlong into the trap. "You probably don't mean to be insulting!" she retorted with an angry little gasp.

"Knowing the circumstances one could scarcely be anything else," he answered with a cool detachment which she envied. "When a woman denies a man his own child she can't expect the world to judge her kindly."

"But she was only one side of it, wasn't she? Perhaps if my father had cared enough to retain some form of contact, if..." Her voice trailed off weakly, her doubts and fears clearly reflected in the extreme sensitivity of her face.

He said brusquely, his eyes unfathomable as sickness held her, "I shouldn't lose any sleep over it if I were you. You could console yourself that you were too young to know anything about it. Very few of us are granted such immunity from the mistakes of others."

The extreme dryness of his tones taunted her. He was a mocking devil, careless that his words hurt as he jerked her body and mind alike. Her head spun as she went helplessly lax. The numbness of the last weeks had been like an anaesthetic. Now feeling returned, yet with a curious emptiness, as if the whole of her unconsciously yearned for some new experience beyond her reach.

She stared at him, desperately frightened, not knowing if she could cope with the enormity of her reactions, knowing she must have time—if only so much. And because she knew that in some way he was irrevocably bound up with these feelings she over-reacted like a distracted child. Unwilling that he should guess that he disturbed her, she disregarded his advice with resentful stubbornness.

Recklessly blind to the glint in his eyes, she said, "You talk as though divorce and separation are irrelevant in this day and age. What, I wonder, would you have done if your wife had left you like that?"

The glint in his eye deepened as he regarded her small defiant chin. "I should see to it that she never wanted to leave in the first place, but we didn't happen to be discussing me. You missed the point at the beginning, my dear Sue. I only intended advising you against leaving Glenroden, should you entertain such an idea. I merely suspected that you might share your mother's tendencies to run at the wrong moment, and that would never do."

He couldn't actually be threatening her? Tautly her slim white fingers went to the low neck of her dress, hiding the nervous pulse at the base of her throat. "You mean because of my father?"

"Another shock wouldn't help him."

"Like—when I came back?" She moved away from him then, alarmed by his cruelty, her eyes resting momentarily and blindly on her grandmother's face, unwilling to admit the logic of what he said, waiting tensely for his reassurance.

But none came. Only his hands came up behind her as she turned, gripping her bare arms, the steely strength of his fingers hurting. Yet he held her impersonally, as if he was shaking a dense child, his voice terse in her ear. "If you like. But for heaven's sake don't torture yourself, girl. It's just not the time for soft words, if that's what you're wanting."

For a moment her lips parted wordlessly as, while mind tussled with body, she slumped back against him. Then, with an almost frantic effort, she wrenched herself free, whirling to face him, the imprints of his fingers red on her upper arms. "I just wouldn't expect any kindness from you, Mr. Findlay. Why should I? And you might be my father's manager, but you certainly aren't mine! Whether I go or stay is none of your business. Please remember that!"

Furiously Sue heard her own voice, slurred and choked with emotion as she almost ran from the room. With a little more dignity she might have given the impression that she had had the last word, but not now.

It seemed equally perplexing that she should feel curiously restless and unsettled during the next few days. So much so that Mrs. Lennox noticed and advised her to go out for a change.

"I'll pack you a few sandwiches, dear. You can take your car and explore, then have your lunch. If you keep to the road you can't go wrong. You could go to the loch and the air will do you good, bring a little colour back into your cheeks."

She had promised to keep an eye on John, but it was reluctantly that Sue went. Although he was now getting up daily, Doctor McRoberts had warned her not to let him do anything, just gentle exercise around the house. Today he had seemed tired and said that he would stay in bed. So at least, Sue thought wryly, as she reversed her Mini from the garage, she knew where he was.

Once out on the road she felt her spirits lifting and was glad she had taken Mrs. Lennox's advice. She hadn't realized it would be so good to be out. A still autumn silence lay over the moors, broken now and then by the abrupt firing of distant guns. John had told her only that morning that Meric took shooting parties out two or three days a week at this time of the year. Sue had been surprised until he explained in detail.

"It used to be my thing," he had smiled wistfully. "I stopped holding shooting parties myself some years ago, but we have an arrangement with the hotel in the village. We provide the shoot, and they provide the shooters. It involves quite a bit of hard work, taking everything into account. I don't know how long Meric can keep it up, but it certainly helps, financially."

"How long has he been with you?" She hadn't meant to ask, but since that night in the drawing-room Meric Findlay had never been far from her thoughts, even if, as she tried to persuade herself, it was only because of his questionable activities.

John had glanced at her quickly, as if he found the wording of her question curious, but all he said was, "About ten years. He came here in his middle twenties, and had a lot to learn. We sort of helped each other, if you know what I mean. His father died in South Africa, so he had no one else."

Sue didn't know exactly what he meant. She was fast learning, however, that when asked to be more explicit he often recoiled into a sort of shell from which it was difficult to prise any explanation. Instead she had concentrated on the South African bit, sudden interest surging through her. But before there had been time to say anything Mrs. Lennox came in, and she had decided to leave it. It would keep until another day.

CHAPTER FOUR

DETERMINED not to dwell any longer on that which worried her, Sue concentrated on finding the loch. Mrs. Lennox was a trained nurse; her father would be in good hands. Yet in spite of her former resolutions Sue frowned. Was it natural at her age to find all illness tedious? Secretly she was ashamed to admit it. Her mother's attacks of migraine, whenever anything upset her, had been trials to be endured, involving as they had done long periods when the slightest noise had been taboo, when even the sound of Sue's transistor turned low had been forbidden. It didn't help much to remember how her occasional resentment had usually propelled her to her mother's side with extra assurances of sympathy. If Sue had ever thought of a father, he had always been a particularly robust figure. While John Frazer pleased her intellectually, his frailness, due to his heart condition, dismayed her. And again, as with her mother, a guilty conscience plagued her unmercifully.

With a little difficulty Sue found her way, back over the river ford, taking the right-hand fork instead of the left which would only take her to the village. The Mini was going well. Woman-like, she had worried that there wasn't enough petrol, but the tank she could see was half full and she recalled filling it up after she had left Edinburgh. The weather was good today, and the countryside enticing, and on the road the dark-eyed sheep scattered before the car. Huge boulders dotted the landscape with hidden crevasses, while rough grass and heather encircled bare slabs of rock. Ideal spots for a dry picnic, she noted as she drove on, not really keen to stop until she reached the loch.

She was not really surprised to pass several cars. After all, it was the tourist season. She remembered that first day and all the people in the village shop. Even so, these roads were deserted compared with similar roads in the south. The south… Suddenly she wondered if she would ever go back. Did she really want to? It might not be altogether easy to stay here. It would be foolish to think so. She would have to make new friends, eventually find a job—she couldn't just wander around Glenroden for the remainder of her days. Her heart gave a downward jolt. If Meric were to marry Carlotte Craig she might not be able to stay here at all.

Then, around the next bend, without warning she came upon the caravan site. Protected, and almost hidden, by a screen of birch and conifers, it stood well above the loch on a flat green plateau, but within easy reach of the lapping water. Startled, Sue pulled off the road on to a wedge of tarmac, and stared. It was one of the nicest parks she had seen, yet a niggling resentment bothered her. It seemed an intrusion of her privacy. All around the mountains and wild, lonely places were at their best, basking in early autumn sunshine, and here was the very thing she had hoped to escape from— crowds of people!

Driven by some inner compulsion, not because of inclination, Sue left her car to walk down the wide track between the vans. She saw a notice which said clearly: Glenroden Caravan Site. No vacancies. She didn't attach any particular significance to it. It was only when she saw Carlotte coming around the corner of one of the caravans that suspicion began to grow.

Carlotte stopped, obviously as surprised as Sue. "Whatever are you doing here?" she asked, her eyes wary.

"Having a look around," Sue stated, none the less bluntly. Which wasn't quite what she had had in mind, but Carlotte shouldn't ask silly questions. Besides, why

should Carlotte act as if she owned the place? Surely—
the thought struck Sue from out of space—surely she
didn't live here? Suddenly she realized she had no idea
where Carlotte lived. She had imagined in the village.
"I'll show you around, if you like?" Smoothly, a cat
with the cream smile on her face, Carlotte waved a
magnanimous hand towards the park, taking little notice of Sue's raised eyebrows.

"Show me around?" Deviously Sue sought to satisfy
her curiosity. "Why should you do that?"

Too easily Carlotte saw through her. "If you mean,
do I live here, or own the place, then the answer is no.
It belongs to Glenroden."

"You mean, the estate?" As she asked Sue flushed
hotly. She hated having to persist. Why had no one told
her?

It didn't help that Carlotte nodded her sleek dark
head, her stare superior. "It seems there's a lot of
things you don't know about. I wonder why?" While
her words were innocent enough her tone was mocking. "The woman who usually sees to the office is away
for a few days, so Meric asked me if I would help out."
Her tone, shifting slightly, implied much more than
that.

Slowly Sue froze. Unpredictably her heart lurched
downwards again. The two of them, in it together!
What did they need with a caravan site at Glenroden?
Surely an estate of this size needn't resort to this? "My
father didn't mention it," she replied stiffly. "But then
he's ill, and I don't see a great deal of Mr. Findlay."

No sooner was it out than Sue regretted the last bit of
information. A smug smile spread over Carlotte's
mouth. "Meric wouldn't wish to discuss these things
with you," she said, "especially as you're a stranger.
He doesn't think you'll stay long, not after John's better, so he would only be wasting his time."

With difficulty Sue restrained a biting retort. Carlotte
might be speaking the truth—she wouldn't put remarks
like that past Meric Findlay—but she was obviously

baiting her. She must refuse to be antagonized. Then she might find out what was going on. She bit her lip sharply, then releasing it, smiled. "I think I would like to see around if you don't mind. Now that I'm here."

The next hour she spent with Carlotte, walking around the park. It was a good one; she soon realized that. Every mod convenience, even a small shop where, as Carlotte explained, such necessities as milk, bacon, and eggs were sold. "Other items can be bought at the village shop," she told Sue. "This site has helped them quite a lot."

The caravans were all occupied, she added, as people liked it, and its reputation in the last two years had spread. And the holiday season now stretched well into the autumn. In fact this was fast becoming the most popular time of the year.

Their tour over, she invited Sue quite cordially into her office for coffee. Sue thanked her and accepted, feeling it would be churlish to refuse after the time Carlotte had spent with her. Carlotte, she thought wryly, would have made a good courier for a travel agent. She appeared to excel at this sort of thing. If she was trying to demonstrate her usefulness to Meric, then she had certainly succeeded.

The office was small and well equipped. Carlotte eased her elegant, trouser-suited figure into a comfortable chair behind the desk, waving Sue to the seat opposite. "Another woman will be along in an hour or two to release me," she said. "The busiest times are early morning and after tea, when new people arrive. Meric doesn't expect me to cope with those."

Which could mean many things, Sue grimaced cynically, a short time later, as she drove away. Either Carlotte wasn't as competent as she appeared to be, or Meric Findlay was over-solicitous for his lady-love. She went on, around the loch where she stopped to eat her lunch in the middle of the afternoon, but somehow, for some inexplicable reason, she hadn't the heart to explore further.

"I've had quite a nice day, though," she assured Mrs. Lennox, who looked at her searchingly, obviously puzzled by her early return. "I'll take tea in if you like, then you can get away. Perhaps I remembered that you need time off as well as I do."

Picking up the already prepared tray, she went along to her father's room, resisting an impulse to ask Mrs. Lennox about the caravan park, afraid that she might get another answer such as Carlotte had given her. It might be better to tackle Meric Findlay himself, when she next saw him.

Then, with a start of surprise, as she opened John Frazer's door she found Meric with him. As she entered he rose, he took the tray from her and placed it smoothly on a small table by the fire before turning, his eyes narrowed on her suddenly flushed face. "I believe you've been out?"

And he wanted to know where she'd been—if she interpreted his tone of voice correctly. Well, his curiosity could remain unsatisfied for a few minutes. She smiled briefly at her father before answering with a question of her own. "You're back early. Where is your shoot?"

"In the capable hands of my second in command. I hope." His voice was light and taunting, as if he guessed her intention to procrastinate and was willing to go along with it—so far. "When I left they were almost through, and will probably be back at the hotel by this time."

"You can obviously dispense with your duties lightly, Mr. Findlay." With uncontrollable antagonism she gave him back look for look. Their eyes clashed, his a shade dangerous, hers glittering like sparkling ice.

"I think," he said, hard and deliberate, "that wherever you've been the air hasn't agreed with you, Miss Frazer. But I'm sure your father would appreciate his tea more than your temper!"

Mortified for a moment, her hands clenched tight, Sue glanced towards the bed, relieved to see John lean-

ing close to the radio and Gardener's Question Time.
Her head came up proudly as a faint remorse left her.
Someone had to put this man in his place. Her father
apparently couldn't care less. She moved away blindly
to the fireplace and started pouring tea, her lashes dark
fans against her cheeks.

Meric said nothing for a long moment as she at-
tended to her father, but his silence offered no comfort, totally more threatening than mere words. As she
passed him a cup—Mrs. Lennox always put a spare one
on the tray—she flicked him one apprehensive glance,
then just as quickly looked away. Today he wore his
usual kilt and tweed jacket. Beneath this he wore a tan
shirt and a plain tie, and at his waist, hanging from a
strap and chain, was a brown leather sporran. A sporran, she knew, was necessary because a kilt has no
pockets. Stockings he wore of tan wool, with garter
flashes, plus heavy brogues. In the top of his right
stocking she noted a horn-handled knife in a scabbard.
His knees were vagrantly exposed. He looked hard and
handsome, not willing to concede an inch.

Her stormy eyes flashed over his wickedly sardonic
mouth and she bit nervously into a cucumber sandwich. "When I was out," she announced sharply, "I
discovered, quite by chance, a caravan park down by
the loch. Carlotte kindly showed me around."

There! At last it was out, laced, in spite of herself
with angry reproach, and as she said Carlotte's name,
an upsurge of unfamiliar jealousy. Immediately she felt
Meric's quick glance, her father's slightly disturbed
one.

It was her father who spoke, with faint agitation.
"I've been ill, Susan. These things slip my memory."

Meric added with intense irritation, "Why make an
issue of it, Sue? Apart from being ill, your father
doesn't care much for caravans en bloc. In the first
place, I'm afraid the whole idea was mine, so perhaps
it's quite natural that he forgot to mention it."

"There are other people in the house besides my

father!" Too late Sue was aware of her injured tone of voice, the flickering resentment in her wide eyes.

His dark eyes explored her own, totally objective, wholly provoking. "Other people happen to be busy, my dear."

Colour flooded her cheeks. "Meaning that I'm not?"

His face darkened and for a moment she thought he was going to cross the room and shake her. He looked a stranger, dark and formidable. "On the contrary," he spoke coldly. "But our affairs scarcely lie in the same direction."

She ignored that with feminine logic. "You can't possibly work every evening. You could have spared a little time to put me in the picture."

Disturbingly the heavy mouth twitched a little at the corners as his dark eyes rested on her.

"If I could be sure you would find my company entertaining, Miss Frazer, I would be more than willing to oblige."

That he meant something quite removed from what she had in mind seemed obvious. His eyes, directly meeting her grey ones, were filled with clear menace, something for her to ponder over. *Until you're ready to meet me half-way, keep your distance,* they seemed to say. Completely shattered by her own crazy interpretation, Sue cried unwisely, "There's no reason to suppose that Miss Craig monopolizes all your free time!"

The glint in his eye deepened at that into clear hard laughter. "You might tell your daughter, John, how I spend most of my evenings. Dining at the hotel, in the interests of business." He ignored her reference to Carlotte. Seeking her father's support might be relevant, but seemed purely incidental.

Mumbling, John stirred himself from his preoccupation with his tea and radio, only half aware of their verbal sparring. "Should have been my job, as I told you, Susan. A lot to discuss of an evening. Used to be a most enjoyable part of the day—in the old days, when people stayed at the house..."

Inwardly fuming, Sue bit her lip, which seemed to be becoming a habit. Her father and Meric together were like a stone wall, and in their different ways, equally impregnable. She could never hope to make headway against their combined forces. Driven by a helpless frustration, she said scornfully, "It's surprising what goes on in the interests of business."

There was a silence. John, refusing, perhaps owing to the nature of his illness, to retain any prolonged interest in anything which worried him, retreated to his radio, turning up the volume, leaving the issue to Meric, ignoring Sue's indignant face. So much registered with Sue before her eyes left him to collide once again with Meric Findlay's dark ones. He was finishing off his tea in one deep draught, his glance still on a curious level between anger and amusement.

Putting his cup back on the tray, he stood up, his forcefulness hitting Sue like a blow. It drove all the nervous reaction from her body and for several seconds as she braved his dark eyes, she regretted her hasty words. Picking up her own cup in order to brace herself against further reprisals, she took a distracted sip.

When he did speak his tone of voice deceived her for a minute. He said softly, "I don't ordinarily go round explaining my actions, Miss Sue, and I don't intend to start now. If you have in mind a private investigation, then you'd better start conducting your own."

"I wasn't..." she choked.

"Wasn't casting aspersions?" His voice, silky smooth, slewed over her. "Wasn't that what you had in mind? Rather an old-fashioned way of putting it, but nothing more original could be so apt."

Sue flushed, colour creeping vividly beneath her skin. Never in a hundred years could she hope to make headway against such a man. His voice, sardonic, drawling, taunted her more by its inflection than his actual words, but his mind was razor-sharp and she wasn't at all sure that she liked it. Defensively she flung fretful fingers across her brow. "You must admit that I'm entitled to be told more? My father is ill; I can lay no blame at his door." Desperate to break an inner tension, she glanced pleadingly towards her father.

He had finished his tea and was fixing one of his cheroots, taking his time over the clipping and trimming and lighting. He surprised her by saying through the trail of blue smoke, "Meric came home early today to show you around. You've been here some time and lately he's been of the opinion that you might like to see something of the countryside."

"That wasn't quite what I meant." She stirred restlessly, startled by what he said, yet only faintly mollified as she looked at Meric again. "I'm not just a passing tourist and to be treated as such. To discover something by chance can put me in an embarrassing position. Carlotte at the caravan site, for instance. It was rather humiliating having to confess I knew nothing about it!"

From his great height Meric looked down at her, his eyes ironical, a hint of mocking despair in their dark depths. "A Scottish glen, especially a Perthshire one, is full of all sorts of enticing things—woods, hills, moors, rivers and streams, rich in wild life. And out of all that you have to find a caravan park!"

So she had been right about the laughter. Her voice was dry as she retorted, "You're convinced that a city-dweller's intuition led me to it? A sort of magnetism."

He taunted, "Or an inborn curiosity, which isn't particularly prevalent in towns. As for Carlotte, she isn't above helping me out, should I ask her nicely. And she does have all the information any holidaymaker might need, as well as being charming."

With a sharp twinge of shock, Sue stared at her hands. He found Carlotte charming! The knowledge struck her, irrationally painful. She took a deep breath. "If I stay I, too, might learn to be useful."

"Not at the caravan park, if that's what you mean."

"Not exactly..." Her voice trailed off, her confused thoughts defying clarification. The emphatic tightening of his hard mouth didn't help or she might have told him she had no wish to remain here as an outsider. Mutinously she shrugged, her eyes going slowly to the patch of bare skin which showed between the bottom of his kilt and the top of his stocking. The skin was tough-looking and firm, like the rest of him; dark brown in colour, weathered by the winds. Suddenly she knew a crazy longing to touch it and, as impulse surged, her pulse jerked and she swiftly looked away.

A piece of coal falling from the fire made her aware of his waiting silence. Hastily she picked up the tea tray and scrambled clumsily to her feet, not attempting to finish off her sentence but starting another. "Perhaps I owe you an apology, Mr. Findlay. If you did intend to show me around, then I'm grateful, but I'm afraid it's much too late. You may not be aware of it, but I usually cook dinner. I'd be perfectly willing to go another day."

But another day didn't arrive too quickly. Meric Findlay, in fact, appeared to forget all about it, and Sue, although eager to be shown the estate and the exact boundaries, was reluctant to remind him. Probably, she decided, as manager he was hesitant about making the first move, but that she seemed unable for some indefinable reason to make one herself proved a bit of a dilemma.

Helping Mrs. Lennox about the house kept her occupied to a certain extent, but not nearly enough. Yet her father still had bad days when he needed both of them. Even so Mrs. Lennox did all the nursing and Sue was determined that as soon as he was really better she would see about a teaching job. Locally, some authority somewhere must need an infant teacher. It might be a good idea to make a few inquiries. According to her map Perthshire abounded in small villages.

She started with Mrs. Lennox. "I'm sure I wouldn't know, dear," the woman replied when she asked. "They've had the same two teachers at our village school for years, and neither of them is old enough to retire."

Sue frowned. "I might have to go further afield."

"You might." Mrs. Lennox hesitated, noting Sue's serious expression. "I should wait until your father's fully recovered, though. He seems to worry when you're out of his sight, and anything like what you have in mind might upset him."

"Of course," Sue's reply was perfunctory. How could she explain to Mrs. Lennox she wouldn't mind staying forever if only she could feel that she was really a part of Glenroden? Her father clung to her because he was thrilled with his new-found daughter, and the idea of introducing her to his friends when he was stronger pleased him. But she wanted to be more than a show-piece. She wanted to belong! Would anyone here really miss her if she was gone?

She said, her mind switching erratically, "Mr. Findlay might be glad to have me off the place more often. He must get tired of having me constantly underfoot." Which was a devious way of seeking reassurance in a certain matter, but suddenly it seemed important.

Mrs. Lennox's eyes rounded with genuine surprise as she glanced at Sue. "I'm sure you're mistaken, dear. I don't suppose he often notices you're here."

Sue's eyes gleamed with derisive amusement. Well, she'd asked for that! Not exactly the answer she had hoped for, but one which she no doubt deserved. Yet she persevered if in another direction. "Carlotte must still be at the caravan park," she went on. "She hasn't been here for some time. I asked Father where she lived, and he said near Perth, so she must have a good way to travel."

Mrs. Lennox nodded absently as she started to prepare lunch. "Her father, who was your father's first cousin, is dead, and she lives with an elderly relation on her mother's side. I think she was the only relation your father had until you turned up."

"Mr. Findlay seems to like her..."

"I expect he does, dear." Sue suspected that when Mrs. Lennox chose, she could be deliberately obtuse.

"She does come a lot to Glenroden, and they've always got on well together."

Sue turned away as her father's bell rang. She wasn't going to get anything out of Mrs. Lennox. To be at Glenroden was like living in a vacuum. The past and future could apparently have little bearing until her father was up and about, and until then she was caught in a prison of her own making. If she was aware that most of her strange restlessness stemmed from an entirely different source she refused to admit it. Meric Findlay had no part in her future plans whatsoever!

One evening, after dinner, she decided to go down to the cottage. As usual Meric was out, but Mrs. Lennox was there, not having gone home that afternoon, and Sue thought it an ideal opportunity. To pass the time she had been helping John research his book, and over the last few days they had both been immersed in the Jacobite rebellion. John had fought Culloden in at least three different ways, and had now passed on to the Hanoverian army of occupation.

Sue's help was invaluable, he pointed out, as, once he was well, he could find in her notes all he needed to complete his thesis. His first rough notes, still at the cottage, he asked her to fetch. There were also two books with additional information which he would like to have by him. Not bothering to put on a coat as the late September night was still warm, she picked up a basket to put everything in, and let herself quietly out by the side door.

The cottage, some distance from the rambling old Georgian house by the road, could be easily reached by following a grassy track through some trees. To Sue's dismay the night was already beginning to darken as she hurried along the patch, although the setting sun enhanced the beauty of hill and glen, slowing her flying footsteps in spite of herself. She liked the smell of autumn woods, the sweet aroma of grass drying out, a ripening reflected in the red of the rowan berry; the darker purple of the blackberry; the gold of the hazelnut. Other things changed, but not these.

Quickly she unlocked the cottage door, cross with herself for lingering until she realized that the electricity supply had not been cut off during John's absence. With a flick of her finger the little hall flooded with light, but she switched it off again. It wasn't yet dark enough to need it, and she had promised herself a quiet look around. If someone saw a light they might come to investigate.

Rather furtively she explored the little house, finding everything much as Meric Findlay had described it on that first evening. Faintly disappointed, she returned to the living room and set down her basket on the still cluttered table. She had asked John several times about coming back to live here, but in every instance he had only looked put out and shook his head.

"I thought you were comfortable here, my dear," was his usual reply. "I've only been using the place to write in since my heart started to play up. Meric doesn't care for me being there alone."

"But you've got me now," Sue had argued. Secretly she was beginning to get fond of the big house, as everyone called it, but Meric Findlay disturbed her, and some instinct of self-preservation warned her to move before it was too late. Her father, however, was adamant. "You're not aware of all it would involve, Susan. Think of all the renovations which would be necessary, and which you couldn't hope to cope with yourself. We're much better off where we are."

Which was a matter of opinion, but now that she had seen for herself Sue could understand his point of view. The upstairs rooms, though structurally sound, were chaotic, with bits of plaster and wallpaper peeling. Stuffed full of junk, they would take a week to clear out. The other room downstairs had obviously been used as a bedroom, but here again it was untidy and smelt musty. It was perhaps difficult to understand why her father had come to live here in the first place.

Once or twice she had tried to broach the subject, but he seemed to find it difficult to talk to her very deeply about anything, apart from his book. Although he had promised to stop her mother's allowance at the bank, he appeared reluctant to discuss anything else. In the end she had had to write to the solicitor in London herself, giving brief details and a promise to keep in touch. Which reminded her that she had also promised to write to Tim. She had sent him a short note soon after she had arrived. It must have stopped him worrying, but he would be waiting to hear further. It was rather surprising that he hadn't replied. He must be waiting cautiously for further details which, because he had always been so good, she must supply.

Carefully she searched amongst the array of writing material on the over-burdened desk. Finding what she required, she removed the pen and pad to the table and sat down to compose a letter. Reluctantly she picked up her pen. Conscience dictated that she wrote straight away, while she remembered, but over the last weeks Tim seemed to have receded into the background and she scarcely knew where to start.

"Dear Tim," she wrote at last, "You will be surprised to hear that my father owns a large estate..."

No! Dissatisfied, she stopped, nibbling the end of her pen. That sounded—well, ostentatious? Frowning, she reached out to tear up the page and start again when a sound at the outside door made her jump. Someone was there. Could it be Mrs. Lennox seeking her? Was there something wrong? Instantly she was on her feet, alarm spinning her to the inner door, only to find it flung open in her face as Meric stood there.

"Whew!" she gasped, half in relief, "I heard something and thought it might be a ghost."

"A ghost would scarcely have given you a whiter face," he said dryly, closing the door behind him before gripping her arm and guiding her to the nearest chair. Bending down, he switched on the fire. "A disused room gets cold," he informed her. "A little heat and you'll soon recover."

Sue thrust the thought from her that it was much nicer to bask in his solicitude, much more warming than a mere fire. Instead she protested weakly, "There's nothing wrong. I just didn't expect to see you, that's all."

The look he slanted her was oblique. "You never do, do you, Sue? I might be wholly flattered if I thought for a moment that I was responsible for all this feverish activity!"

Her lashes fluttered as she tried to sustain his ironic stare, colour creeping like wild rose beneath her skin. Retreating a little, she lay back in her chair, unable to fight against his hard masculinity. She tried to concentrate on what he said. "I thought perhaps it was Mrs. Lennox with bad news. I suppose it was foolish of me."

"Very." He didn't pretend to misunderstand her, and suddenly it seemed his eyes were kinder. "Actually I didn't find you by accident. John told me where you'd gone and I decided to come and walk back with you. It will soon be dark and you might get lost. Besides, I had something to ask you."

Only half hearing, Sue gazed at the flickering fire as a dozen muddled emotions went through her. She was scarcely aware when he turned and sat in the chair opposite, where her father had sat that first evening. What could he want to see her about? Nothing of importance, surely. In a moment of nervous panic she spoke. "I'm helping Father with his research—which is really why I'm here, if he didn't explain. I'm to find him two books."

"It doesn't bore you?"

"Why should it?" She inclined her fair head as she straightened and her hair fell in an arch across her flushed cheek. "I must admit," she confessed, "that I wasn't quite sure when I started, but I'm getting more interested every day."

"You're interested in Scottish history, or is it the way

John fights every campaign as if he'd been there personally?"

There was a glint in his eye again. He could be teasing.

She replied lightly. "His strategy seems good. Bonnie Prince Charlie might have fared better if Father had been there. As for my interest? Well, after all, Scotland is my country, even if I've just found out."

"I haven't been long here myself. Only, in my case, I came back."

"You came back? You mean," Sue glanced at him sharply, "you'd been here before, on holiday?"

"Not exactly," he drawled cynically "I don't suppose John got around to telling you, I left with my parents when I was six. My father was a bit of a gambler, not a soldier like yours."

"A gambler?" Curiosity flickered through Sue's grey eyes, and Meric's mouth twisted with obvious amusement.

"There are many kinds of gambling, Sue. He gambled everything he had and I suppose it paid off, but he lost his life."

She glanced at him, startled, meeting the cool level gaze. Breathlessly she asked, "What did he really do?"

"Gold-mining." He didn't add anything else.

"Oh, I see..." She didn't like his harder expression.

"No, you don't, but leave it. Sufficient to say that I returned."

"But you must have lived in South Africa a long time," she persisted. "Didn't you mind leaving?"

"If I had I shouldn't have left. I had only myself to please. Maybe I felt the pull of my native land. How about you?" Lazily he stretched his long legs to the fire, subtly diverting her interest in his own affairs. "You've lived in London all your life, yet I take it you don't miss it too much?"

"Not really..." Uncertainly Sue paused. It seemed a ready-made opportunity to ask his advice about the flat, and it was inevitable that she asked someone. It wasn't a decision she felt free to make herself. Meric Findlay, in spite of his derogatory remarks about her deserting when he had found her in the drawing-room, was the obvious person to ask. He had been with her father for years, and, in the circumstances, must know him much better than she did. Making up her mind, she said quickly, before she could change it again, "It's the flat. I'm not quite sure what to do with it. If I let it go I'm not likely to find anything so reasonable. Finding anything at all is very difficult."

He flicked her an odd look, his eyes narrowed. "So we're back to that again. You want to go home."

It was a statement, not a question. He had already come to his own conclusions. Anger slipped through her, reflecting in her eyes as they met his dark ones. "You deliberately misunderstand! You enjoy judging me without knowing any of the facts. You must realize that I had to live somewhere before I came here. My mother and I had a flat. Someone she knew let her have it cheaply, or cheaply perhaps compared with prices here. The lease still has some time to run, but that isn't the problem. When I left it was merely to deliver a letter. I intended to return and find a teaching post."

"That isn't a problem, either. You could easily find such a job around here," he said dryly, his eyes as wary as her own.

"That's not the point!" Wildly Sue felt like tearing her hair, but he only laughed harshly.

"You could try explaining exactly why you want rid of that lease but daren't let it go."

"Oh, don't be absurd!"

"I'm not being absurd," he pointed out calmly. "But until you're willing to elucidate more clearly, my remarks might continue to infuriate."

"I was leading up to it!" Defensively, her cheeks pink, Sue dropped her eyes from his to stare down at the fire again. Her hair fell across her cheek and she thrust it impatiently to one side. Did he expect her to

throw all her half-formulated fears in a heap at his feet?
She had only asked about the flat. Not for an inquisi-
tion!

Confusing her still more, he leant forward, his hand
shooting out to grasp her wrist. "I wouldn't want you to
strain those ingenious resources of yours, Miss Frazer.
You just take your time. While you're thinking about it
I might well pass the time making us a nice cup of coffee. The ingredients will all be in the kitchen, right
down to the powdered milk." He grimaced, shrugging
his wide shoulders as he released her hand and stood
up. "We might reach some sort of understanding before midnight, but that's up to you. I'm not in any
hurry."

CHAPTER FIVE

Sue rose to her feet and followed him into the kitchen her wrist still tingling where his fingers had gripped, the sensation, illogically disturbing, running up her arm. Every instinct cried out against having coffee with him here in this old cottage where it was so easy to whip up an atmosphere of intimacy which she wished to avoid. She was too aware of Meric Findlay not to realize he could be dangerous, although, she decided wryly, she was probably insane to imagine that he had any personal interest in herself.

On her round of exploration she had missed the kitchen and she saw now that it was small, more of a kitchenette, something like what they had had in the flat. In the confined space two people could scarcely move without touching and she gazed around, pretending curiosity, but only conscious of the man by her side. There was in the sardonic gleam of his dark eyes, that which dared her to retreat. She didn't even dare a murmur of protest about coffee.

Which left her no good reason for being there. Confused, she sought to explain her presence in another way. "I asked Father about coming back to live here, but he doesn't seem too keen. I can't really understand him."

Meric removed his narrowed glance from her face, turning to the cooker with the kettle he had just filled, striking a match as he switched on the gas before settling the kettle on the naked flame. "Does that mean," he asked softly, "that you don't care for living with me?"

At this Sue looked up, startled that he had applied his

own interpretation, uncertain that she agreed with him, yet unwilling to concede even an element of doubt. "You're quite wrong," she retorted over-vehemently. "As we scarcely see you I don't know what put that into your head!"

"You don't claim any responsibility?"

Was he alluding to his frequent absence, or the latter part of her statement? Refusing to be drawn, she rejected his remark as nonsensical, and went on, "I really would like to live here, but he won't even discuss it."

He lifted his head from the stove and looked her full in the eye, his voice on a thin line of patience. "I've told you before to give him time."

"You mean to recover?"

"Not exactly." He spoke flatly, as Sue might have done to one of her own pupils. "It's a big thing for him at the moment to come to grips with the past. Living with me, at the big house, he doesn't feel committed to anything."

Sue frowned, her smooth brow wrinkling, not fully understanding although she wanted to. In retrospect she considered her father's behaviour. "On his good days he sometimes takes me to see my grandmother's portrait in the drawing-room, almost as if by comparing the two of us he can convince himself that I am his daughter."

Meric passed her a jar of instant coffee. Opening a cupboard, he took two mugs from their hooks, putting them on the sink-unit as she unscrewed the top of the jar. Silently he handed her a spoon. "You're trying to say that he doesn't attach any reality to you?"

"If you like to put it that way." Carefully Sue measured out two spoonfuls of coffee. "I know he doesn't love me, not yet anyhow, I know he likes me, and has some sort of family feeling towards me, but that's all."

"And you expect more?"

She tried to speak more boldly, but her voice quivered. "I don't expect anything. I had hoped, maybe, but I don't honestly know how I feel myself."

His eyebrows lifted, creasing his brows in a way she found disconcerting, while his mouth quirked resignedly at one corner. His patience, it seemed, was being tried a little. "Listen, Sue, it might be better if you looked at the whole thing from this angle. Remember what I told you when you first came? Think of yourself as an orphan, a foster-child, and be content to let your relationship with John develop gradually. If you like each other, then you've got a good base on which to work. But for heaven's sake get rid of all these guilty feelings of inadequacy."

Sue's face registered bewilderment rather than conviction. "The trouble is I'm not a child. Besides, children usually accept situations without curiosity, and I'm afraid I can't do that."

He returned her gaze with long-suffering endurance. "So there are things you want to know. Well, fire away, but don't be too disappointed when I don't know the answers."

"Thank you," she said, with a matching irony. "I didn't make a list. Just the odd thing, perhaps. What my father is really like—deep down. It might be a whole lot easier if I knew."

"Why?"

She hesitated, conscious more than ever of the rock-like arrogance in his face. His eyes held hers, making it impossible to look away. Nothing could be easy beneath that intimidating stare. Stumbling, she attempted to put into words thoughts which she had always kept hidden. "My mother... She never believed in showing her feelings. I can never remember her giving me a hug, or showing any affection, not towards me or anyone I ever knew. It might sound ridiculous, but sometimes I used to think she was partly frozen, incapable of being warm and outgoing, all the normal, natural things a mother ought to be. But I don't seem to be making much headway with my father, either."

His head went back as comprehension dawned, yet his eyes lingered sardonically on her taut face. "And you can't let it go. You've got to delve and dig and dissect, and now you're wondering if you've inherited adverse characteristics, maybe from both of them? What you've got to get into that beautiful head of yours is that experiences such as your parents went through invariably leave a scar, but not one which need necessarily affect their offspring. What makes you think that you're cold by nature, not capable of all the normal responses?''

She drew back startled from the gleam in his eye, her pulse jerking. "You aren't much help, are you! I was only pointing out a possibility."

"And I was merely pointing out that you seem quite well adjusted to me. If you must pursue the matter further, then there are questions you must ask yourself. How do you react when a man makes love to you, for instance? I couldn't possibly know the answer to that one."

Mockery had replaced the even keel of his voice, and Sue flushed scarlet at the bluntness of his words. "I don't know what you mean," she spluttered, knowing very well what he meant but unable to confess, when it came to the point, that she had never known any wild thrill when a man had kissed her. Did that amount to coldness?

His gaze moved wickedly over her face. "I could demonstrate, if you like, but you might not approve of my methods."

"Oh!" Sue felt the colour deepen in her face as he left her in no doubt of his intentions. Still full of nervous confusion, she turned her head. "I think we're talking about two entirely different things."

"But each of which is irrevocably bound up with the other, my little coward."

A minute ago she had trembled when he said she was beautiful. Now he called her a coward. She drew back, her eyes fixed on his face, widely resentful, the thick lashes flickering. "I don't agree. I wouldn't have mentioned the subject at all but for the fact that my problems don't just concern me, personally. I don't want to hurt anyone else."

Those dark eyes examined her face again, and suddenly the kitchen was too small. Heat swept up through her body and, unconsciously, her hand went to her shirt neck, undoing the top button so that the skin of her throat gleamed smoothly white. She had a frightening feeling that she was suffocating. If she had hoped to receive rational advice then she had obviously approached the wrong person. There was no help here in the indolent tilt of dark eyebrows, the mocking speculation in equally dark eyes.

"I don't think you can be a bit like your mother," he drawled, blocking the entrance to the kitchen effectively as if he guessed her desire to escape. "Quite clearly, in spite of her failings, she must have been a person of decision, which you're not. You want someone to make yours for you all the time. Well, to make a start, you can get rid of your London flat right away. If you should ever need another place, then I'll supply it. And second, you can forget about a teaching post, or anything else, at the moment, and about leaving the big house to live here. These sort of decisions are not beyond my intelligence, but don't let my generosity fool you. It's limited. Eventually there are things you'll have to decide for yourself."

"Such as...?" she gasped, no proper gratitude assailing her senses, rather a blind flame of anger at his excessive conceit.

His hand caught her as she began to move away while his hard laughter went over her head. "Such as when you meet the right man, my dear Sue. If you don't recognize him yourself, don't come running to me."

Her grey eyes clouded with impotent fury as she tried to escape his cruel fingers; as she tried to match his laughter but could only manage a flippant remark. "I don't think I should worry you on that account. I hope I'm quite capable of choosing my own friends."

"Which isn't exactly the same thing, and I doubt it."
His reply was as audacious as his grip on her waist. She
stopped struggling. Against his superior strength she
was helpless. Besides, she had a suspicion that he enjoyed taunting her. Probably with the intention of pun-
ishing her a little for pestering him with her problems,
when he must surely have enough of his own.

His voice came, full of soft derision, in her ear as she
stood tensely within his hands. "I don't think you'd
find anything much wrong with your own emotional
responses if you gave them a chance. You can't keep
them in a refrigerated container for ever."

Stormily she swung around, her eyes alight with hostility, an attempted defence against her young vulnerability. Illogically she cried, "How I tick underneath can
be of no interest to you. You don't run my life!"

"I'm willing to take anything on—at a price." Still
the gleam of mockery ran through his eyes, but blindly
she didn't see it. She only saw the size and bulk of him.
The hardness which she coveted but could never
achieve.

Colour smouldered recklessly in her cheeks. "You
may be my father's manager, but you can't expect to
manage me!"

"Is that so?" His dark head went back with considerable menace as he stared down at her polished skin,
the sheen on her fair, heavy hair. "I'll admit I have
known myself to be mistaken about people, but not
often." His mouth moved and she knew he was angry.
"It seems that mere words aren't enough to convince
you. There are other ways which you might appreciate
better."

With deliberate intent he moved his hands slowly to
her shoulders, in such a way as to stop the breath in her
throat. She was conscious of his physical nearness and a
trembling assailing her limbs. He was holding her imprisoned between the wall and his body. The kettle
boiled and his hand went out to switch off the gas, but
he made no attempt to let her go. His eyes had never

left her pale face. "You've succeeded in arousing my curiosity as well as my temper, a rather dangerous combination, would you not agree?"

Sue imagined she felt the impact of his kiss seconds before his lips came down on hers. Desperately she tried to retain the tension in her body, but anticipation clouded her mind as it sharpened her physical response. Strength drained out of her when, as if determined to scatter the last remnants of her resistance, his arms tightened, pressing her softness against him, his eyes stabbing sharply through her as her own closed before the ruthlessness of his.

Against the strength of his arms and his obvious experience she was helpless, yet while instinct warned her not to struggle, her traitorous body wouldn't allow her to remain passive in his arms. Her hands lifted in a feeble attempt to push him away, but only managed to reach his chest where the feel of his hard muscles seemed to shatter coherent thought. With a soft moan she felt sensation explode through her like splintering glass, sending her arms up around his neck, to cling tightly where his hair grew down to a clean smoothness at the back of his head. His lips moved over her mouth, bruising the soft skin, and aroused in her a response which was frightening in its intensity.

At last with narrowed eyes he raised his head, pushing the tumbled hair back from her brow, the better to see her flushed face. It wasn't the hand of a man unused to making love. Sue was quick to realize this, but not to care. It was there, in the thin red line of difference between the boys she had known and a man who knew what he was doing. Her heart beating unevenly kept time with her frantic pulse as she lifted her heavy eyelids and stared at him, stunned. His arms and lips had aroused a mad, dizzy sort of magic, like riding a shooting star, and she suddenly didn't want him to stop.

"Please..." she whispered against his mouth.

But he drew back, his dark face intent within inches

of her own. "Does that mean, Miss Frazer, that you would like a repeat performance, or that you want me to let you go?"

His voice had a note of cynicism, so slight that she could have been mistaken. Only his eyes, curiously watchful, told her she was not. Yet his ironic question startled her, bringing her to her senses, stilling a wild confession that she desired only to stay where she was.

With a jerk she pulled away from him. "Of course I want you to let me go! If it pleased you to kiss me then consider it payment for time spent listening to my foolish conversation."

His mouth quirked with unexpected amusement. "Tut-tut, Miss Prunes and Prisms! Not many girls who enjoy my caresses are capable afterwards of such a lengthy speech. I must be slipping!"

"You beast!" It was all she could think of, a feeble reprisal and not at all effective. Meric continued to hold her lightly, to study her indignant face and tremulous parted lips with the uttermost satisfaction. "Somehow I hardly think you'll question your complete normality again. In spite of your derogatory remarks you might have reason to be grateful to me yet."

"You're hateful!" Furious colour licked under her skin. She felt like a butterfly on a pin, knowing that her naïveness amused him, that while her immature response might have flattered his ego, it had not impressed him physically. Desperately she struggled to be free, a pulse beating painfully at the base of her throat, and he watched it as he held her, seeming to forget place and time. Then, so suddenly that she almost fell, his arms weren't around her any more. She was free as with a swift movement he turned to the still hot kettle and began pouring water into the mugs.

Once filled, he put them on to a tray with a basin of sugar. "Open the door for me, there's a good girl. We may as well have this now that it's ready."

His keen eyes flicked to her face and she felt unpredictable tears stinging her eyelids. Quickly she did as he instructed, hurrying into the other room, suddenly afraid that he should notice. The knowledge that he disturbed her she would rather keep to herself.

She went back to her chair by the fire, scarcely aware that he had put the tray on the table until a smothered exclamation jerked her around. With dismay she saw that his eyes were fixed on the letter which she had been writing to Tim before he had arrived. Uneasily she remembered the exact wording, wishing fervently that she hadn't left it where Meric could see it. Now it was too late! She saw the scepticism, the touch of derision at his mouth as he picked up the sheet of note-paper.

"And who is Tim?" he demanded, slanting a glance at her perturbed face, ominously quiet.

The change in him was barely perceptible, yet it was there. Never had Sue felt more like running away, or wishing that the ground would open and swallow her up. He stood there like the day of judgment, scattering her wits when she most needed them. "Just a friend," she managed to croak at his arrogant eyebrows.

"Just a friend," he repeated with extreme dryness, scrutinizing her closely. "Why write as if you'd won the pools?"

"I don't know how you come to that conclusion," she faltered. How could she confess, in his present mood, that she knew very well what he meant? It wasn't what she had intended putting down, and she had been going to tear it up.

Disparagingly he rapped out, "I'm afraid you don't fool me one bit. Not now. A girl who responds as you do in a man's arms wouldn't be without boy-friends!"

In the half-light his face was grim, and Sue shrank back suddenly cold. "It's not what you think," she gasped, through stiff lips.

"I'm not gullible, nor am I a fool. What happens next? You'll be having dear Tim along to view the promised land? Your rich inheritance?"

"How dare you!" she flung at him, rage replacing

468 The Kilted Stranger

her former dismay, her face white. "You're mistaken in your horrible assumptions. Tim was kind after the accident, that's all."

He brushed this aside with a sardonic grin, his eyes sluing over her. "In your arms, Sue, a man might find it easy to be kind."

"You're insufferable—and forgetting your place!" Sheer desperation hurtled the words recklessly from Sue's lips, as her chin lifted furiously. "If you think I enjoyed your kisses then you're mistaken. Against your brute strength I was forced to submit."

She heard him laugh ambiguously above her head and, as before, she knew that she had aroused him, if without lasting effect. "I shouldn't like to call you a little liar, Sue. The next time we get together I must see you're better pleased."

"Sometimes I hate you!" she said clearly.

"A complete waste of emotion." His gaze rested darkly on her hot face, her bruised mouth, but when he spoke again his voice was level and somehow remote. "I should advise you to wait and see the size of the estate before completing your missive. I intended asking if you would come with me tomorrow. A sort of conducted tour, if you like."

"Only if I have no choice?"

"If you can find a suitable explanation. John is especially keen that you should see around. I shouldn't wish to inflict my company on anyone, but we have quite an expanse of rather wild territory which it wouldn't be safe for you to negotiate alone. Besides, you don't know the boundary lines."

"It's taken you quite a while to get around to it," she accused sharply, because in a curious way his accusations and indifference hurt. "At least Tim Mason knew how to treat me like a—like a lady," she finished, for want of a better word.

"Good for you." He glanced meaningfully at the notepaper, his voice sarcastic again. "Obviously in his case it's paid off, but don't you ever get tired of being handled with kid gloves?''

Again Sue's face flamed with her temper as her eyes locked with his. Did he really intend piling insult on injury? "I suppose in South Africa you had a different approach, but it might not be one that every girl appreciates." She longed, with a pent-up resentment, to fling Carlotte at his head along with all her secret suspicions, but suddenly she dared not. Suddenly her anger seemed to evaporate as quickly as it had come, leaving her tired, oddly drained, and she turned away. "I think it might be better if we both went home," she added simply, and with as much dignity as she could muster.

He made no response, just shrugged his wide shoulders, his eyes empty of both amusement and anger. Smoothly he folded her letter and passed it to her before bending to switch off the fire and hustle her out of the door. "The next time you feel like writing to London," he said, "write to your solicitor instead of Tim, and ask him to look into that lease on your flat."

Unavoidably, it seemed, Sue's tour of Glenroden had to be postponed owing to the state of the weather. During the next few days immediately following her quarrel with Meric rain fell incessantly, while mist shrouded the hills. With autumn scarcely arrived, winter would seem to be following too closely behind, but John assured her that there were many fine days yet to come.

"It's all just part of Scotland, I suppose," he remarked, as they sat in the library one afternoon after tea, watching the rain driving hard against the window. The wind, joining forces, swept through the branches of the old pine forest on the edge of the grounds. Hurtling all before it, it scattered the first fallen leaves untidily across the rough-mown lawns, leaving them lying, fragments of crimson and gold.

"The weather, you mean?" Lazily Sue glanced slowly away from the window, idly contemplating the blazing yellow logs in the fireplace. It had been one of John's good days in spite of the monsoon outside, and they had spent the greater part of it on his book. Today they had almost completed the rough notes on a whole chapter dealing with the history of the old Ruthven barracks, scene of the last act of the Jacobite Rising, where after the Battle of Culloden, rebel clansmen, followers of Charles Edward, had waited, only to receive the heartrending message to disperse. Sue's typing had improved daily, as had her grasp of the whole Rising, which delighted her father, who had confessed that secretly, at one time, he had doubted ever finishing even the first part of his book.

Now, feeling refreshed and rested again, she contemplated going for a walk. "Not far," she assured John, as he raised anxious eyebrows towards the streaming window. "I'll never sleep if I don't get some air. I'll take Bruce," she ruffled the ears of his dog who lay stretched out at their feet. "He's getting lazy, like me. A good walk will do him good. Maybe," she hesitated, avoiding his quiet eyes, "I could take Meric's dog too? He won't have done much today—the dog, I mean—but sit in the Range-Rover, if he's been out at all."

"Well..." John nodded, only half convinced but conscious of his daughter's pale face. "Run along, then. Sometimes the weather does ease up after tea. I think you'll find Rex in the study with Meric. Remember he said he was going to sort out some accounts when he looked in before?"

Sue nodded, not waiting a second bidding, jumping quickly to her feet. Belatedly she tried not to appear too eager, but was unable to restrain her dancing feet. She had seen very little of Meric since that night at the cottage and, in spite of what had passed between them, she found herself thinking of him continually. It was surprising, both living in the same house as they did, how little she saw of him. He usually dined out and took sandwiches and a flask for lunch, and usually had eaten his breakfast and gone long before she was up. Sometimes, stupidly, she found herself longing for winter with its dark cosy evenings, when surely he must spend more time indoors.

"I'll go now," she smiled lightly, calling to Bruce. "If you'll be all right? Mrs. Lennox has gone, but I'll be back in plenty of time to get dinner. Meric will be around if you need anything."

Humming softly to herself, she collected her waterproof from a cupboard in the kitchen, remembering to stoke up the cooker and replace the hob before she went out. The oven should be nice and hot when she returned. Jamming a matching hat on her fair, fluffy hair, she left the room, running over the wide hall to knock quickly on the study door as she pushed it open.

Startled, and not a little embarrassed, she drew back, her breath catching painfully in her throat. Carlotte was there, in Meric's arms. Sue stopped dead and blinked. True, Meric just held the girl lightly, but he was smiling gently into her face, which was clearly that of a girl who had recently been kissed. His expression, Sue noted indignantly, didn't change as he lifted his head and saw her standing in the doorway. Antagonism surged through her so that it took an almost physical effort to remain there looking at them, to keep a smile fixed on her own face so that neither the two of them should guess the chaotic state of her feelings.

"I'm taking Bruce out," she stammered uncomfortably, forgetting to greet Carlotte, attempting to explain her own intrusion when no one spoke. "I thought Rex might like to come with us?" She could see nothing but the inquiring tilt of Meric's eyebrows, the sharp glint of humour in his dark eyes.

It was Carlotte who spoke first, sleek satisfaction glowing over her face as she viewed Sue's discomfiture. "Don't let me stop you," she murmured. "I just popped in to see Meric. The dog's over there."

The soft insolence in her voice must have been audible only to Sue, as Meric didn't so much as bat an eyelid. With a regretful sigh he released the girl, his mouth quirking wryly. "Perhaps Miss Frazer guessed I wasn't getting on with my work, my love. She's been at it all day, I believe, on her typewriter. A proper little slave-driver!"

Sue, her cheeks hot, ignored his satirical remarks as she called sharply to Rex, almost grateful that Bruce was impatiently pushing her towards the door. "I'll see you later," she retorted coolly, returning his dry smile with a blank stare. "I must apologize if I interrupted something." That it seemed impolite to depart so quickly without offering Carlotte even a cup of tea, Sue did not care. She had no wish to subject herself to an hour of Carlotte's sharp tongue. Undoubtedly Meric would supply her with a drink—along with other things! As she hastily closed the door her eyes fell on two half-empty glasses. She need not have worried about a lack of hospitality!

A peculiar rage churned through Sue's heart as she swiftly ran from the house. As if countless demons were chasing her. Yet, as she slowed down on the rough grass track which led to the forest, she was forced to admit she was being slightly ridiculous. That Meric Findlay shared some sort of relationship with Carlotte seemed obvious. But it was equally obvious that it was entirely his own business.

Unhappily Sue tried to collect her senses and keep an eye on the two golden Labradors as they ambled off into the trees. It seemed little use denying, here in the primitive forest, that she was attracted to Meric Findlay herself. Almost in love with him, she supposed wretchedly, refusing to admit the futility of that qualifying adverb. The rain stung her face; the wind tore at her clothing, but she scarcely felt it, as the wildness of the elements found an answering reaction in her own heart. Unleashed in her she felt emotions streaming, and knew a wild, uncivilized urge to rush back and accuse him of philandering. Which seemed even more ridiculous than her previous thoughts, and filled her with dismay. This, she supposed, was jealousy, plain and undiluted!

Impatient with herself, Sue stopped and leaned against a tall fir, striving for some measure of composure, grateful that there was no one to witness her despondency. Meric Findlay had chosen to kiss her as a form of punishment, nothing else. He hadn't liked her alluding to his status as manager. How he could be sensitive about such a small thing, she didn't know. She had been here long enough to realize that Glenroden couldn't be run without him. Her father was really just a figurehead, and she herself could never presume to have any real say in the matter. But, one of these days, she must insist on knowing Meric's exact position, and refuse to be sidetracked by one of John's evasive replies.

If only, she wished, not for the first time, she had known her father from childhood in the normal way. Then she might have found it easy to persist, to expect utter frankness in most things, to find it possible to rely partly on intuition, born from years of association, to be aware of many things without having to ask. It seemed dreadful still to feel so often a stranger, utterly bereft of the warmth and comfort of a deeper relationship. Feeling as she did there was really only one sensible thing to do. If nothing else it would stop her becoming completely obsessed with Glenroden and its occupants. This, she admitted with utter conviction, was the road to disaster. She knew that!

To her surprise Carlotte was waiting in the drive when Sue returned. She had stayed out longer than she had intended, in a vain attempt to get rid of her vibrant unrest. As John had predicted, the rain had eased off, if only slightly, and the walk up through the forest was reasonably sheltered and dry. There had even been a glimpse of sunshine which, as it broke through the heavy layer of cloud, had touched the mountain tops with yellow and pink, making a sparkling tracery through branches of spruce and pine. There was something beautiful in the silence of the forest which she especially loved and as usual was loath to leave. John often talked about the forests, how they teemed with a wild life of their own, but so far Sue had seen little sign of the birds and animals he appeared to know so well. The thing was, she supposed, she didn't know what to look for, or where to find it. Maybe, she thought wistfully, she might find the courage to ask Meric to show her some time.

Damp, but feeling refreshed if not enlightened, she did not particularly welcome the sight of Carlotte sitting in her car, and quickly searched her mind for an excuse not to linger. "It's later than I thought," she smiled politely. "I must hurry or there won't be any dinner!" Then, before she could stop herself, she heard herself saying, possibly because of her earlier lack of hospitality, "Won't you stay and have a meal with us? It will only be simple, but you're very welcome."

As usual Carlotte's smile didn't quite reach her eyes. "Meric is taking me out to dinner in Perth, so I won't need to trouble you. He's picking me up in an hour, so you aren't the only one in a hurry. Right now he's been called out for a few minutes by one of the men."

Sue's face felt suddenly stiff. So this was what Carlotte had waited to tell her! She might have known that it wasn't just a friendly gesture. "Don't let me keep you, then," she retorted with a shrug. "In any case, Meric seldom dines at home."

Again satisfaction gleamed furtively in Carlotte's eyes, but apparently her reason for lingering had been two-fold. She startled Sue by ignoring her note of dismissal and saying blandly, "Meric and I are old friends and often dine together. We have done for years. I'm not quite sure of his exact position with Cousin John, here at Glenroden, but as it's probable that one day I get the lot, I'm not going to quibble over the balance of things."

Blankly Sue stared at her, knowing intuitively that Carlotte's statement, if one could call it that, was a sort of throwing down the gauntlet. Carlotte obviously felt the time had come to let her know exactly where she stood, along with a subtle warning that it had better not be in her way. But she was also trying to find out if Sue was in possession of the true facts concerning the estate, Sue was certain of this.

A small spate of anger rushed through Sue's head. It seemed that Carlotte was prepared to go to any lengths to satisfy her curiosity, to get the information she was after; the information which she insisted was not important. She was quite prepared to use any devious method which she thought might work. Coolly, Sue spoke. "So far as I know, Carlotte, Meric Findlay is just the manager, so there isn't really any mystery. If it's a wealthy husband you're after, then I'd advise you to look elsewhere."

There was a sharp silence as Sue stood back, rigidly polite, waiting for Carlotte to go. The car engine roared abruptly into life, calming down slightly as Carlotte impatiently slammed the door and wound down the window, easing her foot from the accelerator. A faint flush stained her cheekbones, otherwise she appeared quite calm.

"A word in your ear, too Miss—er—Frazer," she replied. "I never did like people who get in my way. It might pay you to remember!"

The letter from London which Sue had waited for came next morning, sooner than she had expected. She read it through quickly, and was just finishing her coffee and toast when Meric thrust his head around the door.

"Not bad news, I hope?" His glance took in the letter and her thoughtful face.

Sue lifted her head and looked at him, surprised that he should be around at this time of the morning, her eyes quick to note the fine lines of strain about his firm mouth, a faint weariness in his dark eyes. Undoubtedly he had had a late night! "Since you ask," she answered, "it's from my solicitor, but not really bad news."

He waited, eyebrows raised, as she hesitated before going on somewhat reluctantly, "He doesn't see any difficulty in getting rid of the flat, this sort of accommodation being so much in demand, but he thinks I'll have to return and deal with the furniture and any personal belongings myself. It's not so much the furniture," she frowned more anxiously than she realized, "the whole lot put together wouldn't be worth very much—I mean, on today's second-hand value. We don't have any antiques, I'm afraid. But there's my clothing and books, and various other items which no one could sort out but myself."

"Of course, not." He accepted her rather muddled explanation with a brief, concise nod, then stepped into the kitchen to fill a mug of coffee from the still hot pot. "As a matter of fact I've had some correspondence from London myself this morning, which necessitates my going there too. It might be a good idea if you travelled down with me, say in a couple of days' time."

CHAPTER SIX

THE plane from Turnhouse Airport to London seemed to be full of wealthy tourists and business men. Sue subsided quickly into her seat, not because she was glad to sit down—she had been sitting all the way from Glenroden that morning—but because she and Meric were not on their own. Carlotte was with them. They had picked her up at Perth, and now she was sitting in front with Meric, her dark head very near his shoulder.

Irrationally, the only grain of comfort which Sue could glean from the situation lay in the fact that Meric had not been directly responsible for Carlotte being here. It was only yesterday, when Carlotte had called, that John had innocently mentioned Sue's pending trip, adding that Meric was going too. Carlotte, quick-witted as usual, had professed to be delighted. It would be an ideal opportunity to visit her mother who lived in Kent, she said, They could all travel together.

Sue had been surprised to learn that Carlotte had a mother, until she remembered when she had first met her in Edinburgh. Carlotte had been on her way to see her mother then, but it seemed strange that she didn't live with her all the time. She had asked John about it when Carlotte had gone in search of Meric, to arrange to be picked up.

"Her mother married again," John told her briefly, "years ago, but for some reason or another Carlotte doesn't get on with her stepfather, so doesn't live with them. She visits, and her mother comes to Edinburgh, but that's as far as it goes. Just as well, really," he had grunted, "as Carlotte likes to rule the roost."

Sue hadn't asked any more questions, content to

leave it at that. Carlotte obviously had a legitimate excuse for her journey, she decided, as she fastened her seat belt following the instructions of the charming stewardess. Come to that it might not be fair to call it an excuse at all. Seemingly Carlotte visited her mother quite often. It made sense that she didn't like to travel on her own.

All this sweet reasonableness on Sue's part didn't stop her glancing wistfully in Meric's direction as the plane took off. This was her very first flight, although he didn't know it, and she would have welcomed him by her side. Instead she had a tired-looking tourist, to whom flying was obviously no novelty as she was already half asleep. Rather frightened, as the huge Trident left the ground, Sue closed her eyes, trying to concentrate her thoughts on something else.

It was actually four days since that morning in the kitchen when Meric had suggested this trip. She hadn't been easily persuaded, and even now she was wondering if she'd been wise. Quickly opening her eyes, she stared at the back of his dark head and broad shoulders, still uncertain that she was doing the right thing.

At the time Meric had swept her doubts impatiently to one side. "It seems the sensible thing to do," he had pointed out emphatically. "You might need help of some kind, and your friend Tim Mason might not be available." This last with a glint in his eye.

Sue had found herself protesting hotly without meaning to. "I should have to let Tim know..."

"Know what?" His question had cut through the sharp morning air.

"That I'm giving up the flat, of course. He's been keeping an eye on it for me."

"Which means that he has a key?" The glint in his eye had deepened, not very pleasantly.

Sue still remembered the heat in her cheeks as she had flashed him a look. "It's not what you think! There was no one else."

"So you keep telling me, Susan my darling, but you

must be prepared to admit that it rather strains the credulity?"

The evening before he had called Carlotte "my love"! Was there no limit to his arrogance! "You must think what you will," Sue had replied stiffly. "You seem to enjoy putting the worst construction on anything I do."

He had stared at her closely for a long tense moment before appearing to shake off his black mood with a mocking twist of his lips which might have been a smile. "Put it down to jealousy if it makes you feel better, Sue. Other women have derived much pleasure in doing just that."

"Where you're concerned?" Her raised eyebrows had imbued the question with a fine contempt, and for a split second his brilliant dark gaze had hardened threateningly.

Then suddenly his dry smile had deepened into a ring of laughter. He was amused and not troubling to hide it. "Just when I feel like putting you over my knee, I find myself wanting to do something else! To be on the safe side we'd better get back to our original discussion."

While her heart had turned over in her breast he had talked casually of flying to London, of going down one day and coming back the next. Only an hour from Edinburgh, he had said, but he didn't mention expense! She had had no idea how much it would be, but surely it was much more expensive than going by car or rail? When she had mentioned this tentatively, he had exclaimed:

"If you're worrying about the cost, then don't! I think Glenroden can take care of that. You haven't been exactly idle over the last few weeks. Consider it in lieu of salary, if it will make you feel better."

Sue's hands clenched angrily on her lap. How he loved to ride roughshod over people's feelings! His few ambiguous remarks had told her quite clearly that he realized she had little money to spare of her own. She

had longed tempestuously to throw his offer back in his
face, but something, she knew not what, stopped her,
and the moment in which she might have refused came
and went, leaving her lips to utter a formal protest, but
only weakly, "How could we both be away when
Father's so ill?"

"So ill?" For an instant she had thought Meric
looked startled. "Yes, I suppose he is," he conceded
guardedly. "But he could go on the way he is for years.
His condition isn't critical. In between attacks he keeps
fairly well. I think we might safely leave him for a
couple of days with Mrs. Lennox. It wouldn't be the
first time she's looked after him, and then there are
plenty of men around the place should she need any
help."

A hundred doubts had continued to plague her
mind, in spite of what Meric said, yet the idea of going
with him wasn't to be resisted. The true reason for
Meric's going might be clouded in obscurity. She had a
suspicion, which she tried to discard, that it was to ensure she returned. John, who was obviously relieved
that at last she was getting rid of the flat, had possibly
asked him to go, and he couldn't refuse. Whatever the
reason, she had been in the mood to clutch at straws
without querying too closely what had prompted them
to blow in her direction.

The plane was comfortable and well heated, for
which Sue was grateful. The coat she wore was thin,
too thin for October in the Highlands. From the flat she
would collect her warmer clothing. At least, if not very
up to date, it would see her through until she was in a
position to earn some money for replacements. After
take-off she found herself enjoying the flight, the thrill
of a new experience dissolving some of her previous
gloom. The wide vista of the British Isles spread out
below them was breathtaking. Viewed from this angle
everything looked completely different, and although
many landmarks eluded her she found the trip absorbing enough to keep her mind off the two in front.

All too soon, it seemed, they were at Gatwick. Incredibly it was little after three hours since they had left Glenroden, the flight from Edinburgh having taken just over an hour. With the whole day still in front of her, Sue didn't even feel tired, and within a short time Meric was dropping her off in Kensington outside the flat.

He told the taxi to wait while he escorted her to the door, refusing her invitation to come in, but staying to insert the key for which she fumbled in her bag. "You'll be all right?" The question could have been a statement, as his eyes swept her paler face.

"Of course!" Inadvertently her glance wavered away from his, going past him to where Carlotte sat impatiently in the taxi. It would be senseless to confess that now she was here, a host of misgivings beset her. While she had been away it had seemed possible to put the tragedy of her mother's death behind her. Now it seemed to be coming back to haunt her, making her curiously reluctant to enter the flat. But how could she explain all this to Meric especially when he was obviously not disposed to linger, and even finding the right words might be impossible.

Besides, she had a sudden feeling he was a stranger. For the first time since she had known him he had abandoned his kilt for a dark blue town suit, in which he still looked extra-ordinarily attractive, but in an entirely different way. With his change of dress came a bewildering sophistication. That he was a man of the world, and of some experience, was quite apparent. It didn't need the added incentive of well-groomed hair and smoothly shaved skin to confirm it. She could think of nothing to add to her brief observation.

A slight frown creased his dark brows as she stood waiting for him to go. "Don't forget," he said, "that you're staying at the hotel tonight." Again he named the well known establishment which he had mentioned earlier. "I'll probably be dining elsewhere, but I'll check before I turn in to see if you've arrived."

Numbly Sue nodded as she watched him drive off, a smile, which she hoped appeared grateful, fixed to her lips. She had no doubt that he would be spending the evening with Carlotte, although he hadn't actually said so. Neither had Carlotte said anything about hurrying down to Kent! The flatness of unreasonable despair almost overwhelmed Sue as she closed the flat door behind her.

For the next hour she tried desperately to adjust her feelings, but somehow the flat didn't seem like home any more and she felt unable to associate herself with the place where she had spent a greater part of her life. Wandering aimlessly from room to room she couldn't attach to any of it much reality. The brief apprehension she had known when she had first arrived faded quickly, and she felt no familiar stirring of distress. At Glenroden she had imagined the different environment accountable for her swiftly diminishing pain, but it was almost as if the life which she and her mother had led together had never been and, as before, Sue searched for some flaw in her own character which might explain her apparent heartlessness.

In the end she gave up trying to analyse her reaction and set to work. The rooms were small, but on closer inspection, in spite of what she had told Meric, the furniture was comfortable and of excellent quality. All of which, she saw bitterly, reflected the generosity of her father's allowance, if she had but known it. It seemed a shame to let it go with the flat for probably next to nothing. Eventually, after collecting and packaging her personal belongings, she decided to ring Tim and ask if there was anything he would like. Perhaps it would be a nice way of saying thank you for all that he'd done.

She had been going to ring Tim in any case to let him know she was here, only she had forgotten that both the telephone and electricity had been cut off while she was away. It seemed more feasible to wait until nearer lunch time, as now she must go to the kiosk at the end of the street. When she was out she would find a café and have something to eat.

Tim was delighted but surprised to hear from her, and immediately insisted on taking her to lunch. "You should have let me know," he reproached her indignantly. "I've been waiting daily for all the details of your remarkable adventure, and then you turn up! I've been trying desperately to get extra leave. I might have passed you on my way to Scotland, which wouldn't have been much good!"

Sue stared at him, aware of a flicker of dismay. Tim had brought her to the same restaurant where they had last had a meal together on that August day before she had gone to see her mother's solicitor. When he had asked her to marry him, and she had refused. Or at least—she tried to remember with painful honesty—she had put him off because she hadn't been enthusiastic, which probably wasn't quite the same thing. Strange that she had almost forgotten such a momentous event. At the moment she could only feel disturbed that he had considered following her to Glenroden. "I don't think it would be a good idea. Not now."

Tim finished ordering before he replied, and a quick glance told Sue that her words had offended. Without much perception it was possible to read Tim like a book. He said now, his mouth pursed, "Surely it would be a good idea for me to come and check up? A wealthy father with a weak heart could need careful handling. Someone should be there to look after your interests!"

"I didn't ever say he was wealthy, Tim!" Sue started at the casual mundanity of his remarks. "That is... Well, I suppose he is quite well off, but I don't know any details."

"There you are!" Tim's voice was laced with triumph. "So easily deceived, my dear Sue. This manager fellow you talk about. In a situation such as you describe, that's the type to watch!"

"But I haven't described anything, Tim. You're

making it up. I've only given you the bare facts. My father's ill. I haven't pried."

"Then you should have done, darling, for your own good. I'm only giving you the benefit of my experience. I'm used to reading between the lines. It's part of my job."

Tim must be indispensable to his tax office! "Please," she tried to stem the self-righteous flow.

He brushed her weak protest aside, his brown eyes sullen, "You tell me that you're giving up the flat, leaving London for good. What am I to think—or do?"

"Tim," Sue stared at him unhappily, "you said when I first went to Scotland that I might find an elderly relation in need of care and attention. Well, my father had this long before I arrived, but I think he does need my companionship, and I intend to stay, just so long as he wants me. It's probably irrelevant that I happen to like Glenroden, but I do. I'm only giving up the flat because it isn't practical to keep it on. It doesn't mean I won't come back one day."

"But it's highly unlikely. This manager fellow..."

"I wish you wouldn't go on about him!" Sue interrupted sharply. "He does a splendid job. I don't think he has any designs on my father's property, and as a matter of fact, he came down with me today."

"Good heavens!" Tim pushed away his soup as if his appetite had gone. "See what I mean? He obviously can't let you out of his sight. Maybe he thinks he'll have you along with the estate when the old man goes."

"Tim!" This time Sue's voice was cold as she stared at him as if he had struck her. "You've no right to say such things. If you must think them then kindly keep such thoughts to yourself. I've explained the whole situation. If you can't accept it..."

"Oh hell, I know that!" Tim shrugged elaborately. "And being a fool I'm deliberately bungling my chances." Remorsefully he leant across the table to engulf her hand with his, his expression pleading forgiveness. "It's you I'm thinking about, Sue. You know I've loved you for a long time."

Which was news to Sue, although she didn't actually say so. True, he had asked her to marry him, but partly she suspected with a view to settling in a comfortable flat. He had made no bones about the fact that he found her home attractive. Also attractive might be a wife with a small income of her own, plus the training and ability to earn a good salary. Besides, wasn't his boss often hinting that the right wife could give a man the kind of stability he needed to put him in line for promotion!

She knew an extra start of dismay when he added smoothly, "If you're an heiress to a Highland estate, any kind of estate for that matter, you need someone to look after your interest. This manager..."

"Meric Findlay is not interested in me personally, if that's what you're getting at," Sue broke in heatedly. Bleakly the truth of her statement paled her hot cheeks. As she stared back at Tim her grey eyes clouded with inner distress, grateful only that he couldn't guess the true state of her feelings.

"And you expect me to believe that?" Speculatively his eyes swept the fine, clear outline of her face, the heavy, swinging hair which seemed to have acquired an extra polish from its weeks of freedom, the sensitive, curved mouth.

Sue bit back an angry answer, not wishing to quarrel with him. It seemed senseless to spend the short time they had together in this way. "We didn't come down here alone." The words fell colourlessly from her taut lips. "There's another girl with us whom Meric likes very much."

"Oh, I see!" Visibly, a knowing smile on his lips, Tim began to relax, finding nothing to doubt in Sue's forced indifference. "Well, that's okay, but you know how things are. One can't be too careful, and you never have been very worldly!" He broke off abruptly and looked at his watch. "The darned time, Sue! I really must go. I'll call you this evening and we'll have dinner somewhere. It's too bad you didn't let me know you were coming. You put me in quite a spot."

"Never mind, Tim." This time she ignored his air of reproach. "Remember you promised to look over the furniture?"

He nodded, as he struggled into his coat. "I'd really like to take over your flat completely. It's a lot more comfortable than my place, but according to your lease, subletting is out. Anyway, in my case, as a new tenant, they'd probably bump up the rent out of all proportion, and I couldn't afford it just now."

Tim's mind ran in circles, Sue grimaced with a wry smile as she watched him depart. It always returned to himself. Still, he was someone she knew and for the first time that she could remember in London she felt lonely. It would have been nice to have spent the afternoon with him. However, there was still plenty to do. Most of the things she wanted to keep were packed. Meric would arrange for these to go by rail, but there were some bits and pieces, old books and such-like which nobody would want. She must ask someone to dispose of those. Maybe the old man with the junk shop in Queen Street would help?

The man said he would, and could call in an hour. Thankful, Sue started back to the flat. It was imperative she should have everything finished so that she could hand over the key to the solicitor tomorrow. In a way, especially if Tim didn't want much, the sale from the furniture might cover the solicitor's fees.

Then at a small boutique on a corner she was side-tracked. It was the display in the large plate-glass window which stopped her so suddenly. Cleverly arranged over a raised pedestal was a chiffon nightgown with a matching negligée in a wonderful rose pink. Entranced, Sue gazed. She could imagine it toning beautifully with her fair hair and grey eyes. Apart from one thin nylon nightie which she had worn during the summer, all her night attire had consisted of pyjamas, usually boys' pyjamas which her mother used to pick up cheaply at sales, which she had always insisted were better value than anything else. Not that Sue hadn't been quite happy to wear them, but this in the window was something special. Not bridal exactly, but very, very nice.

Inside the shop she asked the price and was startled when the woman told her.

"It is really beautiful, madame." The woman eagerly took the set from the window, to show Sue the intricate filigree of delicate silver on the waist. "It was just made for a girl like you." Her eyes flickered admiringly over Sue's slim figure.

Greatly against her better judgment, but with the filmy material between her fingers and unable to resist, Sue agreed to buy. By swift mental calculation she decided she could just about afford it and have enough left over for a warm anorak and a pair of slacks. Her money, she knew, was rapidly running out. There hadn't been as much in her mother's account as she had expected, and she had earned nothing herself since going to Glenroden. The sale of her Mini might be one possible way of raising funds, but without it she would lose her independence. There was no bus service within miles of Glenroden, and if she did find a job, which she must, she would inevitably need transport.

But until she did find work such extravagances as this would have to stop. Hastily she took the carefully wrapped parcel from the pleasant, smiling woman, and left the shop quickly before she was tempted to buy more. How practical such a flimsy garment would be in a Scottish winter, she had no means of knowing, yet, in a moment of temporary light-heartedness, she didn't really care.

Long before Tim called for her that evening Sue was tired. She took him back to the hotel, leaving him with a drink while she bathed and changed. And when he suggested that they ate in the hotel's very good restaurant she was more than willing to agree. It was only afterwards, when he talked of going on somewhere, that she demurred, but seeing his disappointed face she gave in. After all, it could be a long time before she was back in London.

It was after midnight before they returned, later than Sue had intended, but the night-club had been fun and, in a strange way, had seemed to release some of the tensions of the past weeks, possibly because of its very gay atmosphere. They had drunk a sparkling white wine and relaxed, talking desultorily. Tim had surprised her by reverting almost to his old companionable self, and when they had said good-bye outside the hotel Sue liked him better than she had done all day. In the morning he and his immediate superior were on their way to Devon to do an important tax assessment, so she wouldn't see him again before she left.

"You mustn't forget to give me a ring and write," he instructed as he left her. "If you don't I'll be worrying as usual."

With what amounted to nearly a sigh of relief, Sue collected her key from the desk and went up to her room. She had half expected that Tim might be awkward. That he might try to extract promises of marriage or meetings, but apart from the few words as he left her, he hadn't said a thing. Perhaps he had decided that if he was patient she would return to London in the near future. He might have been surprised to learn that almost before she closed her bedroom door Sue had forgotten about him.

Once in her bedroom weariness claimed her, washing everything from her mind but the desire to sleep, making even the effort of getting ready for bed insurmountable. In the adjoining bathroom she creamed her face before taking a quick shower. The warm water revived her a little, and she put on her new negligée. In the centrally heated room it would be much more comfortable than the pyjamas still packed in her overnight case.

Ready at last, she climbed into bed, but no sooner

was her head on the pillow than there came a knock on the door. Uneasily her heart thudded. Surely Tim hadn't returned? But he wouldn't know her room number, and if she had forgotten something he could have left it at reception. Unhappily as the knock came again she got up, not bothering to switch on the light as she stumbled to the door.

Wrenching it open, she was startled to find Meric standing outside on the corridor. Surprise ran through her, widening her eyes. Determinedly throughout the day she had kept him from her thoughts. Even when Tim had referred to him so disrespectfully she had refused to allow herself to dwell on him for a moment longer than it had taken to defend him fairly. Meric had said, she remembered, he would check to ensure that she was in. Unfortunately she had forgotten all about it. If she had thought about it she might well have pictured him retired for the night, or still out with Carlotte.

"If you wait," she said blankly, before he could speak, "I'll put on the light and my dressing gown."

"Whichever way you like," he replied sardonically. "When I think of the time, not to mention the shoe leather, I've wasted traversing between this floor and the two above, another few minutes can't hurt me." He leaned against the door jamb, casual and relaxed, but his voice was edged with sarcasm.

Sue took one look at him and fled, her fingers fumbling for the light switch as she snatched her wrap from the bed. The bedside lamp lit the room dimly but enough. Conscious suddenly of the thinness of the pink negligée, she hugged her arms around herself as she went back to the door. Meric was already stepping through it.

"Just to make sure you don't start combing your hair and all the other things women tend to do when confronted by a man," he muttered dryly. "Even one they don't like."

As on another occasion she decided he had a fine

conceit of himself and her eyes flashed. "I've done no more than necessary," she retorted, "as you can see."

His eyes went over her tumbled hair, her slightly dishevelled appearance. "What I see I like," he grinned. "It's made my wait rewarding."

Her eyes, dark smudges of weariness, stared at him apprehensively, missing the smooth satire of his remark. While she didn't appreciate his humour, she could guess that his patience was wearing thin. "You've been here before?" she asked, rubbing confused fingers across her brow.

"Don't tell me you forgot?" His hard mouth set in lines of mockery and amusement.

"You said you'd check if I was in!"

"And I've been doing just that for the past hour." His voice jolted her wide awake. "I thought you'd have the sense to be in before this." The fathomless eyes flicked over her face, harshly interrogating.

Sue continued to stare at him, her fringed eyes defensive. She need not have worried about being decently covered up. In his present mood he probably wouldn't have noticed had she been naked! "I spent the evening with Tim Mason," she said faintly.

"Now I just thought you might." His voice was a long, cool drawl. "It also crossed my mind that you must have other friends, but undoubtedly it didn't occur to you to let everyone know you were in town?"

Dazed, as her mind attempted to absorb and dissect, she blinked at him, her pupils dilated. "It would scarcely have been feasible," she whispered, her throat constricted. "I wasn't exactly holding a party."

With a shrug he moved slightly away from her, his height casting bulky shadows against the wall. Too late she wished she had used the main switch. The light from the small lamp, which flooded palely, was too intimate. She watched nervously as he turned smoothly to face her again. She lifted her head, braced for the onslaught, and he gave a short laugh.

"So you concentrated on one man—Tim from the

tax office! And what does he think of your next move? Does he approve, I wonder?''

There was a cleft in Meric Findlay's chin, etched deeply below his firm, chiselled lips. Sue fixed her gaze on it, refusing to meet the mockery in the dark smouldering depth of his eyes.

She drew a long, quivering breath, and tried to retaliate with a mock flippancy she was far from feeling. "I could have a tax problem, for all you know. Tim is very obliging. Secondly, he doesn't like the idea of my moving away, but he hasn't actually said much against it. Does that answer your question?''

"Not completely, but then having no personal knowledge of your friend I don't know how his mind works.''

Sue's shoulders moved just perceptibly. If, as Meric claimed, he didn't know Tim personally, then how did he know he worked for the Inland Revenue? But she wondered idly, too tired to probe, realizing she might only get an evasive reply. A man like Meric Findlay would make it his business to know of anything that could touch him even indirectly. Her presence at Glenroden, if only temporary, no doubt provided an excuse for detailed surveillance.

She mumbled carelessly, scarcely looking at him, "If I have omitted any relevant information then I'm sure you can supply the deficiency.''

Just as carelessly his hands came down on her shoulders, a means of emphasizing his point, nothing else. "You'd better decide once and for all that the Tim Masons of this world don't count. Not so far as you're concerned. You can leave him behind tomorrow and start a new life. A clean break is the only way.''

At the touch of his hands an awful feeling of weakness swept over her and she stirred restively, attempting to concentrate on what he was saying, thrusting the merely physical from her mind. Glenroden was important to Meric. It seemed he would go to any lengths to protect it. He nursed the estate along like a baby. No adverse breath of wind was allowed to blow over it. But in doing so, didn't he realize he could be downright hurtful?

"You can't rule everything according to the book," she cried, fire slipping through her, holding her taut within his hands. "You should allow for the human element."

"Your own?" He asked sharply, catching her off guard.

She jerked away from him a little wildly, but he held her still. He looked so strong and unassailable, a man with power to make her feel soft and vulnerable, ready to collapse into his arms.

"Tim and I like each other." She spoke on a little note of desperation, hugging her body still tighter with her arms. "I couldn't hope to be as ruthless as you are."

His wary eyes mocked her. "You don't strike me as a girl who's been swept off her feet, but perhaps you feel happier with both feet on the ground?"

Aroused, Sue's glance clashed angrily with his. "The emotional side of my life is none of your business, Meric Findlay!"

"Do you really believe that?" His dark eyes suddenly narrowed, raking her pale skin, her pink negligée, the curtain of ashen hair about her upraised face. "I remember an occasion when you seemed to enjoy being emotional in my arms. Do you always say please after Tim kisses you?"

A sparkling tension united them, making static the air between them, and her breath escaped audibly through her parted, rose-tinted lips. Irresistibly her eyes were drawn to his mouth, against her better sense. Only too well did she remember the imprint of it on her own from another evening, and longed crazily to repeat the experience. That he should guess the longing which threatened to consume her was utterly beyond comprehension.

"I think I'd like to go to bed," she said indistinctly, her wits departing with her precarious poise.

His head went back at that, a brilliant smile lighting his dark face as his gaze slid again over her sensual young figure, over the lovely curves of her body which her protective arms revealed, had she but known it, more than they concealed. "Could that be an invitation?"

His fingers were burning her shoulders through the flimsy material of her gown, and heat swept through her blood like a fever, like nothing she had ever known before, and she quivered with the shock of revelation. Unable to check her trembling, she sought refuge in words. "Why do you enjoy twisting everything I say? I don't know why you came here tonight, but I do know it's not because you feel attracted to me!"

"You're very charming, Miss Frazer. I shouldn't underestimate your charms if I were you, nor your capacity to enjoy the purely physical in life. Don't tell me that Tim didn't kiss you good night?"

Tim had tried, but she hadn't felt in the mood. At least she had told herself this as she had pushed him away, pleading tiredness. Not that she intended confessing this to Meric Findlay! Resentful that he should even ask, she stayed mutinously silent, until his hands moving over her arms brought sensations which swept everything else from her mind.

Like quicksilver he read the thoughts she tried to hide. "So you feel cheated. Maybe you would like me to supply the deficiency." His slanting dark eyes touched the pulse in her throat. He bent his head, slowly and deliberately, and she felt his lips against the bare skin of her shoulder, lingering and drifting over the bone to the nape of her neck, while his fingers curved, pressing soft flesh until she cried out. As a grand finale, as if to punish her a little for even one small note of protest, his head lifted and on her parted lips he dropped a kiss, brief and hard, hurting her in the split second before he let her go.

"Which might just about prove my point," he spoke

tautly. "That you're not the frozen little iceberg you pretend to be."

He moved away as she collapsed on to the edge of the bed, barely knowing what she was doing. Nothing of what he alleged could be true, but even if there had been some modicum of truth surely he had no right to inflict his views in this manner?

Her flushed face paled as she stared at him, and her heart turned over. Big and powerful, he stepped back and through her blood ran a wild, stormy longing. Desperately she tried to gather every grain of common sense which had been scattered in those few mad moments in his arms.

In her ear she heard him saying, "If you'd had the sense to get back in decent time none of this might have happened."

"So it's my fault?" Childishly she refused to look at him.

"Listen, Sue, I don't intend entering any sixth form argument as to where the blame lies. Maybe," a faint smile quirked his mouth at one corner, "it could be placed with the assistant who sold you that very fetching night attire, if that would ease your mind."

"You surely don't think I bought it specially?" Driven beyond normal constraint, Sue choked untruthfully. "I've washed it several times."

"Liar." His voice was soft, his face full of glinting amusement as he stepped suddenly to her side. "Unless we now have washable price tags!" Swiftly his fingers pounced, filching a tiny slip of cardboard from the frills on her neckline to show it to her.

Meric's voice was light, purposely mocking, but Sue had lost hers, owing to the hard constriction in her throat. But he gave her no opportunity to answer, dismissing the incident with a brief shrug before he went on. "It was necessary to see you tonight, Sue, because I have to meet someone again in the morning. I'll probably just manage to catch the afternoon plane by inches. I've settled everything up here and arranged for you to have a taxi to the airport, but I had no idea how you were getting on. For all I knew you could be having difficulties. I had to make sure you were all right."

He had moved to the door, watching her carefully, his hand turning the knob as he waited. Sue's gaze, in spite of her attempt to divert it, went tenaciously to his face. Silently she prayed feverishly he would leave quickly, ignoring the intensity of her feelings which cried out just as wildly for him to stay.

She made a tremendous effort to pull herself together, to concentrate on what he was saying as she nodded her head. "I have an appointment with my mother's solicitor in the morning. I believe there are a few papers to sign, but apart from that I don't think there'll be anything much. I have the key to the flat ready to give him, and he'll see to everything else. I have all my personal belongings packed, like you said..." Her voice trailed off uncertainly. There didn't seem to be anything more to add.

"Fine, then, I'll see you tomorrow. Go to the airport and wait for me there." His tone had reverted to normal, alert and decisive. "I'm sorry it's all been such a rush. Maybe another time we'll have more time to spare."

Sue flinched as he was gone sharply, and for fully a minute she remained staring at the closed door. If she had been dreaming then her awakening had been too abrupt, almost more than she could cope with. Her hair spilled over her flushed cheeks as despair and taut nerves jerked her into action. Quickly she jumped to her feet, finding her overnight case, tipping the contents haphazardly on to the floor. In a few fumbling seconds she had removed her new negligée, pushing it carelessly to one side before finding her old pyjamas and putting them on. They were a bit short and too boyish, the thin cotton entirely without charm, but in them Sue felt her old, level-headed self.

Satisfied, yet curiously unhappy, she slid back into bed. It might seem a wicked waste of money, but in the morning the pink negligée could go into the dustbin! Or, on second thoughts, she could give it to the little chambermaid with the nice smile. Wherever it went, she never wanted to see it again. If Sue was sure of nothing else, she was sure of that!

CHAPTER SEVEN

ONCE back in Edinburgh Sue tried to view the whole incident sensibly, as merely a trick of the night playing on senses too finely balanced. Meric Findlay was patently not the kind of man to indulge in such interludes, but, she supposed, any man might have his moments of indiscretion. He had probably been as tired as herself, and what had happened had been without design or intent. A clear case of one thing leading to another. Such reasoning, while mundane, was momentarily comforting, and she clung to it as a drowning man might cling to a straw.

They arrived at Turnhouse in the late aftrnoon, and Meric insisted they had tea before leaving for Glenroden. "It's a fairish drive," he said, "and once on the road I'd rather not stop."

Sue glanced at him quickly as they drove into the city but made no comment. She had enjoyed the flight better this time. There had been no Carlotte, and Meric had sat with her naming the various landmarks which had eluded her previously. With the expertise of a seasoned traveller he had answered all the questions, telling her all she wanted to know. Unfortunately there had also been time to sit and think, something she hadn't appreciated quite so much.

While she had seen little of Meric in London, in retrospect his rigorous supervision of her affairs was obvious. His tight schedule, his insistence that every aspect of her life in Kensington be neatly packaged, tied up and disposed of in as short as possible time, had been achieved almost it might seem by remote control. Never once had it occurred to her to quarrel with his authority, or to question the fact that he allowed her little leeway of her own. Having always guarded her independence, Sue knew a moment of disquiet, a sneaking premonition that unless she was careful there could be worse to come.

Yet, in spite of an uneasy apprehension, she sighed, murmuring impulsively, "It's good to be home. Scotland is all I ever dreamed it would be. In two days I've missed it."

His head half-turned. "Dreams," he declared, "can be dangerous things."

Hadn't things worked out as he'd planned in London—in his life? "Do you resent me coming back with you like this?" she asked.

One eyebrow rose. "Why should I? You have every right," he declared. "And your father needs you."

"But you don't," she felt like adding, only it would seem an odd question for her to ask. Her mind wandered unhappily to the occasions he had made love to her, then on tenaciously to his friendship with Carlotte. Was it possible he was just playing with them both until he found out who was to inherit Glenroden? Did he hope to be able to choose? John could live for years, but then again he might not. Frightened by her own thoughts, Sue tried not to look into the future. If she had never loved her mother very deeply she still missed her, and in finding her father it seemed she might just as suddenly lose him too. What was the use of loving people if they could be snatched away without warning to leave only an aching void? Even beginning to care for Meric Findlay could only be inviting heartache.

Swiftly as they went down Princes Street she glanced at him, the knowledge of her own foolishness bringing her sharply upright. She was letting a too vivid imagination play tricks! Her eyes turned impatiently to gaze at the fine shops, the cosmopolitan crowds thronging the pavements. Why should she allow a few kisses, the crazy reactions of her impressionable heart, to cause her such torment? Meric must look elsewhere for amusement, and she herself must learn to acquire a thicker skin than the one she had now.

"The capital has a highly dramatic appearance, don't you think?" Meric glanced at her lightly as they left the car, apparently not at all disturbed by her sudden silence.

Sue nodded as she looked up and her eager gaze fell on the silhouette of the thousand-year old Castle on its rock and the Old Town stretched against the windy October sky. Across the gardens of Princes Street it was an eye-catching sight.

"The next time we can spare you for a couple of days, you can spend them here and have a good look around." With a slight smile Meric guided her through the slow moving traffic towards a hotel, his hand firm beneath her elbow. "It seems a shame we can't stay longer this afternoon, but I'm afraid we'd better push on."

The drive home was accomplished in record time, or so it seemed to Sue, as she remembered her first lone journey in August. For the main part Meric appeared preoccupied and she found herself dozing off at regular intervals, her tired body subduing her restless mind. It wasn't until they were nearly there that she roused herself sufficiently to ask when Carlotte would be returning. She had tried to ask on the plane, but it was only now, by great effort, she found herself able to phrase the necessary sentence. "Father enjoys her visits, I think," she tacked on carefully.

He answered shortly, leaving her strangely unsatisfied, "She didn't say, and I'm afraid I forgot to ask. No doubt you'll be able to survive without her for a few days."

She said, "You don't need to be sarcastic. I just thought you would think it funny that I hadn't asked!"

He replied quietly, "Forget it. It didn't cross my mind. Usually she doesn't stay away for any length of time."

His broad shoulders lifted with seeming indifference as he glanced at her sideways. They were silent, aware of each other, but neither willing to say anything more. Sue turned her head away, deploring the tension between them, yet unable to understand it. Her eyes turned towards the moors, looking out through the window to where they lay drenched and bleak from the recent rains. The solitude seemed to reach out and touch her, bringing comfort in the gathering darkness. It was of little use denying that Meric Findlay didn't want her, nor did Carlotte Craig. But Glenroden was fast becoming home to her and no matter what the opposition she intended to stay.

Now that the days were getting shorter, Mrs. Lennox decided she would live in until spring. Doctor McRoberts was still uneasy about John, who seemed to grow frailer each day, and Sue was daily grateful that the woman was prepared to help look after him. During the winter the road between Glenroden and the village was often impassable when the river was in flood and, as Mrs. Lennox pointed out, she could be marooned in the village for days.

Before she could come, however, she had various things to see to, and Sue co-operated by doing more around the house as well as continuing to help John with his book.

"Sometimes, dear, I wonder who's writing it, you or him," Mrs. Lennox smiled. "I don't think he would ever have managed it without you."

"It keeps my mind occupied, and off other things," Sue returned the friendly smile enigmatically. In spite of Mrs. Lennox's inquiring look she didn't explain that "other things" mostly constituted Meric Findlay.

Clearly, for all her secret opinion that he was a ruthless adventurer, intent on furthering his own interest, Meric continued to plague her heart. As well as contempt he aroused other emotions which she would rather be without. Whenever she saw him she remembered guiltily that in London she had been on the point of asking her solicitor if he could be properly investigated without arousing suspicion. Yet somehow she had found herself unable to parade all her doubts and fears before the detached legal mind of the law. In the solicitor's office it had suddenly seemed impertinent even to think of broaching the subject, but once back at Glenroden she reproached herself for being a fool. The opportunity might not come again. If only she had had some idea what such a procedure would involve! Cowardly, she had shrunk from the consequences of wrongly placed judgment. The chance that Meric might be quite innocent of all she suspected, apart from a more or less normal inclination to feather one's own nest. And if she were to mortally offend him without reasonable justification he might leave. Which, she told herself unhappily, would only leave her father in dire straits, and do no one any good.

Time passed. Meric still took out shooting parties, but with the end of October in sight the caravan park was to close for the season. Or so Carlotte said when she returned from London.

"Next year," Carlotte said smoothly, "we intend to develop another few acres beside the loch. Subject to planning permission, of course. And, if we get it, I might even be prepared to spend most of the summer here at Glenroden. Meric seems to think I'm indispensable. You probably won't be here, but I thought you might like to know."

Sue could have retorted that she would rather not have known, that she found the information curiously unpalatable. But there was no denying that, whatever happened, she might not be here. So she remained silent, listening politely as Carlotte chattered on, trying to give the impression that she was completely indifferent as to what happened next year or any time in this part of the world.

According to Carlotte, Meric was taking her out again to dinner, and it added to Sue's increasing bitterness that he had never once asked her. In fact, if anything, he seemed to make a point of keeping out of her way. When, on departing, Carlotte mentioned that she thought a young teacher would be needed in a small school near where she lived, after Christmas, Sue jumped at the idea.

"Let me know as soon as you hear anything definite," she said, as she waved Carlotte good-bye.

One day towards the end of the month, Meric actually took her around the estate. He surprised her one evening by asking if she would go, and Sue, disregarding her half-formed intention to refuse, accepted with alacrity.

She was ready soon after breakfast on a fine, if windy October morning. Meric had told her to dress warmly, without regard for fashion as the going would be rough, and the weather unpredictable.

"Don't come dressed in a skirt and thin blouse," he had said, "or I'll send you back to put on something different."

His slightly threatening tone had been enough to send Sue searching through her wardrobe for a pair of thick slacks, and a heavy sweater which she wore on top of her shirt. She hoped he would consider these suitable.

Mrs. Lennox had also contributed her share towards making their day a success by packing a light rucksack with sandwiches and flasks which she gave to Sue as she came downstairs. "Enjoy yourself," she said kindly.

Sue smiled as she ran out to where Meric was waiting. He had the Range-Rover at the door and as she climbed in beside him he released the brake impatiently and they were away. Even now Sue could scarcely believe it.

He glanced at her sideways as they went down the drive. "You're looking very bright this morning," he grinned, his impatience forgotten.

She flushed, her smile deepening to laughter as she felt his eyes slide over her miscellaneous attire, right down to her thick stockings and nailed boots. "You can't complain that I haven't followed your instructions to the letter. I'm prepared for anything, to quote your exact words."

"Hum...well," his eyes still lingered speculatively, "maybe that wasn't altogether what I had in mind, but as we're going stalking lighter clothing wouldn't do."

"Stalking?" She stared, her gaze jerking away from the scenery to his dark face. "You mean—really stalking, after stags and deers?"

He laughed again at that, his eyes glinting as momentarily they met her own. "Deer is the plural, nitwit, as you should know."

"Clever Dick!" she laughed back, greatly daring. "We had a name for such as you at school."

"I've known women call me nicer names than that," he taunted with matching humour. "My name happens to be Meric. Once or twice I've heard you use it yourself."

Sue's gaze fled back to the distant mountains. She took a deep breath. "You're very nice when you're friendly," she said primly, "but there are times when only Mr. Findlay will do."

His mouth quirked at the faint note of indignation. He remarked with a touch of mischief, "Well, for my sins, it's nice to know I arouse positive reactions on occasion. Would you not be prepared to agree with me, sweet Sue?"

She would...but wild horses couldn't have dragged from her so much as a nod. Nor a plea that he wouldn't refer to her as sweet Sue when he didn't mean it. Instead, she suggested tartly, "Suppose we stick to the deer?"

"Oh, yes, the deer." His smile mocked. "Women are past masters of evasion—if that makes sense. One thing you might learn one day, Sue. You can't run for ever. But for the moment, as you say, we'll stick to the deer."

"Well?" Her colour heightened, her rather tense

query prompted by a sudden jerking of her heart.

He replied smoothly as he swung the large vehicle out on to the major road, "I hope to show you a stag, several perhaps, and you might see some hinds."

Intrigued, Sue forgot to be defensive, and turned to him eagerly, her face alight. "Will we see them on Glenroden? I mean," she went on cautiously, "right now I don't know much about Glenroden. Is it a large property?"

Nervously she clutched the edge of her seat, her hands slightly damp with apprehension, hating to admit how little she knew, yet willing to subdue her pride if only to find out more about a place she was beginning to love.

Meric, however, didn't seem at all surprised by what she asked. "Yes, to both questions," he said. "Glenroden is big by some standards, but don't confuse size with profitability. We have a deer forest, some grouse moors, a loch which you've seen. Then lower down we have pine woods, lower hills with sheep, and a few rather poor fields of cereals and root crops. These last fields are improving with care, but the ground remains very stony."

She found herself frowning, not wholly convinced. There seemed an awful lot of it. "You say it isn't profitable. Why not? Surely, considering the size, it ought to be?"

For once he must have thought her curiosity pertinent as he appeared quite willing to explain. "You don't make an awful lot of money on this sort of property. If you own a deer forest you must look after it properly, but it costs quite a lot of money and doesn't pay. Ours does now, now that we have an agreement with the hotel. Some owners let theirs for a season, but you never know what people will do. Sometimes it's all right, but it can be a disaster. This way, the way we do it, the head keeper and myself supervise everything."

"You mean you let people kill the deer?"

"This way we cull them."

"By shooting them? That sounds cruel." As soon as she spoke she knew Carlotte wouldn't have made such a remark.

Meric said, smiling faintly, "A certain number must be killed every year to prevent the herd increasing."

Which didn't make sense. Not to Sue, to whom a deer forest was about as familiar as the wilds of Siberia. She considered the information doubtfully. About them there lay plenty of territory, high ground, low ground, miles and miles of it, stretching as far as the eye could see, and not a creature in sight. Surely enough space for hundreds of deer.

"Why can't you let the herd increase?" she asked, bewildered, shifting a little on her seat.

"Because," he explained quietly, "there's only a limited food supply. Our deer forest is high and wild. This means that the herd must be kept down to certain numbers, otherwise the beasts would starve before the grass begins to grow in the spring."

"I see..." Considering the bareness of the higher slopes, this seemed logical. Far more logical than the fact that she had been here several weeks and knew little. Certainly she had never stopped to wonder what all these wild creatures lived on.

They had reached the river by this time, where it ran over the road on its way to the loch. Once across the ford Meric turned right, up a hard but narrow track, running against the river but alongside it, following its rocky bed up through a wood of birch trees, clinging tightly to its twisting path. "Hang on!" he shouted, as the Range-Rover lurched through a bad dip, throwing Sue against him, hard against his shoulder.

He grinned, and threw an arm around her, steadying her briefly until she regained her balance, after which he needed two hands to control the spinning wheels.

Sue jerked upright and away from him, shrinking into her corner, to obliterate the feel of his hard muscles, the steely grip of his arm. Rather than think about it she hustled her thoughts back to the deer.

"Can't you feed them artificially," she asked, "like farmers feed cattle?"

He didn't answer immediately, not until the line of his jaw relaxed to its usual sardonic angle, and his eyes recovered their indifferent dryness. "Suppose you start at the beginning," he said as the track smoothed out and his grip on the wheel eased slightly. "A deer forest looks enormous on a map, but there are only certain places where there's food, so you can only support a certain number of deer. We know the exact number of deer, that is stags and hinds, which can live comfortably here."

"So you don't need to feed them?"

"Oh yes. We feed rock salt, beans and potatoes, early in the morning. But it's only in a very hard winter that we might do this. It costs money, and we couldn't do it every year if we didn't have some sort of recompense. Usually the deer forage very well for themselves."

"You say usually?" Sue's voice quickened with interest.

He nodded, his eyes warmer on her eager face. "It's the long, hard winter which causes the trouble. The winter when snow lies deep in the corries. Corries, if you don't know, are places where the grass grows, the places where the stags find their food. If the snow lies deep it takes time to melt. This is the dangerous time. Once, in such a year, John and I found deer dying of starvation, so weak they couldn't run away, too weak to move when eagles attacked them."

Sue's breath caught. "What did you do?"

"Do? We had to shoot them. Put them out of their misery."

Tightly she closed her eyes, refusing to allow even mental vision. "Poor things... Why don't you always feed them?"

"Well, as I said, or rather implied, it would be too expensive. And if you fed them all the time they would become tame, and there'd be no stalking and then the forest would get overcrowded."

"Would that be a bad thing?" Sue's frown returned. "What would happen if it did?"

"Well, use your imagination, girl. It stands to reason. The deer would come down from the hills, eat the farmer's crops, and the farmers would shoot them. So you see we must cull them. They must be shot by people who know what they're doing. A clean shot is an easy death compared with starvation or bad wounds from a shotgun instead of a rifle."

The tone of Meric's voice hinted that his patience was not unlimited, but his eyes were still kind, giving her courage to say tritely, "I shouldn't like to shoot a stag myself, even supposing I knew how to go about it."

"Fair enough," his eyes mocked slightly her nervous tremor, "but you can get quite a lot of fun out of stalking, without shooting or knowing a great deal about it."

Sue sighed, lapsing momentarily into silence, watching the sun rise higher above the mountains, its beams creeping down the hillside into the valley. It was going to be a fine day. She turned her head to look at him in the closeness of the car. "You say that any novice can enjoy this sort of thing?" Her hand flicked towards the wildness about them.

"You're twisting my words, Sue." He returned her curious glance in full measure. "You shouldn't go wandering around here on your own, if that's what you mean. You must be with someone experienced who knows what they're doing."

"Is that a warning?"

"It could be..." His lips twitched. "I suspect you could be recklessly headstrong beneath that civilized veneer of yours, but just let me tell you this! If I ever catch you up here on your own, I'll wallop you so hard you won't sit down for a week."

And he would, too! Colour came surging, tinting her pale skin, but it wasn't anger which flared between them. The thought of such punishment brought a strange excitement where it should have aroused fury. There was something in their relationship which she wouldn't understand. Again she moved away from him. He tended to talk nonsense. She wasn't as he suspected. Right through she was sensible—Tim always said so. Very rarely did she ever act without thinking. She said primly, refusing to give him the satisfaction of knowing he had so much as ruffled her feelings.

"I don't know why you should feel it necessary to issue such a drastic ultimatum, nor what grounds you have for jumping to such outlandish conclusions regarding my character!"

"Just bear it in mind. You might not appreciate it, but a few well chosen words never came amiss. They could even save your life."

"I think you exaggerate." Deliberately, as a form of self-defence, she forced a cool note of haughtiness, just to put him in his place. "I expect your patience can be too sorely tried by our clients at the hotel. But after all, that's your job."

Instantly his eyes smouldered as with the tilt of her chin his mood swung dangerously, and instantly Sue knew she shouldn't have spoken in this way. It wasn't the first time she had set out to goad him deliberately by implying that he should realize she was the rightful heir to an estate which he obviously coveted. But today he was putting himself out to see that she enjoyed herself, and, if nothing else, she should learn to control her tongue and not antagonize him by way of repayment. John, she felt, would not have approved.

But before she could speak his left hand moved with lightning speed, his fingers taking hold of a thick handful of hair at her nape, jerking her neck painfully, and with each small struggle tightening his grip. "Another word of warning," he uttered softly as she cried out in pain, not attempting to relax his hold. "Look about you, Miss—er—Frazer. Look at the wilderness and take care not to try my temper too far. It's supposed to be quite something when properly aroused—ask my men. So take heed.''

He growled in her burning ear before thrusting her roughly away, and she crouched beside him shaking, her eyes fixed mutinously on the track ahead. Fervently she wished she could fade out of sight, or be endowed mysteriously with larger proportions. Then she wouldn't feel so dwarfed and defenceless against his big, powerful body.

He didn't look at her, and she turned quickly from him so that he wouldn't see how she tried to steady herself by gripping her hands tightly together. His rough treatment must have taken her wits away as a clever retort eluded her and she could think of nothing to say. The minutes ticked by silently while her chastised mind restored itself with youthful resilience.

The country on either side was getting wilder, and the track they were travelling seemed barely discernible in the heather. Obviously Meric knew where he was going, but they seemed to have come many miles from Glenroden. Perhaps their slow speed gave this impression? Masking her new nervousness with an air of composure, she asked coolly, "How much further do we have to go?"

As if aware of her uncertainty and still wishing to punish her a little, he answered smoothly, "Not much further, but I hope you've recovered sufficiently to walk. If not I'm not prepared to carry you, even supposing you make it an order."

She looked at her fingers, so that he could only see the sheen of her downbent head. "I rather asked for that, didn't I?"

"And I didn't intend to forgive you so easily, Miss Sue, but we've the rest of the day to spend together and I'm not much good at sign language."

The touch of humour from him broke the tension and made her laugh shakily. "Well, you usually give as good as is sent," she couldn't resist retorting. "All those doubtful 'Miss Frazers' have the intended effect, which you know very well."

What he might have replied was lost as they swung to an abrupt halt inside what looked to Sue like a ring of boulders, a natural car-park carved from the rock. "Oh, lord," she exclaimed, her eyes round, "what a place!"

"It's the end of the track, where we leave all vehicles," he explained. He looked down into her eyes for a second, searching them for panic. Finding only a lively interest, he nodded approvingly. "From now on we use our legs, and the going is tough."

The going *was* tough, although Sue would have died rather than complained. Besides, she found she was enjoying herself. Meric walked slightly in front, the rucksack containing their lunch slung on his back, and every now and again he paused to let her catch up. The morning mist still clung to the hillsides, but the mist didn't deter him, he knew the path well. The view as they climbed higher was beautiful—mountains, rocks, green valleys and sparkling burns. Sue, following closely, could hear the sound of running water, like music on the air. Presently the mist began to evaporate. A breeze sprang up, blowing the melting shreds of it away, and the hills stood out in ridged and jagged crests agains the sharp blue sky.

An hour's solid climbing brought them out of the heather on to the bare hillside. It was hot and shadeless, so Sue was glad when they turned the shoulder of the hill and she felt the wind on her face. She felt inordinately grateful when Meric paused long enough to let her get a quick drink from one of the burns. The water tasted cool and fresh and very, very clean.

"Thirsty?" He gazed at her consideringly, noting the dark smudge across her wide brow where she had brushed back a tendril of hair with fingers soiled by contact with the rocks. His eyebrow quirked as he put out his own hand to flick off a fragment of sandy soil. "At this rate," he grinned, "you'll need a wash as well as a drink!"

"I don't mind." Refreshed, she looked back at him, returning his smile, her former antagonism forgotten in the exhilaration of the climb. Completely alive, her mind and body possessed by a mood of complete enthrallment with the wild country, she felt happier than she had done for some time. "The air is marvellous. I could climb for hours without getting tired," she said.

"Good." Sardonically his eyes still lingered on her animated face as if held there by her lively expression. "But we have yet some way to go. You aren't really big or tough enough for this sort of thing. You may be congratulating yourself too soon."

Trust him to put a damper on things! "So you require an Amazon?" Her eyes sparked, the antagonism creeping back even while she strove to remain objective. It was probably women en masse he referred to, not just one inexperienced female like herself. A man like Meric Findlay would enjoy lumping everyone together. It was up to her to prove him wrong. "An Amazon," she repeated impatiently, moving beneath his fixed gaze as she waited his reply.

"I certainly don't require one, personally. It's the terrain I'm talking about, not me." Tongue in cheek he grinned derisively as he turned away.

Exasperated, she picked up her anorak and followed. How did he always manage to have the last word!

They worked their way across the shoulder of the hill, climbing amongst rocks and scrambling down screes. The wind, which had been blowing on their faces, now swirled behind them, whistling through the narrow clefts with a strange moaning sound.

Sue shuddered, speaking to Meric's broad back. "It's a bit eerie."

He glanced around at her, nodding soberly. "This is a grim sort of place. But as you said before, the air is marvellous." His dark eyes flicked across the stony ridges, the black boulders, the dark, bare clefts which sunlight never reached, gently mocking her delicate aversion.

"Where is the forest—the deer forest, I mean?" Unable to see even a single tree around or above them, Sue couldn't resist asking, even if it gave him another opportunity to tease.

Meric laughed as he eased his rifle on his shoulder. "Didn't anyone tell you, Sue, there are no trees in a deer forest?"

Sue bit her lip as she walked on. It seemed she couldn't win. Up here, she felt and was totally ignorant. Small wonder he laughed at her!

"Never mind." His glance took in her crestfallen face as his hand gently gripped her elbow. "A lot of people make the same mistake. And don't ask me why it's called a forest. Very few of them ever have many trees."

Feeling strangely grateful for his few kind words, Sue scrambled on. The track was very steep and stony, but presently, it went around an outcrop of rock where it was blocked by a huge fall of stone. Meric had stopped and when she caught up she saw that he had taken out his binoculars and was scanning the hills.

"Look Sue," he murmured, putting an arm out to draw her up close, "there's a stag over there. Look over to Ben Cruan—he's at the entrance to the corrie. If we're lucky we'll get nearer, but first take these and see for yourself."

Sue, too aware of his steadying arm, took the binoculars from him with hands which trembled slightly, focusing the instrument as he instructed on the wilderness in front of her. For a moment she could see nothing but bare hillside, but presently she caught sight of something brown that moved.

"Is it a stag?" she asked eagerly, straining to get a clearer view.

"Yes." His arm tightened unconsciously, the line of his jaw taut as his eyes narrowed into the distance. "It's a big one. We're too far off to see his points, but he's a big beast."

"Can't we get nearer?" Impatiently she lowered the

glasses, her gaze following his, but unable to see the stag without them.

"It's difficult." Meric pointed out the steep decline covered with boulders and loose stones, the boggy patch in the bottom which lay between them and their quarry. "The wind's in our favour," he added in a low voice. "This way it's blowing in our faces again so the stag can't get our scent. Deer, if you didn't know, have such a keen sense of smell they can scent man from an incredibly long distance. But we're certainly going to try."

With a quick, concentrating smile he put her from him, just as the warmth from his body was beginning to spread. With a pang Sue realized that his gesture had been purely impersonal. So intent was he on the deer, he had scarcely realized she was there. Hastily she suppressed a sudden longing to stay within the circle of his arm as she dropped carefully behind him down the slope of the hill. As he had said, it was a difficult approach. If they were to dislodge a stone it could start a small avalanche which would warn the stag of their presence, but Sue found it difficult to move soundlessly over the uneven surface.

To her secret delight she did manage remarkably well, her quick light movements matching Meric's experience, something which she sensed pleased him although he made no comment. His approval lay only in his brief smile as he turned his head to see how she was progressing. Soon they were down the slope, over the swampy patch at the bottom and climbing up the mountainside.

For a while, they lost sight of the stag, but Meric told her he had marked the spot where he grazed. It was very still. In their present position they were sheltered, and nothing moved, not even a blade of grass. Sue, used as she was to city streets, had never known such silence. Then they were creeping slowly, mostly on their hands and knees, until eventually they were on a rock ridge looking down into a narrow valley. A small burn ran down the middle of the valley, twisting amongst the stones, but there was no sign of the stag.

"He's moved to the upper part of the valley," Meric whispered in her ear. "Of that I'm certain. I know the corrie well and the grass at the top is sweet. He'll be feeding."

"Are you sure?" Sue crawled up level with him, glancing anxiously sideways into his face. Unlike her own, his looked cool. Obviously he was hard, and in tip-top physical condition, as after the hard climb his breathing had scarcely altered. Feeling the hot perspiration on her brow, Sue glanced at him again, her eyes tinged with envy.

He was gazing straight across the incline and nodded his head to her question. "Yes. There's a passage between the burn and the mountainside, before the valley widens. Once past the burn the path is blocked by fallen rock, but we can climb on to a ridge and view from above. Not a good angle to shoot him from, but then I'm not shooting today."

They climbed down to the burn. It took several minutes, and as they drew nearer, Sue could see the passage between the burn and the cliff. She held her breath with excitement. Never before could she remember feeling like this, keyed up and brimming over with expectancy. And not a little, she acknowledged, had these feelings to do with the man beside her.

"Now we go up the cliff," Meric said softly, beckoning to Sue to follow closely.

The rock was warm with the sun and the crevices were filled with grass and little pools of water. On some parts it was slippery and she didn't reject Meric's helping hand, but clung to it tightly, pulling herself up. Hot from exertion and quite without breath, she was thankful when they reached the top. Her hair tumbled in disorder about her face, and looking back she could see the woolly hat she had been wearing hooked on the branch of a stunted tree. She would collect it on the way down.

Meric drew her nearer, making way for her in a niche beside him. From their perch half-way up the mountain they could now see the top of the valley. It was small, filled with boulders, which Sue supposed had fallen from the higher crags. Between the boulders the grass looked fresh and green, surprising for the time of year. But it wasn't the grass which caught and held Sue's attention. It was the animal which grazed there completely unaware of the two watching strangers. It was a beautiful, brown-coloured, antlered stag.

CHAPTER EIGHT

In her excitement Sue clutched Meric's arm, only just remembering to keep her voice down. "What a beautiful beast!" she gasped, her eyes widening with admiration and something like awe. It was the first time in her life she had ever seen a stag apart from films and photographs, and she watched spellbound from her high perch on the rock. The animal was about a hundred yards away, grazing towards them head on, and even from that distance, she thought she could count ten points to his antlers.

She was right—as Meric confirmed. "It's not a Royal stag. A Royal has twelve points to its antlers. But this one is very nice, about nine years old, I should think. You won't see anything much better."

To let her have a better view he spread out his legs and settled his rifle against a piece of old turf. Sue lay down beside him, her eyes fixed on the corrie. The stag went on grazing. It was so still and sheltered in the corrie that she could hear the noise of the creature's hoof against the stones. He was coming nearer very slowly, seeking out the tender young grass between the boulders, still unaware of their presence.

"There may be more," Meric whispered, easing himself more comfortably in the confined space. He was so near that glancing at him Sue saw herself reflected momentarily in the dark depth of his eyes. For a minute she was afraid to move or speak, to do anything to disturb her feelings of unreality. The length of his strongly muscled leg was pressed against her own, and when he spoke his breath came warm on her cheek.

She stirred as a flicker of fire shot through her, distracting her attention from the animal in front of them.

Taking a deep breath, she said quickly, "I suppose the stags look more or less alike? Like sheep."

He smiled at that. "Don't make a remark like that near the shepherd—or our head keeper! He knows most of the stags by sight. We try to collect their horns and mark their development. They cast their horns every year, you see, and grow new ones. Once Donald and I had a set of horns from the same beast three years running. It was about eight years old. The horns showed a distinct improvement, although the number of points remained the same."

Somehow it warmed Sue's heart to know that Meric wasn't just interested in the shooting, yet she couldn't stop herself asking, a hint of censoriousness in her voice. "How do you choose which stag to kill?"

He grinned again, without rancour. "Usually those with deformed horns, bad points. These are usually shot as they're not good to breed from. People sometimes refer to them as switches. Then there's another which we call a hummel—a beast without horns at all. Just hard, bony knobs where the horns should be, but he's usually big and heavy. All the same, we don't like the look of him."

"I thought it was always a Royal stag that people went after?"

"Not always," Meric shook his head. "We don't shoot very many of those, but a chap the other day got one, a perfect twelve-pointer, well worth mounting. It's gone to the taxidermist in Dundee. But there again, the guests from the hotel don't always want to shoot. Like you, many of them just want to look and learn."

Sue's eyes wavered and returned to the stag in the corrie. "It wasn't until we came out," she said, "that I knew I was to be given the opportunity, Mr. Findlay."

"Well, it's all part of the service," he mocked smoothly.

The tone of his voice aroused resentment, and she turned sharply, not thinking, and dislodged a small stone. The sound of it falling was barely audible to the human ear, yet the stag below them stopped suddenly and raised its head, listening. His shining brown body turned sideways as he sniffed the air. Then before they could move he gave one bound towards the burn, springing across it with one incredible leap to disappear in seconds around the bottom of the valley. The swiftness of his leaving was almost unbelievable, and left Sue gasping. Nothing else stirred in the silence. Meric stood up with abrupt grace, his kilt swinging. "Now you can understand," he teased, "why a lot of people never get near them."

Scrambling to her feet, Sue nodded, speechlessly. "I suppose I've been lucky," she agreed soberly.

"You could say that," he conceded. "You could also be grateful you were with such a good stalker."

She looked back at him mischievously from beneath her lashes. "I didn't think you were over-fond of gratitude, Mr. Findlay?"

She held his glittery, dark look. "If you call me Mr. Findlay again, you'll never know what hit you, girl!"

Her mouth quirked in a careless smile which disregarded the menace in his face. "You're full of dark threats today, aren't you? Most probably empty ones, but I don't scare easily."

His light teasing provoked, but she doubted whether his mind was really on what he was saying, or her light responses. He was a busy man and quite likely regarded her as a bit of a nuisance, someone he could treat casually while he concentrated subconsciously on his current problems. Someone like a younger sister. Her own mind rebelled unexplainable at her inability to make any indelible impression. Illogical though it seemed, Sue decided, with feminine perversity, that she didn't like being ignored. It might not be wise, in fact it could be quite insane, but the desire was there in spite of his threats to provoke him a little in return!

He hadn't replied to her last remark, as with an indifferent shrug he turned and made his way back down into the valley, leaving her to follow as best she could. With one last wistful look towards the place where the stag had disappeared Sue scrambled after him, sliding down the cliff face to land in an undignified heap at his feet.

"Well, that's one way of doing it!" His eyebrows shot up and his voice drawled sardonically, and he made no attempt to help her to her feet.

She gazed at him scornfully as she picked herself up. Her hands were scratched where she had tried unsuccessfully to retain a grip on the rock, and one leg hurt slightly, but that would be nothing to him! A few well chosen words beat in her brain and it took a great deal of effort to hold them in check. They would only bounce off his hard arrogance, she was sure of that. Even, now, as she dusted herself down, he was picking up his coat and looking at his watch.

"We'll have something to eat," he said, "then it will be time to get back. It's almost two o'clock and we've some way to go." With long strides he set off along the stony path. "There's a good spot up here," he told her over his shoulder. "I've used it before. It's more comfortable than perching on a rock."

Secretly intrigued, Sue trailed behind him up the burn, her movements freer now that the need for complete silence was past. As they went deeper into the small valley she found the isolation exciting. It might have been a private Shangri-la. They might have been explorers in some far off corner of the universe, trekking untrodden ground; the mountains of Tibet; the Great Wall of China. Vividly she allowed her imagination to run riot, through all the places she longed to see and probably never would. This place, she felt, was very old, sculptured in dramatic patterns by the elements, cut into jagged peaks and precipices by the sun and the rain and wind. A long, cold shiver ran down her spine as the thick isolation caught and held her, like a

demon lover refusing to let go. Here a person could be
lost for years before anyone might pass by. There must
surely be ground here where no human foot had ever
trod?

All too soon they came to the spot Meric had mentioned, a sheltered ring of boulders within the backdrop
of mountains, and within the boulders, flat rock covered with grass. Grass, burnt and dried at this time of
the year, but thick enough to provide some comfort in
an otherwise barren landscape.

Meric turned. "Will this do?" he asked, a slight
smile at the corner of his mouth as he handed her the
rucksack with the food.

Without waiting for her assent he placed his rifle
against the cliff. She noticed how he always took the
greatest care of it. Next he took off his waterproof
jacket, spreading it for a pillow before he lay down.
"Now serve the food, woman," he grunted as he
stretched out his legs.

For a moment Sue's eyes dwelt indignantly on the
whole long length of him, then, strangely submissive,
she did as she was told. She tried to convince herself it
was because he deserved it, not because he was so arrogant and good-looking that her heart could no longer
resist him. It seemed the most natural thing in the
world to work while he rested, to lay out the lunch Mrs.
Lennox had provided. On a flat piece of exposed rock
she put the ham sandwiches, the green apples, the
thick wedges of home-made fruit cake and cheese. The
flasks of coffee she put aside until the end of the meal,
but removing the screw tops she went to the stream
and scooped out two cups of the clear, sparkling water.
If they were having ambrosia, food of the gods, then
this surely would be nectar to go with it. Feeling enor-
mously pleased with herself , she carried it back to their
rocky table.

Meric opened his eyes as she sat down beside him,
propping himself up on one elbow as she passed him a
sandwich, noting her still damp cheeks which she had

rinsed before returning from the burn. His gaze lingered appreciatively on the matt bloom on her skin before dropping slowly to the feast she had spread out. "You'd make quite a good handmaiden," he said amiably. "In another age I might have purchased you."

"I suppose," Sue rejoined primly, "I should feel flattered. You would have haggled over me in a market place?"

"I might have been tempted."

"Provided the price wasn't too high?"

His eyes swept over her lazily, and her cheeks flushed at what he thought she read in his glance, something which smouldered there, causing a pulse to jerk in her throat. He laughed softly beneath his breath. "You said that, not I, sweet Sue. In a moment of weakness you might tempt a man not to consider the cost."

"But you would regret it later!" What foolishness made her persist with this inane conversation? It was like sliding down a precipice, once started one seemed unable to stop.

He continued to look at her, his expression sardonic. "That would depend on several things, wouldn't it? The price of some things, Sue, is far beyond their true value."

Quickly, to still a flicker of anger, she bit sharply into a green apple, crunching the white flesh with even white teeth. "You don't like women much, do you, Meric?"

His eyes glinted, mocking her patent innocence. "Of course I like women. You have a genius, Sue, for asking silly questions. Now, my opinion of them...? Well, that's another matter altogether. I suppose you refer to women in general?"

What did he mean? With an almost physical effort she drew her eyes away from his enigmatical face. She wasn't going to ask him to elaborate. It would be wiser, she knew it instinctively, to change the subject. She shrugged her slim shoulders, suppressing a small yawn, deliberately giving the impression of boredom as her hand went out to a flask to pour coffee. Her appetite had suddenly gone, she wasn't even thirsty any more, but it was something to do and might distract his attention from her hot cheeks.

"I have enjoyed myself today," she assured him, studiously polite as she measured brown sugar into his cup. She knew from experience that he took two spoonfuls. "The stag was wonderful... So is this place," she tacked on haphazardly, staring around her.

He raised his eyebrows at her delicately tinted face, making it understood he was aware that she had ignored his last question. "So much enthusiasm," he murmured indifferently. "I seem to have heard it all before."

Of course he had! Crossly Sue flung herself on her back on the hot grass some feet away from him, preferring not to look at him. Guests from the hotel—women like herself from the cities. Their exaggerated expressions of delight would waft unheard about his cynical ears. "It's known to be possible," she retorted stubbornly, "to fall in love with a place after only a short time."

Lazily he put down his cup which he emptied in one long draught. His voice was soft but ironic. "You're not cut out for places like this, Sue, You're sweet, and rather lovely, but don't try to fool yourself otherwise. Hothouse plants should stay in their proper environment, not seek to flourish where only the hardiest can survive."

"I came with you here today! I kept up over all that rough ground, and you dare say that!"

Taking no notice of her indignant gasp, Meric rose to his feet, carried both their cups to the burn and rinsed them out. "It's more like July than October," he remarked quite casually. "I've rarely known it so hot."

Watching him from beneath her thick lashes as she lay on her back, Sue curved a hand compulsively around a hard piece of rock. Why did he enjoy raising a fine anger within her, such a turmoil of emotions she could never hope to sort out? "You don't like me, do you?" she accused sharply. No sooner were the words out than she felt she had uttered them to him before.

"I don't think I do." Noiselessly he turned to drop down lightly on the ground beside her. "But liking needn't always enter into the relationship between a man and a woman, or don't you agree?" His eyes, clearly indicating his meaning, roved slowly over the curved outline of her young body. With an easy strength and without hurry, he pulled her into his arms, lying with her on the softly sensuous turf, one arm curved around her waist, the other beneath her head, his hand holding the fine bone of her shoulder.

A long time afterwards Sue wondered why she hadn't attempted to escape. Afterwards she blamed the heat which partly drugged her senses, and the atmosphere with its almost hypnotical silence. The feeling that Meric Findlay and she were quite alone in the world, and what was happening was a natural continuation of the pleasure she had experienced in the morning.

She did not stir, not wanting to after a long moment, yet subtly aware of the danger of staying where she was. But with easy strength he controlled her first tentative movement, his hand tightening on her shoulder, his chin pressing just a little more firmly on the top of her head.

"Be still," he ordered, his voice low, lazily indifferent, as he stretched his long legs out against her. "You told me before you were grateful!"

But that didn't mean ... ? Somehow, when she tried to speak, the words stuck in her throat. A curious inertia which she had felt before in his arms seemed to be taking over, rejecting any desire to protest. He was holding her gently, as if seeking to reassure her, almost as if she were one of the small animals of the forest which he held captive in his embrace. She said, because she felt she must, "Do you always exact payment in this fashion?"

He laughed deep in his throat. "I can't think of anything more gratifying."

She was silent, turning the word over in her mind, not liking the sound of it. She was aware that he could, if he wished, be utterly ruthless, that he was too dangerous to play with, and yet she didn't care. It could be an opinion that by appearing totally acquiescent she was inviting trouble, but the experimental rapport of just lying in Meric's arms seemed curiously irresistible. After all, it was just for a few minutes, it wasn't necessary to go any further. At twenty-one it was perhaps time she began to live a little more dangerously, to lose a little of her former inhibition. No man would want an inexperienced schoolgirl. If only, she thought, with a small despairing sigh, she had a few guidelines to go by!

Unexpectedly he raised himself on one elbow, traces of a question on his dark face as he looked down at her. "Why the sigh, sweet Sue? Are you wondering how you're going to cope?" The timbre of his voice was amused and sardonic, stiffening her diminishing resistance.

"I'm not wondering anything of the sort," she lied lightly. Attempting to substantiate her statement, she glanced directly into his eyes, a warm wave of air dancing between them, but her faint little smile never quite made it. Something in his expression made her tilt her face defiantly, and her smile faded as a dark wave of apprehension washed over her, as softly and very gently he lowered his lips to hers.

The touch of his lips was like fire going through her, but before she could free herself his hand slid under her hair and pinned the nape of her neck. Carefully the pressure of his mouth increased as his fingers moved back to her hair, raking through it slowly, gently smoothing the heavy silkiness of it from her forehead and ear. Her head seemed to swim at the warm crush of his mocking mouth on hers. As he drew her sensuously closer, his heavy body held hers to the heady scent of the crushed grass. Flushed and tormented, her fair head thrown back, she returned his exploring kisses with a kind of helpless hunger.

Something within her leapt crazily, jerking through her being, a whirlpool of emotion, striving for expression. Involuntarily her arms went up around his neck, her fingers threading through the dark thickness of his hair, as his hands went down to linger hard on her waist before going up under her blouse to rest, his fingers wide-spread over the soft skin on her back.

Then suddenly his mouth eased slowly from her own, just enough to allow her to draw one deep shuddering breath.

"Poor Sue," he murmured, his mouth trailing fire across her face, holding her to him as she tried to draw back, his lips dropping to the soft hollow in her throat. "And you thought you could cope!"

His words stung through the flame which threatened to consume her. His voice was low but as sardonic as before, as he mocked her inability to fight the wilfulness of her devastated emotions.

"I might, if you let me go," she gasped unsteadily. "If it wasn't for your brute strength . . ."

His eyes glittered as he dropped another kiss on her lips. "Must you always seek excuses, Sue? You'll be telling me next you have a built-in aversion to this sort of thing."

"Not exactly." Through a haziness of mind Sue thought it better to stick to halftruths. "It rather depends who I'm with."

"Tim Mason, for instance?" One of his hands left the warm flesh of her back and returned to her throat, encircling it forcibly. "I wonder—are you usually such a liar?"

"You don't believe me, then?" she asked, helpless under his infinitely exciting touch.

"The devil I do!" he muttered thickly, and drew her savagely to him again, this time parting her lips with the force of his own.

Regardless now of what he thought, Sue returned his

kisses eagerly, frightened yet revelling in the tide of feeling which was rising between them. Her body went soft and curiously boneless against his, and his hand moved across her back, gripping the bare skin, inflicting a fine pain which shot through to her breast, moving her lips in a wide little gasp under his own. Crushed against him, she clung to him feverishly, losing all awareness of everything but the needs of her pulsing, hungry body.

He could feel her trembling, and lifted his dark head fractionally, muttering against her lips, "Just how permissive were you in that college of yours, dear Sue?"

"It doesn't matter..." Through the thick drumming of her heart Sue heard herself answer, again diverting from the truth, filled with a crazy desire to stay in his arms. If she confessed her innocence, he wouldn't want her, and, in a moment of insanity she knew she wanted him, as she'd never wished for anything else in her life before!

"Sue!" For a long moment she imagined she was to get what she desired. As the closeness of their bodies became charged with tension, she tried to hide the torment in her eyes. All her life she had waited for this, a moment when she might let her mind sink beneath mounting sensation. And, as he roughly spoke her name and his mouth hardened on hers again, her doubts faded against a wave of feeling so intense that she had no wish to fight it.

"Darling," she whispered, beneath her breath, but the soft sound she made must have reached him. In an instant he lifted his head, seeming to retreat from her as with one fluid movement he rose to his feet.

Quickly he pulled her up with him, still holding her, but lightly, waiting until she recovered some form of balance. His voice came, faintly indulgent if very dry. "What did you expect this time, sweet Sue?"

Transfixed and blazing blue, her eyes fastened on him, all the turmoil inside her reflected in the colour which flared across her white face. "I hate you!" she cried, attempting furiously to defy him, truly hating his male arrogance, even while she longed to be back in his arms.

"No, you don't." Remorselessly his fingers bit into her arm, keeping her still. "But you might do if we stayed here longer. Grow up a little, for God's sake, Sue!"

Her slight figure seemed to droop on his arm. "I don't think this conversation is doing either of us any good." Her voice came low, tinged with strain and a gathering bewilderment.

Meric's mouth quirked, but his smile held no mirth. "You would never have forgiven me, Sue. You might even have said that I deliberately tried to compromise you in order to get the estate, that I was trying to keep the heiress chained to my side."

His lips, which had been so gently persuasive just a few minutes ago, tightened as she stared at him, and he felt her body stiffen. "You can't be serious?" she choked.

For a brief space of time something in her face seemed to hold him oddly, then with a grin he said suavely, shattering still further all her preconceived little notions, "I suppose we're really a couple of fools, Sue, and neither of us too pleased with the other. I certainly didn't mean to hurt you intentionally—but let it pass. Nothing will have changed come the morning. In any case, we must get going if we hope to make Glenroden before dark. I don't think you'd really enjoy spending the night with me out here!"

Feeling distinctly chilled, she followed him along the burn, on to the rough downhill track where she had almost to run to keep up with his loose-limbed stride. Unhappily she stared at his broad back, scarcely aware of where she was walking. Never could she remember feeling so deflated. On the mountain, protected in Meric's arms against the elements, she hadn't cared at all about getting back to Glenroden, but now all she felt she wanted was somewhere to hide her head. She could

only feel grateful that at least he didn't know how
much his rejection hurt.

The Range-Rover was waiting for them as they
reached the lower ground again. To her surprise, after
putting their gear in the back, Meric actually came
around and opened the door for her to help her in. With
one foot on the step she turned swiftly to look at him.
Tall and rugged as the country around them, he was
handsome in a compelling sort of way—his quick observant eyes, his firm mouth and determined-looking jaw,
his hair, thick and vital and very dark. She knew in that
instant that she loved him and quickly she lowered her
heavy lashes, that he shouldn't, with his keen perception, read what must surely lie behind them. If nothing
else it brought a grain of comfort that her behaviour in
the corrie hadn't been completely wanton. That it had
been evoked by an emotion as old as Eve, stronger than
one inexperienced girl. But momentarily stunned by the
knowledge of her own involvement, she remained quite
still. There was no way in which she could possibly tell
him, so she must be prepared that he should think the
worst. Maybe better this than he should know the truth,
and be amused by it?

"A penny for them, Sue?" He was waiting to close
the door, his brows raised sardonically but his eyes curious.

"Not for sale," she managed to reply briefly, a faint
smile touching her curved lips which still felt bruised
from the pressure of his.

"From the expression on your face," he said, "I
thought they might be interesting."

"I suppose I was day-dreaming," she admitted.
"Anyway, it wasn't important."

To her surprise he suddenly grinned, his eyes alight
with laughter, but for once his laughter sounded kind.

"Maybe tomorrow I'll ask you to be more explicit,
Sue. But right now we must get a move on or John will
be worrying. And he did trust me to look after you
safely," he pointed out amiably.

So amiably that Sue's heart gave a small lurch in her breast. He was in good spirits over something and not troubling to hide it. Maybe—the thought was fleeting, but it brought her gaze back to his face—maybe after all he did like her a little? There seemed to be a promise in his laughter about which she dared not begin to think. Instead she nodded cautiously, but made no comment as he gently closed the door and climbed in beside her.

It was getting dark as they reached home, the colour fading from the west, but as they passed the loch there was still a flare of red across the water against the darkening sky. There seemed a strange savagery about the land bathed in this half-light which made Sue shudder in spite of the warmth of her thoughts. Autumn was a nostalgic time of year in the country, when the heather was fading and the leaves turning colour. In the whispering morning mists and the shadowed clouds across the hills there was sadness, a brooding, a feeling of finality as the season drew to a close. Unpredictably she felt hot tears stinging the back of her eyelids, tensing her throat, until it was almost with a cry of relief that she saw they were back at Glenroden.

"I'll go straight in and see Father," she said quickly as they left the Range-Rover. "He's probably been lonely without us."

But in thinking this she was wrong, and afterwards she wished fervently that their homecoming could have been different.

Mrs. Lennox met them at the door, or near it, as she was just coming down the great oak staircase. "Oh, it's glad I am to see you back," she cried rather nervously. "You have a visitor, Susan, a Mr. Mason, and I wasn't quite sure what to do with him."

Behind her Sue felt the rigidness of Meric's hand which had been resting lightly on her waist as he walked with her to the house. It had been nothing, she assured herself, but a friendly gesture, but from it she had derived great comfort, an indefinable sense of happiness.

Now, for a split second, as his fingers bit into the curve of
her hip, she sensed his anger and restraint.

His hand dropped sharply and she felt bereft. Tim
couldn't surely be here? And yet he must be, as Mrs.
Lennox was adding quickly, "He came early after
lunch and seemed quite put out that you weren't here,
Susan. However, your father and he have been getting
on like a house on fire, talking their heads off all afternoon. I've prepared a room. I've just shown Mr. Mason
up, as a matter of fact. He'll be staying of course. At
least Mr. Frazer said he thought so."

"Of course," Meric was nodding smoothly by her
side. "Susan's boy-friend is very welcome. I hope you
made that clear, Mrs. Lennox?"

As he spoke dismay flooded through Sue, tightening
the nerves of her stomach, fading the pink glow of her
cheeks. It was no use suggesting there had been a
mistake, that it might not be Tim, when instinctively
she knew it could be no one else. But why, why had he
come all the way to Glenroden? At this moment he
was the last person on earth she wanted to see. Carefully, aware of the pregnant silence, she moistened dry
lips before asking Mrs. Lennox, "Did he say why he's
here? What he wanted?" which sounded ungracious
and slightly stupid, and which would have been better
left unsaid. Only something in Meric's face as he stood
regarding her grimly prompted her to indiscretion.

Before Mrs. Lennox could reply he murmured ironically, "You shouldn't ask foolish questions, Sue.
Obviously the fellow couldn't wait, and I repeat, he's
welcome to stay a few days if he feels like it. In fact,"
his eyes narrowed consideringly, "it might not be such
a bad idea, providing he behaves himself."

The arrogance in his tone stung Sue as she gazed up
at him. He was like a stranger, not the man who had
held her in his arms on the wild mountainside, who had
given the impression on the way home that their relationship had moved subtly to a different level. Now she
could only stare at him with a leaden heart as involun-

tarily she tried to excuse Tim's behaviour. "Tim probably had a spell of leave due and thought he'd surprise me. He wouldn't realize that it mightn't be convenient."

Mrs. Lennox interrupted, glancing quickly from one to the other. "It's no inconvenience, Susan, so don't let that worry you. If Mr. Findlay doesn't mind, I'm sure we'll never notice the extra work."

"It need not concern Mr. Findlay!" Again words ripped indiscreetly off Sue's tongue. It wasn't what she'd meant to say at all.

"Sue!" Meric's brief exclamation hit her sharply as, confused, she turned to go. Startled, she looked back at his face, noting that he seemed to go white beneath his tan. She was also aware that but for Mrs. Lennox's presence he might have lost his temper. Instead he pushed derisively past her, striding to the far side of the hall. Over his shoulder he said tautly, "Another time you feel like entertaining, please let us know beforehand. If only for your father's sake," he added, as if under compulsion.

But it seemed that Tim's visit to Glenroden didn't have an adverse effect. At least, not on John Frazer. John, in fact, seemed to enjoy his company, and the two men often talked or just sat together for long periods. Sue realized with a pang that their friendship, though in some ways surprising, had developed easily. There were none of the somewhat forced attempts to find something more permanent than a friendly camaraderie, none of the sometimes uncomfortable straining after a deeper, more lasting relationship which plagued Sue's own daily contact with her father. As Meric had pointed out, it was maybe because they were both too impatient, but, apart from their shared pleasure over John's book, nothing seemed to be changing very rapidly. Hearing John talking and laughing so easily with Tim seemed to emphasize her unspoken doubts—that the gap caused by the missing years was too wide ever to properly bridge. And unless something changed she could never feel a genuine daughter of the household, or be willing to accept any part of Glenroden should anything happen to John.

Tim, however, was plagued by no such doubts. Like her father he seemed continually amazed by her likeness to the Frazers, and never missed an opportunity of noting this aloud. Like her father, when she had first come, he never seemed to tire of arranging her in front of one of the many family paintings, or of contriving to go with her through the heavy family albums of Frazer photographs, pointing out how in both figure and face she resembled them closely.

"There's no doubt about it, Susan," he exclaimed, on his third morning at Glenroden, as they stood together in the drawing room, held there, unwilling prisoners by the wind and rain outside. "It's quite clear to see that you're a Frazer all right! It was a good move when I allowed you to come here. Anyway, John has been telling me his solicitor had verified it through and through, so there can be no mistake. Just look at your grandmother's picture. There's no question about it at all!"

Rather blindly Sue stared up into her grandmother's face, wondering if she imagined a slightly enigmatic smile. Tim did go on so! Half-heartedly she nodded and shrugged. Why should she feel a twinge of resentment that Tim should call her father by his first name so easily? Her father preferred it, she knew, but Tim might have desisted for a little while. She also knew a twinge of resentment that he should have so easily gained John's confidence. Already after only two days, Tim seemed in possession of more facts concerning Glenroden than she herself was after all this time? Already, too, John seemed to have the impression that she and Tim were to be married, and try as she might he appeared to think that her protests just amounted to a schoolgirlish embarrassment.

"I know you're right, Tim," she answered, a trifle impatiently, "but please don't go on about it! You never let us forget a minute, and it gets a bit tiresome, don't you think? It's as if you're trying too hard to convince somebody."

"That manager chap, for instance?" Tim's face grew sullenly determined. "I rather think I could put him in his place if I were here long enough."

"But you've only two weeks...At least, that is what you said?" Sue's brow creased anxiously. "And I'm not really sure of Meric's position..."

"Then it's time someone was!" Tim's voice held an oddly threatening note, and Sue's breath caught in her throat. Unaccountably she felt a little shiver of fear. The face Tim turned to her seemed still with determination.

"Please," she whispered , staring at him as she tried to marshal her thoughts. His attitude filled her with a growing apprehension, making it impossible to deny that since he came she had been unable to relax. Again and again she found herself wishing he hadn't been here at all. This late holiday which he hadn't expected to collect owing to the pressure of work was, so far as she was concerned, turning out to be a fiasco. As she had guessed, he had intended surprising her by arriving unannounced, and had obviously not even noticed her lukewarm welcome. He had been much too busy making himself pleasant to John and Mrs. Lennox. Meric he treated coolly, with the offhand politeness of an important visitor towards a lower member of the staff, and at times Sue found herself cringing helplessly at the tone of voice he employed.

"Well—please what?" Tim prompted impatiently as she hesitated.

With a start she pulled herself together. "What I meant to say, Tim, is that you mustn't start interfering. Meric Findlay, in many ways, is indispensable. You haven't had much time to realize this, but do try to remember in the future. My father wouldn't be very pleased if you did anything to upset him."

"So..." Tim's eyes narrowed suspiciously on her

flushed face, and she noticed with confusion that he seemed relatively unimpressed. "I'm beginning to wonder," he went on shrewdly, "who would be the most upset! But don't get all hot and bothered, Susan. I'm only trying to look after your interests."

"I haven't," she retorted, her chin tilting indignantly, "any interests to look after, Tim. So please don't..."

"Don't what...?" he mimicked suavely. "Don't upset the great Meric Findlay, you mean? Are you scared of him, Susan, or what? It seems to me," his eyes gleamed suddenly beneath his sandy lashes, "that you're almighty anxious to keep on the right side of him!"

"Just because we couldn't run Glenroden without him!" Sue insisted. "Of course I'm not scared of him! You get such ridiculous ideas, Tim. I rarely see the man." Which wasn't so far from the truth, she thought miserably. Meric had scarcely been near her, other than at mealtimes, at which he now chose to appear regularly. But for the most part he seemed to ignore her, apart from the barest of civilities—a state of affairs which might only have coincided with Tim's arrival, having more to do with the incident on the mountain. Anything Tim might say or do obviously couldn't make things worse as far as she was concerned, but for John's sake she must try to retain the modicum of politeness he still showed towards her.

Preoccupied, she watched Tim moving thoughtfully around the room, examining closely the fine paintings, the valuable objets d'art which filled the antique cabinets and decorated the mantelshelf of the beautiful Adam fireplace.

"There are other men," he said sharply, "who would be quite capable of running an estate like Glenroden. Once we're married, Susan, I shall probably see about getting someone more congenial."

"I'm sure you would!" Furiously, her voice laced

with sudden sarcasm, Sue spun away from him, only to suppress a startled gasp as she heard a small noise in the doorway. Carlotte Craig was standing there gazing at them.

CHAPTER NINE

How long had Carlotte been standing there? Sue, the
pink in her cheeks deepening to red, put a hasty hand
to her face in a futile attempt to hide her embarrassment. Carlotte, however, was smiling quite gaily, and
gave no indication that she had overheard anything,
but with Carlotte one could never be quite sure. Sue
could only hope fervently that she had only arrived in
that second.

"Aren't you going to introduce me to your friend?"
With raised brows, Carlotte obviously waited, her
glance going past Sue to rest curiously on Tim's equally
speculative face.

Somehow Sue managed to perform the small ceremony with dignity, but her mind was anything but cool
as she watched Tim shake Carlotte's hand, his face full
of expansive cordiality. Her thoughts flew angrily back
to what he had been saying when Carlotte arrived. How
dare he put her in such a spot, assuming so loudly that
she was willing and eager to marry him? Why, oh, why
hadn't she said definitely no in London, instead of not
taking him seriously? The sooner she straightened
things out the better, but it was scarcely possible to do
so in front of another person.

Uneasily she realized Carlotte was probing blatantly,
her brilliant smile covering a determination to discover
Tim's exact status. "You're Susan's boy-friend from
London, I suppose? I didn't quite catch what she said."

"Well, you could say that," Tim answered, before
Sue could speak. "Actually I'm rather hoping to be
something more, but there's nothing official at the moment, you understand?"

"Of course," Carlotte agreed smoothly. Obviously, by the way her smile widened, the news suited her more than a little. "I've just returned from London myself," she confided with a charming grimace. "I must confess to feeling rather flat, but this spot of romance has cheered me up considerably. Have you and Susan known each other long?"

"Oh, yes," Tim was not reluctant. "We've known each other a long time. I looked after Susan and her mother, you might say. We lived near each other, and her mother was always glad of my advice."

When she gets Tim alone Sue thought desperately, she'll be asking all sorts of questions. Yet how could she do anything to avert it when there wasn't really anything particular to hide? Tim's only fault was perhaps that he was too impulsive, that he had construed a situation incorrectly. It had nothing to do with his basically generous self. It was probably more her fault than his that he was here. She had been mistaken in thinking that once out of sight he would automatically forget her. And now that he was here how could she possibly ask him to go?

Confused, she brushed a strand of hair back from her hot brow. Carlotte was still smiling, apparently well pleased with herself. Instinctively, in spite of her friendly demeanour, Sue distrusted that smile, and her uneasiness increased as Carlotte suggested blandly:

"We must all get together one evening and go down to the hotel. Meric will know the best night to go. Perhaps we might have something official to celebrate by then. You never know!"

What did she mean? Sue blinked, her eyes wide and startled as dismay flooded her heart. Was she hinting, not perhaps at Tim, but at some relationship between Meric and herself? "I'll keep it in mind," she replied cautiously, trying to appear gracious. "It will all depend how John is."

"And that reminds me," Carlotte nodded her head

agreeably, "it was John whom I really came to see. How is he?"

On safer ground, Sue found herself assuring her that her father was fairly well. "He was talking to Meric a short while ago," she said, not thinking.

"Oh, good!" Satisfied with the news, Carlotte turned to go, a smug smile on her dark red lips. "I've arranged to go with Meric to Perth this morning," she explained. "He's going to a livestock sale. I'm returning with him this evening and staying to dinner, so I'll see you both then."

With a light lift of one hand she was gone, leaving them both staring silently after her.

Tim was the first to find his tongue. "At least she appears to be a girl with a head on her shoulders," he spoke appreciatively as they heard her opening and closing John's door a little further along the hall. "Certainly she seems to know what side her bread's buttered on—or is she just busy buttering it?" he joked rudely.

"Tim! I wish you wouldn't talk like that," Sue pleaded stiffly, not knowing how much more of it she could stand. Her head ached. "I'm sure Carlotte has no ulterior motives. She just pays friendly visits. Actually," she added, "she helps to run the caravan park in summer, so we see quite a bit of her."

"Caravan park?" Tim's official ears pricked. "Whose is the caravan park, might I ask?"

"Not if you use that tone of voice you may not," Sue retorted coldly. "It's on the estate, so I suppose it's ours, but it's all legal and above board, with a proper office and facilities and that sort of thing. So you needn't be suspicious!"

"Susan, do be quiet," he interrupted sharply, looking slightly affronted. "I wasn't even hinting at such a thing. I only intended pointing out that a caravan site can be a real asset as well as a lucrative means of profit if properly run, as you say this one is."

Restively Sue glanced at him, a tiny frown between

her winged brows, wondering, not for the first time, why she couldn't think faster. Tim saw things which never occurred to an ordinary individual. With him it was second nature, something which made him good at his job, and quick to gain promotion. But to Sue, who usually accepted things on face value, it wasn't so easy to delve beneath the surface.

"On a place like this," she said at last, "one thing usually balances another. The caravan park and other enterprises, such as deer-stalking, must help subsidize the lack of profit from other parts of the land."

"Deer-stalking, too?" Tim looked up quickly from his examination of a small Canton enamel dish. "It seems to me, Susan, that you could be heir to quite a property, one way and another. Have you ever been right around the estate? Have you any idea what size it is?"

Mutely Sue shook her head, wishing distractedly she could find the courage to tell Tim to mind his own business. Yet it might be foolish to allow him to disturb her so deeply. But how to shut him up without being rude? Perhaps the wisest way to divert him would be to use a little diplomacy?

"I have been deer-stalking," she said listlessly, "Remember, I was out with Meric on the day you arrived."

Tim leaned forward. "Doesn't it seem strange that this was the first time you'd been out on the estate, in two months?"

"Not really." Sue moved away from him, hoping he hadn't noticed the uncertainty in her eyes. Not easily could she confess to thinking the same thing herself. His questions echoed too closely her own doubts. Helplessly she tried to push them aside. "You see, Tim, Father is far from well, and I don't want to do anything to upset him—or Meric Findlay."

"Upset?" Out of sympathy, Tim stuttered crossly, "I can understand about your father. Actually, I like him a lot, old girl. But, regarding Meric Findlay, it's up to you to assert yourself a little, or you'll be trodden into the dust!'' Taking no notice of her small protesting gasp, he continued, ''Didn't your cousin Carlotte say that she and dear Findlay are off to Perth for the day? Well, while they're away, how about you and me having a look around? Just see if you can get hold of a map, John must have one somewhere, and I'll do the rest. It's amazing what can be ferreted out with the aid of a good map and a little ingenuity.''

''But, Tim...'' Not liking his tone, Sue glanced back at him, startled. ''I shouldn't feel happy doing all this behind Father's back, so to speak.''

''But we're not doing any harm, and no one need know, if it will make you feel any better,'' Tim argued. ''Besides, if the others are out enjoying themselves, why shouldn't you?''

Tim was goading her deliberately, Sue realized this. But when she reluctantly agreed to do as he suggested, it had nothing to do with the motive he had uppermost in mind. It was the thought of Meric and Carlotte spending the day together that prompted her to give her assent. She knew, in a moment of truth, that she couldn't bear to be here brooding about them until they returned. And, as Tim said, there could surely be no harm in exploring the estate. When one thought about it rationally, perhaps he was right. She should have been taken around sooner.

In the end, however, it wasn't altogether easy to approach her father, especially when she found it impossible to be completely frank. ''I would just like to show Tim the district,'' she told him, when she went to his room. ''I was wondering if you had a map of the area. Perhaps one showing the boundaries of Glenroden, just so I can point them out?''

A curious expression flitted across John's tired face as he eased himself up in his bed. It wasn't one of his good days. Carlotte, he said, had wearied him with her chatter, and he didn't seem disposed to talk any more. Sensitive to his moods, Sue decided that if nothing else, it would be a good thing to take Tim away for a little while—while John rested. It was obvious, though, that he didn't seem very pleased by her request for a map, and she wondered if he would rather she stayed by his side. But he refuted the idea when she put her doubts into words, although he still didn't appear very happy about her previous suggestion.

"You'd have been better," he said testily, "to have gone with Carlotte to Perth. There would have been more of interest to you there. I think Meric has most of the maps in the office, but if you look in the top drawer of that cabinet over there you might find a small one."

"I could always get one from the office, I suppose," Sue looked at the map dubiously when she found it. It was faded and somewhat tattered, and she could see at a glance that it wouldn't be much help.

"No, don't do that!" Her father surprised her by speaking quite sharply. Don't ever go there, Susan, without asking Meric first, I mean," he added oddly hesitant, "I wouldn't like you disturbing anything and perhaps giving him extra work."

"No, of course not," Sue, her eyes anxiously on his pale face, thought it better not to argue. "I won't go near the office, but if you could just point out the boundaries on this, then we'll be off. The rain has stopped, I can see."

John, however, had turned away from her on to his side as if he couldn't be bothered. "Just go, Susan, please. There are plenty of places you can visit without getting lost. Meric took you up the mountain, but I wouldn't advise you going there today. If you were to get lost you'd soon find that Tim Mason is no Meric Findlay," he finished enigmatically.

Feeling slightly hurt, Sue departed. Why was her father always so reluctant to explain anything about Glenroden? It wasn't as if she was ever very curious or probed, but if it was mortgaged up to the hilt, or something equally disastrous, he had only to tell her. Many estates went through bad times; it was nothing to be ashamed of. If it was something like this, at least it would squash her niggling suspicions that his secrecy had something to do with Meric. A transitory wave of self-pity smote her, as she went to collect her coat. Why couldn't John consider her position more? It wasn't easy when her heart refused to believe that Meric could do anything wrong, but her common sense told her otherwise.

"We'll take the Mini," she told Tim. "I still have it as one day I intend to get a job and will need it. The car, I mean," she tacked on hastily. She didn't intend telling him that she needed a job rather desperately for some spare cash. He would only laugh.

Tim, fortunately, was too busy perusing the map to pay much attention to what she was saying. She doubted if he had even heard. To her surprise he was smiling in an altogether satisfied manner. Apparently, to him, the age and shabbiness of the map was no deterrent. "You ought to be keeping your eye on this little lot," he exclaimed, tapping the faded lines with one finger, "and not worrying about a job! As far as I can see your father owns a huge stretch of territory. No wonder Mr. Findlay doesn't want you to know."

"Tim, please!" In her agitation Sue changed gear too quickly on a corner, jerking them forward in their seats. "I'm sorry," she muttered through Tim's warning shout. "But please don't agitate me any more. If you insist on going on about Meric, then I'm going home!"

"Okay, calm down," Tim's eyebrows rose unrepentantly. "You know your mother relied on me to look after your interests. I'm only trying to point out one or two things, as I did before. It isn't impossible, nor would it be the first time, that a man in your father's state of health has been taken advantage of."

Sue remained mutinously silent. It was bad enough thinking things herself without having him put them into words. They were passing the river ford on their way to the lock, and Tim insisted on getting out at the caravan park.

"Just for a quick look," he said, ignoring her glum

face with a smooth smile. "I might even come here on holiday myself." He ran an expert eye across the near row of vans. Wincing, Sue watched him wandering about, her gaze straying behind him to the loch where the light wind blew ripples across the deep water. Where larch and pine flanked the white-sanded shore and the sky hung cloudless above it. Now that the rain had gone, the clearing skies would bring frost, a first taste of winter, and Sue shivered. What was winter like in the Highlands? she wondered. In her mind's eye she saw the long, dark evenings, the cosy log fires, the isolation which must surely be part of winter in these parts. Her own position at Glenroden might be obscure, but such a picture more than made up for any feelings of insecurity. Winter here meant Meric and John, and Mrs. Lennox. She refused to think about Carlotte—and Tim would be gone.

When Tim returned from his tour of the caravans he seemed in excellent spirits and for the rest of the day remained in a good mood. Afterwards Sue was never quite sure how far they went. Tim, to her surprise, proved a first-class map reader, seemingly quite capable of guiding her through the wildest of places. If it hadn't been for the faint, unexplainable uneasiness at the back of her mind she might almost have enjoyed herself.

At one place the road, no more than a rough track, went up through a sort of rocky canyon, running close to the edge of a deep ravine where they seemed to cling precariously to the cliff wall, and as they looked back they could see nothing but the tops of firs and the gleam of bright water far below.

"You'd better keep your eyes on the road," Tim remarked dryly, as Sue caught her breath. "We should be nearly at the top, but I want to get there, not to the bottom again!"

On top the view proved well worth the perilous journey.

Beyond the loch, beyond the ridges, the background

of mountains looked across at them, magnificent against the skyline. After careful consideration Sue decided she could see the mountain which she and Meric had climbed after the stag.

She told Tim about it. "It really was a wonderful experience," she said, and wondered why he gave her a funny look.

They walked back to the car which they'd left on the track. "Just a little further on," said Tim, putting a friendly arm about her shoulders, "we dip back down to the main road, then back to Glenroden. Are you satisfied with your day today?"

"Umm." Not paying much attention, Sue glanced at him uncertainly. It seemed rather an odd way of putting it, but she supposed she was. "I've enjoyed the run around, if that's what you mean," she found herself saying. "And I should never have managed it myself."

"This is what I've been trying to tell you," he declared with emphasis. "I know we don't see eye to eye about many things, but at least allow me to guide you in some. I don't want to see you hurt."

She gazed back at him blankly. "Hurt?" she repeated.

"Oh, never mind. It doesn't matter!" Appearing completely exasperated by her lack of co-operation, he slammed the car door. "Sometimes I wonder, Susan, if you're being deliberately obtuse. It doesn't do to place too much trust in the wrong person."

"Well, that's plain common sense, of course, and I've surely got enough of that?" Sue tried to keep the conversation in a lighter vein, but wasn't sure she had succeeded when he asked abruptly:

"Has John always been ill?"

Unprepared for his question, Sue replied with some confusion. "Yes. At least I think so, for these last few years at any rate. That's what Doctor McRoberts told me. When I first arrived he'd hurt his ankle—Father, I mean, and that very same night he had a bad heart attack. He hasn't really properly recovered since. Doctor

McRoberts did say that the ankle and my turning up unexpectedly might have been culminating factors."

"This Doctor McRoberts doesn't beat about the bush."

"I know, Tim, but I did ask him, and he gave me an honest answer. It wasn't any use avoiding the issue anyway. I knew it was partly my fault. This is why I mustn't be the cause of any further upset. It's important to me that Father doesn't suffer any more on my account."

"Enough said..." Tim shrugged impatiently. "You always did make a habit of blaming yourself for everything! I should have thought, regarding the circumstances, that you'd find it easier to settle down if you had everything cut and dried."

"In what way?" Sue's own voice was ringed with impatience.

"Well, if I were you, I should make one definite attempt to regularize the situation without worrying John. There must be an agreement somewhere concerning Meric Findlay, possibly in the office, not even tucked out of sight. If you could find it, then you might know exactly how things stood. This estate is large, and I think with your father so ill you ought to feel some responsibility."

Meric had rung while they were away. Mrs. Lennox had answered the telephone, and he had told her that Carlotte and he were staying in Perth to dine with friends. The same friends would run him home afterwards.

"It would save Miss Craig a journey," Mrs. Lennox quoted. "Fortunately," she added, "I hadn't started to prepare anything, but then Mr. Findlay is always very considerate."

He isn't always, Sue muttered, half aloud, as she went upstairs to bed. After a light supper she had decided to have an early night, and had left Tim listening to the radio. There was no television at Glenroden. Meric made love to her, then scarcely spoke for days. He roused her feelings so that she couldn't rest, and expected her to continue as if nothing had happened. So far as he was concerned probably nothing had! Men! She shrugged, with the careless lift of her shoulders attempting to hide an aching heart. How foolish she had been to imagine she could spend the winter at Glenroden. She would never survive! She must remember to ask Carlotte if she had heard anything more about the teaching vacancy she had mentioned. It might be necessary to get away sooner than she had thought.

A few days later Meric surprised her by announcing at breakfast that he had booked a table for four, for the following evening. "There's a hotel near Pitlochry," he said, unsmilingly, "which I think you might enjoy. Usually on a Saturday evening there's entertainment of a sort thrown in."

Tim perked up immediately, almost prepared to be civil. "It will make a change," he agreed. "Susan and I would like to go."

Although Meric had addressed her, Tim obviously took it for granted that he was included in the invitation. In spite of a twinge of irritation at the way in which he included her in his answer, Sue couldn't suppress a small smile as she watched him attack his bacon and eggs with renewed zest. The anticipated pleasure of an evening out had cheered him. He might not realize it yet, but the pace of life at Glenroden was, for him, too slow. In time the quietness would only bore him. Unlike herself he was more suited to life in a big, bustling city.

On the evening of the outing Carlotte arrived late, and it was after six before they started out for Pitlochry. The autumn light was beginning to fade, but even so Sue enjoyed the change of scenery. She was surprised to find how quickly they arrived at the famous resort which lay in the beautifully wooded valley of the Tummel. To the east, Meric pointed out the mountains, faint shadows through the gathering darkness, and in the middle of the town the famous Clunie dam, part of the hydro-electric scheme with its fish-pass and observation chambers.

"You must take Tim before he returns to London and show him around," he said smoothly, as they continued on through the town. "You'll find more of interest there than you did on your tour of Glenroden."

So he knew? Dismayed, Sue stared at the back of his strong dark head. Neither Tim nor she had mentioned where they had been, nor had they seen anyone who might have told him. When she had returned the map John hadn't even asked if they had had a good day. With a faint tinge of colour to her cheeks she tried to imagine how Meric could have found out. Was there anything going on at Glenroden which he didn't eventually hear about?

Carlotte broke the uneasy silence with a laugh, but she only managed to make things worse by saying, "Are you returning for Christmas, Mr. Mason? I'm sure you would have fun, and Susan is going to be very lonely when you go back."

Whatever Tim might have replied was lost as Meric swung abruptly through a pair of tall, wrought iron gates, jerking the car to a sudden stop in front of a large, imposing-looking hotel. "It stays open all year round," he told them, as if anticipating Sue's query. "But during winter months they rely quite a bit on local trade." He opened the car door and got out. "Come on in," he said.

Nothing loath, they allowed him to pilot them indoors. Carlotte and Sue went to leave their cloaks in the ladies' room before joining the two men in the cocktail bar. Again Sue thought how splendid Meric looked in the kilt. He had a breadth of shoulder and height which made every other man in the room insignificant. Beside him she didn't notice Tim at all.

As they were late they carried their drinks to the dining-room. Sue sipped hers as she gazed around. It was a beautiful room with a tartan carpet and long wide windows, which during the daytime and the long summer evenings must provide wonderful views of the Scottish countryside.

She sat beside Tim, but Meric sat on her right and all through the varied, well-cooked meal she was aware of him—aware of him, it seemed, with every part of her being. Time and again her eyes were drawn to his darkly handsome face as if held there against her will. She had worn her black skirt, still all she had with her, but with it this time a soft clinging top of matching silk jersey with long sleeves and a low, rounded neckline which showed the pure, graceful lines of her throat and shoulders. Her heavy fair hair she had brushed until it clouded around her shoulders, spilling across her cheeks, giving her an occasional line of retreat.

Meric thought she looked attractive. She could see it in the appreciative gleam in his eyes as they rested on her slim figure, but he didn't say so in so many words. Somehow she ached that he should. Tim had no such inhibitions, yet his openly expressed admiration proved no balm for her sore heart.

After dinner they went into the ballroom and had coffee at one of the small tables arranged around the dance floor. A piper came in dressed in full Highland costume, and an impromptu concert was followed by dancing to a small Highland band. Later Sue found herself circling the room in Meric's arms.

"It's good of you to condescend to dance with me, Miss Frazer," he murmured. "I wonder that you trust your toes to a clumsy chap like me?"

"Don't apologize, Mr. Findlay," she smiled, in the same vein. "If you tread on my toes I shall no doubt find some means of retaliation, you may be sure."

"Don't you always?" he retorted suavely, glancing keenly down at her. "Is Tim Mason your latest form of retaliation?"

"Tim?" Her feet stumbled and she almost fell against him. "How could he be?"

"Well, he certainly doesn't exert himself to please me." Meric's hold tightened with slight cruelty on her

waist as he swung her around, and his voice grew
cooler. "I might last out over the week-end, but I
couldn't guarantee my temper much longer than that."

Sue flushed, whether with dismay or annoyance she
couldn't say. Perhaps it was a mixture of both. "He's
due to leave on Monday or Tuesday," she replied stiffly.

"Just so long as he doesn't extend his visit," he said
dryly, "Or that you ask him back."

"You've not exactly gone out of your way to make
him welcome," she said sharply, stung to open rebellion by his derisive tone. "What about your famous
Highland hospitality?"

"It isn't always extended without discrimination.
Not everyone is greeted with open arms."

"But you can't slay people with a claymore these
days just because you don't like them!"

"True." His eyes glinting beneath raised brows
brought a flare of colour to her cheeks. "Words are
about the only weapons left to us, but we have been
known, even in this day and age, to use something
stronger."

Sue shivered slightly as his eyes slewed over her.
Was he referring to their deer-stalking trip to the
mountains? The thought of that day tinged her next
words with an unintended hint of desperation. "I can't
imagine Tim will want to come back, even if you were
to ask him!"

"Don't worry, I won't." The glint in his eyes hardened, confirming that he misconstrued her reaction.
"He's no good to you, Sue. He's not your type at all
with his mealy-mouthed ways. And the sooner you forget about him the better."

"Why, you . . ." Quickly furious, Sue tried to escape
from his arms. She hadn't a great deal of enthusiasm
for Tim herself. From the time he had first called on
her mother, a pleasant young man from the Tax Office
obligingly leaving some forms on his way home, he had
become more of a habit. But, she assured herself, if

nothing else, she owed him a little loyalty. "If I wanted to ask him, or any of my friends, to Glenroden, you couldn't stop me," she gasped.

"Just try me and see!" Meric's grin was wholly mocking as he pulled her closer, stilling her struggles as the lights faded low for the end of the waltz. She felt herself slump against him, completely without defenses as his breath quickened in her ear. "I should enjoy a fight with you, sweet Sue, and I know who would be the victor."

When the lights went up again with the close of the waltz, she left him, retiring blindly to her seat, aware that he followed at a more leisurely pace. Tim she found deep in conversation with Carlotte, who had her hand on his arm, obviously giving him her whole attention. Uneasily Sue remembered thinking Carlotte would not be above questioning Tim if she got the opportunity, and she had little doubt what those questions would be about. Carlotte had been told little except that Sue's parents had been separated, but Sue imagined her curiosity knew no bounds.

"You don't seem to have enjoyed that very much." Leaving Tim, Carlotte rose to her feet, a mocking lilt to her voice as her eyes went from Sue's flushed face to where Meric lingered a few yards behind, exchanging a word with another man. "You seem to be running away."

"I didn't run away," Sue drew a deep breath , adding with daring indifference, "You do like to give the wrong impression."

"It was you who was giving it, not I, dashing down the room as if wild animals were chasing you." Undisturbed, Carlotte countered, "As a matter of fact I've been enjoying a cosy chat with Tim. He's been telling me a little of your previous history. You're on the make, he appears to think, by coming to Glenroden. I really must relate the gist of it to Meric."

Bewildered, her mouth slightly open, Sue stared after her, as she turned to join Meric for the next dance. She had been foolish to imagine she could ask Carlotte about a job when she was so patently her enemy!

The evening continued with Highland dances, mostly reels, until it was time to go home. Tim didn't dance, but Meric, to Sue's surprise, danced a lot, although he didn't ask her again. But they joined with another party, comprising several young people from the neighbourhood, so Sue suffered no lack of partners. Fortunately she had taken Highland dancing in evening class, as part of a keep-fit curriculum at college, and being particularly light on her feet was no mean performer. She took part eagerly, hoping her rather forced enthusiasm successfully hid the longing in her heart for a tall, handsome Highlander who never came near her.

The two girls were tired when they arrived back at Glenroden and went straight to their rooms. Carlotte was staying for the night as it was too late to return to Perth. Unhappily Sue wondered if Meric had deliberately arranged it this way. Yet if he had romance in mind he didn't seem inclined to linger with Carlotte in the still warm drawing room where Mrs. Lennox had left out sandwiches and coffee in a flask in case they were hungry. After a very short time he followed them upstairs to bed. Sue heard him walk past her bedroom door, then there was silence apart from the wind blowing down the glen.

The wind usually lulled her to sleep, but on this occasion, an hour later, she was still lying awake. Her thoughts disturbed her, refusing to allow her to rest. Wholly they concentrated on Meric, clinging to him feverishly, turning the whole problem of Glenroden over and over in her mind. She knew beyond doubt that she loved him, although she realized the hopelessness of such misplaced affection. If she had ever had cause to hope, those hopes had been more than dashed this evening when he had practically ignored her existence. Sue shivered and tilted her head back on her pillows, letting a cool stream of air from the window play over her face and neck as she pushed back her heavy hair from her hot forehead. Then, exhausted by tossing and turning she lay still, trying to remember everything he had said during their one dance. Not that there was a deal of comfort to be gained from that! He had lectured her about Tim; on whom she might not invite to Glenroden. He had talked as if he had actually owned the place! Suddenly, as her thoughts turned back, Sue sat straight up in bed.

Frowning through the darkness, she recalled how, when they had toured the estate, Tim had suggested that she search the office to try and discover Meric's true position. Of course she had refused to have anything to do with such a scheme, and he hadn't mentioned it since. Now, at this very moment, she found such an idea curiously tempting—not from Tim's completely mercenary point of view but rather regarding her own relationship with Meric. From a personal angle it would make no difference to her feelings whether he was manager or not, but there was a possibility that he really was her father's partner. Or worse than that, he could probably own half or even more of Glenroden. The thought had never occurred to her before. She couldn't think why not, but suddenly it seemed imperative that she knew the truth.

As she thought this, her eyes flew open, and with a quick twist of her supple body she pushed back the blankets and slid out of bed. Not stopping to put on her dressing-gown or slide her feet into a pair of slippers, she made for the door and gently opened it. She dared not switch on a light, and if she were to fumble after these things, someone might hear.

She need not have worried. The big house was silent, but she felt the palms of her hands go moist and sticky as she waited to make sure there wasn't anyone around. Reassured by the quietness, she slipped through the door, closing it carefully behind her before running down the thickly carpeted stairs to the hall, her bare feet making no sound.

The library which Meric used as an office lay along a passage at the back of the stairway. Wraith-like, Sue moved towards it with only memory and instinct to guide her. Otherwise there was only a very faint gleam of light from the moon coming in through an uncurtained glass pane high up on the wall. The only noise she could hear was her own heart beating too loudly in her ears.

At the library door she stopped, of a sudden drawn back within herself in an agony of uncertainty. Then resolutely, feeling that her decision had been a right one, she thrust open the door and went in. Once inside she stumbled, then paused on the threshold, wishing she had remembered to bring a torch. There was one in the kitchen, but somehow she didn't dare risk returning for it. The kitchen was full of bits and pieces, she might easily knock something over. As her fingers nervously flicked down the switch she waited apprehensively, but no one was likely to see a light at this time of night, and the sooner she found what she was looking for the better.

A quiver ran through her as she stared around the room. She had only been here once or twice before, once when she had come to collect Meric's dog for a walk—Carlotte had been here then—and another occasion with a message from a caller. She remembered the desk, but little more. Now her gaze wandered tentatively to the high bookshelves, the comfortable chairs by the wide fireplace before coming back to rest on the large oak desk with its leather-covered top. Then, suddenly, her heart was beating so heavy and fast it was unbearable, and her eyes widened with perplexity. It was a frightful thing, but now that she was here she found she couldn't go through with it. It had been an idea, impulsively born in a moment of stress, but Sue knew, standing there, that whatever secrets the old desk contained it must keep them. To start and search, even though it was her father's property, was something quite foreign to her nature, if only she had had the sense to realize this before. Perhaps, she thought despairingly, if after Tim was gone she came here and asked Meric frankly, he would tell her all she wanted to know.

CHAPTER TEN

IN a moment of enlightenment which should have brought only relief, Sue suddenly found herself freezing into immobility. Instinctively she knew that someone stood outside the door. And when the door opened slowly, although it scarcely made any noise, the faint creak of the turning knob rang like an explosion in her ears.

After one suspended crystalline moment she spun, like a top out of control, stunned disbelief illuminating her features as her shattered glance fell on Meric. Taut with despair, she stared at him, wondering speechlessly if he intended to strangle her. Every vestige of colour left her face as she heard him mutter some violent exclamation beneath his breath. As if the sight of her standing beside his desk aroused feelings of unrestrained anger.

For the first time since she had known him, his fury appeared to leave him incapable of words, and, because she couldn't seem to stand it any longer, she managed to speak.

"I'm sorry," she stammered stupidly, through the heavy frightened beating of her heart. "I didn't mean to disturb anyone, I don't know how you came to know I was here."

His dark eyes narrowed even further as his cold, glittering glance went over her; the thick fall of hair, bare feet; the thin blue cotton boy's pyjamas. "I came down to see if John was all right," he said grimly. "I followed you downstairs. It was dark and like you I didn't put on a light, but I didn't know who the cat-burglar was until

I opened this door. I thought perhaps it was your friend Mr. Mason, taking a look around.''

"Is Father ill?" Fear took her breath, stinging through her head, so that she scarcely heard the last bit about Tim.

He replied harshly, "You're changing the subject, Sue. He hasn't been well lately. You know that."

Remorse caught her, but with a flicker of indignation which seemed to dispel a fraction of fear. She met his eyes. "I should have looked in myself when we came home, but I did think he'd be sleeping. And I'm not changing the subject!"

"No?"

It was just one word, but seemed to speak volumes. Her eyes clung to his, widening apprehensively. In his dressing gown he looked larger than usual, the breadth of his shoulders solid beneath the dark blue silk. He seemed older, entirely unapproachable, his hard face completely devoid of sympathy. He took a step nearer, continuing to watch her. The room was intensely quiet, and she wondered if he could hear the frantic thudding of her hear.

"You haven't told me what you were doing in my desk?" he rapped out, with such force she winced.

"I wasn't in your desk." Stiffening with resentment, she tried to conjure up some gesture of defiance as she tilted her chin. From this angle she could see the terse set of his jaw, the dark, downy hair on his chest where his pyjamas lay open at his throat. Her resolution wavered as, with a quickly indrawn breath, she dragged her eyes away. She was aware that he waited, that if he was to believe her she must think of something convincing to add to her brief statement. But for a second time, her mind refused to function and she remained silent—an uncertain, self-condemnatory silence.

Meric's dark eyes scanned her face. He insisted without mercy, "If you weren't here to go through my desk, then what exactly were you doing? You'd better have a good explanation!"

Once before, Sue remembered, he had accused her of being a liar. It had only been said in jest, but she didn't want him to have an occasion to accuse her seriously. Yet what could she say? Despairingly she stepped backwards, away from that unnerving gaze. How was she to get out of this one when she didn't have the courage to admit the truth?

He gave her no longer than ten seconds before his patience broke. With one stride he reached her, his hands clamping down on her shoulders, gripping tightly through the thin cotton. "Mason put you up to this, didn't he? You're trying to cover up!"

His question, like his hands, hurt. Hurt because in a way, he was right. Yet how could she possible explain that her involvement was completely divorced from Tim's suggestion! It was impossible to involve Tim when she hadn't intended to share with him anything she might discover. And if she did confess any of this to Meric he would never believe she had changed her mind at the last moment. It was all too irrational to ring true.

Helplessly she shook her head, attempting to squirm from his hold. "Tim doesn't know I'm here tonight in your office. That I swear."

"Which doesn't really answer my question, as well you know!" Disregarding her feeble struggles, his fingers bit deeper as his temper increased.

Sue found herself stammering wildly, "I know it was silly of me to come here. Perhaps I was sleepwalking, but I've done no harm. I haven't even touched your desk, and I certainly haven't stolen anything, in spite of what you suspect!"

If her tone of voice was meant to annihilate then she failed dismally as his mouth twisted sarcastically. "You're wasting your time. You certainly weren't sleepwalking, although you might have been, dressed as you are!" His eyes, once more, went narrowly over her thin attire in such a way as to bring a deep flush to her white cheeks. "I must admit," he went on, "that those pyjamas are better than what you were wearing in London, but even those don't leave much to the imagination. Maybe because they're too small."

"I hate you!" Pent-up emotion released the words in a rush, as stunned, she realized for the first time how very scanty were her pyjamas. Defensively she tried to wind her arms about her nerveless body.

He taunted, "When a man finds a girl going through his property at this hour he's not usually bothered as to how she feels exactly."

"You wouldn't have found me," she cried witlessly, "if you hadn't been sneaking around yourself. You gave me a horrible shock, creeping up behind me, and then you accuse me of all sorts of things..."

"Sue!" He interrupted the hysterical flow, shaking her none too gently. "Are you going to tell me, or do I have to drag it out of you?"

His face was now as pale as her own, and his dark eyes cold, but keyed up, nerves jangling, she ignored the danger signals. Lips tightly closed, she made no response, just stared at him mutinously.

"So..." he ground out, his voice hard with anger, "you enjoy being insolent! I've told you once in the past few hours and I'm telling you again. I don't have to spell it out. Get rid of Tim Mason, or heaven help me, I'll do it for you—which could be a lot more humiliating for him!"

Sue gasped on a wave of pure apprehension. "Don't you dare say anything to Tim, do you hear me! Or he won't be the one to go, I can tell you."

"Could that be a threat, Miss Frazer?" His fingers tightened ominously on her shoulders before sliding to grip the soft flesh of her arms, imbuing swift terror.

How could she answer him? How could she say—"I have to find out your exact position at Glenroden? Not knowing is driving me crazy"—But there was her father to be considered. Suddenly, as confession trembled impulsively on her lips, this angle struck her. It was John who must tell her what she wanted to know,

not this grim-faced man who held her so hurtfully because she refused to give him the explanation he asked
for. She must have been blind not to have seen this
before!

Little beads of perspiration appeared on her upper lip
as her bewildered mind veered back to Tim. At all costs
she must save him from Meric's anger. "I don't like to
see people hurt," she faltered, "especially Tim."

He treated her short statement to the contempt he
obviously thought it deserved. "You seem determined
to protect Mr. Mason," his voice slurred sarcastically,
"so why isn't he around to protect you now from the
scoundrel who runs Glenroden? Is he sitting up in bed,
I wonder, waiting for whatever it was you intended to
bring him?"

"You're quite, quite horrible!" Her face scarlet with
temper, Sue felt she was stifling beneath the force of
her indignation.

His hands left her so suddenly she almost fell. He
spoke with soft violence. "So—in your estimation I'm
quite without virtue?"

"You could say that!" she retorted recklessly, her
only desire to hurt with primitive intensity as she
backed away from him. She swallowed something hard
in her throat, moved again as the expression in his eyes
changed darkly. She felt herself beginning to shake and
knew that for the rest of her life she would remember
this moment. There was a peculiar tenseness in the air
between them, then no air at all, just an inexorable sensation of disaster as Meric advanced, his arms reaching
out, this time not asking for explanations.

He came straight on, not stopping, taking hold of
her, hauling her to him, ignoring her brief, futile
struggles with a hard laugh. "You must allow the devil
to live up to his name," he demanded, as with unleashed savageness he pulled her softly sensitive body
into his arms.

Desperately she tried to fight, to escape, but he
scornfully stilled her protests with brute strength, one

hand hard on her throat, forcing her chin upwards, his
lips hurting as they crushed heavily down on her own.
Wildly the blood seemed to thunder through her veins,
coursing like fire. It wasn't exactly like the time in
the cottage, or on the mountain. He wasn't playing
with her now, but neither was he loving her as his lips
held her quivering mouth with a cruelty she had had no
idea he possessed. Flame leapt through her body as
weakly she tried to resist him, to hang on to one last
shred of saneness. But her ineffectual movements he
curbed with the strength of his arms, caressing her
slight body until she slumped helplessly against the
hard muscles of his chest.

Sensitively, driven by a surge of feeling, her arms
lifted, locking behind his neck, her fingers moving unconsciously across his face, losing herself entirely in the
violence of emotion which swept through her.

Only once did he lift his head, and only so his hand
could explore the soft curve of her shoulder, linger on
the bare, soft skin before sweeping the warm, silken
hair back from her neck and burying his lips in the
white pulsing hollow of her throat. His hands held her,
allowing no protest, inflicting punishment, taking a
cruel revenge for her rebelliousness. But, inadvertently, as his lips returned to hers, his love-making
aroused a response which she had never known was
possible, a shattering sensation of nerves and impulses,
dissolving any self-control she might have left. Deliberately, it seemed, he set out to demonstrate how ineffectual was her resistance, what he could do to her if he
wished. So that, when he stopped kissing her, her arms
pulled his mouth down to hers again, uncaring whether
he thought her wanton or not.

She had no idea how long afterwards she was aware
that he lifted her in his arms and walked out of the
office, back up the stairs in the moonlight, her soft,
fluid body held close against him, her hair floating
cloud-like through the cool, scented darkness. As he
thrust open the bedroom door she heard him murmur

inaudibly against her cheek, his lips soft on her hot skin, his tone speaking of a fast dwindling restraint. Then, so suddenly that the shock of his rejection shattered, he dropped her unmercifully back on to her bed.

His voice, as it came to her dazed bereft ears, was coolly sardonic, full of total mockery as he moved away. "There comes a time, Sue, when the truth has to be forced upon us. A girl like yourself who's too blind to see otherwise..."

There came a sharp click of the door and he was gone, leaving her bruised body and mind to try, with hopeless incompetence, to grasp the implications of what he had said.

The next day being Sunday, Meric took Carlotte back to Perth after lunch and didn't return until late evening. On Monday Tim departed for London, and on the Tuesday afternoon John Frazer died. He died quietly in his sleep while having his afternoon rest. In spite of the fact that it wasn't unexpected, Sue was stunned by the suddenness of his going, when Mrs. Lennox broke the news.

Sue had been out walking, exercising the dogs, trying to rid herself of a measure of heartache. She hadn't seen Meric all day, nor, she assured herself, did she want to. Not until her mind came to terms with her problem and found a solution. Failing this, she knew she couldn't remain any longer at Glenroden. If she hadn't been aware of this before, she knew it now, definitely. To stay could mean utter humiliation. After what had happened in the office she couldn't trust herself where Meric was concerned. How could she place herself in a position where her precarious self-control might slip any time when he disliked her so strongly?

Before going to Perth, to the station with Tim to see him off, Carlotte rang. "It's about this temporary job, darling," Her voice had been warm and friendly, as if they'd parted on the best of terms. "I believe," she continued, "it's yours if you want it. You would have to see the Head, of course, and if you're really keen, it might lead to better things."

Sue had called at the school and been accepted—just, she believed, because of availability. With one or two minor details to be complied with, she could start the following week. She could either stay in digs and return to Glenroden each week-end or, if John was not agreeable, she would travel in each day. Either way it would give her the breathing space she so desperately needed.

But before she could find an opportunity to even tentatively broach the subject, her father wasn't there any more to confide in. Sue could scarcely believe the shock could affect her so greatly. Perhaps it was the culmination of several things, but she seemed to feel much worse this time than when she had lost her mother. Meric and Mrs. Lennox took everything off her hands, seeming to understand her grief without explanation. Carlotte sent a brief note of condolence, but didn't appear at all.

"She doesn't care for this sort of thing," Mrs. Lennox explained dryly. "No doubt she'll turn up for the funeral!"

Meric was friendly but completely detached, dealing with everything with sober competence. Always he seemed there to see callers and answer the telephone, unobtrusively in the background, yet providing a veritable tower of strength, his own sense of loss only apparent in the faint lines of strain about his firm mouth, the sombre darkness in the direct gaze of his eyes.

The next few days, Sue found, passed in a sort of daze. If ever she thought of the future it was only with her teaching post in view. About Glenroden she didn't think at all. It seemed the natural sequence of things that the estate should go to Meric, although how this should be dealt with she had no idea. To her surprise she could muster up no interest.

But the day after the funeral she decided to go to Perth, to see John's solicitor and ask his advice. It had been arranged that he should come the following Monday, but on Monday, Sue knew, she wouldn't be here. Guiltily she realized that Meric should have known this. In fact she had been going to tell him, but hadn't got round to it. During the week-end she must find the courage to approach him, but before this it seemed imperative that she saw the solicitor in Perth.

She left on Friday after an early lunch, having managed to get an appointment for two o'clock. To her relief Meric was out. In spite of the difference her journey to Perth seemed strangely reminiscent of that day in summer when she had seen her mother's solicitor about the letter which had brought her all the way north to Scotland in the first place. She remembered she had lunched beforehand with Tim. Erratically her thoughts roved as she drove swiftly towards the city. Maybe she ought to have let Tim know about her father? It would have been polite, only she had forgotten all about him since he had returned to London. He had simply faded from her mind since she had seen him off at the station. He didn't seem real any more. Only Meric Findlay occupied her heart and thoughts, but, after the unhappiness of losing John, not even Meric could dissolve the encompassing numbness.

Parking the car, she wandered along Marshall Place, to find the solicitor eventually some way further on, in a very ancient-looking building of no architectural distinction but which was probably known as a rare relic because of its obvious age. It was hemmed in by warehouses, public houses, and factories, with nothing to recommend it to the eye, but Sue was so relieved to find it she didn't notice these things. Inside, the dim interior managed to give an air of surprising comfort even though it was a trifle austere, but there was nothing comforting in what the solicitor had to say.

"You know, of course," he began, "that your father didn't own Glenroden? Not since he sold it ten years ago. He was indeed fortunate in finding a buyer like Meric Findlay. But there, that's water under the bridge, long since past."

Aghast, Sue stared at him, unduly grateful that in his
concentration with some papers he hadn't seemed to
notice her start of surprise. So Meric owned Glenroden, not her father! And this man took it for granted
she had known. Despair surged as she wondered desperately why John hadn't told her. Why he had kept
such a thing from her. And, without the humiliation of
confessing she knew nothing, how was she to acquire
all the facts? She didn't even feel able to ask why her
father had been forced to sell in the first place, as the
solicitor would expect her to know this, too.

The man talked on. It was apparent he had known
her father for years, her mother, too, after John married, although, true to his calling, he was studiously
discreet.

"You're very like your grandmother, my dear. She
was a fine woman," he observed shrewdly, some time
later as he personally saw Sue out.

When the door closed gently behind her, Sue realized that, apart from the one devastating piece of news,
she was not much wiser than when she had come in.
There had been something, she couldn't seem to remember the exact details, about a small legacy, but that
was all.

Afterwards she had no clear recollection as to how
she spent the remainder of the afternoon. For a while
she just wandered. In a small café she ordered tea, but
could not remember eating it, nor leaving after she had
paid the bill. It had long been dark before she found her
way back to Glenroden, and it was only as she crossed
the ford that she decided to say nothing to Meric of
what she knew until she left again on Monday morning.
Then it would necessarily have to be brief. A short
apology—a word of farewell and thanks before a quick
departure. It would all be over in a few minutes, saving
a lot of embarrassment. Meric would probably be grateful. Explanations, should he choose to ask or give any,
would be almost impossible because of time. At all
costs, Sue argued with herself, she must keep every-

thing down to a bare minimum, otherwise, in her present highly emotional state, she might say things which she would later regret.

This evening Meric would be out when she returned. Thankfully she recalled that he had an appointment which he had said couldn't be put off. Deliberately she had tarried in Perth until she knew he would be gone, not realizing she was getting cold. As she walked aimlessly around the streets, the air had been chill, and she hadn't remembered that the heater in the car had developed a fault during the summer which hadn't been put right. Now she was indeed frozen, and longed suddenly for a hot cup of tea.

Her headlights swept the short drive brightly as she drove up to the front of the house, and she switched them off swiftly so that she might no longer see the old stone façade of a house which could be home to her no more. Quickly she jumped out on to the gravel, leaving the car where it was, and ran with stumbling feet in through the main front entrance.

With numbed fingers she caught and slammed the door behind her, only then becoming aware that, in spite of all her precautions, Meric was there, striding down the hall towards her, his shabby old working kilt swinging, his hard face grim. He was almost on top of her before she could think of a means of escape.

"Sue!" His terse exclamation jolted her to a stop as his glance took in her white face, the wide, shadowed eyes, the nervous tremor which ran through her slight figure, oddly attired in a thin summer coat. "Sue, for God's sake, where have you been!" Impatiently he grabbed her shoulders and shook her, the force of his emotion transferring through his hands, so that all her newly made resolutions crumpled and tears started streaming in torrents down her cheeks.

"Sue!" For the third time he uttered her name, but this time his voice held more than a hint of desperation. "Please tell me what's wrong, what's happened?"

When she made no reply because she couldn't, he

caught her shaking body to him, one hand behind her head, holding her against his shoulder, cradling her in his arms until the force of her pent-up misery exhausted itself. And all the time he kept repeating, "Sue darling, I love you."

From somewhere, it seemed a great distance, eventually she heard, yet unable to take in the full implication of what he was saying. Stupidly her mind clung to what she had learnt that afternoon, as helplessly she tried to free her hand, to scrub away her tears with a clenched fist.

"Why didn't you tell me?" she whispered brokenly.

His body went instantly rigid against her own, and the hand which had been stroking her hair stopped suddenly as he withdrew fractionally. He went on holding her, but his eyes were inscrutable, his mouth tightening grimly as he realized her question was quite divorced from what he had been murmuring. "Just where the devil have you been this afternoon?" he insisted curtly.

This time there was no possible evasion, yet she hesitated, guilt that she hadn't trusted Meric sweeping through her, mingling with despair. "You didn't guess?" she whispered, her breath catching in her throat.

"Sue, how could I?" His eyes lingered with attempted patience, a growing anxiety, on her tear-wet cheeks. "Mrs. Lennox thought you'd gone to Perth, but when you didn't come back I began to worry. I've been nearly out of my mind!"

"You were going out to dinner." There was still a sob in her voice which she couldn't control.

"It wasn't important." He dismissed his engagement with a terse shrug of his shoulders. "You are! I took Mrs. Lennox to the village, expecting to find you home when I returned. But that doesn't answer my question."

There could be no escape. Apprehensively she forced her head up to meet his eyes. "I went to see Father's solicitor in Perth," she said.

"Ferguson?"

She nodded mutely, feeling faintness. What had she done? Meric's face swayed strangely. She cried out as his grip tightened, but before she could speak he picked her up, and, with the dampness of her cheek against his jacket, strode with her to the library. With a resounding thud he closed the door.

Through a haze Sue sank willingly into the strength of his arms, conscious that here was great joy. Yet also she was aware of growing consternation when she thought of all which must be said, all of which she had hoped to avoid. Vaguely, as Meric held her, sat down with her on the great leather settee, she recalled some whispered words of endearment. He might only have intended bringing comfort? Whatever—he certainly wouldn't care for her any more when he learned how she had gone behind his back!

Nervously weak, she forced herself to speak. "I was only trying to find out about the estate. I had a horrible feeling that things were not as they should be. Sometimes I thought you were only a domineering manager, but, at others, I had a frightening conviction that Father and I were living on charity."

"Poor Sue—so mixed up..." Above her head his warm voice deepened to tenderness. "Suppose," he suggested firmly, "we start at the beginning, you and I? Something we should have done long ago."

She looked up, meeting the stern concern in his eyes, and felt the grip of his hands tighten. "This solicitor, he told me you own Glenroden, not Father, but I didn't ask him anything else. He seemed to take it for granted I should know. I could scarcely tell him I knew nothing. Besides, it didn't seem important any more."

His eyes held hers, not condemning but full of regret as he regarded her pinched, colourless face. "If only I'd known where you were going, Sue! I could have saved you all this heartache. I intended explaining everything over the weekend. I was only giving you a breathing space which I thought you needed. I was definitely going to tell you before Ferguson came on Monday."

"I see," she said, but she didn't, and waited silently for him to go on. He still held her and her heart fluttered in her throat, threatening to choke her. She dared not move for fear he left her and, if nothing else, she must have this moment to hold for ever.

"When I bought Glenroden ten years ago," he told her, "I was a callow youth of twenty-five who didn't know the first thing about farming in the Highlands. Glenroden was on the market and I bought it."

"Just like that!"

"Just like that, sweet Sue. Haven't you discovered that when I see something I want I must have it?" Her pulse jerked again as he punished her small interruption. He went on, "The estate wasn't entailed and John's brother—your uncle, I suppose—had sold off most of the farms. From what I gather he lived very much beyond his means. There had only been Glenroden left, and this was heavily mortgaged. John fought against losing odds for years. He had no family—he didn't then know about you. But having to part with Glenroden hurt him a lot."

Sue flinched, asking as he paused, "You let him stay?"

His mouth quirked ruefully. "Not then from any feeling of benevolence, I'm afraid. To me it made sense. John knew everything there was to know about the running of a Highland estate. I had no knowledge whatsoever. We came to an arrangement."

"You mean...he was the manager?"

Meric shook his head. "No, Sue, not that. I liked to manage my own affairs, even then. But he taught me all I had to know and lived with me here at Glenroden. In fact, very few people knew the true position."

"But surely, when you bought it..."

"It suited me, Sue, for reasons of my own. Remember I once told you my father died in South Africa? Well, my mother married again and I didn't exactly see eye to eye with my stepfather. At twenty-five one is young enough and often crazy enough for anything. I took my share, pulled out and came here. But I didn't want my family following on my heels, which, if they'd known about Glenroden, they might have done. My mother is Scottish born, too, you see."

"And the family now?"

"Oh, nice and tight in S.A. It was the step I was seeing in London when I took you down. He wanted to see me about some shares I still have in the mine."

"So that was what you were doing?"

"What else?" His eyebrow tilted.

Sue stared hard at a leather button on his jacket. "I thought perhaps you were with Carlotte..."

"And I thought you were painting the town red with Mr. Mason! It seems we both jumped to the wrong conclusions, my darling."

There was silence, a long-drawn-out moment when Meric's arms drew her closer, while Sue tried to take in what he'd just told her. There were still several things she didn't understand. "Why didn't Father tell me about it," she whispered at last, "when I first came?"

His eyes met hers soberly. "We should have told you, but John begged me not to. I think subconsciously he was frightened of losing you, as he did your mother, and he imagined, rightly or wrongly, that if he told you the truth you might go. He did intend doing so after a while, but like most deceptions the knot became increasingly difficult to unravel. And, on top of this, his health didn't improve, which made it daily more difficult for me to insist on a course of positive action."

In spite of the warmth from the fire and Meric's arms, Sue felt suddenly cold. "Why didn't he trust me?" she said sadly. "I was his daughter, I should never have left him. That is—" Her face whitened as she remembered her new job. How was she to explain this? Yet somehow it was easier than she'd thought. Everything seemed easier now with Meric. "I only intended staying away during the week," she finished, "or even going in daily; whatever he wanted. I just felt I ought to be earning my keep." No need, she decided hollowly, to mention to Meric that it had really been a means of escape from him.

But Meric glanced at her keenly, almost as if he guessed the truth. "Your father would have told you eventually, Sue. Perhaps on the whole life had proved too disillusionary for him to trust people too easily. In many ways he certainly seemed happier after you came, but, as things turned out, he wasn't given the time to prove it."

"As you say," Sue mused sadly, "maybe neither of us was given enough time, but I didn't realize until after he'd gone that I was beginning to love him dearly. It is some comfort to know I helped a little. But," she added dully, "he must have trusted you implicitly."

"I think he did." Meric paused, regarding her thoughtfully. "Ten years, Sue, is a long time. We got on very well together, he and I. I think he regarded me as he might have done his own son if he'd had one. Certainly I grew fond of him. It's been heartbreaking this last year to see his good health diminish so rapidly."

He regarded her a moment longer, then in the ensuing silence slid her gently from his knees on to the settee, proceeding with deft fingers to remove her coat. As she shivered slightly he jerked it from her shoulders, examining the thinness of it sombrely. "You needed money, I expect, to replace this sort of thing? I told John to ensure you had enough, but he obviously never got around to it."

Sue shook her head, evading a direct reply, startling herself by answering his question with a totally impulsive one of her own. "You never wanted to get married?"

"Yes," he replied softly, "many times."

So it was Carlotte! Apprehensively Sue stared at him, her eyes wide, dilating, the newly restored colour fading from her cheeks. The dizziness returned and she was scarcely aware that he was back beside her on the settee until he placed a glass between her shaking fingers, commanding her to drink it. "I should have given you that when you first came in," he frowned, "but I was too distracted to think straight. Drink it up, there's a good girl," he ordered with mock sternness, "then take a look at what I'm going to show you."

As she sipped the brandy nervously, Sue's colour returned, but her eyes still stayed on him fearfully.

From his pocket he took his wallet, and from it a small miniature, gazing at it for a moment like a star-struck teenager. Then he put it in front of her on a small table. It was a small oval miniature of a girl, a young girl in a flowered dress. Her fair hair was looped back into ringlets, and tiny feathery tendrils of hair escaped at her temples.

Bewildered, Sue stared. The girl in the miniature was an exact replica of herself, only it couldn't be! The high neck of the dress and the hair-style spoke of another age. Yet the likeness was amazing. "Who is she?" she gasped. "Where did you get it from?"

"I found it," he exclaimed, with great satisfaction, "by accident—in one of the bottom drawers of this desk. I did ask John if I could keep it, and he agreed. I knew then that she was the only girl I could marry, which was crazy, as I could never hope to meet her. Or so I thought—until one evening in Edinburgh..."

His meaning couldn't have been clearer. Sue's heart missed a great beat as her gaze left the other girl in the miniature to cling to Meric's face. "You thought it was me?"

His hand clamped possessively over hers. "I knew it was you," he stated positively. "Or, if you like, your grandmother reincarnated. That evening you obviously thought my behaviour peculiar." He gave a slight smile. "I suppose it was, but when a man sees a dream coming true he doesn't usually stop to think. Even when you took fright—very properly, I might say, and ran away—I knew beyond a doubt you would turn up at Glenroden."

"And you waited on the crag," she whispered, "and you were annoyed about something?"

"I waited on the crag," he repeated, his arms going around her. "And to begin with I was suddenly alarmed that you might upset John—thus the bad temper. I was annoyed more with myself than you, for not thinking of it sooner. Then you weren't a bit like the meek Victorian Miss of my dreams. You've been quite a little handful! Sometimes I wanted to shake you, especially when your Mr. Mason appeared, but," he added wryly, "in spite of all the misunderstandings I could never resist an opportunity to have you in my arms."

"Darling," Sue snuggled aginst him, warmly content. "You don't need to worry about Tim. I never loved him, nor did I ever let him think I did. I think he was confused by many things, but I don't suppose he'll ever come back to Glenroden." She finished helplessly, "I've loved you for so long."

"Not as long as I've loved you, Sue." He kissed her deeply, tenderly. Then, on a lighter note, "I'll admit when I first heard about Tim Mason, I thought you couldn't make up your mind."

"I thought exactly the same about Carlotte Craig," she retorted, but not quite so lightly.

He ran his fingers through her hair, brushing it back from her smooth forehead. "What we have, Sue, is something stronger than lesser passions." His deep voice vibrated. "Do your teaching stint, darling, if you must, but marry me before Christmas. I refuse to wait any longer."

"We'll spend Christmas at Glenroden?" she pleaded, hiding her hot face against his rough jacket. Everything seemed to be happening so quickly, she could scarcely take it in, but the knowledge that Meric Findlay loved her sent the blood singing wildly through her veins.

"Yes," he agreed slowly, his dark eyes faintly smiling. "We'll spend Christmas here at Glenroden, then I'll take you to South Africa for a proper honeymoon, and to meet the family. You'd like that?"

Sue nodded. Just so long as Meric was there she didn't mind where they went. They would come back to this old grey house amongst the mountains. From now on Glenroden would always be home—Father would like that...In her heart she knew a warm prayer of thankfulness as Meric, as if understanding her thoughts, held her close.